Looking for Sweet Love

R.L. Byrd

R.L. Byrd
PUBLISHING

Published by
R.L. Byrd Publishing, a brand of R.L. Byrd, LLC
PO Box 98334
Atlanta, GA 30359-2034
www.richardleonbyrd.com

Cover Design by WINC Atlanta

The publisher does not have any control over, endorses, or assumes any responsibilit for third-party websites or their content.

ISBN: 978-0-9905577-0-8 (PB)
        978-0-9905577-1-5 (EB)

Printed in the United States of America | First Trade Book Edition: June 2010

Reissued: July 2014

Other Books by R.L. Byrd

Black Coffee, the sequel to *Looking for Sweet Love*
www.richardleonbyrd.com

Acknowledgements

My gratitude and sincere thanks goes out to Debra Dawson. Without her assistance, this book would not have been completed.

The author and publisher wish to thank the songwriters and music publishers for permission to use the following copyright material.

12 Play
Words and Music by Robert Kelly
Copyright (c) 1993 by Universal Music – Z songs and R. Kelly Publishing
All Rights Administered by Universal Music – Z Songs
International Copyright Secured   All Rights Reserved
Reprinted by permission of Hal Leonard Corporation

Ain't No Need To Worry
Words and Music by Marvin L. Winans
Copyright (c) 1987 by Zomba Enterprises & Selah Publishing, Inc.
Performed by The Winans and Anita Baker. *The Very Best of the Winans*. Rhino/Wea, 2002.
Reprinted by permission of Marvin L. Winans Music

Come Ye Disconsolate
Winn, Ted. "Come Ye Disconsolate." Lyrics.
Performed by Ted and Sheri. *The Healing Starts Right There*. Church House Records, 2001.
Reprinted by permission of Ted Winn, Teddy's Jamz Music

I'm Catching Hell (Living Here Alone)
Words and Music by Charles Jackson and Marvin Yancy
Copyright (c) 1976 by Chappell & Co. and Jay's Enterprises, Inc.
Copyright Renewed
All Rights Administered by Chappell & Co.
International Copyright Secured   All Rights Reserved
Reprinted by permission of Hal Leonard Corporation

Last, but definitely not least. I would be remiss if I didn't mention the lady that provided the insight and words of encouragement that put my feet on this *new road and journey*. Although the road has been bumpy (WHEW! has it been bumpy), what . . . a . . . *journey* it has been. Thank you Dorothea (www.dorotheaonline.com) for your insight!

Dedication

Finding love, whether true or not, takes you down many roads. Some roads may take you for the ultimate thrill ride. Others may just lazily wind you through the country-scape called life. A few, may just slowly lead you back to where you began, while others, without notice, just abruptly end. But all roads, regardless of the one you're traveling, will have at some point, hills to climb, pot-holes & bumps to endure, and many break-downs and trials to overcome.

In sight of this, I now realize that it's not the road you're given or the direction you take, but how you chose to navigate, through life's many situations, which gets you from the beginning to your final destination.

This book is soulfully dedicated to all the beautiful sisters I've encountered as I've journeyed on my road through life. With a special thanks to my Mother Lois (my joy and inspiration), Grandmother Lucy (light extinguished by Alzheimers) and Aunts Gwen and Cecil (keep the jokes coming).

Love you and God bless.

Prologue

Atlanta. May 2, 1998. Graduation day. Spelman never looked so good! The campus was decked out in blue and white streamers, gorgeous flowers all over the place, and handsome black folks dressed in their Sunday best—I almost thought it was Easter—lol! And all that beauty was set under the prettiest sky—it seemed like the sun was smiling on us, just for us, like it was just as proud of our graduating as we were. The commencement was at the Fox Theater in downtown Atlanta, and if you haven't been to the Fox, girl, it is no joke! Just grown! I was so proud of my girls. And I was especially proud of myself, as I had fallen in and out of love like it was the style or something, and maintained my grades through it all. We had put in four years of hard work and now our "real" lives could begin. College hadn't been my easiest feat, in the academic or man departments, but it was done and I was ready for another beginning. I was sad, though. Most of my friends were moving to find jobs and I was staying in Atlanta to take care of Big Momma. Her health was failing and I couldn't leave her. I'd have to build my future and care for her at the same time. That's what family does. And believe me, I never thought, for one minute, to do otherwise. But there was that burning question of *What if?* running all through me, quick as my own blood. What if Big Momma had been perfectly healthy and my mother wasn't too busy to take care of her full time and I could spread my wings wide open, use all their strength and go out into the world and see what I was really all about? Unfortunately, I got to answer that question way sooner than I wanted because Big Momma was dead four years later. And I was on a plane to Dallas to work for DataComm—at the entry level.

After the graduation ceremony, all my girls gathered outside of the Fox to say goodbye, good luck, and "Bitch, you look fierce. They don't see you." Before taking oh so many pictures, we reminded each other of our promises: to stay in touch no matter what; to hold our friendships dear to our hearts; to have one another's backs through the fire. The previous night we had partied and partied and gotten drunk and partied some more and gotten our freak on, more or less, while living it up with those sexy-like-a-mothafucka strippers from Club Water. Damn, they know they some fine-ass Negroes with some big-ass dicks! We talked trash all night, play-fussing about who we thought was the best catch at Morris Brown, Morehouse, and Clark. We gossiped and died laughing about all the guys we had dated and whether or not their reputations lived up to the hype. We exchanged high fives for the ones who had done their reps well. Thumbs down to the ones who hadn't! Boooo! Now it was time to put the big-dick strippers to the side (or at least slow down the visits to once every couple of months), and find big-dick men who could pay half the mortgage, be good daddies, and help us make our dreams come true.

Despite being sick and unable to attend the ceremony, Big Momma had been overcome with pride. I was the third generation of girls to graduate from college. I was upholding the tradition and fit right in with all the women in our family who were blessed with brains and ambition. The only problem with all that drive and intelligence was that none of us Harris women could hold a good man. Oh, we found plenty of them. Keeping them was a whole other story. Some say it was so bad our family had been cursed. Of course that depended on which family member you talked to. Some said the Harris women preferred it that way . . . if you know what I mean. We could be some evil little somethings, and you know how evil likes to be left alone most days.

Even Big Momma had been bugged by the spell: One day, back in 1947, in the dead of winter (she said Atlanta had never been so cold), after three years of marriage and two kids (it's like I've heard this story a thousand and one times), Big Daddy went to the five and dime for some chewing tobacco and never came back. Big Momma swore up and down the Klan had something to do with it, but that theory was never proven or even supported with evidence. The years rolled away like leaves in the wind but Big Momma did not entertain the passing of time. She never married again. She only waited for Big Daddy to come back. She knew in her heart that one day he was gonna find his way back to her and walk through the front door, just as surely as he had walked out. (This hope, of course, did not match up with Big Momma's Klan theory. But I never pointed that out. I never said, "Big Momma, I thought you said the Klan got him?" because I knew she had just said that to blunt some of the embarrassment of being left like that.) To her deathbed, when you asked her what she'd do or say if he ever came back home, she'd tell you, with a smile taking up her whole face and her head tilted to one side, in a little girl whisper, "I'll welcome him with open arms and question him not." Can you believe that? The same answer given in the same sweet voice after fifty-one years! Fifty-one!

But maybe it's me that needs the attitude adjustment, because six years after Big Momma's death and ten years after graduation, I'm still looking for my husband and I'm beginning to believe in that stupid curse. At graduation, I vowed to have it all—the career, the marriage, the kids. Now I'd be happy to get a man to call me every once in a while. I'd think I was doing pretty good if I looked on my caller ID and a little chill went up my spine from the strength of the number. And good God, if I could get a few nights of even mediocre sex now and then, I'd feel like I'd hit the damn number. Don't let the sex be halfway decent! Except none of those things—half-ass sex or a man to give me the chills—seem to be in the distant, let alone immediate, future. I mean, I'm no bragger. Big Momma never stood for conceit. She said, "Pretty don't pay the bills," and she never lied. But your girl is very easy on the eyes. Ha! My legs last till the middle of next week, damn near. My silhouette is like Ping! Pang! Pow! I look like a damn bottle of Ms. Butterworth's syrup if I keep my butt in the gym a couple weeks straight. I got the body, the house, the car, the career. I mean, what the hell does a woman have to do around here?

Chapter One

A Little Birthday Therapy

June 21, 2008. "Whew! It's raining cats and dogs out there. Michael? Mike, I'm home." I put down my briefcase and walked towards the kitchen. Even beneath the safety of my umbrella, I had gotten soaked. At least all that damn rain had missed my hair. I was ready to get out of those clothes, though.

"What's up, baby girl?" Michael was waiting in the dining room in a bright white robe looking good enough to lick.

"What you doing, crazy boy?" I took off my jacket.

"Hey, it's your birthday, ain't it?"

"Yes, silly." And then I giggled like a young girl myself. We were acting like two kids. "What's all this?"

There was a cake with the words "Happy Birthday Baby" in bright purple letters on the table. That was one of the many reasons I liked (maybe loved) Michael so much. He always paid attention to the details. Purple was my favorite color. And he knew I loved chocolate cake—so I could bank on that deep dark brown underneath the frosting. (Though I was more interested in the deep dark brown under his robe.)

"Just a little something for my baby." He walked over and hugged me. It felt like tiny feet marching all along the base of my back. I was ready to skip the cake and see about that bulge between his legs.

"Yo, ain't you gonna blow out the candle?"

"What candle, boo? I don't see any candles!"

I stared down at the cake, puzzled. There were no candles but it damn sure said "33" clear as day.

"Oh yeah. Hold on, baby. Let me take care of that." Mike moved towards the cake on the dinning room table. "I decided you only needed one candle." He opened his robe to reveal a rock hard chest, stomach, and best of all, a big old dick. "So, um . . . you wanna blow it out?"

"Hmmm? And how should I go about blowing that candle?"

1

"Well baby, you can start by—"

"Ms. Harris? Ms. Harris! The doctor will see you now." I was shaken out of my reverie. And just when it was starting to get good too! *Now that's the kind of therapy I really need.* I'd have to settle for Dr. Wilma, the psychotherapist, though she was *far* from what I had in mind. Girl, who would have thought that me, of all people, would be seeing a shrink? Well, let's be politically correct here—an emotional therapist.

You'd think a birthday would be a joyful occasion, but after the year I'd had, thirty-three was just another number after thirty—not that thirty was all that itself. Or thirty-one . . . or thirty-two! And let's not even discuss the job I hated (deplored is a better word), the boss, whom I hated worse than the job, and the fact that I had not one prospect for a husband—not a one (I mean, I wanted Michael, but did he want me was the better question . . . can someone be your soul mate and you not be his?). And if that didn't beat all, I was swimming in a sea of debt with only one arm and one leg . . . and the leg had a big deep gash put there by all the creditors hounding my ass. That was the icing on the motherfucking cake. But then again, at least I had a fierce collection of handbags and shoes to stare at when I was feeling too sad about being broke! Gotta find the silver lining in everything, right?

Knowing all my business (like good girlfriends do), my girls had treated me to a wonderful spa—Spa Eloná (something I would never have paid for myself). Girl, it had everything from mud facials and body wraps to all the rubdowns and therapies you could ever imagine. Swedish and aromatherapy massages all the way down to anxiety therapy. Humph, guess which one I was going to? Here's a hint—it didn't have a thing to do with massages. My first of six therapy sessions and I was thinking, *Dr. Wilma? A psychotherapist!?* Oh my god . . . who would have thought . . . me . . . Jessie . . . seeing a shrink! I mean, not that there is anything wrong with getting a little help, I just didn't think I needed any and I didn't know what the hell I was about to face behind those doors—and for two hours at that. What could we possibly have to talk about that would fill the space of 120 minutes?

"Jessie Harris?" Dr. Wilma definitely betrayed her name. With a name like Wilma, I expected a frumpy old lady wearing thick-soled shoes and a too-tight wig. Ha! Dr. Wilma made *me* hot, and I'm strictly dickly!

"Yes, I'm Jessie Harris. Thank you for seeing me." She walked out from behind the frosted glass doors. Her suit fit like a sleeve, highlighting her figure-eight shape. She was thicker than a snicker and I was happy for it. I needed a good-looking, smart woman telling me what to do. She could lead by example. Even behind those designer glasses, I could see her lashes, long as my damn pinky fingers. I wondered where she got them done. I wanted to ask her, but was trying to match her professionalism.

"Welcome to Spa Eloná," she said, extending a manicured hand. "I'm Dr. Wilma Mathis. Thank *you* for making your appointment with our office. I'll be working tirelessly to assure that your sessions are rewarding and fulfilling. Please, do step into the Sanctuary." She motioned behind her and my eye caught the Movado making her wrist glitter like the night sky. *Okay, Dr. Wilma Mathis! Let me find out my therapist is a bougie-ass baller. I love it!*

Stepping beyond those frosted double-glass doors was like walking into the White House. If I ever make it that big . . . no wait . . . *when* I make it that big, I want an office just like hers! Honey, as soon as you walk in, the first thing to snatch the breath right out of your throat is the glorious wall of ceiling-to-floor windows overlooking the spa's courtyard. Not a damn smudge, not a damn forehead print, not a damn fingerprint on that glass. Just clarity and beauty and the courtyard landscaped to a tee! Flowers I've never heard of, in colors I've never seen, run wild all over. A grand and impressive waterfall cascades from the upper floors down to its center, and there are these big-old statues in all four of its corners. It's magnificent. And then you come back inside to the magnificence of the Sanctuary itself. The décor is taupe and beige accented with a deep blood red. The furniture is classic, and the artwork—from premier black painters of course—speeds up your heartbeat! I was overcome with pride walking those halls. I wanted to pat Dr. Wilma on the back and tell her, "Go on, girl!" But I just said, "This is really lovely."

"Have a seat, Jessie." She sat behind a desk that said "money" and took up a pen and notepad in her hands. The Sanctuary was just that—money come to life. I was hoping some of it would rub off on me. "So, this was a birthday gift? Care to elaborate?" she asked me.

"Well, my girlfriends think I'm getting a bit uptight. They think I'm stressed out."

"Hmmm . . . how so?"

I was thinking about the plush feel of the leather chair massaging my ass as much as I was to the answer to that question. The cost of this chair probably would have paid my mortgage! "Well, probably over my job, career, finances . . . and love life, or lack thereof, and everything else that falls in-between. They pitched in and treated me to the spa, and as you know, one of the amenities is the sessions with you."

"I'd say those are some pretty caring friends."

"Yes. They're crazy but caring."

"So Jessie, what do you hope to gain from this experience?"

"Well, Dr. Mathis—"

"Please, call me Dr. Wilma. All my clients do."

"Oh, okay. I mean, I really don't know what to expect. I have to be honest and tell you I'm a little skeptical. I don't come from a family who relies on shrinks—I mean psychologists." I probably turned red as a beet when "shrinks" came out my mouth. I couldn't believe I had just called this professional woman a shrink! I tried to cover up my slip. "I mean, what can I expect from these sessions?"

"Well Jess . . . you don't mind if I call you Jess, do you?"

"No, not at all."

"First, we're going to determine why your friends think you need to be treated to a weekend at Spa Eloná and to these sessions. And FYI, the sessions aren't included with the weekend pass—it's an option added upon request."

"Oh, really?"

She smiled, revealing a smile bright as the morning, and I thought, *Lady, do you have a flaw?* "Yes, really. Just a little food for thought."

Dr. Wilma's point was not lost on me. I knew my girlfriends had likely forked over a good amount of cash. That made me weepy. First for the love the act demonstrated, and then for the idea behind the love. My girls obviously thought I was in trouble. Maybe they were right.

"So Jess, tell me a little about yourself—where you're from, how you ended up in Dallas, where you work, and of course, anything else you'd like to reveal."

"Well, let's see. I'm thirty-three and originally from Tulsa, Oklahoma. I graduated from Spelman College with a BA in Marketing. I've been here in Dallas for a little over five years working for a marketing and research company as the director of sales and marketing."

"And have you been happy with your life thus far . . . so to speak?"

"So to speak? Girl, no! Since I've been in Dallas, I've met some characters, and I do mean characters, Dr. Wilma. My most notable accomplishment since stepping foot on Dallas soil is the friends I've made. I've also become closer to some of my old, life-long friends. But one thing's for sure, I haven't been successful in Dallas's dating game."

"And are you comfortable with that?"

"Oh no! I mean, I'm thirty-three this week. And I guess you'd think a birthday would be a joyful occasion, but after the year I've had, thirty-three is turning out to be nothing more than another odd number after thirty."

Dr. Wilma giggled a bit. "Interesting—about the dating woes I mean. Why do you think you haven't been successful in Dallas's dating game?"

"I don't know . . ." I paused to consider the idea. "Maybe I'm too aggressive or business focused? I always put business first, and everything else falls second, and I do mean a distant second. Like, visiting you has been the only non-work thing I've done in over a month. Looking back, I've let some good men fall by the wayside, and before I knew it, thirty-three was staring me dead in the face—and by the way, thirty-three is not as cute as twenty-three—and suddenly my career didn't mean as much to me . . . not that it was sky rocketing anywhere anyway!" I sighed. "I don't know, but right now finding love means the world."

"Okay. Stay with me here. I want to delve a little deeper." Dr. Wilma put her pen and pad down on the desk and sat back in her swivel chair. She pushed her glasses above her head and looked up at the ceiling. "Help me out. We're going to play a little word association game, and I want you to say whatever comes to mind when I ask a question. Okay? All right then. So Jess, what one song illustrates most effectively your emotions, feelings, and/or thoughts at this very moment in your life?"

"Well, I guess if one song could sum it all up, it'd have to be the gospel song by the Winans and Anita Baker 'Ain't No Need to Worry.' Because while things aren't the best, I do trust that they will get better."

"That's a deep and powerful song. If I recall . . ." She paused, and then began singing, *"Ain't no need to worry what the night is going to bring, it will be all over in the morning."*

"Yes! That's it, Dr. Wilma. Hallelujah!"

We laughed a bit and suddenly I felt completely at ease. Dr. Wilma was a doctor, yes, but she was also a sista.

"Good. I take it you're a spiritual person, then? A person who seeks solitude in desperate times and looks for answers from a higher power? Interesting, very interesting. So far you've indicated that things in your life are not going as well as you'd like them to. But if you hold on and lean back on your strength, the Lord, if I may say this to you, will bring a solution your way. Is there a song that describes your job?"

"Oh, that's easy. That would be Vanessa William's 'I Got Work to Do.'"

"A Stylistics remake, but a good one nonetheless. What song best describes your home situation?"

"Gladys Knight said it best with 'Home Alone.'"

"Okay, and lastly, what song best describes your personal, or should I say love, life?"

I sat a minute, combing through the decades of music I'd fallen in love with, music I had bumped and grinded to, music that had touched me in some way, that reflected my life. "I'd have to say Luther Vandross's 'A House Is Not a Home,' but Natalie Cole is running a close second with 'I'm Catching Hell.'"

Again, I had tickled Dr. Wilma. She laughed, and while both she and I knew nothing was really funny about my situation, it felt good to be able to step outside of it and find some relief in laughter. I felt like I could trust her.

"Good, I think we're making good progress here," she said. "It's interesting how you've chosen two songs that are somewhat similar to represent your home and love lives. It appears there may be some issues or confusion when it comes to making a happy home life and a fulfilling love life. Now, why don't you tell me how you think you ended up here, in that chair, opposite me?"

With that question, I let out a gallon of breath. The sigh was bigger than even I expected. "Dr. Wilma, I'm overworked. I'm stressed. I'm struggling over the fact that I'm not at my salary potential. I'm drowning in a sea of debt. And I don't have a man or any worthwhile prospects. My biological clock is tick, tick, ticking away. All that has made me a mean, bitter woman."

"You mean you're a bitch."

"I'm the Queen Bitch. I don't even like myself. I can't see how anybody even wants to be bothered with me lately."

"What do you think would solve the problem?"

"I honestly don't know. I thought maybe changing jobs with a higher salary would at least help me out financially, but I'm not sure that would be the total fix."

"You're right. Good observation, Jess. As you've figured out, in many cases, there needs to be a combination of fixes to make a person whole again. I think in our coming sessions identifying problems and discovering the best solutions will be our goal. We both want you to leave here a whole and happy individual. Once *you're* complete, and most of all, happy with yourself, then everything else should fall into place."

"Yes." I sighed softly. "That sounds good. And I'm open to that. I mean, I want that. But, quite frankly, I'm wondering if I really even have any real issues?"

"Well, in many cases, my clients are already quite aware of their problems. Granted, they may be in denial or they might simply be refusing to confront them; while others might not know how to address their problems with good, workable solutions. So Jessie, it may not be that you have any 'real' issues, if by that you mean definable psychological ailments, but your issues are certainly significant because they are tearing your life apart. Tell me, when things start getting really bad, how do you cope? Do you exercise? Take long walks? Listen to music? Is there someone you can just call and talk girl talk with?"

"Oh yeah! I can always talk to my girl Melissa about anything, and her ears . . . and mouth . . . especially her mouth, are always open, willing and eager to listen to whatever I need to talk about. She's there whenever I need her."

"Good. Who is Melissa and how long have you known her?"

"I've known her for about four years now. I met her on my first real marketing assignment when I started working at DataComm International. I was doing some research for Warner-Merritt Communications in regards to radio station K103.5, and she was the new disc jockey on the block. Being new, she had a little more free time than others, so they also made her the station's ambassador. We met and hit it off immediately. Since then, we've been the best of friends."

"Good. You're doing very well. Listen, the chair you're sitting in reclines. I want you to lean back and begin talking about K103.5, your relationship with Melissa, and whatever else comes to mind. Oh, and by the way, Jess, Melissa Morgan is one of my favorite DJs as well."

That was a hefty task. I didn't know where to start and I told Dr. Wilma so. She suggested that I describe a typical day in my life.

"Start at the beginning, when your alarm goes off to the moment your head meets the pillow again. Just relax. Drift away . . . focus. Focus in on whatever day you choose. Relax. Inhale, exhale, inhale . . . now what do you see?"

Chapter Two

K103.5 The Power Station

"Dr. Wilma, I don't know about a typical day, but I know last Tuesday was a nightmare."

"How did it differ from any other Tuesday?"

"Well, usually I just go to work and bust my behind, maybe catch a happy hour—once in a blue moon—go home, and do it all over again. But last Tuesday took a turn. I remember it clearly, because I was plain old exhausted from the day before. The whole company had been preparing for a big meeting with one of our major clients—Daisy Chain—and the pressure and late nights were taking their toll. I was so tired! As *soon* as I had gotten home that night and before my head caressed that pillow, I was out. And no sooner had I laid my aching body and big head down, the alarm clock started going off like a siren, bouncing off the walls of my little town house. Anyway, I dragged myself out of bed, switched over the alarm to the radio, and from there everything began."

"K103.5! This is your boy DK 'Love' Niles along with the sweeeet Melissa Morgan—girl, you know you fine! And we're here to relax your mind and soothe your soul during your early morning commute through the busy streets of the big D-town. Melissa, what's going on with traffic and the weather?"

DK and Melissa were on the radio already. And while I always enjoyed the show, I would have rather been sleeping.

"Well DK, the listeners are going to have to listen to something really deep to keep their minds off being stuck in all that traffic in this heat. I-35 South is packed jam tight from the Belt Line all the way down to 635, due to an earlier wreck, finally in the clearing stages. Medical personnel are on the scene, so please approach the area with caution. And if you're in a hooptie, and DK, you and I both know there are a lot of them out there, make sure you turn the air off so you don't overheat the car and just plain add to the already horrific traffic problem. As for the weather, Dallas is scorching this morning, as usual, with a temperature of seventy-eight degrees. Expected high in the low hundreds. And we won't even talk about the heat index. The time is seven-oh-eight. This traffic and weather report is brought to you by Big Jim's Rib Shack: Big on food, not on price. I'm Melissa Morgan with K103.5 bringing you traffic, weather, and a little bit of fun during this hot Juneteenth week. Back to you, DK."

"All right, for all the eager listeners out there waiting to hear about Tequila's *looove connection* from our hook-up line, Tequila's in the studio, tapping her feet, and waiting to tell it all—so is Robert, her love connection date. Tequila, I took the liberty of checking out his bio for you. You know DK looks out for the sisters! I was raised by a woman!"

The Tequila chick said, "I hear you, DK. Weren't we all . . ."

Melissa belted out that outrageous laugh she has, "Hee-hee, you know I checked the stats!"

I had finished washing my face and was feeling a little more awake.

"Remember, the 'love connection' is also an adult database where listeners call in and browse through the many men and women who leave their bios for other men and women to check out. If you like what you hear and want to respond, then you simply set up your own bio by following the voice prompts. We ask that if you make a love connection and are going out for the first time that you let us know. K103.5 will put your name in a weekly drawing that qualifies you to have that date on us. That's right. K103.5 will take care of the bill for you. There is one catch though. You have to come on *The DK and Melissa Morning Show* and tell us all about your first love connection . . . And Melissa, we have certainly had some interesting first dates the last couple of Tuesdays."

"Yes we have, DK. Lord knows we've had our share of first date busts. But first we have some advertisements from our sponsors. And to get Tequila and the listeners in the mood, we'll set it off with a little Stephanie Mills, 'So Good, So Right.'"

By the time Melissa put on Stephanie, I was brushing my teeth and thinking, *I tell you, every day it's the same damn thing.* I had been waking up to the DK and Melissa show, kneeling down to pray, reciting the same prayer over and over again for far too long. *Lord, thank you for allowing me to see another day. I ask that you please guide me through this day Lord, letting me touch lives in a manner that will be pleasing and beneficial in your sight. And Lord, be with me at work today. I need your guidance. I also need you to give me the strength to deal with that bitch of a boss Harriet. Excuse my language, Father. And God, if it be your will today, please send a tall, dark chocolate, extremely fine man into my life. I'm not asking for much, just let him be attractive, employed, own a car, and we'll talk about the rest later. These things I do pray and ask, Amen.* I would get up off my knees and start getting ready for work. And not too soon after, I was out the door, heading out with the countless thousands of other Dallas commuters to the downtown business scene. That Tuesday was a little different though. "The Love Connection" segment of the morning show, which airs only on Tuesdays, was one of the best because there was actually a connection and not a date bust. But girl, what happened next during the "Speak Your Mind" segment was a trip.

I put on my slippers and turned up the radio before dashing to the shower.

All the while I was singing, "*Good when you touch me, so right, right when you hold me.*"

"Yes, Stephanie. You know it was good, girl. Yeah. Sing it."

Under the warmth of the shower water I heard Melissa yell, "We're back! Okay, Tequila girl. Now you know everybody wants to know, what's up with the name?"

"Girl, you so crazy. My mother wanted something different. Why she chose Tequila, Melissa, I just don't know."

Melissa said slyly, in a low voice, "Shout out to all the drunks. Whew! Just kidding. Okay Tequila, so tell us about your date. How did it start?"

"Well, Robert called, and we made plans to hook up at the Fisherman's Wharf about eight PM on Friday. He was late getting there."

"Typical man! What time did he finally get there?" That was Melissa's voice, and damn that shower felt good pounding all over my back. I just wished I wasn't taking it to go to work.

"He got there 'round eight thirty, which was fine. At least he ain't have me waiting no hour. I saw one of my homegirls there, and we talked while she and her fiancé waited for their table."

Obviously Tequila's ass had low expectations. Why was it acceptable for him to show up half an hour late? See, I don't play that shit. I was drying off by then and yelling at the radio like Tequila could hear me, "Girl, he done started off all wrong. That's a bad sign already. Don't go letting that nigga take you another damn place. Cut your loses. Say thank you for the free food and just, oooh, walk away!" I was out of the shower and rubbing on lotion by then.

"Okay, so you told your girlfriend to be at the wharf, just in case. When Robert finally arrived, what did you think?"

Tequila laughed like a straight hooker. I could just see her rolling her eyes and probably twirling her hair. She said, "Girl, where do I start? The brother is just fine!!!"

I turned up the radio like that would make me see him or something. I stopped getting dressed for a minute so I could imagine him.

"He had told me he would be wearing some Fubu gear."

"Fubu?" DK said, and I knew it was coming. I didn't know why Tequila or Robert set themselves up like that. "You mean he had on some Fat-Ugly-Broke-and- Unemployed gear?"

"Whew! The hate is in the room, and whatever, DK, he looked good. Anyway, when I actually saw it on him, I thought I was going to faint. He had said he was a tall brother, a little on the slim side, with a baldhead, slim mustache, and connecting goatee. Girl, when that man walked through that door, honey, the room all paused, and I truly was about to Klimaxx."

"Girl, please! You must still be drunk from Friday night—too many tequila shots, I guess. No offense Robert baby!" Melissa said.

That girl is a complete fool. Then she turned on the fake "oooooh" sound to back up the dis.

"Audience, I'm just tripping. The brother definitely has it going on."

I was climbing into my dress suit by then imagining what Robert must look like. I said, looking in the mirror, "Melissa, I know your ass like the back of my hand. 'Has it going on' means that nigga is a troll with a big dick. Stop staring between that man's legs."

"All right, Robert, my man. So what did you think of Tequila when you first saw her?" DK wanted to know, and so did I.

"Nice, DK. Real nice."

He was obviously a man of few words.

Melissa said, "Okay, okay, okay! So what happened next?"

The Tequila chick said, "Well, we both decided to get the seafood buffet and it was just like I was hanging with a homegirl. We hit it off just like that, talking, joking, just, you know, having a good time."

"You mean like a boy/girl homey type of friend or a girl/girl homey type arrangement?"

"Yo, I don't swing like that, Melissa. It's strictly boy/girl homey, lover, friend with me," Robert said.

He spoke up for that!

"Just checking, baby. We are in Dallas, boo! And listeners, as I've said before, you have to ask a man the one A and three Ds before you proceed, and even if he tells you what you want to hear, you still have to tread with caution, okay!? And ladies, what are the one A and three Ds? Let's all say it together now: A. Are you married? D. Do you like women, men, or both? 'Cause I need to know! D. Do you have a job? 'Cause I don't make enough money for both of us. And most importantly, the third D—Do you have a car? 'Cause Negro, I may pick your ass up, but I'll be damned if

I'm gonna drop your black ass back off! Ladies, you heard!? DK it sounds like everything was going fairly well for Robert and Tequila on this date. This might just be the first success story!"

"Most definitely, Melissa! So you two, how did the date end? Tequila, why don't you let us know since Robert is being so reserved. And we want the real scoop!"

"Well, we decided to go to the lake and just walk and talk under the stars. But girl, it was too damn hot, so we ended up just sitting in the car tripping, and then kissing. Then—"

"Whoa! This is still a family show, girl. We *do* get the picture—believe me! So Robert and Tequila, do you think there's a spark that might turn into a blazing love inferno?"

Robert finally said a piece. "Oh, most definitely, Melissa. Tequila's definitely my homey-lover friend and we're about to set the D-town on fire!"

"All right, Tequila girl! Okay!"

"Yeah! This is what I'm talking about. The beginnings of sweet, sweet love. I want to thank Robert and Tequila for coming on the show and sharing their first date with the K103.5 family and really showing the D-town that two people can meet, greet, and have a good time. Once again, thanks. And I wish the two of you much joy and success in the beginnings of your relationship. I don't know why y'all humped so damn fast, but that's your business."

Tequila and Robert spoke in unison like a true couple. "Thanks, DK."

"When we come back, Melissa, we'll go to the phone lines to take calls for 'Speak Your Mind.'"

"Oh yeah! And remember, DK, I'm doing the first taping of *The Love Forum* tonight with Mr. Kirk 'Magic' Wonder during the evening love hour."

"Oh, yeah, yeah. That's right, so can you give the listeners a taste of *The Love Forum*'s first topic?"

"Sure, I'm going to introduce the audience to six women who are close associates of mine, or in other words, my sista girls. And we're going to talk about life, love, and relationships.

But what's interesting is that each week after our Wednesday night premier, we're going to track how each one is doing in the love slash relationship department. And to help each participant, we're going to include the advice of Dr. Laura, Dallas's relationship guru. And of course the K103.5 listeners will have an opportunity to ask questions and/or comment on the situations at hand."

"Sounds like this is going to be an interesting spin-off of 'The Love Connection' segment in the morning. What's the difference between the two and how long will the ladies have to put their lives on 'public display' per se?"

"Each participant has the option of not disclosing any information she considers too personal, but we encourage openness because we all know that hearing someone else's story helps our own. And as for the time, each lady has agreed to six months of continual dialogue about her personal love life. So, don't worry, DK, we're not going to put 'The Love Connection' out of business. The morning show basically focuses on putting people together. My show will focus on bringing people together and *keeping* them together by discussing situations that will keep the spark and fire in their relationships."

"Sounds like a winner, Melissa. I will definitely be checking you out tonight."

"Thanks, DK. I appreciate the support."

I didn't even know about Melissa wanting me to do the show until the night before, and like an idiot, I had said yes. And now I was volunteering to have my life put on display for months. I thought that maybe it would bring something good. Like a man. Big mistake! I didn't know how I got entangled in Melissa's nonsense, but I figured out real soon it was going to be a big mess—for me and all my girlfriends—before it was all said and done, and it all started with that day's segment of "Speak Your Mind."

"We're back. And of course every morning we allow our audience to call in and voice their opinions about anything and everything. We ask that you keep it clean, of course. So Dallas, let us know what's bothering you or just call in to get something off your chest. Just, you know, speak your mind. Now, last Tuesday the listening audience got on the 'dating outside of your race' bandwagon. And the sisters got too real and took it there with the brothers. I must say, it was quite an interesting show." Melissa laughed.

"Interesting indeed, Melissa. I thought I was going to need an armed guard escort out of here after that show. I do not date white women, by the way, Dallas! I was just talking a little junk, playing the devil's advocate, putting a little pep in the show!"

"As usual, DK! But you know I got your back, baby! Anyway, before we get real up in here this week, let's see if we can pull a track from way back. Play me a little bit of one of my favorite jams 'cause we gotta come correct and be real with this here. Here's the real-deal—Ms. Cheryl Lynn and 'Got to Be Real.' Soo-hoo, soo-hoo, soo-hoo . . ."

"Go, go, go, go, go, go Melissa, go, go, go!"

"Go head. Go head. Go, go, go head. All right, get it, DK. Break it down now. Ha-haaaa!"

"Yeah, Melissa! That was the jam back in the day. I mean the JAAAAAAAAM!"

"Okay. All right, now! Going to our first 'Speak Your Mind' caller. Caller, are you there?"

"Yes, I'm here. Good morning. I need some advice, DK and Melissa."

"Where you calling from, caller?"

"I'm calling from Fort Worth."

"Girl, am I sensing pain?" Melissa heard in her voice the same thing I heard, and I knew she recognized the voice just like I did! "What's troubling you my sister?"

"Ooooh lord, Jesus . . . Oooooh lord, Jesus, okay! Okay, so this guy started working in my department about three months ago right . . ."

"Right."

"And I'm attracted to the brother. I think he's single, very attractive, intellectual, and has his act together."

"You *think* he's single? Hmm . . . you better double-check that one. But until then, does the brother have a car?

You know your sister has to look out for you. Let me tell you, you don't want any man that does not have his own transportation. You should not be picking up any man for the booty and dropping his tired ass off at home, or wherever he needs to be, or go afterwards. Ain't nothing worse than having to get up out of bed and drive a Negro home—and then have to turn right back around and drive yourself back. Ya heard?!!!!!!!"

"Girl, you are crazy! But yes, he has a car. A nice BMW, I might add. But Melissa, listen, back to the problem. I have this insecurity, and after some personal experiences, and reading E. Lynn Harris's novel *Invisible Life* some years back, I want to know if it's quote, unquote politically correct to ask him a question."

"What's the question?"

"Well, I want to know if he might be gay."

"Ah, man. You hear that, Melissa? What makes you think that the brother might be, humph, straddling both sides of the fence?"

"All right! Or just one side for that matter, DK!" DeDe yelled.

"Yeah, even I need to know the answer to that question. Come, come, inquiring minds do want to know!" Melissa said.

"It's just some of his actions and his responses—physically and verbally—to things."

"Oooooh! No, girl! Like what?"

"It's like when he's upset at something or somebody he sucks his teeth and rolls his eyes."

"Uh-huh, girl, you're on point about that one," Melissa said. "We all know what that means—B-I-T-C-H—but I'm going to let DK handle this."

"Well ladies, I haven't had that happen to me, and I never roll my eyes or suck my teeth, but I still don't know! We definitely have to see what the listeners have to say about this one. And sister, if the listeners feel that the vibe or answer is, well, yes, how do you plan on asking the brother the question?"

"Well, he asked me on a lunch date, which is today . . . well, um, I kinda invited myself . . . and this has been on my mind all weekend long. I know what my girlfriends think, but I want some outside feedback."

"So the brother is taking you out to lunch, and you want to know if it's appropriate for you to ask him, during lunch, that he's probably paying for, if he's gay?"

"Well, yes. Something like that."

"Okay listeners, you've heard one of our Tuesday 'Speak Your Mind' comments and it definitely needs to be our question of the day. So call in, let us know what you think."

"Oh, DK, this is going to be an interesting question of the day! And with that said we'll be back!!!"

I knew that voice better than I knew my own. That was my girlfriend DeDe posing that question. I knew DeDe had had a real bad experience before, where she busted our girlfriend V's husband in the act in her motherfucking bed (the nigga was supposed to be fixing a pipe leak in DeDe's bathroom but was in there taking the pipe from a twenty dollar crack-head instead), that sure was a mess. I didn't know she was still letting it haunt her, though. DeDe was in love with a married man—who was good and crazy—so why she was calling up asking about a whole other man on live radio, I couldn't understand. But that was DeDe for you. By that time, I was in the heart of Dallas traffic, listening to a string of boring commercials. Before I knew it, I was looking at Melissa's number on my cell phone's caller ID. I picked up knowing just what she was about to say.

"Jessie speaking."

"What's up, girl?"

"Stuck in all this traffic. I wish y'all would devote more time to traffic and the news instead of cutting the fool all the time."

"Girl, please. Who wants to listen about traffic all hour? There are only three things you need to know: yes, there's traffic; no, it's not moving; and yes, your slow black ass is going to be late like every other day. Anyway, girl, you know who just called the station right? I don't believe her crazy ass!"

"Yeah, I heard." I busted out laughing. "You know how DeDe is. She wants to know if every man she dates is gay or has bisexual tendencies. If she investigated their marital status as much, she'd be straight. And meanwhile, the rest of us are just looking for a man with a job, car, and who don't live with his momma. I don't blame her, though. She just wants to know, straight up, if he likes dick or pussy—or dick and pussy."

"Jessie girl, you are a trip. You know she ain't right. You know she ain't. Even after we've gone through this over and over again, she still has to ask that man how he gets down."

"Girl, just leave it alone. If that man doesn't put her in check, some other man will. Like how Malcolm is gonna put her in check tonight. You know that looney toon is probably on his way to her job—with his wedding band on!"

"You know I'm about to put her on the spot."

"About what, Lis? Not Malcolm, I hope!"

"No, girl. Malcolm's wife is going to handle that one day real soon. I'm talking about her asking every damn man if he's gay."

"Oh, well go ahead, girl. I need a good laugh this morning before I go in and deal with that bitch Harriet."

"Got to go!"

"Wait, Melissa. You know I just did my living will with that life insurance agent. You need to make sure you get one ASAP."

"Well damn, Jessie. You going to kill me off?"

"No, girl. You know what I mean. We're getting up there . . . got to put our shit in order."

"Yeah, I do. I'm going to get to it in the next few days."

"Okay, good. Call me later."

I turned up the radio a bit and prepared for both the remainder of my commute and the circus about to beat up my car speakers. Dallas traffic was a pain in the ass, but at least I had Melissa's crazy tail and DeDe's crazier tail to get me through it.

"Yeah, this is DK with the sweeeeeeeeet Melissa Morgan. Caller, you've got a comment?"

"Yes, I'm the friend of the caller who wanted to know if she should ask the gentleman if he's gay or not."

"Okay. So friend, do you want to give your name?"

"My name is V, short for Vanessa."

"Okay. So V, you have the inside scoop on the deal. What's your take on the situation?"

"Well, in De—" A loud beep smothered the rest of DeDe's name, "case—oh my goodness! My bad, girl, for saying your name on the radio. But anyway, she asks every man she dates if he's gay, so if she really wants to take it there—and I know she will—all she has to do is just say that she asks every man if he's gay, or has gay or bisexual tendencies, nothing personal. That's my MO, and trust, I must know."

"That's all fine, V, but regardless of if she asks every man if he's gay or not, I think the question is, is it appropriate to ask a man if he is gay? From a male perspective, if a female asks me that question out of the blue, I'd be offended . . . Okay, I think we have a male caller on the line. Caller, what's your name? Where you calling from and what's your take on the situation?"

"Yo, man, my name is Reggie. I'm calling from Oak Cliff. Hey DK, if a woman that I was taking out to lunch, and paying for, came at me that way, that bitc [*beep*] would be paying for her own damn lunch."

"Whoa! The language my brother."

"My bad, but yo, man, it's incorrect for a sister to ask a brother something like that, regardless of what's happened in her past. If you have doubts now, regardless of what the brother says or does for that matter, the sister's probably always going to have some shadow of a doubt in the back of her mind. I don't think that's the way to start a relationship, and I think she should just keep it on the friendship tip and move on to a brother who she feels comfortable with to where she doesn't have to ask that question, or have any doubts."

"That's a point well taken my brother. Thanks for your comment. So what do you think about that, Melissa?"

"DK, I agree. If it comes to the point where you're unsure about a man's sexual orientation, I say move on. Any man will know when someone is interested in him whether gay or straight, and if he doesn't give into your advances it doesn't necessarily mean that he's gay. He may just not be interested! If he does show interest, and by chance he happens to be bisexual, do you really think he's going to admit that he likes to, as you put it DK, straddle both sides of the fence? I agree with the male caller. If you have to ask, then you've answered the question yourself . . . Hi, caller. Talk to Melissa. What's on your mind?"

"Hey, Melissa. Hey, DK. I just wanted to let you know that I love your show! You guys are doing a great job and really touching the community. DK, can you sing happy birthday to me? And um, are y'all still giving away those tickets to the singles Pajama Jam for this Saturday? It's going to be on my birthday, and that sho' would be a good birthday present."

"Okay! Girl, you do know that the K103.5 Pajama Jam is only ten dollars, but since it's your birthday and all, maybe we can break you off a twenty. What do you think, DK?"

"Oh, no doubt, Melissa. Two tickets to the K103.5 Pajama Jam. What are you gonna wear? You sound good, girl . . . all sexy and stuff!"

"Oh my goodness, DK. You so crazy! I don't even know, but whatever it is, it's gonna be sexy."

Melissa said, "Unh-hunh, whatever, girl. Hold on, we need to get some information from you. Well DK, it's time to see what's cooking for lunch at Big Jim's Rib Shack . . . ."

Melissa and DK had gotten me to work safely another day, and as I walked through my company's doors I was wishing I could be back in the car listening to their fool antics. To say I hated my job would be putting it very mildly. I couldn't stand it. I felt like I knew too much to be dealing with the mediocre bullshit they gave me to do. And let's not talk about that bullshit title: Director of Sales and Marketing. It's just that—a damn title. I did have one thing to be grateful for though (look at me, always finding something good in even the worst situations—Big Momma would be proud!). Working for DataComm had put me in the path of Tracy, a sorority sister who actually pledged the same year I did. While she was pledging at Grambling I was pledging at Spelman and after discovering we were sorors we hit it off instantly—mostly comparing our pledging experiences and talking about being AKA sorors. Oh, and less not forget seeing who had the fiercest sorority call—Skee Wee. Tracy had hooked me up with her husband's good friend, Michael. Michael and I certainly weren't an item at that point, but I really liked him. And if nothing else, I could say DataComm had brought me love. Hell, if Michael and I worked out, all those miserable years working like a slave up under Harriet would be worth it.

Any who, that Tuesday was the day of the big meeting with Daisy Chain, a small but reputable cosmetics company trying to improve their image and increase their profits by launching a new cosmetics line. Their parent company, Daisy Chain grocery stores, wasn't helping their image either. As director of sales and marketing, it was my responsibility to drum up their business. However, it was the promotions/advertising department's responsibility to sell them on the marketing strategy, and my success depended on their success . . . fucked up, huh? Well, of course, what can you do with a name like Daisy Chain? Daisy Chain! Like sisters would be busting down the doors and fighting in the aisles for the last container of Flower Basket Brown lip shade #12. Anyway, I was nearly to my desk, I wanted to go over the marketing proposal again before the meeting, when none other than my boss, Ms. Don't-Have-a-Life-and-In-Everybody's-Business Harriet, stops me in the hall.

She says, "Well Jessie, are we ready for the big meeting today?"

I said, "Harriet, I'm on top of my sales pitch. I just hope advertising has a good idea to work with so we can hook this deal. It would be a shame if we created a great marketing package and advertising doesn't get the word out."

Then Harriet said, "Well, I've given your presentation some consideration and believe that you're still too green to handle such an important deal. So, as vice president of sales and marketing, I'm going to present the marketing pitch to Daisy Chain before and after advertising wows them with their pitch."

I could not believe the shit coming out of her mouth. But I kept it on the straight and narrow. I said, "Well, do you think that's wise? I mean, I've been working on this for almost four months now, and I know all the details in and out."

"Just follow my lead, Jessie. I'll see you at ten thirty."

I almost said, "No this trick didn't," out loud. No this trick didn't! Damn! I'm the one who got the client in the door, slaved over the numbers according to advertising's and promotions' ideas, and this bitch was going to present my idea to Daisy Chain and our company executives. Ughhhhhhhhhh! All I could keep saying was, *No this trick didn't*, inside my head. Oooooh, I was so damn mad, I couldn't even sit down and think. Ooooh Jessie, Jessie, Jessie, breathe girl, breathe . . . I tried it all and I was still steaming! That bitch! Aarrgh! No this trick-ass bitch didn't!

Chapter Three

The Presentation

Ten thirty and all of us were sitting in the executive boardroom talking and making idle chitchat when Ms. In-Everybody's-Business showed up. In my head, I was saying, *Look at that bitch. Ughhh! I just can't stand her.*

"Good morning, everyone. I'm Harriet James, and I'd like to extend a warm welcome to the Daisy Chain Corporation. On behalf of DataComm International, I'd like to thank you for taking the time out of your busy schedules to meet with us and discuss how we can market your new cosmetics line to make it as well known and profitable as the CoverGirls and Estee Lauders of the world. I'd like to start by introducing the DataComm International staff, and then I'll introduce the Daisy Chain executives who are, I'm sure, eager to hear how DataComm can improve their image and enhance their business portfolio. Starting to my left is Vic Ramsey, director of advertising and promotions; seated next to him is Sharon Wisely, director of accounting services; next is Wes Parker, director of public relations followed by DataComm's chief operations officer Nancy Pruitt; directly across from Nancy is our president and chief executive officer David Housmann; and last but not least, a familiar face to the Daisy Chain staff, Jessie Harris, director of sales and marketing, whom you've been interacting with since day one."

Ms. Nosey went on to introduce the Daisy Chain Corporation representatives—Jay Folsom, director of advertising and sales; Tracy Cole, director of marketing and public relations (I gave her a little wink hello); and senior vice president of sales and marketing Daniel Van Johnson. She welcomed us with the phoniest smile. I wished I could slap those big teeth down her throat. I sat back and opened my eyes and ears wide, though. I needed to see and hear exactly how she was going to take all the credit for my sleepless nights and countless hours of research.

"Jessie? Could you please hit the lights for me? I'd like to set the milieu."

Milieu? What the hell was she talking about? I *knew* she had just watched me sit back and get myself comfortable for her charade. I felt my eyes on their way up to roll all over the place, but I knew everybody was watching me. I returned her phony smile and got up to dim the lights. All the while, I was thinking, *What the hell is wrong with your feet? You couldn't walk your skinny ass over here and hit these damn lights yourself?* Before I got back to my seat, she was running her mouth again.

"Daisy Chain . . . Daisy Chain . . . Daisy Chain . . ." The bitch was chanting like a damn monk—and with her eyes closed. "Stay with me here." She lifted up her hands as if in prayer or something. "Imagine a glorious field of daisies. Can you see it? Can you see it?" She opened her eyes to look around the room. We all stared at her in the same— bitch, are you crazy?—way. She must not have liked what she saw because she shut those eyes again right quick. "Imagine a glorious field of daisies. They are swaying in the wind, reflecting not only their own color, but the color of the sun. Now imagine women of every shade emerging from this field of daisies. Suddenly white, yellow, red, brown, black women stand among the flowers, their makeup flawlessly applied, their smiles wide as rivers . . ." She opened her eyes a final time and rushed over to lift the lights. She jogged back to her seat to gauge the reaction of the Daisy Chain representatives. The whole time I'm thinking, *Oh . . . my . . . god. If that wasn't the most ludicrous marketing pitch I've ever heard. Not only did the heifer present the idea, she threw a curve ball and changed the entire presentation—that's what you get bitch! Who the hell would associate a field of daisies on a warm summer day with all the skin tones of the world? The last daisy I saw was pure-T white. Not black, not brown, not even red.* The Daisy Chain people looked about as puzzled as I felt. The silence was long and awkward.

So I intervened. "My apologies, Mr. Van Johnson. If I could offer another idea for thought?"

"Jessie, I don't think that will be necessary or appropriate," Ms. Field-of-Daisies said.

"No, no Ms. James. It's fine. Please. We've been meeting with Jessie for the last four months, and no one—as clearly evidenced by that marketing pitch of yours—knows how our company operates and what we're looking for better than Ms. Harris."

"Thank you, sir." I stood and took my rightful place before the members of the meeting. "Well, after countless visits to Daisy Chain and after speaking with a number of its employees and then going further to talk with dozens of customers, I've come to the conclusion that Daisy Chain must offer the public at large an idea built upon a dependable, reputable image. From the information I've researched, a single problem has surfaced again and again, and that problem is that Daisy Chain does not appeal to everyone—much like Ms. James's field of daisies analogy." I didn't even look at Harriet because I would have busted out laughing. I continued, "I can offer Daisy Chain, not only a way to sell its *current* product line, but a way to sell the proposed product and all its future products as well. Why pay to market something that only appeals to a small subset of people? A subset that cannot sustain the line's financial goals? Why not expand on Daisy Chain's original idea—to beautify the faces of the country's lighter ethnicities—and welcome women of all ethnicities? Of all shades? Take a look at Daisy Chain's current advertising campaign. Ms. James, would you mind getting the lights for me? I have a PowerPoint presentation for our clients." Unlike me, Harriet had a hard time containing her anger. She stomped to that light like a damn toddler with a soggy diaper.

The slide lit up the screen and I was commanding everyone's attention. Good thing I had gone with the red suit. And good thing I hadn't eaten breakfast. The curves were like Oww! I kinda wanted to holler up to Big Momma, "Sometimes pretty does pay the bills." We all looked at the dull face of an elderly white woman on the screen.

"I only see white. And while there's nothing wrong with white, and the Daisy Chain products do a wonderful job of minimizing this woman's flaws and highlighting her strengths, it simultaneously shuts out millions of other women. Now take a look at this slide."

The next slide portrayed a group of older women of every possible shade. They were beautifully "painted" in experimental Daisy Chain products. Each of them smiled. Their eyes twinkled.

"Here we have black, yellow, red, *and* white women."

"Excuse me, Jessie."

"Yes, Mr. Van Johnson?"

"Well, Jessie, this is an absolutely stunning campaign, but whose products are these women wearing? We only manufacture for, as you say, those members of 'lighter' ethnicities."

"Oh, Mr. Van Johnson, I had a few of the makeup manufacturers in your creations studios whip up some experimental formulas for me. All the products, per your company's policy, were tested without harming a single animal."

"Wow, Jessie. I am truly impressed."

"Thank you. I appreciate the recognition, but what I am most interested in is assuring that Daisy Chain commit to producing products that address the skin care needs of all women . . . Mr. Van Johnson, if I can have you walk over and stand in front of the mirror, please."

I accompanied Mr. Van Johnson over to the wall-length mirror behind the projection screen after raising the lights. It was quite the intimate meeting for a moment as we waited for the screen to lift, and I was happy to have him so close to me for a while. Not that I was trying to holler at Mr. VJ or anything, but I knew I'd be able to give him all my positive energy. I shot him my million-dollar smile. Finally, the screen revealed the entire boardroom in the crystal clear mirror.

"Okay, so now you're looking in the mirror and you see a reflection, right? It's you and everyone else. You don't have to study too hard to see that this mirror offers us a variety of images. We're all uniquely beautiful. Now multiply our numbers by millions. There are millions of women in this country yearning for a skin care system that not only considers, but addresses, their needs. You want a product that will be a perfect reflection of this image of diversity.

"Please, Mr. Van Johnson, have a seat. And Ms. James, do you mind getting the lights for me one more time? Thanks."

As he returned to his seat and Harriet huffed and puffed over to the lights, I released the projection screen and assumed my pose before the table of eager listeners.

"Now, what product can accomplish this for you?" A slide with the word *Egami* appeared on the screen. It was coated in gold and set against a deep purple background. My favorite color never failed me. Just the word alone was beautiful. I said, "You pronounce this word E-ah-me. It is nothing more than *image* spelled backward. But it is, in fact, much more. The word promises what Daisy Chain will deliver—skin care for the very original and special image each of us see in the mirror. What better way to push Daisy Chain products than with a new and invigorating concept—the concept that we are all beautiful and all deserve individualized skin care? *Egami: The perfect image of you.*"

I was quite pleased with myself, but I was staring into a room of closed mouths. To diffuse the silence, I went to raise the lights a final time. By the time I turned around everyone was grinning from ear to ear. I thought, *Okay, I think this is a good sign, but will somebody say something?* A smile can mean a few things. I mean, psychopaths run around smiling all over the place the same way regular old happy people do.

Mr. Van Johnson broke the silence. "Jessie, all I can say is brilliant! With this idea, Daisy Chain Corporation would like to establish a working relationship with DataComm. We trust that you will make Daisy Chain cosmetics a household name. CoverGirl, Estee Lauder, Fashion Fair—watch out!"

"Thanks, Mr. Van Johnson. That has significant meaning coming from you. Now with all that said and done, can we go over these numbers again?"

"Let's start cracking, Jessie. Or should I say partner?"

Finally, I had gotten to show them what I was made of. Not only could I go out and drum up the business, I could market the product, and reel the deal in, too. It took five years, but I had finally showed them. Now bitch, what you got to say about that? Kiss my black ass! Humph! I just knew she was saying, *No this trick didn't!*

Nothing could have stopped my high, but something did strike me as a little strange. On my way out of the boardroom, Tracy caught up to me. We gave each other a hug and she congratulated me on the presentation. Then, out of the blue, she said, "So, are you and your girls hanging out tonight?"

I told her, "Well, not really. We're actually all going to be participating in this love forum on K103.5. Girl, I would tell you to listen in but I think I'm going to end up embarrassing myself!" We laughed, and she promised she'd tune in and told me not to worry, I'd do fine.

"So all your girls are going to be discussing their business? I bet there's going to be some scandalous talk on there!" Tracy was a cute, petite girl. Her hair was always fly. Shoes always sharp. But the bullshitting she was doing wasn't becoming.

"Whatchu mean, Tracy?"

"Well, you know how we women can be." She play tapped me on the shoulder. I was getting uncomfortable with the corniness. "Sleeping with each other's husbands and stuff!"

"Unfortunately, I do, girl. And unfortunately, there might just be a story or two about that! But I think the premise of the show is to find good, healthy love. So hopefully everyone will move away from the negative and closer to the positive."

To the casual observer it might have just looked like two sorors chatting, but Tracy and I had never really discussed my girlfriends. And she had never behaved that way with me. In fact, I couldn't even recall a time that I'd even said Melissa's name to her, and Melissa and I went together like peanut butter and jelly. Everything from the forced hug to the tap just seemed contrived. I didn't know what it was, but something came over me. I asked myself, *Why is she asking about my girls?* You know how some things just don't sit right with you?

Chapter Four

K103.5 The Love Forum

I went home that evening feeling real good about myself and about all the possibilities the relationship with Daisy Chain would lead too—one that I hoped would put me out of that little-ass cubicle I was calling an office. But I got the reality put right back in me when I realized I had to head over to the radio station. In just that short space of time, I had forgotten all about it. Damn, I was nervous about exposing my intimate self to hundreds of thousands of people in and around Dallas. Girl, I was a wreck, but Melissa knew how to calm everyone down, despite being a wreck herself. I didn't know what was going on, but the deal with Dr. Laura wasn't going too well, so she was worried about the show not having any credence. A Stacey Lattisaw song was playing, and we were sitting around the DJ booth singing and reminiscing about what we were doing when we first heard the song.

"That was Stacey Lattisaw with 'Don't Throw It All Away' ending our old-school triple play and easing you into the first love forum with the sweet, sweet Melissa Morgan. I'm Mr. Kirk 'Magic' Wonder getting ready to throw a little hot grits on you with a little 'Love and Happiness.'"

"K103.5, this is Melissa Morgan. Ahhh, something's going on baby. I want to welcome you to the very first edition of *The Love Forum*—a forum to discuss life's issues as they relate to, as Al Green would put it, love and happiness. Our first show will revolve around introducing the K103.5 listeners, not only to the show's format, but also to six beautiful sisters who have committed to sharing their personal lives with the K103.5 family for six months. Yes, you heard it right—six months. You might be asking yourself, what are these women going to talk about for six months? Absolutely everything! From the men they're currently dating to the breakups they'll have two weeks later—just kidding—to what a sister really wants from a relationship, and how to get it too. Hmmph, and the best part for me—the down and gritty sex. You know, which type of man can get down with it, and which type of man needs the coaching. Oh, and let's not forget exploring why money, or the lack thereof, can enhance or hurt a relationship.

"It should be an interesting voyage, to say the least, and to help us out on some of our personal issues, and yours, we've brought in Dr. Laura. Dr. Laura is our in-house radio psychotherapist, and you know she's always on point, and more importantly, she always keeps it real!"

The more Melissa ran her mouth, the more nervous I became. By this point, I was tapping my feet beneath the table like I was Gregory Hines or something. I couldn't even stomach a peek at my girls sitting around the table. If they were nervous too that'd make me more nervous, and if they were calm and collected, I'd drive myself crazy wondering what was wrong with me.

"But first, I need to introduce you to the six beautiful sisters, sitting ever so patiently, and give you a little bit of their background information. Let's see where each of them is coming from!"

I swallowed a big gulp of air and started coughing right into the microphone.

"Oh lord! That's Jessie, y'all. And she is far prettier than she sounds! She's just a little nervous. Jessie, girl, get it together over there. First, K103.5, we have Pat. Pat is a housewife who married her college sweetheart Donnell, the football jock. She has two kids: Matthew, six, and Chanté, four. They are the typical American family with a nice house in the 'burbs, two cars and an SUV, active in their community and, of course, their church. Makes you want to say, 'Hmmpphh! Whatever!'"

I took a quick look at Pat. She looked as nervous as me. She held her hands in her lap and hunched her shoulders like a little old lady.

"Brit is a flight attendant for American Airlines. Needless to say, she's about as big as a pencil with hair big as the sun. She thinks she has it going on, but thinking has never been one of her strong suits." We all laughed at that, nervous or not. "Just kidding, girl! Now, Darlene is a real estate agent who is banking. You go, girl. The only problem is, she's sworn off black men and is now dating exclusively outside of her race. Girl, you know I'm going to tell ma dear, but then that Brazilian man know he's fine! Humph, I'm here to tell you, girl, watch your back!"

"I ain't got to watch my back, Melissa. Miguel, whose name means 'who is like God' by the way, ain't going nowhere. And you know God is all the time faithful."

"Amen, girl."

I looked at Darlene a while as I had started to calm down a bit. I thought, *Well shit, maybe I need to start shopping in some other aisles too!*

"Jessie is the Spelman graduate who is beautiful, conservative, and one of those on-the-fast-track executive black women. Still, she admits there's a void in her life. I just hate her." Melissa opened her mouth wide in laughter. "You know I'm kidding, girl. Skee-wee.

"Vanessa, affectionately known as V, is a single divorced mother who lets everyone know that her man just came home one day and said he was leaving her quote, 'fat ass for someone else.' Little did she know it was for another man. Oh, and please don't let me forget to add—'and after eleven and half years of putting up with that Negro's mess'—but y'all know she used way worse words than those! But that surely isn't the most important thing about this lovely lady! She is thinking of opening her own business. Ain't that right, V?"

"Wheeewww, speak it girl! Make those blessings fall down. You know I need to open up that shop!"

"I'm trying to make it pour down on you V," laughing, "and speaking of *in need of some blessings!* My girl, DeDe, is a third grade school teacher—props for making school teacher of the year girl!"

"Yes!" yelled DeDe. "Couch Elementary in the house!"

"Girl, we do not do shout-outs! Anywho, DeDe is also an aspiring songstress who's actively trying to get her singing career off the ground. Humph, good luck, girl!" laughing. "And finally, I'm Melissa Morgan, co-host of K103.5's morning show with the mad-cool disc jockey DK Niles. I've been here in the big D-town for over six years now, coming from the Dirty South's Hotlanta. I'm currently dating a very special man and we've been exclusive for a little over a year now. Just waiting for that question, Quentin! You heard! Welcome my beautiful sisters, and thanks for being a part of K103.5's *The Love Forum*."

In one big voice we all said, "Thank you."

"I'm sure all the listeners, especially the fellas, are interested in learning more about all of you, so I want to start to my left and ask each of you to give a brief description of yourself. Better yet, if you had to rate yourself, tell the K103.5 family what you consider yourself to be on a scale from one to ten. Magic will let the K103.5 family know if you're on point—as only he can do. So, starting to my left . . . go, Brit girl."

"Hi, K103.5. I'm Brit. I'm twenty-nine-years-old, and as Melissa said, I'm a flight attendant for American Airlines. I love quiet evenings at home with that special man, and if I had to rate myself, I would say that I'm an eight."

"Magic," Melissa said, "Is she on the money?"

Magic played "Super Freak" by Rick James and started singing adlib to the music, "She's a freak . . . freak . . . my girl is just a freak—"

"Oh no, he didn't!" Brit gestured like she was about to get out of her chair, but Melissa waved her down.

"Girl, Magic just calls 'em like he sees 'em!"

It was Pat's turn. "Hey, K103.5. This is Pat, the housewife. I'm thirty-six, married to a wonderful man—hey, Donnell baby, I love you—I have two wonderful children, and we all work hard at making the space within our house a wonderful home."

"And Mrs. Wonderful-Home," Melissa interrupted, "how would you rate yourself on a scale of one to ten?"

"Why bother, Melissa? I'm off the market."

"Okay, Magic. What do you have to say about that?"

"Well Melissa, I think the song that sums it all up for Mrs. Wonderful-Home is from Chanté Moore, with a different spin on it of course. *My girl V gotta a man at home and he's so good to V*—"

"Humph, whatever. K103.5, this is DeDe, and I'm a twenty-nine-year-old aspiring songstress."

Melissa said, "Girl, the hate! Anyway, you sure you only twenty-nine?"

"Yes, girl. That's how old I'm going to be for this show! Any who, I'm a twenty-nine-year-old aspiring songstress and I have one thing to say about the man I'm dating."

"Uh-oh. Tell it, girl!"

"Oh, I'm going to sing it for you!"

"All right! Blow, girl."

DeDe silenced us all with her beautiful voice. "My girlfriend *Shirley* called me, and I couldn't believe her call. She told me that my man, wasn't, really, my man after all. Ooh, she knows she hurt me, but I needed to hear that call. *The man I loved had a wife and kids, beyond these four walls*. Yes, he did! He had a wife, and kids, beyond these four walls."

"Ooh, no he don't, girl!"

"Yes, he does, Melissa. And if I knew his damn address the night I found out, I would've driven over there and kicked the black off of his natural black ass." I knew Melissa was glad that she'd have the opportunity to go back and "bleep" out all the personal information and cursing DeDe had just done, but she had a hard time holding in her laughter, especially as Magic started playing the theme music from *Psycho*.

"Magic, you just wrong for that!"

"Anyway, Melissa," DeDe interrupted, rolling her eyes at Magic, "on a scale from one to ten, I say I'm a nine."

"Magic, take it away for Melissa!"

"Melissa, nine is stretching it a bit. I think En Vogue said it best." And then he played, En Vogue's 'Lies.'"

DeDe wasn't paying attention to Magic, though. She was on her BlackBerry, probably texting Malcolm. She had been talking about leaving him for months now, but she still hadn't found the strength to do it. She made me think of the conversation Tracy and I had had earlier that day. So sad my girls couldn't defy the stereotype! They had to live right up to it!

Vanessa was no better with her bitter self and laughed at DeDe with the rest of us as she began her introduction. "103.5, 103.5, 103.5! I'm V, short for Vanessa. I'm thirty-four, and I'm an around the way girl, in every sense of the word. I'm searching for a man who's not afraid to show his emotions, and who knows how to work that thang and get up in all this! Who can handle an independent woman who's an entrepreneur. I don't want a hater, okay? Because men do be hating! Yes they do!"

"All right now, V."

"Okay! Come on girls, you've got to give up the dap on that one!" V gave Darlene a high five. "On a scale of one to ten, bump that seven, eight, and nine mess 'cause modesty don't live here baby. I'm a ten and plus some! Magic, whatcha got for me?"

"Only one thing can touch that V." Magic began playing 'She's a Bad Mama Jama' by Carl Carlton, "36, 54, 36—"

"Heyyyyy! I know that's right, Magic—fifty four and everything. Go 'head, boy . . . I'ma get 'cha later!"

"Whew, girl, you are too much for Melissa!"

It was finally my turn. I had calmed down a bit, though my palms were a bit warm. I hadn't been that nervous presenting to Mr. Van Johnson! And my job was on the line with that. "Hello, K103.5. This is Jessie. I'm thirty-two about to take that turn onto thirty-third street. I'm a hopeless romantic at heart, and I'm looking for a man who's true in every sense of the word. On a scale of one to ten, I say I'm an eight. Okay, Magic?" I gave him that look.

"Baby girl, I just have one thing to say," as he began playing "SuperModel" by RuPaul, "you better work Jessie Harris—with yo fine self . . . You ain't no damn eight. You'sa dime! A ten all day!"

"And of course K103.5 listeners, last, but nothing says least about her, Darlene, the banking real estate broker."

"Hi, K103.5. This is Darlene. I'm thirty-one-years-old, a former Ms. Black Texas, and I'm currently in a relationship with a beautiful man who treats me like a queen. And girl, it feels like he throws rose petals on the ground I walk on."

"Well, just to move us along before the break, not to rush you or anything, girl, but how long have you been dating the Brazilian?" Melissa cut right to the chase, and I can't lie, I started to worry a little more about her getting all up in my business. I mean damn!

"We've been dating for about two months now, and I think it's turning very serious."

"Serious? In two months, girl? Okay, okay, let me stop! And on a scale of one to ten, how would you rate yourself?"

"I say that I'm probably a nine."

"Aw shucks now, girl! Melissa ain't mad at you. Go on with your bad self. Sounds to me like you may be in love too. And listeners, what would be more appropriate in taking us to our commercial break than the queen of soul Aretha Franklin, singing like only she can do, 'I'm In Love.'"

During that first break, Melissa received dozens of calls praising the show and letting her know it was already the talk of Dallas. Over the course of the night, we all talked and laughed and just had a good time with Magic and all the callers and listeners. I actually looked forward to the official premier on Sunday, during the quiet storm hours beginning at ten. Thursday, and Friday were like different days for all of us. It was like we had been transplanted into a different world and time. Being on *The Love Forum*, for that one night, made the six of us into local celebrities, to say the least, and all our lives changed just as quickly. I can't lie. I began to feel a little hopeful about finding love.

+++

I figured Dr. Wilma probably had a good idea of how a typical—well, not so typical—workday went for me. I looked up from my seat to find her flawlessly made-up face. She was studying her notepad. I can say I definitely appreciated being listened to so well. It was like talking to a much smarter Melissa.

"Jessie, now that Dallas has been officially introduced to the love forum ladies, well, the built up façade that all of you have established for the audience, I want to know the 'real' love forum ladies. What's going on behind the scenes? What's holding you ladies back from finding what I call sweet, sweet love?"

"What do you mean, Dr. Wilma?"

"I mean that sometimes you can learn a lot about someone by the people they associate with. Many times, things that are happening amongst friends impact one's life or all the lives involved. So, I hear what you want Dallas to know, but what's really going on? And hopefully, you'll feel comfortable enough to be candid and open about summing up your friends."

"Well, I guess I'm as comfortable as I'll ever be, and as for the Divas—that's what we call ourselves—I guess there's a lot of hurt, anguish, and confusion in all our lives. We all want that perfect life, the great job and career, the wonderful husband to come home to and share our lives with, and the family held together by love. But even with those who appear to have that on the outside, it's a far cry from what's going on in the inside."

"I'm assuming you mean Pat and Donnell's relationship?"

"Yes!"

"So what about Brit? And I'm just going to go down the line. You let me know where they are in their lives, and maybe I can determine if it's having a negative or positive impact on yours."

"Well Brit is the special one. She has no common sense—at all—and men just treat her like shit . . . Well, the ones she's attracted to, who are usually the bad boys. She believes that she needs a man in her life to complete her, and she'll put up with all kinds of shit to keep him in her life. Believe me, there are some stories with that one!"

"And Darlene?"

The mention of Darlene's name made me laugh. "That girl can sell anything. She could sell you used toilet paper and make you believe you need it. But I truly believe she's pretty happy. After all the brothers she's dated, and been dogged by, she took a bold step and decided to date outside of her race and met a man who treats her like a queen. The only thing is, all those bad relationships are now affecting this one, and I'm not sure he's going to wait around for her to let them go. She's hounding him all the time about why he loves her. She thinks it's suspicious that he likes her so much just when his work visa is about to expire."

"Good, and what about Vanessa?"

"V has a wonderful personality, but she believes that her weight is keeping her from true happiness. Every week there's a different diet plan or gimmick that's going to make her lose the pounds, and make her more attractive. It's so sad. What she fails to realize, and what we keep telling her, is that she's fine just the way she is. There are plenty of men that want, and only want, a BBW."

"Yes, there's nothing wrong with a big beautiful woman." Dr. Wilma and I laughed a good bit at that one. "As you can see, I happen to be one myself, and I do all right."

"Well, maybe she should come and see you. Maybe you can talk some sense into her!"

"So, what about Ms. Sing-Every-Word DeDe?"

"You got it, Dr. Wilma. Yes, DeDe is the twenty-nine-year-old aspiring songstress who, with every year, gets older and her dreams fade a little, but the girl can definitely blow. For some reason, she keeps attracting the same type of man, who just happens to be the wrong type of man, and usually married. Though I will say she usually drops the attached ones when she discovers she's the other woman. Malcolm, though, she hasn't been able to push away."

I smiled a bit and then sighed. This particular combination always came out when I was about to talk about Melissa. "And then there's Melissa. She appears to have it all—the career, the spoils of her career, and the love of her life to go along with it. You know, some people are with someone and they may love them, but they're not in love with them. That's not the case with these two. They're in love with each other, and the rest of the Divas are trying sooooo hard to get there. Melissa's so secretive, though. I hope she knows she can always count on us in case she needs us . . ."

"And what about you, Jessie? How is Jessie doing?"

"I really don't know at this point. I think I've given up. I want to find my soul mate. I want to find the man that every hour of the day I think of him. I want a man who, when we're together, it's not only the physical, but it's mentally satisfying as well. You know where we communicate and can talk to each other without even talking to each other. And those seconds, minutes, and hours of time that we're together or apart makes our relationship grow even stronger. I want a man who wants to be with me for me, and only me. Is that asking too much? Does it even exist, God? I just don't want to grow old alone. I see it every day, and I pray that I can escape that life!"

"Well Jessie, I think we've made tremendous progress. Unfortunately, our time is up. You mentioned an old-school party going on tonight. Do you have any plans to attend?"

"Well, actually, Melissa arranged for all of us to be there tonight so the listeners can come out and put faces with the names and voices. So I think we're all going to be there minus Pat."

"And will this be a first time you've participated in one of the radio station's events?"

"Pretty much. I'm a homebody, I guess."

"Hmmm . . . Well Jessie, it's been a pleasure meeting you, and I look forward to our next session. I want to start scheduling a normal time, so if Saturdays at two work well . . . ?"

"Yes, that's fine."

"Then Jessie, we're set. I think the second or third Saturday of each month will be our standing meeting time. So I'll see you next month, okay? If you'll just see Rochelle at the front desk, she'll put you on the calendar. Thanks again, Jessie. And enjoy the old-school party tonight."

"No, thank you, Dr. Wilma!"

As I made my appointment with Rochelle, Dr. Wilma buzzed her and asked if I was still in the office. In the midst of writing, Rochelle raised her eyes to look at me, and then answered yes.

"Can you ask Ms. Harris if she can spare fifteen more minutes? I just looked at my notepad and saw that I had circled something I wanted to go back to prior to her leaving for the day."

I looked at Rochelle and with a puzzled face said, "That's fine."

Rochelle indicated that I was available, and Dr. Wilma asked when her next appointment was. Rochelle looked down and told her in two minutes. Dr. Wilma swiftly asked Rochelle to see if her next appointment would be willing to wait fifteen minutes and, if so, she would give her the first thirty minutes of their session as a gift. She said to buzz her if she encountered an issue and to send me back through. I thought to myself, *now this is one classy bitch.*

"Thank you for consenting to come back, Jessie," Dr. Wilma said as I entered the office. "In looking at the complete picture, I'm a little puzzled. You said that DeDe, the songstress, was involved with a married man, right? Well, I'm sure your circle of friends is very tight-knit, and who doesn't listen to K103.5, so tell me, did anything transpire between Malcolm and DeDe after her call into the radio station?"

Chapter Five

DeDe and Malcolm

After the K103.5 fiasco, DeDe walked into her condo exhausted after a long day at the school. Whoever said teaching third graders was a joy had not met her students—they were hoodlums in little people's bodies! Little midget hoodlums who sometimes peed on themselves. It was days like this one—when Jarrod's badass hoodlum self decided to dump the whole class set of math books out of the window—that she wanted, worse than anything, to be a famous singer, and nothing more. She was too wrapped up in thoughts of lesson planning and the parents she had to call to notice that Malcolm was standing in her living room looking like hate come to life.

Malcolm was a handsome man, and that could not be denied. Never mind the fact that he was helping DeDe with her bills. If he could just get that married thing handled he'd be her dream come true. He stood there with his fists balled and beads of sweat decorating his flawless skin.

"Now what the fuck you on that radio show talking about?"

DeDe was shaken out of her daydreams. He had obviously used his key to get in. Mean as those words sounded and angry as that face looked, she couldn't help but remark his beauty. Still, she wasn't up for Malcolm's pretty-ass antics.

"What, Malcolm? If you heard the shit, what you asking me what I said for? You heard with your own damn ears."

"The hell are you doing going out to lunch with some gay nigga from work?"

DeDe looked down at her left hand, turned it back and forth like she was searching for something. "Um, excuse me? But I am not your wife! Oh wait. You already have one of those!"

"DeDe, don't start that shit. You sure ain't leaving my married ass alone."

"Oh. And why is that Malcolm? Could it be that you made sure I was good and in love with your tail before you revealed that little bitty fact?"

"We ain't talking about me right now. We talking about you and how you about to drive that Benz back to the dealer if you don't cut that nigga off."

"Don't threaten me, Malcolm. You pay the insurance on that car, not the note, and if I have to, I'll pay that too. Don't make no damn threats until your ass is divorced and on your knee in front of *me*."

Malcolm snapped hearing how DeDe was just going to blow him off. He brought his hand all the way back and smacked her. DeDe didn't think she was the sort of woman to take physical abuse but he had surprised her, so she just stood there. She stood there until Malcolm began choking her. And he choked her until she cried and cried, "STOP IT—*Please!* Let me go . . . Malcolm . . . W-what . . . you doing? You said you'd never hit me."

DeDe looked at him out of lost eyes. She had been the other woman for going on thirteen months. And while the setup was getting tired, and she was dating other men in her spare time, she couldn't build the nerve to leave Malcolm alone. She wasn't even going to leave him after this incident. That's exactly what those lost eyes said. It likely had a whole lot to do with him putting a little something on her bills, but on top of that, she honestly did love the man. After he held her awhile and apologized for tripping out, they made love to make up for all the anger and hurtful words and violence. But he was dressed and out her door before she found where her panties had landed. She was nursing her bruises and questioning whether or not she could put up with this much longer.

Chapter Six

The K103.5 Old-School Party

June 26, 2008. Just being in Dr. Wilma's presence had put me at peace. I mean, I knew it probably wasn't a permanent thing . . . that it might not last longer than the damn weekend, but I was grateful to just breathe in and out a couple times without the feeling that something was lodged in my chest. I thought about calling my mom as I drove home from Spa Eloná, but then decided against it. I love my momma down to her bunions, don't get me wrong, and I missed her something terrible (damn, I wished I could eat some of her fish and home fries just then), but I didn't need to hear that sadness in her voice. I was beginning to think she was depressed, and I just didn't want to bear the weight of that at the moment. I made a conscious decision not to think about everything that was wrong with my life. And anyway, me and the girls had decided that weekend was ours. We were going on a little retreat. Broke as they were, the girls had rented the suite next to me at Spa Eloná. We had them for three days: Friday, Saturday, and Sunday. We were gonna party hard, drink ourselves silly, and not even discuss the men—real or imaginary—in our lives. Well, that was the plan.

When I got home, I packed a bag, but that was a little more difficult than it seemed. That stingy salary DataComm gave me not only affected the big things, like me making my mortgage and car note on time, but the little details too—like the extent and newness of my wardrobe! It took me a good three hours to pack a damn bag. Can you believe that? I must have tried on twenty outfits that made me look like I was wearing a paper bag. Thank God for these beautiful legs. Oh, and the ass and boobs still got lift! Not to mention the smile. My body and looks have saved many outfits, believe me. The old-ass dress I threw on to take the ride back to Spa Eloná, where we were meeting to check in and get ready for Melissa's homeboy Shakim's house party, would have looked hurt clinging to something less perfect than me. I was real thankful for Big Momma's genes on that ride over. When I got to the room, all the girls were already there. They might have cussed me out for being so late except they were already lit. Melissa was waving around a big old bottle of Hennessey when I walked through the door.

"Bitch, where you been? The fuck you think? We got all night to be waiting on you?" Melissa's mouth went a mile a minute when she was drunk. She cursed like a goddamn sailor, too. The only good part about it was you might get a little information out of her. Where Melissa was usually tight lipped about her personal business, a little dark liquor kicked down her walls.

I said, "I know you better watch your mouth. I'm not your child, and this ain't K103.5, bitch. You don't run a damn thing here."

"You know not to pay her any mind, Jessie. She drunk as a skunk. She was fucked up before I got here, and I was the second one to walk through the door." V looked nice. I hoped she realized it. Big as she was, she was curvy as the damn highway. That black one-piece pantsuit was fitting her like a motherfucking glove.

"You look real good, V."

"You say that like you don't catch me this way too often."

"I ain't mean that! I'm just saying that pantsuit is hot!"

We laughed and gave each other high fives. I rolled my suitcase into a corner, though I should have probably put it in my own room all the while, keeping my eyes on Melissa. Something wasn't right. Something was bothering her. I mean, I knew the plan was to get it popping, to have a nice relaxing weekend, but what the hell was she doing pissy drunk at ten thirty?

"Everything all right, Lis? You might want to slow it down over there."

"Don't fuck with me, Jess."

She took off and almost ran into the bathroom doorframe. I looked at the other girls. If I wasn't so surprised by Melissa talking to me that way and running off like that, I might have remarked how good they looked. I had a good-looking set of friends.

"I don't know what's wrong with her, Jess." DeDe was shaking her head. "She been upset all night. Coming out her face any kinda way. You know that ain't like Melissa. First of all, she usually act like she made of stone, and then second, she just ain't never upset! Things seem like they always going right for her. But anyway, she won't tell us nothing."

I started walking towards the bathroom. We were all girlfriends, and good girlfriends at that, but Melissa was *my* best friend. I needed to know what was going on with her. Before I could even reach the door, though, she came out looking fresh as ever. I don't know what she did in there, and I especially don't know why it only took her three hot minutes to pull her shit together, but she came out smiling and acting like she hadn't just cussed me out.

"Let's go, y'all. I'm ready to party." She stumbled a bit. I grabbed that bottle of Henny right out of her hand.

"That's enough of that."

"Jessie, you crazy. I'm fine, girl."

We filed out of the suite one behind the other, looking good as all get out, and smelling like a liquor store. We took Melissa's truck. I was obviously the designated driver. I don't know how happy I was about that. I mean, I wanted to get fucked up, too! But I guess that's what I got for showing up two hours late. The conversation was going before we left the parking lot.

"Okay, y'all. I got a question," Darlene said.

"Oh lord," Melissa said. "I already know what it is. You want to know if it's too soon to suck Miguel's dick! The answer's yes!"

We all busted out laughing. We knew Darlene too well. She had what you might call an oral fixation. She was addicted, I guess you might say. And giving head too early, and um, a little too eagerly, had gotten her in trouble many, many times before. She was always telling us stories about how some dude had told her, "That was the best head I ever had," and then never called her before one in the morning again.

"For real, y'all. I'm serious. Don't do that. I need to know."

"Darlene! You have known that man two months!" Melissa yelled.

"Yeah, Darlene. Why you always so eager to stick some dirty man's thing in your mouth? I mean, that shit ain't even sanitary, but then again girl, do you and we know you gone do you," V said, with a hint of disgust, as she rolled her eyes and sucked her teeth. I was beating the steering wheel, I was laughing so hard. Why was Darlene always in a rush to get on those knees? She was so conservative in every other way.

"See, that's why I hate sharing shit with, y'all. Everything's a fucking joke." Darlene crossed her hands like a seven-year-old and looked out the window, but not before she got her hands into V. "Now V—bitch— if you were doing a little more of the head game maybe you would have a man . . . with your bitter ass." After that sting, it was quiet as hell. V, didn't even try to make a comeback. We tried hard to hold back our giggles and did a good job for a while, but then Melissa let out the biggest, wildest laugh, and we all had to let loose after that. For a full sixty seconds, we laughed.

"All right, y'all," I said. "We know this is Darlene's thing. We gotta be there for her. Help her figure this out. Have y'all slept together?"

"Girl . . . please! Jessie, you know they did," Pat said, as she shook her head.

Laughing, I said, "Well, okay. Two months is a reasonable time to wait to give up the coochie."

"Girl, I ain't wait no two months. I been fucking that motherfucker since the first date."

And just when I thought we had it together! We laughed another five minutes.

"Damn, Darlene. You don't waste no time."

"What I'm waiting for, Jessie? I'm a grown-ass woman and this ain't 1965. If I want it, well I want it. And I ain't gonna wait for him to tell me he want it too, to get things popping."

"I know that's right. Well tell me, did he eat the pussy?"

"No."

"No? No? So the hell you talking about whopping him off for then? What you contemplating his dick sucking for and he ain't contemplated your pussy eating?"

"He said he don't do it."

It was like we all had one mouth because in unison we yelled, "Oh hell no!"

Pat took over the conversation then. When Pat takes over, you know it's serious, because Pat is a "taken" woman and she leaves a lot of stuff to us. I couldn't believe Pat had decided to party with us in the first place. I mean, she's not stuck up or anything, and she doesn't judge us, but as she says, "I just don't have nothing to say about some things." But Pat came out of the woodwork for this one. I reminded myself to ask her what had changed her mind.

"Darlene, what the hell you mean he *don't* do it?"

"He said it's nasty. And he don't like that all the holes so close together. He say we pee outta there, fuck outta there, and shit outta there, too. I mean, I understand what he saying. I don't know if I'd do it either. Plus, y'all know how I feel about head. I just love giving it. I don't mind really."

"Girl, what you love is your damn business. I can live without it. My husband's dick is too big in the first place. It's too much fucking work in the second, and in the third, I don't like the taste of nobody's fluids! Shit, I'm strictly a Kool-Aid girl!" Pat said.

"Amen!" hollered V.

"But we ain't talking about me. Whatever you love is your damn business. What I want to know is how any grown man on this whole earth can say he 'don't eat pussy.' Darlene, you do understand that by saying that, he saying *you* nasty?"

"That's right," Melissa said. "He can't separate you from your pussy. That's what the fuck make you a woman. How that nigga—oh wait, he ain't a nigga . . ." Melissa cracked herself up with that realization and couldn't even make her point. "Wait, wait, wait, ain't this motherfucker from Brazil, I hear them mothafuckers don't eat nothing but the pussy!"

"What Melissa is saying is you shouldn't be comfortable with a man who don't eat pussy. We all got our preferences.

Like I said, I can do without it. I don't wanna suck and I could care less to be sucked, but there's a big difference between it not being my favorite hobby and refusing to do it. If you are his woman—you are his woman, right?"

"Yeah, I'm his."

"Okay. If you're his woman then he should be more than willing to do whatever it takes to please you."

"But, Pat, I don't even care. It ain't a big deal to me. I can do without it."

"Okay, but you're missing my point. He's saying it's nasty. In other words, he don't love pussy. He don't love women as a whole. If he don't love pussy and women as a whole, he ain't never gonna love you. He ain't never gonna give you what you need."

"You taking it too far, Pat."

"Watch what I say, girl. Watch my words. I don't trust no man who don't eat pussy. I'm not saying they got to like it, and I'm suspicious if the first thing they do is jump down there with they mouth wide open, but they got to be willing to do it. Watch what I'm saying to you, and girl, Donnell loves to eat this pussy and it's *pussy real good*!"

"So is it too soon to suck his dick, though?"

We laughed again. "Go on, Darlene," I said. "You know you going to anyway."

You would've thought Darlene just won the lottery, she smiled so big. I knew she was probably mad she was going back to Spa Eloná with us instead of over to Miguel's house. I wouldn't be surprised if she skipped out on us, or better yet, had him meet us at Shakim's house and handled her business in the bathroom!

We arrived at Shakim's and looked for parking a good ten minutes. It looked like the spot was jumping. The whole street was lined with Range Rovers, Benzes, and BMWs. Maybe my husband was waiting for me inside! Maybe I'd be asking the dick sucking question in a couple of months myself!

Melissa was still stumbling and it didn't look like the liquor had worn off much, but she was quiet. Still, I had a few words for her in the front seat while the other girls talked behind us.

"I don't know what's going on with you, and you ain't got to tell me right now, but you need to get yourself together. You have a very high-profile job. And all eyes are on you, especially since the kick off of *The Love Forum*. Do not go in there and act up and have somebody e-mailing or calling the station telling your business. You just got in there good. You don't need nothing fucking that up. You hear me?"

"Yeah, I hear you, Jessie. I love you, girl. I got it together now, but let's just say my life ain't as sweet as it seem."

I wondered what Melissa meant, but then I didn't. I mean, what could she be talking about but a trifling man? If Morgan Freeman's old ass cheats, who don't? Even though Melissa and Quentin were really in love, I didn't put a damn thing past him. He was a man. Nothing more, nothing less. Whatever Melissa was talking about I would find out later, but right then, I just didn't want her going into Shakim's acting up. This was one night, and neither her house nor car was paid off!

We got out of the car looking like a bunch of hoodlums. Everybody except me was tipsy and their voices were rising to the occasion. Melissa rang the doorbell. My heart beat a little quicker, I can't lie. I knew it was just a stupid house party, but first of all, Shakim's house wasn't your run of the mill house. He lived on Summer. The houses over in that part of Dallas went for half a million, easy. One of those damn Ranges parked along the driveway was his, and his finger was bare as a chicken bone. He was a little more feminine than I liked, but I was on a new kick. I wasn't gonna cancel a man out for just one turnoff anymore. He could just be metrosexual—you know, a clean-cut ladies' man. As we were walking in, I noticed Darlene was typing away on her BlackBerry. I knew she was telling Miguel to get his ass up here on the double. And I knew one of Shakim's bathrooms was going to be christened, if it hadn't been already, before the end of the night.

The house was as beautiful inside as it was outside and the men were giving it a run for its money with their fine-looking selves. Too bad for us we had the wrong house! While we were busy looking around and admiring the scenery, the host asked Melissa whose guests we were.

"Oh, we're here for Shakim," Melissa said.

"Shakim? Oh, Shakim. I'm sorry, ladies. You have the wrong address. Shakim lives down the street at . . ."

As he gave Melissa the correct address, I felt my heart sink. Oh well, I wouldn't be catching any of those brothers. Maybe my husband was down the street. We all climbed back in the car. Before all the doors were shut, I noticed Melissa's shoulders droop. I knew whatever was bothering her was taking over her mind. I asked her what the hell was wrong with her. She said, "Girl, Quentin ain't never gonna marry me."

And just like that, nothing was funny anymore. Forget turning the music down. I punched that pause button and pulled that truck over, almost on top of the curb.

"That's what's bothering you?"

The Divas, who always had something to say—rain, hail, sleet, snow—were stone quiet. It was like they didn't even have mouths they were so quiet. And the quiet was obviously not what Melissa needed because she burst into tears. The nasty sort. Big ones that make your makeup run and push your snot out of hiding. I wanted to tell her, "Stop that! Your mascara running!" and "Girl, fuck that nigga!" and "I love you, girl. Stop that crying!" all at once. I was on the verge of crying my damn self when V stepped in and saved the show.

"Okay. So what you gonna do? And be honest with yourself. This us you talking to. What you gonna do about it? You gonna leave him? I mean, Lis, you gonna leave him? It's only been a year. He a good man. You gonna leave him because he ain't went out and took out a second mortgage after only a year? You talking crazy. A year. Bitch, I got enough girlfriends to take up both my hands who waiting on a nigga to marry them. And ain't none of 'em been with those fools less than five or six years. And you boo-hooing, acting stupid over a goddamn year. A year! You ought to be 'shamed, Lis. You ought to be 'shamed. Especially running that radio show good as you do.

Giving out that advice like you know just what you talking about when you a scared little girl yourself. You need to dry them damn tears, reapply that dang-on mascara, ask forgiveness for making Jessie almost run up on the curb, and shut the hell up."

I thought, *Well damn, V.* So much for compassion. I was gonna rub her back and tell her everything would be all right. I was gonna say some shit about Quentin not knowing what the hell he was missing, but when she put it that way it made sense. It made a whole lot of sense. We sat with that for a while. It was beginning to feel a little awkward, though. I was about to go for the keys to start the engine and drone out some of that silence, but I didn't have to. Melissa laughed her Santa Claus laugh before I could even turn the key. She laughed and laughed. And started slapping her knee like an old grandpa. She said, "I know that's right, V. Start the motherfucking car, Jess. We 'bout to hit up the old-school joint. Pat, pass me some baby wipes. I know you got some in that damn bathroom cabinet you call a purse. And one of y'all give me some mascara so I can get this pretty-ass face back in order."

"So, *no* to Shakim's?" I asked.

"Yeah, we'll have to holler at Shakim later. We're running a little more than fashionably late to our own party. We gotta get there and mingle."

And we were on our way to the old-school party just that easy, as if Melissa hadn't just had a minor breakdown and V hadn't just swept up all the pieces. We pulled up to the old-school joint, and I let them know I was no longer the designated driver. "One of you bitches is good enough to drive right now. Stay that way!" I led the Divas through the door looking for the bar. I was on a mission until I set eyes on the last thing I wanted to see. A big black good-looking loser named Marvin. My eyes might have rolled right out of my head if my eyelids weren't there to stop them.

Marvin was standing at one side of the bar, which was my cue to make my way to the opposite side.

DeDe said, "Jessie, girl, ain't that Marvin's fine ass over there?"

"Yeah, that's Marvin's fine, broke, no-good-dog ass."

"You gonna speak?"

"For what?"

"Don't be rude, Jessie," DeDe said.

"But more importantly, don't front like you didn't think you were gonna marry that no-good-dog!" Melissa always knew how to put me in my place.

I ordered an apple martini. For real, I was calculating the price in my head. I sincerely didn't have money to be blowing on drinks. When I reached for my wallet, Melissa slapped my hand down.

"Uh? This is our party, love. You know? *The Love Forum*? All drinks for the Divas are on the house."

"Whew, girl." I let out a big sigh. That just about made seeing Marvin not such a bad thing. Maybe I would speak to his trifling ass. I swallowed that martini in three gulps and hit the bar with my hand demanding another. By the time the bartender had mixed me up another—this one watermelon—Marvin was in my face. Looking like my own personal *nightmare* on Elm Street. Not that the brother wasn't fine. Believe me, the nigga was sharp. But after someone has hurt you, even the most handsome face turns butt ugly. He might as well have been the bottom of my damn stiletto. And not the heel part either. The sole—the part that picks up all the dirt and gum and trash.

"Yo, what's up, Jessie?"

Exactly. Sharp as all get out. He was handsome all the way down to his toes, but he opened his mouth and turned you off in three seconds flat. I know I was not looking like a woman you say, "What's up?" to. I mean, the dress was inexpensive and old as the Bible, but lying against my body and beneath my face it looked red carpet ready. And here this fool was talking to me like I was seventeen.

"Hello, Marvin. How are you?" I took a sip of my martini. I wanted to tip my head back and take that bitch straight, but I wouldn't give him the satisfaction of thinking I needed some liquor to handle his trifling ass.

"I'm good. Now that I see you."

"Hmmm. Oh, okay. Well I guess you're about to turn deathly ill 'cause, baby, now you see me . . . and now you don't." I held my drink up over my head (I wasn't going to lose a drop over that clown), and started trying to work my way away from the bar, to find my girls. The man started following me like a dumb-ass puppy dog. Funny how when I wanted him to hound my ass I couldn't find him, and now that we're through—I mean he was as useful to me as my last dump's toilet paper—he wanted to come wagging behind me.

"Aw, girl, come on. Why it got to be like that, Jess?"

I turned around to give it to him eye to eye. "Because Marvin, you're trifling. Flat out. Ain't no ifs, ands, or buts about it. And what I don't need in my life right now, even if it's just to say a simple hello, is another trifling Negro. Beat it!"

"Oh. Okay, Jess. You acting brand new, I see. It's like that?"

"Baby, it's been like that." I gave him a whole lot of neck and evil eye to go with it. My girls were in my periphery by then. I could spice it up a little for them.

"Fuck you then, bitch."

I busted out laughing. I had to save my drink from spilling, I was laughing so hard. That was some funny shit. A dog's favorite way to *try* to affect you was by calling you out your name. If I wasn't a Spelman graduate, if I wasn't a full-damn three-decades old, if I wasn't Big Momma's baby, I might have lost my cool. Might have thrown that watermelon martini in his face. But I was cool as a cat, and I'd be hot damned if he was gonna get even a swallow of my martini down his face. Free or not.

"Fucking this bitch is one thing you will never have to worry about again, love. You could be the last man on Earth—and your dick ain't even good—and you wouldn't get none of this."

I walked off like Naomi goddamn Campbell. I know his bum ass couldn't resist watching my butt the whole way either. The girls were signing autographs and having a regular old good time. I couldn't believe we had gotten so "famous" in such a short period. Melissa's face was a little swollen from her momentary breakdown, but she was in high spirits. Pat pulled me aside.

"Whew, girl! What's up with Marvin? He looking all mad. Like somebody stole his bike. What you did to him? You told him he wasn't getting none no more?"

"Pat, I did what I should have done a long-ass time ago."

"I'm scared of your pretty, celibate ass!"

"You ain't have to point that out, Pat!"

"I mean, that's what I'm here for. I got to offer you both sides of the coin. I'm proud of you for cursing that joker out, don't get me wrong. But I also know those legs ain't had nothing between them in some time now!"

"You ain't never lied, but I wouldn't fuck Marvin if there were cobwebs growing in there." I gave her a high five.

"Well come on, girl. We got to get our celebrity on. We're about to be officially introduced to the crowd."

"Huh?" Before I could question her, Pat was pulling me to the stage where all the Divas, Dr. Laura, Melissa, and a few other people were standing.

"K103.5 family, this is your girl, the ever-so-sweet Melissa Morgan. Y'all, I know that this is the old-school party, but your girl gotta come out on this new jam 'Just Fine' by Mary J. Blige 'cause I'm that type of girl. Yah Magic, play that jam. Wheeeew! I like what I see, y'all. Where the mirrors at, 'cause it looks like everything is *just fine*." Melissa laughed. "Old schoolers, welcome! I'm about to introduce the love forum Divas to all the single fellas. And boys, the girls are hot! But first, I want to introduce y'all to my boy Kirk Magic Wonder up there in the DJ booth, boy you know you just too fly!"

"You fly too Melissa, you better dance girl, get it ma!" Magic yelled over the mic.

Oooooh, Magic, I'm feeling it baby! And next, she doesn't need any introductions because she's Dallas' favorite emotional guru, old schoolers, give it up for Dr. Laura. Magic, play that 'Dr. Love' by First Choice. Dr. Laura, girl, you know you're telling your age with this one!"

Dr. Laura made her way to the mic as Pat and I settled into the line of people on the stage. I had asked Pat where Donnell was. She said a curt, "With the kids," so I let it go.

Dr. Laura was wooing the crowd. "Well hello, to the ninth best city for singles according to the latest *Forbes* magazine. Yes, Dallas, out of forty metropolitan cities, we're ranked number nine behind San Francisco, which is number one, followed by New York, Los Angeles, and Atlanta. Where the single ladies at?" The women in the crowd hissed. "And where are all my single men?" The fellas couldn't be outdone so began barking. "That's what I'm talking about, because Dr. Laura is going to come at you with only the best of her love! How many married couples are out there?" The married folks represented with some wild yelling, and Dr. Laura applauded them. "Well, if you're a couple or happily married, then you're in the right city as Dallas is number one according to *Forbes*'s '2007 Best Cities for Couples' article." The married couples loved that because they got even louder. I looked at Pat, and she didn't seem fazed by the statistic.

Melissa joined the doctor at the mic. "Thank you for that, Dr. Laura. It's nice to know we're in a city conducive to love. Ain't it, y'all? Oh, and for my folks out there confused by the big word, *conducive* means favorable—read a book! Ha! Anyway people, we now have Ms. Brit coming to the microphone. She is accompanied by her man Brass. Give them a round of applause, y'all."

Brit and Brass walked up to the mic and started dancing as the DJ played Rick James's "Super Freak."

Pat said, "Well, that's the perfect song for his ass! He been in ten different women's faces in the last hour alone."

"What?" I said. "And what did Brit have to say about that?"

"Absolutely nothing, Jessie. You know better than that. You know that girl ain't none too bright. He probably fed her some bullshit and she ate it up. Now look at her playing herself. Dancing with that fool in front of all the women he just got finished kicking it to."

Just as Pat finished summing up Brit's relationship, Melissa was calling her to the mic. Chanté Moore's "Chanté's Got a Man at Home" played in the background. Pat said into the mic, "Yes fellas, sorry to disappoint you, but the beautiful Pat is taken." A host of "aaaaah mans" were heard throughout the crowd. "And the ever so fine Mr. Donnell is at home with the kids. I'll tell him y'all said hi!"

"Well all right, Mrs. Pat! Don't rub it in our face too hard. Geesh! Can a single woman get some peace! Magic, put on Carl Carlton's 'She's a Bad Mamma Jamma' because none other than the fabulous Ms. Vanessa is on her way to the mic."

Vanessa fit that song almost as well as she fit in that pantsuit. She even dropped it real quick. The crowd went wild.

"Don't do that no more, V. You know you ain't no spring chicken. Next time you might not get back up!"

"I ain't no spring chicken, Melissa, but your girl ain't dead. And as you can see, I can still drop it like it's hot!"

"Ha! I know that's right, V. But tell me, what kind of man does, V, look for? I mean, give us the physical. What floats your boat?"

V surveyed the audience until her eyes landed on the sharpest high yellow man I'd seen in a long while. They say light skin men are making a comeback, and this brother was leading the pack! Even I was gawking.

V said, "Now that's my speed, Melissa."

"Okay! You hear that, Mister? Maybe you want to holler at your girl before the end of the night."

The sexy man winked his eye and Melissa rolled hers. "Get outta here, girl! Come on up here, Jessie."

I couldn't imagine what the DJ was going to throw on for me. When I heard RuPaul's "Supermodel," I showed all the pearly whites. I strutted my way to the mic where Melissa grabbed my hand.

"Aside from relating to RuPaul, my girl Jessie also relates to Toni Braxton. Magic, throw on that 'He Wasn't Man Enough'!" I realized Melissa had seen Marvin's trifling ass in the audience. I started to laugh when she got on the mic again. "Marvin, bring your trifling, but sexy, tail up here!"

The audience turned to look as Marvin made his way through the crowd. If I put on someone else's eyes, I would have definitely recognized all his splendor. Marvin was certainly fine, no doubt. He stood next to me at the mic, and I tried to maintain my composure and not turn my nose up.

"So tell us, Marvin," Melissa said, "what the hell is wrong with you?"

Marvin said, "Whatchu mean, Melissa?"

"I mean, do you see what I see? Jessie is a magnificent creature. Am I right, y'all?" She motioned to the crowd, and I saw a man in the distance lift his glass in agreement. He was fine!

"She is fine, Melissa. But you know what they say, 'The more beautiful she is, the more likely she is to be driving someone crazy at home!'"

The crowd busted out laughing and I couldn't hold it in myself. It was funny in the first place, and in the second, both Marvin and I knew it held no truth. I couldn't get mad at what wasn't so.

"You hear this, Jessie?" Melissa asked me.

"Yeah, Melissa, I hear this fool. And I'm brushing those comments off just like I brushed his ass off."

The crowd said a collective "ooooooooooh!" and Marvin and I went to separate ends of the stage. Magic threw on "He Wasn't Man Enough" one more time for good measure.

Darlene came to the mic hand in hand with Miguel. I knew they would find each other somehow, some way! They were introduced to Aretha Franklin's "I'm In Love," and I almost threw up in my mouth watching them act all lovey-dovey—giggling and shit—at that mic.

Pat said to me, "Ooh, girl, DeDe's about to sing. Some lady from Electra Sounds, Alicia something, said she wanted to hear her blow."

Melissa brought DeDe to the mic with EnVogue's "Lies" and got on her a little about dating a taken man, but soon pushed that to the side and told her, "Let us have it, girl. You know you got a set of lungs on you."

While the DJ was introducing Anita Baker's "Just Because," I figured out who Pat had been talking about.

"You mean Alicia Myers is here to see DeDe?"

"Yeah, that sounds right."

"Girl, I don't know jack shit about the music industry, but I know Alicia Myers got some pull. Come on! Let's get off this stage and watch De do her thing!"

We women are something special, I tell you, because Pat and I dipped through that crowd with drinks and heels and didn't spill a sip. We found a spot right up front to watch DeDe do her thing.

Like I said, DeDe could blow. Listening to that girl sing was like listening to Aretha Franklin or Whitney Houston or something. She had that sort of ability. You listened to DeDe, and you wanted to just go lie down and make a baby with somebody. Any damn body! She opened her mouth and shut the old-school party down. She sang that Anita Baker almost as good as Mrs. Anita herself! I guess she wanted to show Ms. Myers she could hang with the best of them. When she finished, the club erupted in applause. We all screamed out, "That's my girl! That bitch is a fucking diva!" I looked right into Alicia Myers' eyes. I wanted to see if I could get a feeling off her. I didn't have to look long or hard because she had a big "cheese" smile on. Before I knew it, Pat and I were watching Ms. Myers, Melissa, and DeDe walk into the DJ booth. That couldn't be anything but good news.

Pat said, "That little evil bitch wasn't even gonna come out tonight. Good thing she did!"

"Neither were you!"

"And I'm not about to get a record deal, either. I should have just stayed home and tried to save my marriage."

"Huh? What's going on, Pat?"

"Nothing, girl. Let's just enjoy this moment for De. We'll talk later."

Other than that sharp little turn, I was satisfied with the crazy events of that night. My girls were happy—well the majority of them—I was just about feeling my buzz, and they were playing Rob Base in the background. I dipped off to the middle of the dance floor and danced my pretty ass sleepy.

Chapter Seven

The Love Forum
Long Distance Relationships

June 27, 2008. "K103.5, this is the ever-so-sweet Melissa Morgan, and I'd like to welcome all of you to our first 'official' broadcasting of *The Love Forum*. Now you met all our lovely participants last week, and if you were lucky, you were able to put faces with that talking we did at last night's old-school party. You were even luckier if you stuck around to hear the lovely DeDe tear up that Anita Baker song. Ooh, DeDe girl, that voice, that voice!

"But, we'll get back to DeDe 'Baker' later. Tonight, we're going to talk about relationships in general, and then go further to discuss long distance relationships. To get things started, let's bring Dr. Laura into the conversation. Dr. Laura is joining us via phone, ladies and gentlemen. Dr. Laura, are you there?"

"I'm here, baby-girl! How are my Divas doing tonight?"

"We are fine, Dr. Laura. Now what is this I hear about some dating statistics you have prepared for us about our beautiful city, Dallas?"

"Well Divas, those of us who had the pleasure of joining the love forum members at the old-school party have already heard of some of the good news I'm about to bless you with. And it's such good news, I have to shout it all across the airways— Hallelujah! Whew! I'm here to tell you, Dallas, that you have it far better than some cities. For instance, did you know that according to the latest *Forbes* magazine, in the article 'Best Cities for Singles,' Dallas is ranked as number nine? Oh, but you didn't hear me though—number nine out of forty metropolitan cities!"

V chimed in, "Well hell, I can't tell!"

"Who is that disturbing my statistics, Melissa? Is that V?"

"You know it, Doc! V can't keep the hate bottled up long."

"Hush, V. You can find your mate here! Actually, there's thirty-nine thousand Black single men for you to choose from. You have got to keep your eyes and heart open—and maybe shut that mouth every once-in-a-while! Ha!"

"Dr. Laura, you said thirty-nine thousand eligible bachelors. Do the men outnumber the women?" Jessie asked.

"Yes mam! So many cities have a shortage of men, but not in Dallas. Divas, ya'll are in control—there's a little over thirty-eight thousand eligible black women."

"Well, amen for that!" cried V.

"But Divas and K103.5 listeners, things get even better because *Forbes* ranks Dallas as the best city for couples. That's right, we're number one! So you can find your mate and live it up as a couple, too."

Melissa said, "Well I'm not married yet, and I'm not rushing you or nothing, Quentin." She fake coughed. "But I will say that we have had some wonderful times here in Dallas as a couple. What else do you have for us, Dr. Laura?"

"Well, Divas, Dallas ranked number five in *Black Enterprise* magazine in 2007 as one of the top ten cities for African Americans. This means we're making money here. And where there is money, there is love!"

"And cheating men," I said. I just couldn't help myself. I was learning a bit from Dr. Laura, but I didn't want to ignore the reality of things. "It's me Jessie, Dr. Laura."

"Hi, sweetie. You're right. There are cheating men out there. As a matter of fact, our black men engage in *polygamous* relationships three-and-a-half times that of white or Hispanic men. But don't lose hope. Now are you ladies going to let me get through these statistics or what?"

"Yes, Dr. Laura. No more interruptions, we promise," Melissa said.

"Good. So ladies, let's knock down some misconceptions of why we can't find good men. *Number one*, most black men are in prison. Yes, there is a disparity here. Most of the men in prison do belong to us, but there are currently more black men enrolled in college than locked behind bars. *Number two*, there are too many gay and down low brothers out there adding to our relationship woes. Well this may be true, but according to the Williams Institute on sexual orientation—and there are varying reports on the numbers but we'll just use these for now—4.1 percent of Americans age 18–45 identify themselves as gay, lesbian, or bisexual. Only 4 percent!"

"Wait, Dr. Laura," Pat cut in, and like I said, Pat only cuts in when necessary. "I hate to interrupt you again, and this is not an issue I have personal experience with, but isn't the DL lifestyle, by definition, secretive? So down low brothers wouldn't tell the survey taker they were gay, would they?"

"True, Pat, but my point was that the down low lifestyle has been blown out of proportion. If there are only 4 percent of openly gay people in our country, you figure those with similar lifestyles can't very well outnumber them. I think the down low brothers are more alive in our minds than in real life. Now, back to these misconceptions. *Number three*, our good eligible black men are marrying white women. Yes, some are. And I don't see anything wrong with that, I might add. I say find love where you can find it. However, only 6 percent of our black males are on the other side."

"So bring it home for us, Dr. Laura. Are you saying single black women need to lower their standards?"

"Well, yes, Melissa. At least on paper. What I mean is that as long as a man works hard to provide for you, loves you, is respectful, and faithful, then why not push those other requirements, floating around in our heads—and when I say floating around in *our* heads, I mean *us* women ya'll—a little further down the list? I also want to encourage the women listeners to think outside the box. I have one more statistic for you: 6 percent of black men will date outside of their race, but only 2 percent of black women will do so. Maybe your Prince Charming is an Asian man, a Mexican man, or, a white man, for that matter!"

"Amen, Dr. Laura," Darlene said, and smacked her teeth.

"Well, Dr. Laura, as usual, you were 100 percent thorough. We definitely have a lot to think about. Let me pay some of these station bills, Dallas. We will be right back to expand our discussion to long distance relationships. Again, thanks so much, Dr. Laura. I know you have some patients or something to see! We'll talk to you soon."

The commercial break sped by and before I knew it, Melissa was calling my name.

"We're back, Dallas, and I know, I know, we're all still trying to digest Dr. Laura's information. I guess we have to open our minds a bit, huh? Well, one of my sister girls, Jessie— sitting in the studio ever so beautifully I might add—saw one of her old flames at the old-school party. I don't know how willing she is to open her mind after her experience with Marvin, but we'll see. Marvin is from Houston and, quite honestly, Jessie thought he was the one. Ain't that right, Jessie?"

I laughed. "Well, that's about right, girl."

"So we're coming to you, Dallas. We need your help. Do long distance relationships really work? I mean, is it possible for love to thrive across hundreds of miles? To get us all in the mood for this discussion, Mr. Kirk 'Magic' Wonder is going to play some of that old-school magic as only he can. Magic, what you got for us?"

"Melissa, I'm pulling out the 8-track and taking you way back, getting you in the mood with that smooth dude . . . here's 'Distant Lover' by the incomparable Mr. Marvin Gaye."

I didn't expect that the love forum's topic would center around me, and I was sure hoping Marvin wasn't still in town listening to Melissa give him all those props. I wanted him to continue to believe he meant jack squat to me, but then I guessed that was what the forum was all about. What is it they say? Go hard or go home? I couldn't hold anything back.

Waiting for Mr. Gaye to finish up, I thought about my Marvin. I thought about how much I had invested in him, and how I just knew—I mean you couldn't have told me different— I was going to marry that man. I had met him years ago on a business trip to Houston. I remember it like it was yesterday. I know that's a little cliché, but I'm serious! I was eating in a mom-and-pop diner I had heard I must visit while there. What was the name of that place? Something like Lilac . . . or Lavender. Something like that. Anyway, the food was fabulous! It was soul food, and I could afford to put down a whole plate because I was a little too skinny then. Not to mention that it is a complete myth that all black folks can make soul food! I do not eat everybody's mac and cheese! Hello! And I've met many a women who can jack up a pot of greens. Yes, greens. And all you got to do is boil the things and throw a ham hock and seasoning in there. Anyway, I was sitting at the bar. I was alone, so I didn't want to hog up a booth and look more pitiful than I felt eating alone. But I swore it was my lucky day when Marvin marched his fine ass through the door. Girl, he was sharp. I mean, from his shape, up to the trim mustache, to the beautifully pressed shirt and tailored suit, to the shoes shiny as two brand new pennies. Marvin was always sharp, down to the moment I left his ass. What I didn't know was that he was hardly responsible for his wardrobe or anything else for that matter. I guess he thought he was a pimp or something. When it all came out, I found out he had been juggling me and three other women—and one turned out to be his wife! As heartbroken as I was, I wasn't the biggest loser in it all. I was making less money at that time than I was when I saw him at the old-school party, so I really didn't have the money to blow on him. Though I was so in love, I can't pretend I wouldn't have done what Lala (yes, lord, his wife's name was Lala) and Rhonda and that other chick were doing—supporting his grown ass. I was shaking my head and trying to hold back tears when Melissa pulled me out of my daydreams.

"What you thinking about, Jessie? You better not be thinking about Marvin's sorry ass. That chapter's done, love."

As much as I loved Melissa, I sometimes hated that we were so in sync! I mean damn, I couldn't even have a daydream to myself!

"Yes, I'm thinking about him, Lis. But I damn sure ain't thinking about going back."

"Well, good. You ready to talk bad about his ass? We're about to come back from break."

"Naw. He ain't worth the energy. I'm going to keep it strictly grown-woman style up in here."

"Okay, Jess! Let me find you moving up in the spiritual world. Trying to behave like the Christian woman Big Momma taught you to be."

"Yeah, that's where I'm headed."

"Welcome back, Dallas. The love forum ladies didn't leave you. They're still here. Prettying up this DJ booth like a bouquet of flowers. But while they are pretty as all get out, they got some problems, y'all. Dallas, we need you. Can a long distance relationship survive? Caller, you're on the air. Thanks for calling in. What's your name?"

"Rebbie."

"Hello, Rebbie. Thanks for calling in and joining the Divas' discussion. Can you help my girl Jessie out here? Maybe tell her where she took a wrong turn?"

"Melissa, I'ma tell you like this. Love, like anything else in this life, is what you make it. I have been in a wonderful long distance relationship for the past six months."

"Hold up, Rebbie! Six months? Girl, that ain't enough time to figure out if you like a car. I got to have a car at least a year. Wash it a couple dozen times, almost get in an accident, you know, wear it in, before I know if it's gonna be a meaningful relationship. You mean to tell me you're qualified to tell my girl Jessie here if long distance love is worth its trouble? What kind of issues have you and your man had?"

"We haven't had any yet."

"See, that's what I mean. Y'all are still at the beginning point. Y'all in that new love where nobody can do any wrong. How often you see him?"

"Oh, I've only seen him once. That was the first time we met."

Vanessa chimed in on that one. "Oh hell no! Excuse my language, Melissa, but how she calling up here giving somebody some advice, and her man is sleeping with someone else?"

"Aw man, V. Why you say that? What makes you say her man is sleeping with someone else?"

"Didn't she just say she ain't seen him since she met him?"

"Is that what you said, Rebbie?"

"I said that, but I don't see how that qualifies me as getting cheated on!"

Vanessa said, "If you ain't sleeping with him, Ms. Reebie, who you think is?"

Obviously Reebie didn't think she owed our diva asses any sort of explanation because she let us speak to her cousin Tone. Homegirl hung up on us. Magic started playing New Edition's "Mr. Telephone Man" right on time . . . and we died laughing.

Melissa said, "Okay, Dallas. I love y'all like family, I do, but don't call up here giving us theory. Call us with something we can hold on to! I know there's someone out there with an honest story. Caller, you're on the air. Good evening. Tell us your name and fill us in on your story."

"Hello, Melissa. My name is also Melyssa, but I spell mine with a *Y*."

"Oh, okay. It's always a pleasure to speak with a sister whose parents have as much sense as mine did! Tell us, Melyssa with a *Y*, what can you do for us?"

"Well, I've been in a long distance relationship for three years now. It is just now transitioning into that not-so-new phase. You know, where you start to get on each other's nerves?"

"Yeah, girl. I know about that phase. What has your experience been? Would you recommend long distance love?"

"Yes and no. I mean, knowing what I know now, if I knew it would be this hard, I would have never allowed myself to fall in love. Then again, I love this man more than anything in the world, so I'm sort of stuck. I mean it's hard. Say I need George . . . oh, his name is George by the way—"

"Yeah, we figured that out."

"Well, say I need him. I done had a terrible day at work, right? Which I do all the time! Girl, I work for Verizon. Anyway, I want to come home and fall in my man's arms. Tell him how things went. Have him tell me those fools at my job don't mean nothing. Have him rub my feet. Psssh! No! I fall into the arms of my pillow. I talk to the telephone, maybe the computer if we can get online, and I rub my own damn feet. That everyday love and affection is sacrificed in a long distance relationship. And then you really have no idea what it's like to really *be* with that person. Like our visits are always pleasant because we know our time together is limited, but I'm honestly worried about my move to New York."

"Oh! You're moving, Melyssa with a *Y*?"

"Yes. I'm moving in a few weeks. Packing up house and home and moving in with him. And honestly, I'm scared. I love him, I do. I love him down to the soles of his feet, girl. But do I know him? I mean, do I know him?"

"Melyssa with a *Y*, you have given us a lot to think about. Look here, stay on the line for me. I'm going to pay some bills and run some of these commercials, and after all that's done, I want you and my girl Jessie to rap a little. Can you do that for me?"

"Sure."

Man, Melyssa with a *Y* wasn't lying! It was tough loving someone from far away—and I guess when you had a dirty dog like Marvin, things became even more difficult. The Divas around me started talking about what Melyssa had said, and I drifted back to that first day I met Marvin's pretty, trifling ass. He had asked for a bite of my macaroni. Yes he did! Hell no, I didn't give him any! But I did think about it. You know how some men just have that hold on you? Right from the jump? I mean they can say things to you that you'd slap the next nigga down for. That was Marvin. From the beginning, his mouth was reckless . . . and I loved it. He talked all kind of shit. He walked up to me sitting at that damn bar and said, "What's your pretty ass doing here all alone? Your man in the bathroom? He ain't gonna come out here and whoop my ass is he? I'm a lover not a fighter."

"No!" I said, then laughed. "He's not in the bathroom. I'm here by myself."

"Oh, so I can sit down then. And let me have a bite of that macaroni and cheese. I know that shit's good. I'm a order a big-ass plate, but I want some right now. Give me some."

"Nigga, I ain't giving you none of my macaroni! I don't even know you."

"So what that mean? You don't know a nigga so you can't share?"

He had me dying laughing, and I swear I almost went for my fork to feed him, but I stopped myself. As smooth as he was, I should have known he had way too much practice with women. He picked me up and put me in his pocket as easy as if I was a goddamn dollar. It took all of me—you hear me?—it took all of me not to drop my drawers in that goddamn parking lot. I took his number and gave him mine. I was going to be in Houston for another week. That was one of the best weeks of my life. I worked during the day and met Marvin on Houston's club scene at night. We danced for five days straight. He took me to all the well-known restaurants—and paid for every damn thing (probably with Lala's credit cards). He even filled up my rental's gas tank. I think I might have fallen in love that damn week. I know, I know. I mean, this man just put it on me. And I fought like a pit bull in a skirt not to give up the pussy. And I lasted all the way till my last night there. We both knew I'd be gone the next day and that there was the possibility we might not ever see each other again, and, for real, I was just so damn attracted to the man! We ended up at the Four Seasons in downtown Houston.

I was a little skinny, I'll admit, but the body was toned! And I had on the cutest bra and panty set. I hadn't planned on fucking him that night, but then maybe I did! I mean, why did I decide to wear that black lacy shit? Maybe I was planning that shit and ain't even know it! Anyway, that night goes down in history as one of my top three. Trust! Marvin's dick made the black man/big dick myth anything but a lie. And before him I wasn't the type to swear by a big dick. I was more of a "work with what you got" girl. I mean I was hardly a slut. I had only had a handful of partners before Marvin, but I'd seen every kind of dick. I'd fucked the president of the itty-bitty committee on up to a solid medium-sized dude. All my experiences were okay up until then, and, really, the small-dick dude was no worse than the medium-sized one. But Marvin? Goodness. He turned me out. I can't lie. He whipped that thing out in the Four Seasons, and I gasped! I literally took a few extra drags of air. And like I said, Marvin was the kind of man who could talk to you any kind of way.

"Calm down, Jessie girl. I know you ain't never seen it like this before. I'm a bust that pussy open. Straight up. You ain't never gonna leave me alone after this baby. I'm telling you that right now."

Mind you, I have had far less disrespectful, nasty, crass things said to me and cursed the men out bad, but to Marvin I said nothing. Not only did I say nothing, I giggled—and then stuck my tongue down his throat! And he wasn't a liar. We fucked till the sun was busting through our window. He did bust me open. In both the literal and figurative sense. He drove me to the airport, and I swear I almost started crying in the terminal. I was not acting like the strong woman Big Momma had raised her girls to be—but like the soft, vulnerable woman, she said any man would have no problem walking over—so I pulled it together. On the plane, I wrote him a letter, mailed it the next morning, and had booked my next flight back by five PM the next day.

"All right. Welcome back to *The Love Forum*. We have given a whole lot of attention to our girl Jessie's case tonight, and that's okay. That's the point of this here thing. We want to solve our love problems. Before the break, we pointed out some general issues with long distance relationships, as pointed out to us by our wonderful listener Melyssa spelled with a *Y*. Now, let me ask you, Jessie. Did you find some truth in what Melyssa revealed? Can you tell us a little about your relationship woes with Marvin?"

"Well I mean Marvin and I started off fine. I was visiting Houston quite regularly, and he was here on the weekends I wasn't there. I didn't begin to get worried until it dawned on me—and please don't ask me why it took me so long to see this—that I had never been to his house. I had been flying to Houston for three months before the question—where does this man live?—crossed my mind. Melissa, I remember it like it was yesterday."

"Ooh, girl, what happened? Don't leave us hanging."

"Well, like I said, we were about three months in. I had been to Houston four or five times by then and had yet to walk in this man's house. We were still brand new, and you know us women don't like to rock the boat until we feel we're entitled, so bringing it up was awkward."

"How'd you ask him, Jess?" That was Brit asking as only Brit could ask, so I knew I was revealing too much! Brit is nosey as all get out. If I had her ears perked, I knew that was probably some information I should not have been sharing! *Oh well*, I thought, *I've come this far.*

"Brit, I just said, 'How far to your house, I got a surprise for you and I need to decorate a couple of rooms to get the mood right.' Well little did I know the surprise was on me! You should have seen his face. He went pale as a ghost. And that man was brown enough that he shouldn't have been changing colors! He started stuttering all over the place. Finally he said his place was being renovated and we couldn't sleep there. That was his excuse."

"And of course, instead of taking the reaction as what it was—a clear sign that something wasn't right—you dropped it," Pat said.

"You're right, Pat. Looking back, it all makes sense. But I wanted to believe he was telling me the truth. I wanted to believe that his house was being worked on."

"Excuse me, ladies," Melyssa said, chiming in from the phone lines. "But Jessie, how long did that go on?"

I said, "What do you mean? That 'my house is being renovated' excuse? Um, I guess about eight or nine months. It was coming up on a year when he finally told me the truth. And girl, by then, I was gone. I was so in love he could have told me he was married with eight kids. I would have forgiven him and started the wait for the divorce."

"Dang, Jessie! It was like that?"

"Yes, Lis, like that."

"So what was the truth?"

"The truth was he had a woman. She wasn't his wife, but she might as well have been. They had been together five years, had two kids, and there was another in the oven, due in a couple of weeks."

Brit said, "No, Jessie!" like she was really hurt. I heard the empathy in her voice.

"Yeah, Brit. That's how he did me. I don't think I've felt a pain so deep since."

"So did you continue the relationship?" Melyssa said.

"I tried to cut it off right then. I mean I boarded that plane quick as grease lightning! I left my favorite pair of pumps in that hotel room, I was moving so fast. Both the shoes and the last minute plane ticket cost me my utilities that month. But if they would have cut off my water, I'd have had enough tears to bathe in, wash all my clothes and dishes, and cook with, too! After about a week, he started calling again. I was so mad. Y'all, know what I'm saying? And as women do, we need to know what we need to know and then we just move on. Granted, I was pissed, but I needed answers. I needed to know how he could have done that to me. You know, I had questions like how could you? And I wanted to know if all we had shared was a lie. He had painted a picture that when I listen to it now, I get sick to my stomach. But back then, it sounded so right. He wasn't happy. He was leaving her. He was only staying because she had his kids. Blah, blah, blah. It wasn't until I spoke to his wife—yes, he married her on me—that I got the true story. Girl, SHE was taking care of him and their three kids. I guess she was a fairly successful hairstylist and came from a little money herself. She let me know I was one of many. She had been coming across his 'sideline hoes,' as she called us, for years."

"What?" DeDe said. "I feel sorrier for her than I do you! What kind of life is that? Don't nobody want to be putting up with that bullsh [*beep*], I mean, excuse me, bull crap."

"Yeah, Jess," Melissa said. "Did you ask her about that? Why she put up with that?"

"She said what my own Big Momma had told me years before—that a man ain't worth two cents, and she wasn't gonna leave the father of her children to go be with a man just like him. At least her children got a father out of the deal. And for all his many, many flaws, he was an incredible, kind, and patient father to their children."

"Mmm. Can you believe that? Did she ask you to leave him alone, Jess?" DeDe said.

"No, girl. She said, and I am not lying, she'd prefer to know what she was up against. She asked me if I was planning on coming back out there anytime soon because she needed to know when to plan a visit to her mom's. I told her, *no!* Not ever again. I vowed that was the last time I would utter the name *Marvin*, and as Rameses said in *The Ten Commandments*, 'so let it be written, so let it be done!' Well, that was up until last week."

Pat said, "So really, your issue wasn't so much distance as it was just having to deal with a dirty-ass dog."

"I mean, I guess you could say that, Pat. But I think if I was in the same city as him, I would have figured that mess out a lot sooner. So I mean the distance did have some effect."

"Well since we're talking about issues other than distance, I got an issue I would like to discuss." V was moving her head like it was a well-oiled machine. It was just a rolling! She was mad about something.

"And what's that?" Melissa said. "Oh, but wait one second, V. Let's say goodnight to our wonderful listener, Melyssa with a *Y*. Thank you so much for your time and for bringing such insight to our conversation. It was a pleasure speaking to you."

"Oh, no problem, Melissa with an *I* and the Divas, it's so good to hear women discuss relationship issues. As we all know, a good man is hard to find; finding a good black man is even harder." She laughed and we joined in. "I am really looking forward to listening in to you guys for the rest of the time. I hope *The Love Forum* stays on the air. Thank you."

"Okay, V. Do you think you can tell us what you need to say in the next few seconds? We do have to get off of here and let our sponsors have their say."

"Oh, it won't take but a minute. I just want to point out how at that dumb old-school party I got no play."

"What you mean, V? And how you gonna call a party in your honor dumb?"

"I mean every single brother in that stupid party was busy gawking at you skinny bitches."

"Oh lord, V. Here we go. First of all, you need to watch that foul mouth you got. Your mother ain't teach you no manners? You don't just go off calling girls skinny bitches. You don't know what kind of issues I got. I might be sad about my lack of curves."

"What, Lis? What problems you got? Not having enough time to wear all your skinny jeans? I walked my big self up-and-down that dance floor a good ten, twelve times. Ask me how many 'hellos' I got, let alone propositions for a date."

"How many, V? How many men asked you on a date?"

"Not a one. Not one man in that whole party opened his mouth to ask me out to eat."

Magic butted in, "Well, V. Pretty as you are, you are a lot to hold. Maybe the brothers were thinking about the tab you would run up at the buffet."

"See, Magic. That's the mess I'm talking about. That was inappropriate. I don't have time for your jokes. I'm here spilling my guts, giving all of Dallas my business to cut up and judge, and here you go cracking jokes."

"Oh I ain't joking! I am real sincere, ma. These are tough economic times. Don't nobody want an extra mouth to feed. Especially a mouth that eat seconds and thirds."

Melissa said, "Aw, Magic, you ain't right! For our less ignorant listeners who see past the size and appreciate a beautiful face, V is one pretty woman—even though she just called me a skinny bitch. We're about to get out of here. Our hour is almost up, but y'all brothers who are interested in a woman with a little more to hold, as Magic says, hit me up on my e-mail. Let's see if we can't get something cracking between a good man and Mama V. Because I ain't gonna be called too many more *skinny bitches*! Ya hear? This is K103.5 and it has been a pleasure. I thank you so much for listening in, and I can't wait to meet you back here same time next week. One love."

We all looked at V. Calling us "skinny bitches" was kind of funny, I had to admit, but I was concerned about the tone of her voice. She sounded upset. Really. Pat must have heard the same thing.

"V, honey, what's going on? You feeling bad? You don't sound too good."

"I'm just tired, Pat. I'm tired of having to prove myself. Nobody looks at me and sees me. They see this weight. Oh, I get the 'You have such a pretty face,' or the 'If you would just lose that weight,' but I'm tired of that. Why can't anybody see past my size?"

My little heart was aching for V. I mean, I couldn't necessarily relate. I had always been a slim woman, but I definitely knew what it was to look in the mirror and not be pleased with what was looking back at me. Messing with all those television programs and commercials, box-office movies, and fashion magazines, you'd think that women are suppose to be thin, beautiful and perfectly manicured—all the time. Well, I'm here to tell you it ain't so! I grew up hearing how beautiful my body was—little in the middle, plump in all the right places, long athletic legs (I do look fierce in a pair of pumps). But I could always zero in on the flaws. I have large hands, for example. And my shoulders are a little broad. I would never reveal these flaws! But you know how once somebody points something out you notice it a whole lot better then? So anyway, I could dig where V was coming from, though it didn't sound like Brit did.

"Look, V, I'ma need you to get your tail on the treadmill. Flat out. You doing all this complaining, and I agree that the world is a fucked up place and that all this attention shouldn't be put on the exterior, but the bottom line is that looks matter! Lose that damn weight and stop all this whining. It'd be good for your health, too. You trying to stick around to see that baby of yours married and successful, ain't you?"

"Now Brit, you know that was a low blow," Darlene said butting in. "The last thing V needs to hear is that she needs to lose weight. She's already battling the little-ass women in magazines and even being around our tiny asses."

"Naw, Darlene. I'm tired of us tiptoeing around V. Y'all know just like I know that V needs to lose some of that weight. I'm not saying she needs to look like a toothpick, but what's wrong with taking care of yourself?"

And with that, V busted out crying. It wasn't some little whimper either. I mean, she lost all control of her jaw, and those tears looked like they were in a race to her shirt. We all jumped up and ran to her.

Darlene said, "See there, Brit. Your ass don't never know what to say out of your mouth. Everybody can't look like you."

"Aw, damn. I'm sorry, V. I didn't mean to hurt your feelings. I was trying something new . . . saying what I really wanted to say. You know I love you, girl."

Between her crying and sniffling, V said, "Mean and ditsy as Brit is, she's right. She's right, y'all!" She cried even harder after that. Her shoulders were just a shaking. I took some Kleenex out of my purse and handed it to her. She said, "I mean, if I'm honest with myself, I know that's why I lost that stupid old Jerome. Maybe I should just go on and get that gastric bypass surgery—"

"Fuck Jerome!" I said. "I'm sorry, V, and I feel your pain, but don't you take on the weight of that. Nobody who loves you—for who you are—is gonna roll out because of a few pounds. Excuse my language, but fuck that nigga. And fuck a damn gastric bypass. That is drastic, life-changing surgery. You need to love yourself, not staple your stomach. You get a stapled stomach and to mess around, but you'll never be able to eat a hamburger again."

Magic walked over to us. He looked like he had just eaten something sour. He was probably feeling bad about joking with V.

"Vanessa, look, I'm sorry for playing around with you. You know how I do. Always playing around. For real, though, you are a beautiful woman. Any man would be lucky to have you. Real talk."

"Aw, thank you, Magic. I appreciate it. And I appreciate all of y'all, but something has got to give. I'm sick of this. I'm sick of being alone. I don't want to die by myself."

We all took turns hugging V. I wished I could have just zapped those extra pounds off her. It wasn't until I was in the car with DeDe (we had driven to the station together) that I started thinking about all the good stuff I could have said to V. I was always watching Auntie Oprah, and I could have given V some of her advice. Oprah was always talking about fat people not just liking the taste of food. She said they were feeding some sort of hurt. I should have told V that! She needed to start figuring out what void she was trying to fill. I would call her when I got home. DeDe on the other hand was looking like she was floating on cloud nine. I kept peeking over at her and catching smiles waving across her pink glossed lips.

"Where am I dropping you to, De? You meeting that no good Malcolm or you going home?"

"Both. He's at my house now. And I don't want to hear your mouth. Just drop me there so I can ride that dick to sleep."

"Girl, you know you going to hell with gasoline drawers on, right?"

"Probably with a goddamn gasoline sweat suit, hat, and sneakers! Ha! I ain't no good, and I know it. But it's something about that nigga. I mean the dick is good, no doubt. And the money is good, too. I ain't got to tell you how a little extra every month makes life so much easier, but I'm pretty sure that even with sex half as good and no money, I'd still be stalking his ass. I don't know what it is, Jess. Something about when I look in them eyes. You know I never played this other woman shit before him. Remember that one dude . . . what was his name?"

"You talking about Boobie."

"Yep, Boobie. Remember I had been dating that fool, what, six months? Was talking about moving him in and everything when I found out he was married. I dropped that man like he had the goddamn monster. I hung that phone up and never picked it up again."

"Well that shit don't matter anymore because you sure don't have those morals now."

"You ain't never lied. And this nigga is jealous as shit! Remember when I called into the station the other week?"

"When you were asking about the dude at your job being gay, right?"

"Yeah. Well I get home that night and this nigga starts choking the shit out of me, talking about what the fuck do I think I'm doing dating, or thinking about dating someone."

"And what you smiling for, De? That shit is not cute."

"I know. And he got a lot of fucking nerve being jealous when he get to fuck a whole other set of legs every night."

"And maybe more than that."

"What? What you heard?"

"I haven't heard anything, De. But I mean if he's cheating on his wife with you, why wouldn't he be cheating on you with someone else?"

"Naw, it ain't like that, Jessie. I'm not his wife, but I'm his woman. He takes care of home. He can't afford nobody else. Look what he just bought me."

She showed me a simple set of earrings. Nothing too flashy, but they were nice. I guess the love in her eyes made them extra beautiful. They would have gotten a half smile out of me. By then we were pulling up to her condo. And that *was* nice. I knew women who were the sideline hoes for far less. My homegirl Lita was the side chick getting her ass beat for a happy meal every other Friday. Malcolm's 745 was in De's garage next to her Benz. I mean it was only a C class, but it was a Benz. And more important than that, it was a Benz she didn't have to pay the insurance on. The insurance on luxury cars is high!

"Ooh, yes, girl. My baby is here! My panties sopping just thinking about him."

"Ewww, DeDe. Well don't think too hard about his wife while you in there tossing him across those sheets."

"I won't! Ha! You ain't got to worry about that. He might have a little something to worry about though."

"You pregnant?"

"Girl, hell to the *no*! You know I make that nigga strap up—twice sometimes. I'm stupid, but I ain't that stupid. I know full well he fucking his wife every night. And now that you say that, let me pop this damn birth control."

"So what he got to be worried about?"

Right then, Malcolm came through the garage. He was in a pair of sweat pants. No shoes. No shirt. Beautiful as he wanted to be. He took a few steps in our direction and I thought my heart stopped. Just like in the movies, I saw a past scene in my mind's eye. DeDe was steady yapping, but I didn't hear a thing she said. I saw this same "Malcolm"—pretty as they come—sitting at my soror Tracy's kitchen table. He was eating a roast beef sandwich and laughing at the television secured beneath a cabinet. I remember I said, "That is so neat," and *Martin* was on.

"Malcolm, this is my soror, Jessie," Tracy had said.

"Hey, Jessie! Nice to meet you." That's what he said to me, and then he shook my hand after wiping his hands on a napkin.

He had flashed the same pearly-white smile this Malcolm standing before me was flashing. I knew they were the same man. I had watched him as he picked up the telephone and called his friend, my beautiful Michael, and invited him to meet me at their upcoming informal affair. They were having a little something at their house and thought it would be a good opportunity for the two of us to meet. And then we spent so many hours together, laughing and drinking and having a good time! I could not believe that DeDe's Malcolm was Tracy's Malcolm. I just couldn't believe it.

And then suddenly, I was back to reality. My stomach was turning. I was just disgusted by that man. By what he and DeDe had going. He was standing all out in the open in front of her house—no shame. At all. None. And poor Tracy! I just didn't know what to do.

"Jess? Jess? Are you listening to me? Girl, I been asking you all sorts of questions and shit! Did you hear what I said about Alicia Myers?"

"Huh? What? Oh no. No, girl. What did you say about her?"

"Jessie, you look like you just saw a ghost. Are you sure you're okay?"

"Yeah, I'm fine DeDe." Inside my heart was breaking, both for my girl and my soror. This was some fucked-up shit here. "What were you saying?"

"I was saying—before being so rudely interrupted by your weirdo daydream—it ain't official, but I'm on my way. Girl, Alicia Myers says I'm probably gonna have to relocate to California."

"Really, De? That's good news! That's what y'all were talking about in the DJ booth?" I swear I was asking those questions with my mouth and not my mind or heart.

"Yeah, girl. She doesn't think I can accomplish much staying out here. I need to be where it's at to get this thing going. You know I'm getting up there. I gotta go hard while my ass and titties still got some lift." She grabbed her breasts. "But girl, let me get outta here. Look at his fine ass just staring at me."

"Mmm-hmmm. I see him. *Heartbreaking ass*. Well, maybe you'll get to L.A. and find you a one-woman man who will release Malcolm's death grip on you and allow him to go back to his wife—who I'm sure misses him a whole lot."

"Maybe so, but right now, I'm about to get up under that grip and his wife just gonna have to keep on missing him . . . I'll see you later, boo. Love you."

"Love you too, De."

I sat there a minute, being nosey I guess. I watched Malcolm scoop DeDe up in his arms like she was, well, his wife! Like she was Tracy! I was shaking my head in disapproval and just imagining what Tracy was doing at that moment . . . what their children were doing. Before I knew it, I was taking short, short breaths and on the verge of screaming. Tracy's husband was DeDe's Malcolm and DeDe's Malcolm was Tracy's husband! I just couldn't digest it. I mean, you should have seen these two. If I didn't know any better, I would have thought they were married! He held her with such intensity. Grabbing all in her ass. And she was holding the back of his neck—like it was her hand that was supposed to be there. Like that neck and her hand were puzzle pieces. I think my mouth might have been hanging open. My poor girls. Looking for love in all the wrong places. Shit, poor me. Maybe I wasn't the other chick, but I wasn't anybody's wife either. Maybe DeDe was better off than me and I didn't even know it. She at least had a neck to hold. A damn car to drive! And a house to fuck him in! But that was stupid. I turned my attention back to the matter at hand—what in the hell was I going to do? I pulled off from DeDe's and fished my cell phone out of my purse at the same time. I dialed Melissa who dialed V. I ran the story down for them as I drove home.

"So DeDe's trifling ass done took a step closer to fucking one of our men," V said.

Melissa said, "What are you talking about, V? DeDe is in over her head and doing some messed up shit, I admit, but when have you known DeDe to come onto one of our men? Or to even date a married man outside of Malcolm's ass?"

"She always dating married men!"

"You know what I mean! When she finds out, she drops them . . . usually."

"My momma always told me, 'People tell you who they are. Listen.' If DeDe is capable of fucking any married man, she's capable of fucking ours. And this is a little too close to home for me. Tracy is Jessie's homegirl. Next thing you know, one of us is going to be the homegirl."

I could dig where V was coming from, but wasn't too worried about DeDe trying to get at my man. Number one, I really didn't have one. Number two, that wasn't the issue. "But what should I do, y'all? Here this girl has set me up with a man I *finally* like, and she's such a sweetheart on top of that." I was somehow still talking on the phone and getting into my nightclothes. I couldn't even remember how I got home.

Melissa said, "Well, you can't tell Tracy. That's not your role. DeDe, however trifling, is where your loyalty lies. I feel bad for Tracy, I do, but you're just not in a position to butt into her life in that way. I mean, y'all aren't even really friends, Jess. Didn't you say you barely spoke to her before she hooked you up with Michael? You go to De, tell her to break this shit off, tell her you know the wife—you know the kids—tell her have a fucking heart! Damn!"

"Well we all know it ain't gonna be that easy," V said, "but that's all you can do. I agree that DeDe is your girl before Tracy is, but I see why you're torn. Your only option is to depend on DeDe to get her shit together."

I went to sleep understanding exactly what I had to do and not looking forward to it in the least.

The next morning at work, Tracy was waiting for me in my cubicle. I thought to myself, *Now this is the last thing I need!* I mean, Tracy and I were cool, and I liked her a lot, but she generally didn't just pop up in my cubicle on random days. The Daisy Chain office was a good twenty minutes away. I felt like God was trying to tell me something. I was hot with DeDe at that moment! I tried to play it cool, though I suck at lying, and figured I might as well make sure all my ducks were in order before I started wrecking people's lives.

"Hey Tracy, honey! How are you?" We shared that same fake and awkward hug.

"I'm fine, Jessie. It's good to see you. I love your hair. Listen, I was just stopping by to drop off these figures." She handed me a stack of papers.

Then I knew something was up. Tracy was a big time executive. Why wouldn't she have sent a messenger? I just knew she was about to open fire on my ass. Ooh! That damn DeDe!

"I heard you and your girls on the radio, by the way. That DeDe is a mess," Tracy said, and just stared in my eyes. It was so creepy, and I was beginning to feel like I was just gonna confess on the spot.

"Yeah, she is." I gave a fake giggle. Now I was acting as phony as her!

"So what are you up to this weekend? You and Michael should stop by so we can get those brothers together. I think the last time they were together was when you and Michael met."

"Oh, they don't get together often? They seemed like such close friends."

"Friends? No *brothers*, Jessie. Michael and Malcolm are brothers! Real life brothers." She laughed, but this time it was genuine.

"What? Are you serious? I thought you were saying 'brothers' like . . . you know, homeboys. You never told me they were brothers, Tracy! All this time I'm thinking I'm dating a friend of Malcolm's!"

"I told you they were brothers, girl. You didn't see the resemblance? They favor all the way down to the teeth! You must have ignored me or something."

"But you don't have their last name."

"I sure don't! I kept my maiden name, girl. I just couldn't give up that part of my identity. I mean, on paper I'm a Crawley, but in day-to-day interactions, I'm my momma's child! Oh! I see. You're thinking I'm calling them brothers like they're homeboys, and I got my own last name—girl, we are a mess. Confusing each other. Anyway, get Michael on the phone and y'all come on over this weekend. Malcolm has been busy, busy—you know I make the real money in the family. He really couldn't make it without me, and I am perfectly okay with that, but he insists on working all this double and triple overtime to contribute to the bills as much as he can." She said that like it was a joke, like she didn't believe it. "Anyway, he finally has a weekend free, and I wanna fill up all his time with fun. You don't have anything planned with those crazy girls of yours, do you?"

"Oh damn, Tracy! I wish I knew in advance! I can't make it this weekend. I . . ." I was thinking, *Please God, give me an excuse real quick!* "I'm going out of town to see my mother Friday. I won't be back until late Sunday night."

"Well, don't worry about it, girl. We are going to party hardy anyway. Give me a call next weekend. Maybe we can get together then. Tell your homegirl DeDe this feels like a weekend for wives. Maybe she should go to your mother's with you, and she should try to find a man of her own."

"Huh?"

"You know, just a little friendly advice, Jess. I look out for my fellow women . . . as we should."

"Oh, okay. Well look here, Tracy. That sounds good. Hopefully we can do the double-date thing real soon. And girl, thank you for these documents. I have so much work to do."

Tracy was on her way out of DataComm, and I was on my way out of my seat. I almost slipped to the floor I was so taken with all that information. So it was true. DeDe was fucking Tracy's husband, and on top of that, I was dating that dog Malcolm's brother. I sure as hell hoped Mike wasn't anything like Malcolm outside of the looks department. *Damn, DeDe.*

Chapter Eight

The Love Forum Internet Dating

July 13, 2008. We were back in the DJ booth for the third time. I had grown comfortable with the setup and looked forward to spending the time with my girls—even if I was leaving as single as I walked in. Natalie Cole was singing in the background and we were sipping on beverages. I had a mug of green tea soothing my throat, and it was even helping my mental state a little. It felt good to be among friends . . . even with all of Dallas listening.

. . . I'm catching hell, living here alone
I never realized, oh lord, that you mean so much to me.
I'm catching hell, living here alone. I want you to come
back baby come back, 'cause here's where you belong . . .

"Sing it Natalie girl." Melissa joined in with Ms. Cole. "*I'm catching hell . . . well, well . . . living, living, living here alone. Whew, yah, to tell you the truth, I'm going out of my mind . . .*"

That girl ought to have been ashamed subjecting the listeners to that voice. She sounded like a cat in heat. We laughed at her so hard we had to push the mics away. But we all chimed in and DeDe blew it out of the water.

"Keeping you on track with that old-school flashback. This is the ever-so-sweet Melissa Morgan and that was Ms. Natalie Cole with 'I'm Catching Hell.' I'm dedicating this to all my sisters out there catching hell messing around with these trifling Negroes."

V said, "Amen to that. Girl, V got your back on that one!"

"Oh, you can relate, V?"

"You know it, Melissa. Everybody knows your girl V got left for a man! And he the biggest, ugliest thing you ever seen. Magic, you talking about me eating seconds and thirds, I don't see how my ex affords his big greedy ass."

"So then where does a woman find a good man?" Melissa asked. "Yeah, you've looked in the church, and you've tried the clubs and the bars. You've done the social circuit, and *still* no prize. Ladies, what can Melissa do to help the sistas out? Jackie get me some callers on the line. We gonna work this out."

Jackie was Melissa's new intern. She was a sweet girl, just a sophomore in college, who reminded Melissa of herself when she was finding her way, career wise.

"Divas, Jackie is informing me that Dallas is bombarding the phone lines tonight! Our first caller is Keisha."

"Hello, mama! You're speaking to Melissa. The Divas are catching hell up in here, what hell has some man put you through, girl?"

"Hello, Melissa! Hello, Divas! Big fan of the show. I saw you lovely ladies at the old-school party, and I'm rooting for each of the girls, especially you, V."

We all said, "Thank you" into our mics.

"Girl, I know that's right!" said V.

"Well Keisha, you sound like you got it together over there. Y'all noticed how she said she's rooting for *y'all*? She don't need no help! So tell me, Keisha. What you got going over there? Are you with a good brother? And if so, tell us a bit about that thing there."

"Well, Melissa, people don't want to believe this, but I met my man on the Internet."

"What? Really? What do you mean you 'met' him on the Internet?"

"I mean I answered an ad on that website E-Dating.com— you probably heard about it—and he ended up being the man of my dreams! We've been together over a year now and are talking marriage, kids, all that."

"Get out of here, Keisha," I had to butt in on that one. "I mean, don't get me wrong. I'm open. I'm open to meeting all sorts of men in all sorts of places, but I think the Internet is a little freaky. You don't even know those folks. You could be setting yourself up to get raped, or even killed. I'm sorry. I just can't get with that . . . this is Jessie speaking by the way."

"Oh, hey Jessie. Look, you don't have to tell me! I understand exactly where you're coming from. I still can't believe that's how I met Damon. I'd signed up for the site on a whim. I was a little depressed, you know? I had just broken up with my boyfriend. I was drinking a little. Watching a little porn."

Melissa said, "No she didn't!"

"I'm just trying to set the stage for y'all . . . let you know this ain't just a route for losers. I had never done this before! I wasn't some weirdo and Damon is a stand-up guy."

"Had he used the Internet to meet women before?"

"That was one of the first things I asked him, Melissa. He'd tried it a few other times and was on the verge of giving the whole thing up. He had gone on a couple of dates and said the women had, you know, misrepresented themselves."

"Ha! In what way?"

"Well, you know, Damon said they'd put up a picture of themselves from like 1985 with hair to their hips and bodies like a video chick. Then he'd meet them at Red Lobster or something and walk right past them thinking, 'I know that big old lady ain't my date.' One lady came into the restaurant rocking a goatee thicker than his."

Oh, Keisha had us just about on the floor. I knew Internet dating was not for me. The men wouldn't have anything to worry about—I was the same size I was in high school. But what about me? I might get a crazy, fat, bald serial killer. I was open to different sorts of men, but I needed to be able to look at him. You know, wake up next to him in the morning.

"I find this interesting," V said. I thought the Internet might actually be a good avenue for V. She could weed out the jerks. She could be completely up-front and find a man who loved her exactly for who she was.

"So what's the process?" V asked. "I mean, how would go about this, Ms. Keisha?"

"Uh-oh! Sounds like you done hooked somebody, Keisha. Do you think this Internet thing might help you with the issues you've been having with dating concerning your weight, V?"

"I do, Melissa. I mean I've never been a liar, you know that about me. I have no problem putting a very current, very realistic picture of myself up on, what was the site? E-Dating? That way the fellas know exactly what they're getting and I don't have to suffer that feeling of rejection. I know there are some brothers out there that appreciate a *big-boneded* woman. Ha!"

"I know that's right, V. Well look here, I'm quite serious about the love forum finding love for my girls. So guess what, Dallas—we are taking the show to the Internet waves! Jackie, go on and pull up that E-Dating site while we pay these bills. When we return, we'll let you know how it's gonna go down, Dallas. We'll also have a much needed convo with Dr. Laura. Dr. Laura is going to expose us to the other side of Internet dating. She's going to let us know all about those addictions many of our brothers—and some of our sisters—are dealing with. You know, the not-so-pretty side of things."

While Melissa ran a few commercials, Jackie pulled the E-Dating site up, and we set our tongues to curse.

I said, "Melissa, what the hell do you mean we're taking it to the Internet waves? I am not going on that website!" Most of the other ladies were nodding their heads in agreement.

But before Melissa could defend her idea or convince us to give it a try, Pat shut us all up. "I'll try it," she said.

We all swung our heads in her direction.

DeDe said, "Let me find out I ain't the only one who had no respect for marriage."

"No, De, it's not that. Y'all know I love Donnell! I'm saying I'll take the little survey, indicate that I'm married and just looking for a friend . . . you know, be completely honest. I'll just participate as a good sport."

"Okay, so if Pat is going with the flow, when she is the only one who has a valid reason not to, then the rest of y'all better get with it!"

Just then Dr. Laura came into the booth. She was a sharp woman. She reminded me of Dr. Wilma, except Dr. Laura was slim and tall. I wondered if they knew each other. We said our hellos and Dr. Laura introduced herself.

"Divas! Good evening . . . my lord, you all look stunning!"

I thought to myself, *this bitch is fierce!*

"Aww, Dr. Laura, that is so sweet," Darlene said.

"Well, I'm not lying. It's no wonder you girls are having relationship woes. You know they say the pretty ones never settle down in love. It's the price you pay for being so lovely to look at."

"Well, take this little bit of pretty I got and give me a man. This sista is horny as a dog!"

"Vanessa!" I said. Damn, that girl just said anything she had the feeling for.

"I'm sorry, Dr. Laura. But it's been that long! I no longer have any couth."

"That's all right, V. You're among friends. Just don't let the men see that side of you, okay?"

"Deal."

"Okay, ladies. We're ready to get back on the air. Dr. Laura, would you like any tea or coffee? My assistant can get you a cup."

"Oh yes, Melissa. Tea sounds good."

"Jackie, go on and get Dr. Laura some tea, and Dr. Laura come on over here and sit next to me. We're ready to get this started. Right, Magic?"

"Yes, ma'am. Let's rock and roll."

"Welcome back, Dallas! It's your girl, the ever-so-sweet, Melissa Morgan. The lovely ladies of the love forum are now set up on the E-Dating site! Even the lovely Pat has agreed to participate—but hold up now. I don't want to have to answer to Donnell when I get outta here, so let me be sure to say that she's going the friendship route. In their free time this evening, the ladies will be taking a compatibility survey. They'll date, or in Pat's case, converse, and we will hear back from them in a month or so. Sound good, ladies."

All but Pat said a dry "Yeah" into the mic.

"Well don't sound so happy! Dallas, I am not thinking about these Divas. They're going to open their minds if I have to crack them open myself! Now, on to the spooky side of things. While I want us to find love, I refuse to be stupid in the process. We are now joined by Dr. Laura, nationally renowned relationship therapist. Fellas, I think you'd be interested to know that Dr. Laura is in here heating things up. She is lovely as a rose with a smile that will, as my daddy would have said, knock your socks off! The bad news is she's happily married—and has been so for how many years, Dr. Laura?"

"Oh now, Melissa, if I tell you that, I'd be giving away my age. Let's just say I've been in love a long time. Dr. Ethan and I go way back."

"That is just wonderful. Now Dr. Laura, you have been on K103.5 several times in the past, and I must say you have given our listeners some of the best advice I've ever heard. You have taught many of us how to free ourselves from unhealthy relationships and how to foster new, loving ones. I want to first thank you for that, and then ask you to give us your take on this whole Internet dating thing, specifically its dangers as we have already discussed its positive possibilities."

"You and all of Dallas are more than welcome, Ms. Sweet Melissa. Having such a wonderful marriage is not something I've ever really wanted to keep secret. I love my husband—his whole self—and he loves me, cellulite included."

"Dr. Laura, you ain't got an ounce of cellulite on that body."

"Well if I did, he'd love it. And it has been a tough road that requires lots of work, but I have always been driven to share our 'secrets' if you will. That said, I haven't had a relationship develop from the Internet. Dr. Ethan and I were married before E-Dating.com was even around—but look at me about to tell my age anyway. What I have had is plenty of patients on my couch crying about the Internet."

"Tell us about that, Dr. Laura."

"Yes, please, Dr. Laura," Pat said.

"Ooh, Pat. What's that eagerness I hear in your voice? Don't tell me the Mister has been locked up in the den on the family computer talking about give him a couple of hours."

"Well no, Melissa. Not exactly. But you know me, I like to be prepared. I like to know what I'm up against."

"Melissa, Pat is a smart woman. It's best to approach this whole global obsession with Internet relationships with lots of information and facts. First of all, I want to point out that

Forbes, in 2007, ranked Dallas twentieth in terms of Internet dating. That means out of forty cities nationwide we're smack in the middle. It's also important to know that 25 percent of all marriages have experienced issues with cybersex."

"For our listeners who may be unfamiliar with cybersex, please define it, Dr. Laura."

"It's exactly what it sounds like, Melissa. It is sex that is engaged in over the Internet. Now, it's virtual. That means that two, or more, persons—"

"Freaks!" V yelled.

"No, Vanessa, not freaks. Just individuals who engage in the visitation of pornographic websites, chat rooms with a sexual emphasis, and general relationships developed through e-mail and other online communications. It may sound harmless, but it is anything but."

"How so, Dr. Laura?"

"There's the issue of addiction. For example—and no disrespect to our Nubian kings. But once your man or husband has experienced a woman who has promised him anal sex, oral sex, and offered to do his best friend as well, it's hard to compete with just your t-shirt and panties on—"

"Ooh, Dr. Laura, I heard that rapper Lethal Mayhem—girl, I just love his music—was addicted to cybersex!" Brit could be such a ditz, I swear. She sounded like a dumb blonde.

"That's true, honey. He was on all the talk shows and everything.

"But to wrap things up—I see Jackie's giving me my cue. Pornography puts unrealistic images and ideas in people's heads—typically men—about the opposite sex. Still, cybersex is much different from what your lovely caller Keisha told us about. Some wonderful things have come of dating websites like E-Dating. I do want my lovely ladies of Dallas to be careful, though. Screen those men well, ladies, and always take a couple of folk with you on those first couple of dates!"

"You ain't never lied, Dr. Laura. I am not trying to hear about any of my listeners on the eleven o'clock news. Ladies, do not jump on those sites and rush out to see the first goon you interview. Make sure all his stuff is legit! Well, thanks so much, Dr. Laura. As usual, you have enlightened us."

"Anytime, Ms. Melissa. It was a pleasure."

"Well, D-town, I have saved the best for last. I know, I know! You thought it couldn't get any better! Well it can. Magic is gonna hit you with a couple of hits real quick, and we're gonna set up in here. Don't miss this, Dallas! I'm telling you! Don't miss it!"

Just as Magic took over, a little old lady walked through the booth's door. She had the tightest little curls in her head—salt-and-pepper colored—and a big old pair of glasses swallowing up her whole face. Melissa had lost her parents some time ago and all I could come up with was maybe her grandmother had come to visit. The lady adjusted a large bag on her shoulder.

"Ladies, this is Doretha. Doretha is my psychic. Y'all know I talk to Ms. Doretha at least once a month to keep me on track. Well now I want to share her wisdom with you all."

V's face said, "Oh hell no," but her respect for her elders wouldn't let her spit that out. We said our hellos, and suddenly I wasn't as sleepy as I'd been. I was intrigued. I mean, not that I believed in psychics or anything, but she couldn't have caught me at a more vulnerable time. I needed some answers about my future, and I was willing to give anybody a shot at helping me figure it out. I mean, I was in therapy! I told Jackie to fix me another mug of tea and got comfortable in my chair. The other ladies, V included, looked to be doing the same.

"Hello, ladies. Melissa has brought me here to give you each a bit of guidance. A reading is a very private and personal event, so before we proceed, I'll need your permission to reveal what I'll learn about you on air."

Ms. Doretha got adjusted in her seat, taking out all her paraphernalia while we considered that. We were sharing looks, mostly looking at Melissa trying to see if she really trusted this lady. She looked cool and collected. I can't lie, it all felt a little creepy to me, and I could tell the girls were feeling the same. And nobody spoke for a long while. Finally, Melissa interjected.

"Divas, she's the truth. I've been telling you guys this for years. You're always asking me, 'Melissa, how come everything seems to always work out for you?' Well, you're looking at her. I give this lady here all the credit."

Ms. Doretha was looking like she couldn't care less if we consented or not. That nonchalance made us trust her even more.

I said, "I'm with it." And meant it. "I mean, you will keep it clean, right Ms. Doretha? I mean if it's just too personal, can you keep that information for off the air?"

"Absolutely," Ms. Doretha said.

It was like we were in the presence of greatness. Man, I was about shaking in my boots sitting there waiting to hear what that lady had in store. We didn't even speak to one another, which is quite unlike the Divas, to say the least. Magic faded out that last bit of music and it was on.

+++

"Well Doretha, what's going on? You know we talk on the regular. Has anything changed since we last got together?" Melissa asked Ms. Doretha. I guess she was going to rest our worries completely and put herself on the line first.

"Well Melissa, we don't have to pull any cards. I know your journey all too well. You're still on course." Ms. Doretha gave Melissa a wonderful smile and avoided her eyes. She turned her attention towards me and after seeing how she avoided Melissa's eyes I felt somewhat uneasy about what she was about to say.

"Jessie dear, what's on your heart? What can Doretha do for you?"

"Well, I guess I'd like to know what the future holds for me . . . in terms of love."

"Prepare your heart for a successful man dear. He is one who has pursued you wholeheartedly and won't rest until he has you. But even that won't work out."

"A successful man? Is it Michael?"

"I can't tell you a thing about any Michael. He is not in your future. He may very well be the object of your heart's desire for the moment, but this won't last, and neither will the successful man I speak of. Oh, you'll find true love and it will be someone who cares for you deeply. More than anyone you've ever known. At the moment, this love isn't clear to either of you, but after a series of very painful events it will shine through, bright as the morning sun. And rest assured that a close friend will show the way through all this."

I, like Melissa, was completely disappointed with what I was hearing. Ms. Doretha had ignored Melissa and now she was breaking my heart. Despite the rainbow at the end of the tunnel of Ms. Doretha's story, I didn't want to hear anything about lots of pain, and I especially didn't want to hear that me and Michael wouldn't make it. I just couldn't believe what I was hearing. No Michael? A successful man that won't last either? But I'll soon find love—that could be ten years from now! Well, I definitely was not liking what I was hearing, and with that, I sat there thinking, *this all sounds so typical, like something she learned at some psychic school. And the last time I checked, Miss Cleo, of the Psychic Friends Network, was in trouble somewhere for fraud.* While I was discrediting this woman on the inside, outside I smiled and thanked Ms. Doretha.

Ms. Doretha said, "Dear, I was put here for no other reason than to predict. I have seen into the future since I was a small, small child. My very own mother feared my gift. Please do not doubt me." Oh . . . my . . . god, did this woman just read my thoughts? I blushed as I watched Ms. Doretha—sizing her up—while she huffed on her glasses, cleaning them with a pink silk cloth.

Brit was next. She was sitting right across from Ms. Doretha. Something about the energy around Brit was disturbing the psychic. She shuffled the cards and set them before Brit.

"Pick a card, dear."

Brit did as she was told and Ms. Doretha let out a heavy sigh. "Hmmmmm. Put that back. Shuffle the cards for me. Shuffle them good. And when you are through, pick another card."

Again, Brit did as she was told. The card was the exact same one as before.

"Mmmmm," Ms. Doretha said. "One more time, dear. One more time."

On the third try, Brit's hand still caressed the same card.

"Mmmmmm." Ms. Doretha was obviously disturbed. "Okay. It seems this path is inevitable. You're obviously dealing with a man with a dark cloud around him. If you don't distance yourself from him, the cloud will consume you. I see two roads of travel for you, dear. It will be up to you which path you travel."

DeDe didn't have much luck with her first card either. In fact, her first try tickled Ms. Doretha. She laughed and told her, "You're a mess, dear. Try again. Pick another."

"What's going on, Ms. Doretha? Don't be trying to change my future. Just read the cards girl. Just read the cards."

We all laughed as Ms. Doretha told DeDe, "Well, I tell you what, you're going to make it as a singer, and more importantly as a song writer. It's going to be a little shaky at first, but you will evolve. And this evolution will lead you in a direction quite different from the direction you envision for yourself. I also see that you keep asking God why he hasn't answered your prayers, why you're still where you are, fighting the same battles over and over again. But the truth of the matter is, you haven't learned what you need to learn just yet. You've been given sign after sign, but still you refuse to take the lesson and move on."

I just couldn't hold it in any longer, "Well at least somebody has some half-way decent news!" Everyone looked at me like I was plum crazy. I looked at Melissa and she was looking at me all cross-eyed like, *bitch I know you are not disrespecting my guest like this!* She quickly and swiftly corrected my outburst while trying to assure us that we were in good company and in good hands. "Divas, Doretha is the truth, believe me when I tell you this!"

"Well, we'll just see about that Ms. Melissa. Just know, that if my reading isn't the bomb, then we know something's wrong, 'cause can't nothing be bad with all this fabulousness sitting right here!" V said, in her snarly little way.

We all looked at V, shaking our heads. Suddenly, Pat, out of nowhere, got up and walked over to Ms. Doretha and put her hand on her shoulder—I guess to comfort her with some kind words as she said "Ms. Doretha, good comes in all packages, maybe God has given one of his children a special gift and maybe you were put in our lives for a reason. I don't care what these crazy friends of mine are saying . . . I have faith that you are who you say you are."

"Thank you, dear," touching Pat's hand, "I use my clairvoyant abilities to grasp the energy and aura of each of my clients. This allows me to give them not only the answers they want to hear, but need to hear. And dear, the answers that I'm about to share with you—the answers you so desperately seek—may not be what you want to hear, but what you need to hear.

"Dear, I must tell you that you can look forward to what will seem like insurmountable mountains to climb and enduring storms to bear. For a while, your faith will falter, but it will be the only thing to see you through to the end. These challenges will require all the fight you have in you. And as I said, for a while, you'll think you won't make it, but you will. Trust me. The storms will pass, the clouds will clear, and before you will be the clearest rainbow, shining across the horizon. At its end will be a hefty pot of gold with a love blessed by God himself."

We all looked around the table like what did she just say. I don't think anyone paid any attention to the insurmountable mountains nor the enduring storms part, all we heard were those six words at the end—*a love blessed by God himself.*

"What? What is that suppose to mean Ms. Doretha, what kind of love? Blessed by God himself? So what kind of love are the rest of the Divas suppose to have? Girl, I want a love blessed by God too! I'm ready for my reading Ms. Doretha. Let's get to the reading Ms. Doretha!" V shouted, getting a little agitated as she shifted in her seat.

"I know that's right V." said Darlene, "I want that kind-of love too!"

"Well . . . Darlene dear . . . just because you have been blessed with a good man does not mean the relationship will succeed." *Lord, you could have slapped Darlene with a bag of bricks and that shocked expression on her face probably would not have changed.* It was so bad I couldn't even look at her anymore. I glanced over at Ms. Doretha and noticed she had paused and closed her eyes—tears soon began to run down her face. We all looked at her with crazed eyes, and as several minutes passed, with eyes that were mortified. DeDe and Brit looked at me and I shook my head and shrugged my shoulders as I glanced over at Melissa.

"Doretha are you alright? Ms. Doretha?" questioned Melissa, as she got out of her chair to rush to her side. But before she could take a couple of steps in her direction, Ms. Doretha held out her hand—motioning her to stop—then continued with Darlene's reading with closed eyes and a face full of tears. "Darlene, dear, you must get past all your prior hurts . . . I see you have been hurt beyond words my sweet baby."

Suddenly—at that moment—my doubts about Ms. Doretha slowly began to lift. It was apparent that as many lives as she had probably read, and as many tragedies she had probably seen, Darlene's reading had touched her. Touched her to where she had to take a break, place her hand over her heart, and stare into Darlene's eyes. It was as if she was trying to convey, without language, how far down she ached for Darlene. "Even from an early age . . . mmmmm. Baby, you have to let go of this pain or it will consume you. It will eat you alive. If you don't, you'll never be able to love this man the way he loves you. You will miss out on this opportunity to be loved the way you deserve."

Ms. Doretha pushed back from the table and hugged Darlene, who was sitting beside her and was now overcome with emotions herself. "What those men did to you will continue to haunt you until you have handled it properly. Killing those past demons is the key to you and your man's future. If you want to lose him, keep doing what you're doing— questioning his love—and he will tire of it and leave you like all the rest. But if you want him with the same vigor he wants you, and if you believe in his love, then fix yourself. The sooner you are accountable, the sooner you can heal."

Everyone in the Studio was fixated on Darlene. Some looking with concern, some with horror, some questioning what was really happening. And all of us were either teary-eyed or boo-hoo crying—mainly because it was our girl who was filled with so much pain and worst of all, none of us knew. I could just imagine what the K103.5 listeners were thinking about all of this drama. But that moment didn't last long . . . thanks to V.

"Ms. Doretha, come on with it girlfriend! What about all this fabulousness sitting over here? Girl I'm ready, what you got for me?" V said, as she perched her elbows on the table, with head in both hands, looking dead at Ms. Doretha.

As she made her way back to her seat, Ms. Doretha leaned against the back of her chair, lowered her head, and stared at V over the top of her glasses. She stared at V for quite awhile. So long, we all began looking around the room, as if to say, *what in the hell is going on now?* and out of nowhere, with a sharp tone, Ms. Doretha answered, "Vanessa, you will accomplish nothing—not the opening of your business (yes, your future is bright if you commit to it), not emotional freedom—until you decide to rid yourself of the hatred towards your husband and his lifestyle of choice."

"What? What did you say Ms. Doretha?" asked V as she sat up straight in her chair, "Did you just say I will accomplish nothing . . . not even the opening of my business?"

"Wait dear . . . if you commit to opening up your business you'll make it, but you must rid yourself of the hatred towards your husband first, then you will see your wildest dreams realized. As long as you continue to take your husband's decisions personally, to see his lifestyle as a reflection of something you've done, you will not know peace. Once you have done that work, you and a relative will go into business together. Yes, you and a relative have the same dream. Change will come swift, if you allow it. The world will open up for you and the happiness you seek will find you. A man will fall in love with you for who you are. He will be quite smitten with you, young lady."

One by one, we heard Ms. Doretha tell our futures, and one by one we entered into a state of shock. A strange sense of privacy overtook each of us, and without even discussing it, we decided not to discuss our predictions with each other. Ms. Doretha, on the other hand, appeared neither to be fazed by the quietness of the room, nor the questioning looks she was receiving. None of us even noticed Melissa was back on the mic and the six of us, not even looking at one another, just sat in our own separate and private worlds.

"Wheeeew! My head is spinning ya'll . . . and there you have it, Dallas. The Divas have been warned! Chile, I'm going to have to let that marinate—too much drama for me! I'm not even gonna question the Divas or ask you guys to call in. Just trust me when I tell you, Doretha is the truth. Anyway, it's time for us to get out of here. I know, I know, it's like we just started. But you know we'll be back same time, same day next week! And believe me when I say you will not be disappointed. Next week's topic is 'maintenance men.' Yes, those brothers that keep you single ladies well oiled in times of drought! And oh! What was I thinking? We have one more very important bullet on the agenda tonight. *The Love Forum*, as you know, is striving to get these ladies here . . . well, in love! In our efforts to try and hook our lovely Divas up—the single ones! I don't want Pat's husband waiting outside for me—we're asking one of them to write a poem for the next show. This poem will be used to help us discover a match for the diva. So . . . who's going to be our poetess?" Melissa looked around the table at all of us. I was thinking, *Not me! I am not a poet! I enjoy the occasional poem here and there, but I am not trying to be the next Nikki Giovanni or anything.* "Come-on Divas, where's the enthusiasm, I know Doretha hasn't wrecked havoc on my girls, although she is powerful, and the truth can be unnerving," Melissa, as she walked around the table, said "Okay . . . Jackie! Bring me that hat with those numbers in it. You B-I-T-C-H-E-

S's done made me have to bring out the hat! Alright . . . you know the drill! You pick the piece of paper out the hat. I'll call a number between one and ten. And whoever has the number I call, better come with it next week."

Jackie walked around the studio allowing each Diva, minus Pat, to draw a number out of this big ole stupid hat. I held mine in my lap and said a short, *please Lord, don't let it be me*. Melissa picked a number. She said, "K103.5 listeners, what ya'll think? Humph . . . what number should I call? Oh, I know just the right number, how about lucky number seven? Yes number seven—my ring size. In case some of you out there are wondering." And of course, because I was the last person thinking about writing some stupid poem, I had the number seven . . . her ring size. I looked that girl dead in the eyes and wanted to curse. But all I could do was think, *ain't this 'bout a bitch*. And by my actions and that look, Melissa knew I had picked the number seven.

"K103.5 listeners, I think we have a winner! Your girl the ever-so-sweet Melissa Morgan is standing right beside one of the prettiest Divas, holding my ring size. Yes ya'll, number seven. Who is it? Well, the one that really needs to find a man—Ya'll, it's Ms. Jessie S. Harris! You better come with it girl, Dallas will not be forgiving if you don't!"

With all the hoopla and drama at an end, the show finally wrapped-up and soon we were walking from the station, in a daze, recounting what we had just been through. Each of us contemplating what we had just been told by Ms. Doretha. She had known the intimate details of our lives. Hadn't asked us much. Hadn't touched us. Barely looked at us. And then dismissed us sooner than we understood the gravity of her words. Even V, who, at the beginning, was absolutely skeptical of Ms. Doretha's powers, was gradually won over and had been moved by Ms. Doretha's uncanny understanding of her life. So we didn't even notice that Melissa hadn't left with us. While we were driving home with heavy hearts, Melissa was receiving a private meeting.

"What's up, Doretha? I know you. You brushed me off because there's something you didn't want everyone to know. Let me have it."

"Meli has arrived . . . she's here, Melissa." Ms. Doretha touched Melissa on the arm, and the women stared at each other in acknowledgment of the conception of the baby Ms. Doretha had told her about so many times before.

"She's here? You mean already?" Melissa took a seat and Ms. Doretha did the same.

"Yes, dear. You're with child!"

Melissa was so filled with emotion she began to shake. Ms. Doretha held her hands.

"And I hate to say it, but that's not all I see. And I'm so sorry I have to deliver this news, but you know our policy—no secrets."

Melissa gathered herself temporarily. "That's right, Doretha. We keep it funky." She cracked a spare smile, trying to prepare herself for what would come.

"Melissa dear, I'm sorry to say that you'll never hold her. You'll never hold Meli, and you'll never know her."

"What do you mean? What are you talking about, Doretha?"

"Dear, you must understand that my visions are not always crystal clear, and I cannot always answer questions to a tee. I won't always tell you what you want to hear. All I can tell you about this child is that you will not know her."

Melissa thought Ms. Doretha was talking crazy, despite how on point she'd always been, and began to feel bad about subjecting the girls to her. She nearly cursed at the woman. While she was balling up her face, Ms. Doretha closed her eyes and held her own forehead, as if praying for strength.

"And still, there's more, Melissa. I have to tell you about the man you love," she said, eyes still closed, head still cradled in her hand.

"Quentin?"

"Yes, him."

"What about him?"

"He'll break your heart. But you already knew that. And even though your girlfriends tried to tell you different, and I've told you time and again, you've always known." She opened her eyes and looked Melissa head on.

"Quentin? You mean we're not going to be married? But we're having a child?"

"Yes."

"Well do you have any good news for me, Doretha?"

"I do, but it may strike you as strange."

"It can't be any stranger than what you've already told me."

"Melissa, Quentin will be an excellent father to your daughter Meli, and he will find an excellent woman to help him parent in your absence. This woman will be someone very dear to you. Someone you love deeply."

"Oh lord, Doretha! You are hitting me with one-two punches back to back! So Quentin is going to get with one of my girls?"

"You can't put that spin on it, Melissa. Their falling in love will be anything but malicious. Remember that you will not be present to raise the baby or love Quentin. I know this is a lot to handle and that it's difficult to put into perspective. But trust me, love. In the end, everything will work itself out."

Melissa didn't know what to do with the information she'd just been given. And she didn't appreciate being told so bluntly despite this being the way she and Ms. Doretha always operated. She really wasn't even ready to get up from her seat, but she certainly didn't want to remain in Ms. Doretha's presence just then. She thanked her and escorted her to her car. She had too much to think about. Far too much to digest. She excused herself and walked, as fast as she could, to her car, and then drove even faster home.

+++

Each of the Divas enjoyed taking the E-Dating survey far more than they imagined they would. It asked them lots of personal questions that allowed them to reveal their innermost yearnings and desires. Not a one of them had a problem talking about herself. None minded listing all her positive qualities or what each expected in a companion. The questions made them feel hopeful. And even validated them. Pat was particularly moved by the process. When she got to the question, "What are you missing most in your life?" she almost busted out crying at the computer screen. The children and Donnell were asleep and something about the silence surrounding her and the depth of the question tore her up. She couldn't help but feeling hopeful as she hit "send" on the form.

The funny thing was Pat's survey was the first to receive a response. Karl was also married, and he had also only taken the survey hoping to gain a friend. When Pat opened his message she finally admitted to herself why she had agreed to participate. She was so tired of the distance in her marriage. Donnell was off somewhere living his life and she was off somewhere else living hers. Maybe if she gave him a little competition he'd see the value in their union. She replied to Karl's introductory e-mail with a little too much information, revealing the rocky terrain her marriage was crossing. She almost regretted spilling the beans so early, but Karl was so sweet . . . so understanding. He responded with kindness, urging her to stick by her man and remember her vows. A little further down the page, though, he was flirting and complimenting her picture. He had a wonderful sense of humor, and she found herself rushing to the computer just as soon as the house was asleep. Her attraction to this very married man only heightened through the weeks, and before she knew it, a month had passed and she had a full-blown crush. She couldn't believe it had gotten so far out of control. She was feeling like maybe her behavior was a little inappropriate, but then she couldn't help herself. She and Karl shared at least a dozen e-mails each day, talking about every detail of their lives. She was sharing things with him she'd never dreamed of telling Donnell. And while the closeness and respect and pure fun were exhilarating, she couldn't help contemplating the state of her marriage. Enjoying the company of another man as much as she did could not be a good sign. She wondered if the other Divas were enjoying this e-dating stuff as much as she was. She was eager to hear their tales by the time their month-long hiatus from the show was over, but she was a little nervous about what she would say. She couldn't very well get on the radio and reveal what was in her heart. She decided to keep it professional and protect Donnell's feelings at the same time. She could no longer deny the state of her marriage, though. It had to be looked into, and fixed, before she and her man went their separate ways. Had she given the psychic Doretha any credence, she might have seen the state of her marriage as a sign the lady knew what she was talking about, but she'd forgotten Ms. Doretha no sooner than she'd left her. In fact, Ms. Doretha's image didn't present itself again until it was just nearly time to go back to *The Love Forum*. Pat had gone for a routine mammogram back when she and Karl started conversing, and by the end of her whirlwind crush, her life had changed. And decidedly so.

+++

Pat sat in Dr. Manning's office shaking. Her left hand held her right and streaming from her eyes were the tears of the largest proportions. They would well up high in her eyes and then just splash all across her cheeks.

"I'm so sorry, Pat," Dr. Manning said. He was a sweet old man who had been making strides in breast cancer research for decades. Pat recalled their first meeting, when she thought she was just coming in for a routine mammogram. He was pleasant and put her at ease.

"You have what is called ductal carcinoma—it is the most common form of breast cancer," he said. "It has spread to the surrounding breast tissue, and it is my opinion that you will need both a mastectomy and chemotherapy. I am sorry to deliver such devastating news, but together, you and I, along with your family, will see you through this."

Pat had stopped listening a long time ago—back when he'd said he had bad news. She just knew what would follow. Her mother had had breast cancer, her grandmother had had it, her aunts, her cousins—it was like an inheritance. As much as she had braced herself for the possibility of carrying on the family tradition, she was unable to hold herself together. All she could think about was her husband and her children. What would she tell them? How could she explain that they could possibly lose her? How could she do that to them? In the time spent half-hearing Dr. Manning's words and crying like a young child, she resolved not to tell them. She wouldn't tell Donnell or the children a thing. This would be a secret battle—one she would not bother them with.

Chapter Nine

The Love Forum
Maintenance Men

August, 2008. Lately, I had been measuring my life in weekly intervals. It had been over a month and I couldn't wait to get to the station or to Dr. Wilma's office to talk things through. While no definite love had materialized, I had the feeling I was on the verge of something. I don't know. It was like déjà vu . . . I've been here before . . . I was in grade school all over again. What an eerie but powerful feeling . . . so powerful, it made me damn near want to start carrying a pad and pen like Dr. Wilma . . . jot stuff down . . . a diary . . . my journey to finding sweet love.

"Hey! Oh yeah, oh yeah. That's what I'm talking about, Magic."

Melissa started up that singing again (that's one voice that could bring anyone back to reality). I didn't know how Dallas could stand her.

"'12 Play.' Oh yeah, oh yeah. *Whether it's morning, noon, or night, I can make you feel all right. Sing it. 12 play* . . . Dallas, this is your girl Melissa Morgan here with another episode of *The Love Forum*, and tonight, I promise you—it will be a scorcher! We're discussing our dirty little secret, ladies—maintenance men. And girls, Magic has all the songs that will help us set the D-town on fire, and of course, we're going to introduce you to our girl Jessie Simone Harris like only K103.5 can. She has whipped up the sultry writings of a damsel definitely in distress. So grab those towels, drinks, or whatever else you need to get you through the night 'cause it's definitely gonna be a forum to remember! Magic, bring it back. Whew! All right R. Kelly, boy you can do me any day . . . *12 play, 12 play, 12 play* . . . Dr. Laura, whatcha got?"

"Whew! Melissa, you're too much, girl. Good evening, Dallas. And Divas, good evening to you. It's been awhile, but I think we're going to bring it to you in full force tonight. Tonight should be very interesting and therapeutic because we're going to be exploring relationships from different perspectives."

"Dr. Laura, I'm ready, girl! Bring that therapy on sista." V said as she laughed and perched up in her seat.

"Well V—girl, you're looking too fly tonight, I must say— first, we're going to see how we can heal hurt, or make things clearer, through the medium of writing. I hear Ms. Jessie has written a scorching poem. Audience, I had a chance to take a peak . . . the diva is bringing fire and brimstone ya'll, you don't want to miss. Second, we're going to get the feedback from several of the Divas who participated in the K103.5 e-dating service—K103.5 listeners, you don't want to miss this one either. And last, when all else fails, ladies, who do we typically call on? Girl, I must be psychic 'cause I think I heard someone in the listening audience say the p-busters, and the good Doc's not talking about getting rid of ghosts either. Yes, maintenance men. Get them glasses up, 'cause we're sending a special shout out to you. So sit back, relax, and enjoy tonight's edition of *The Love Forum* during K103.5's quiet storm."

"Whew! Dr. Laura, that's a full plate for the forum tonight and it definitely sounds like one to remember. Yes girl, I love it! Magic, take us to break, bring that '12 Play' back. Hey! Yes! Yes boy, do it, do it." Melissa started singing again, "*12 play, 12 play, 12 play . . .*"

Oh my god, Melissa and Dr. Laura had built everything up with such anticipation that I suddenly became mortified and started fumbling through my purse for my poem. I knew where it was—right in the side pocket folded up like a note you'd write in middle school. You know the ones where you drew two boxes and wrote, do you like me? Check yes or no. Just when I had started getting used to the whole love forum thing, Melissa had to throw a curveball and put this challenge before the Divas and me. I just had to be the one to draw the lucky number from the hat. Honestly though, I'm glad I had to write the poem because it made me realize what I was looking for in a man, and what I could live with, and what I wouldn't settle for. It also summed up everything I had ever felt about my ideal mate and at that point, it was all about the physical—physical pleasure that is—because it had been quite awhile, and frankly, that was the only thing on my mind lately. Um, maybe putting it out there would attract the right man with the right kind of energy (and a job and a car and a little bit of money too, oh, and let's not forget, one who knows how to put it down oh-so-good).

"Jessie mama, you know I love your writing. Ever since you wrote that poem about Marvin . . . you know, before we found out he was damn near married. Get ready, girl, 'cause it's about to be about you in five . . . four . . . three . . . two . . . one!

"Whew Magic, you're putting it out there tonight boy . . . my body, Melissa's body's calling for you, oooh R. Kelly, R. Kelly, R. Kelly . . . K103.5, this is your girl, the ever-so-sweet Melissa Morgan and it's that time. We have a special treat for you tonight. What better way to express our emotions than with written words, and we have Jessie S. Harris 'bout to break us off one of those sultry, seductive poems, and if you really listen, you'll find the true meaning behind the words. Magic, start the music, 'cause my girl has hooked it up with some slamming notes. Family, introducing Jessie Simone Harris with 'Black Coffee.'"

V said, "Owwww! I know that's right, girl. I'm drinking my cup of strong, black . . . but you didn't hear me though . . . strong, black coffee as we speak. Go 'head girl!"

I closed my eyes, took a long deep breath, and let it go. Then started reading:

Intoxicating to my every sense,
emotions rise, with every move of my sweet, full hips.
Slow, rhythmic, grinding moves,
strive for that perfect brew.
Umm, I love that grind

Intoxicating to my every sense,
eyes revel, upon seeing that smooth, black body,
feverishly brewing out of control
and its intoxicating addiction is strong and bold.
Umm, I love that body

Intoxicating to my every sense,
I lick the remnants from my full red lips,
which still possess that pungent smell
from the masculine aroma of its strength.
Umm, I love that smell

Intoxicating to my every sense,
I tremor, from the passion, that hurls me into deep
eternal bliss.
Sending joy throughout my mind, body, and soul,
curling red painted toes into white yarns beneath my
feet.
Umm, I tremor for that passion

I wish this second, captured
within this moment, will only be superseded
by the man, who will be
my strong, black, cup of coffee.
Signed: Mr. Starbucks, where are you?

"Well hot damn, Dallas. Ms. Harris is in the building!
Callers, please chime in. Let us know just what you're thinking.
But wait, I'm going to give that poem some time to marinate.
While y'all think about making and sipping on your own cup of
strong black coffee, Magic is gonna play us a little something.
Magic, what you think about Jessie's 'Black Coffee'?"

"Aiight Melissa, how about we keep the R. Kelly theme
going strong with 'Skin,' 'cause that poem ain't nothing but
sexy, sexy, and drenched with more sexy."

"Well, I think that's exactly what Ms. Jessie was going for.
Put that on for us, Magic, and Jackie, get me some folks on the
line—particularly some men—so they can talk to us about what
type of brew they may be and how they're representing that
strong, black coffee, and fellas, keep it clean."

Off the air the Divas just gushed over my poem, all with their
cups of coffee in hand and clink-clinking as we toasted. It was a
terrific testament to how well the poem had been received.

Pat said, "Jessie! Girl, that was fantastic! You sure are in your element. I mean maybe you should be trying to write for Mahogany, American Greetings, or Hallmark."

"For real, Jess. I felt like a young girl, discovering myself all over again," DeDe said.

"Thank you, Divas. I'm not a writer, lord knows that. I'm just putting everything—within my heart—on the lines of the pages in my new journal I'm calling *Looking for Sweet Love*, and I have Dr. Laura to thank for that."

Jackie interrupted us to let me know a doctor was on the line asking about me. Okay! That's what I'm talking about. If I knew all I had to do was write a poem to cop me a doctor, I would have done that week one.

"Get him ready, Jackie. Let's hear what he has to say to Ms. Jessie live."

R. Kelly finished serenading us with 'Skin' and my palms were getting a little sweaty. I mean I knew what I was getting myself into being on the forum, but damn, did all of Dallas have to listen as a brother tried to romance me?

"And we're back, Dallas. This is your girl, the ever-so-sweet Melissa Morgan, and just like you, I've been trying to recover from Ms. Jessie Harris's poem. Quentin, baby, it ain't nothing but pure heat up in here, you need to meet me in the boudoir straight after work, 'cause I got coffee on the brains thanks to Ms. Harris! That was something serious, Jessie. Why don't you tell us about your thoughts when writing 'Black Coffee.'"

"There's really not all that much to tell. I took something that makes me feel wonderful each day—yes, something as simple as coffee. And simple, yet wonderful, is how I want my man to make me feel. From the moment I get out of bed to when I lay my head back on the pillow at night, I want to feel passionate about him, and in return, I want him to feel passionate about me, passionate to the point it makes both of us tremor."

"Okay, well maybe that man is Dr. Xavier Houston. He's on the line right now, and it seems he was quite taken with those beautiful words you just shared with us. Hello, Dr. Houston.

What would you like to say to Jessie's hot tail? You might have to watch out for her, Doc!"

"Good evening, Melissa, Divas, and especially you, Ms. Harris. My name is Xavier, calling from Gilford Hills. I have to say, I was blown away by the depth and complexity of your words."

"Ooh, Jessie! Dr. Houston knows some big words! Girl, you might want to keep this one around. Quite an improvement from the last couple of scrubs trying to holla!"

"Melissa, girl, you're a mess!" Sending out a soft laughter, I said, "Hello, Dr. Houston. Thank you for the compliment. I was just trying to capture my feelings about my ideal mate, intertwined with my feelings about love. Yeah, I know, sounds a little corny."

"Corny? Not at all! You did an excellent job. And as an avid coffee drinker, all I can say is that you have a strong cup of dark roast, café mocha style, right here at your fingertips, waiting to be sipped."

"All right, damn boy! Hold up, Jessie girl, I might have to take this one for myself. Whew, he came on strong with that one! Now Dr. Houston, I know you're all dark roasted and café mocha style, but my girl Jessie likes her coffee dark and bittersweet."

"Dark, yes. Bitter, no. But definitely can be sweet to the right one," Dr. Houston corrected Melissa.

"Well damn," V said.

"Girl, I know that's right," said DeDe.

"Well Dr. Houston, I think the Divas around the table are in agreement—you definitely have everyone's attention. And I mean *everyone's* attention, including Magic's. And to tell you the truth, I've never seen Dr. Laura searching for words as you've left her speechless. Look here. Doc, would you be interested in taking Jessie out on a date? I'll vouch for her—she is one sexy bitch!"

"Melissa!"

"What, Jessie? You are!"

Dr. Houston said, "I would not only like to take Jessie out on a date, I'd be honored to do so."

"Well what do you know, Dallas? The love forum is good for something! We done hooked up the nasty poetess, Jessie Harris, and the big-time doctor, Xavier Houston. How much y'all wanna bet they gonna get it on the on the first date! Ha! I'm just playing! And to show you how much I support this union, I'm going to pay for the first date. That's right, K103.5 will front the bill. The only requirement is for both of you to be registered in the new and improved 'love connection' database, or what we like to call our new E-Dating Service, and agree to share your experience on the DK and Melissa Morning Show. And speaking of e-dating experiences, we have been showcasing the Divas e-dates all week long on the DK and Melissa morning show, and we'll hear from several of the Divas recapping their e-dating stories in just a few, but back to you, Dr. Houston."

"Uh, no thanks, Melissa," Dr. Houston said. "I have more private, intimate, and romantic plans in mind for a lady like Ms. Harris."

"Oh okay, Doc! If you want to handle this, I'm all for a man taking charge and taking care of his lady like he's supposed to, *but* we will be doing the background check to ensure you're legitimate, and not some stalker or serial killer."

"Yes," he said, laughing. "I appreciate that and rightfully you should. Ms. Harris, do you have a pen? I'd like to give you my telephone number, you can call whenever you would like that sip."

"Boy, you just keep coming with it! You ain't right, and before you say another word, we're going to have to slow your role. Now Dr. Houston, do you know how many hungry women are listening to this station right now? Just itching and scratching to get the digits of a fine *dark roasted* brew, and we want even touch the successful doctor part. You hold on for a minute and give that information to my assistant—off-line! We'll talk to you next week to see how the rendezvous went down."

Brit interrupted Melissa, "Um, excuse me. I love my girl Jessie, I do, but should this match making be taking up the whole damn show? I'm trying to get to our discussion on maintenance men!"

"Oh lord, Brit. Green is not your color tonight, girl! Well K103.5, I believe Ms. Harris has her doctor's number in hand, and with that being said, we need to take care of a little station advertising business and let you know that Big Jim's Rib Shack now has later hours and as always, Big Jim's: Big on food and not on price! Dallas it's a cool seventy-three degrees, and I'm your girl, the ever-so-sweet Melissa Morgan, putting it down during the quiet storm with the bad boy himself, Mr. Kirk 'Magic' Wonder. When we come back, we'll hear from Brit, Pat, and V on their e-dating stories, two successes and one total mess of a disaster, which we just couldn't pass up replaying for the K103.5 audience. And to get you in the mood, we'll have Magic put on a little something sexy."

When Melissa returned from the break, she was howling right along with the song as usual.

"All right, Magic, I think I have blessed Dallas enough with my beautiful voice. What do you think?"

"Uh . . ."

"Don't get hurt, Magic! You know my voice is heavenly."

"Okay, sweetie. Why don't we just get back to the subject at hand."

"Divas, y'all better let Magic know about my voice!"

"We're on Team Magic, Lis, sorry! You sound just terrible," V said.

"Okay, Ms. V, I know a hater when I see one. Why don't your hating tail tell us just how your e-dating experience went."

"Well, Melissa, I am happy to say that I have fairly good news!"

"Hallelujah! I thought we'd never get you a man. Just kidding, V. Explain the process to us."

"I took the survey as soon as I got home from the station a month ago. I was eager; I have to admit. Even after hearing Dr. Laura's horror stories. I say it as an opportunity to weed out the ass—oh, excuse me, I mean jerks. So I took the survey, I submitted it, and I waited. I waited five whole days, in fact. I was getting a little impatient and I kept checking my profile picture like, Uh? I know these brothers see my fine ass posted on this screen. Anyway, I finally get a response on day six. It's from a fairly decent looking guy named Sheldon. He's tall, dark, and most importantly, employed!"

"Amen! Go on."

"We share e-mails for a few days, just getting to know each other, seeing where we stand on things, etc. That next Monday Sheldon decides to raise the stakes a little and asks me to video chat with him."

DeDe said, "Video chat? My dude asked me if he could come over after the second e-mail."

"Oh, well like I said, Sheldon was decent. I don't know what hoodlum you attracted, De, but you know they say who you attract is a reflection of you."

"Do they now? Okay, V. I got something for your smart butt when we get off air."

"Don't wait till we off air, boo! Say whatcha feel."

"Uh," interrupted Melissa, "can we stay on track please?"

I was so happy to be back in the presence of my crazy girls.

"Anyway, as I was saying—before I was so rudely interrupted—Sheldon and I get on the video chat and that just takes our connection to the next level. You know e-mail can only express so much. Actually speaking to him made me really fall for him."

"Fall for him? So is this your new honey, V?"

"Maybe. Maybe not. Look here, Melissa, I know the ropes. I been at this life thing awhile now, and I know way better than to put all my delicate eggs in one basket. Sheldon and I will continue to video chat, and we've even arranged to meet out this weekend, but like I told him I'll tell you, I'm keeping my options open. Wide open."

"Beggers can't be choosey, you know!" DeDe said and cracked up laughing. "I'm just playing, V. You know I wish you well."

"Well, DeDe, since you're throwing so much salt in V's game, why don't you tell us how your e-dating thing went."

"It went nowhere and it got there extra fast, okay? Like I said, the fool asked to come over quick, fast, and in a hurry. I am extremely selective about who gets to see the inside of my house, okay? And he did not pass the test."

"What was his name, DeDe?"

"Girl, I don't know. I done forgot. He wasn't worth remembering. Note to all my Internet-dating brothers out there, don't push the first visit, 'kay? You come off a little stalkerish and way too desperate."

"Okey dokey. Moving right along," Melissa said. "Our girl is obviously a little salty about the whole online dating scene. By show of hands, let me see who also had a negative e-dating experience." Everyone but Pat and V raised their hands. "Whoa, Dallas, you should see what I see. Or should I say smell? A whole lot of musty pits pushing their stink in my direction."

"No you didn't, Melissa," I said, putting my arm down.

"I'm just kidding! Dallas knows we only deal with divas up in here. Let's go around the table and each of you give me a quick description of why your e-dating experience flopped. Then we'll focus on the good news—'cause I'm trying to spread the cheer up in here! Jessie, start us off."

"He looked nothing like his profile pic, Lis. I, like V, decided to go on and video chat, and when that cookie monster came on the screen, I jumped back. I almost fell out my chair. Now don't get me wrong, ugly people need love too, and I might have been willing to entertain Quido a little longer had he told the truth. You know I don't dig a liar."

"But Quido, though? The brother's name was Quido?"

"Yes, Quido."

"Oh, I woulda dumped him off that name alone," said Brit.

"And you, Brit?" Melissa asked. "Summarize your experience for us."

"Thumbs down. Boo! Wack! Never again. He was this square dude with big old bifocals taking up all my computer screen. He was just, well, corny."

"Aw Brit, we already know your problem. If his pants ain't hanging low enough to show his drawers, then he ain't stepping one foot over the threshold, right?"

"You got it, baby girl!"

"Dallas, come get this woman 'fore I pop her a good one. Darlene, how about you?"

"Um, Lis, my e-date lasted three seconds. Miguel shut that thing down just as soon as I answered the first question on the survey."

"I know that's right, Miguel! Let your woman know! Shoot. So we have a room full of Internet busts? Now I see why Dr. Laura told us about our twentieth place ranking! But I did notice that Mrs. Pat 'Locked Down' Carter didn't raise her hand in disapproval! Does Donnell know about this, Missy?"

"Oh, Melissa, please. Donnell has nothing to worry about, but I did meet a lovely gentleman named Karl. He's also married, and we found that we have many similar interest. We have become really good friends in just a short amount of time."

DeDe said, "Uh huh, that's how they get you, girl. And before you know you done ended up launching an affair! Believe me—"

"No, no DeDe, nothing like that at all. Karl has never tried to cross the line with me. As a matter of fact, he just sent me the proofs of his family portrait today. We're strictly friends."

"Nothing wrong with that," Melissa said. "Well, Dallas, there you have it. As a whole, the city is batting about half. But us here on *The Love Forum*, we couldn't even match that. Magic, I think it's safe to say, e-dating is NOT the move!"

"That is precisely why we need maintenance men!" V said.

"V, you ain't never lied. Sistas, e-dating can be a fun and exhilarating experience, but at the same time, it can be a disastrous mess. Trust me, your girl Melissa knows, and as the saying goes, 'Hope for the best and prepare for the worst.' Dr. Laura, any final words?"

Laughing hard, Dr. Laura said, "Girl, you hit the nail dead on the head. One thing most people seem to throw to the wind, besides caution, is that you can be who or what you want within the cyber world, just don't think that the person you built with false imagery, history, or credentials will be able to journey outside of that world, because it never works—the person you built is the individual the other person wants to see. Anything else will be a disappointment. That idea of *'if they get to know the real me'* rarely, if ever, works. Humans

114

are visual creatures—especially men—so ladies, if you're not coming correct, expect the worst."

"Always on point, girl. So, any comments or advice for the Divas concerning their e-dates?"

"Well Melissa, I'm an ole saying type of woman, so let's start with DeDe and her dapper yet clownish man's date: 'Clothes may disguise a fool, but his voice will give him away.' As for V, William Shakespeare said it the best: 'Do not be like the cat that wanted a fish but was afraid to get his paws wet.' Girl, you have to get out there, big-boned and all, but remember, be honest with yourself and with your virtual partner—disappointment awaits if you don't. And Pat, you were the perfect example of how an e-date should happen."

"Well, Dr. Laura, I hope our listening audience got some pretty good pointers on Internet dating and the pros and cons with using this venue for meeting eligible brothers and sisters in the Dallas metro. Well Dr. Laura, Divas, and Magic, it's that time, as Dr. Laura said, time to put those glasses up playas. Maintenance men, we're sending love out to you, and we hope our Brit has calmed her hot behind down, always in a rush to discuss sex. Okay girl, why don't you start it off for us then? What is your definition of a 'maintenance man'? Do you have one in your life now? Why or why not?"

"Finally! A maintenance man does just what it sounds like—he maintains things. He makes sure all your equipment stays in tip-top shape. Especially when there's a drought. You know, when you haven't been so blessed to find that steady one. A maintenance man can be called out to work at two o'clock in the morning and oil those pipes. Holla!"

"And do you have a maintenance man, miss?"

"Not presently. I have a big chocolate wonder at home taking care of all my needs. So all my previous maintenance men have been put on leave. The black book has been tucked away."

"Just tucked away? Not burned."

"Oh, it's never burned, Melissa. I might not even burn it for my husband. That just wouldn't be wise."

Pat said, "Now Brit, that's just ridiculous. When you marry, you're saying you've found the ultimate maintenance man. What in the world would you still need a black book for?"

"Pat, you don't understand. You've been blessed with Donnell. If I had me a Donnell, maybe I'd think differently. I mean, Brass is worth his weight in gold, but you never know. Talk to me in a few more months. Maybe I'll be closer to striking a match and putting the black book out of commission."

"Divas, going around the table, tell me some of your most memorable maintenance men stories. Pat, I know you're locked down and that marriage is working beautifully, but why don't you share a story with us single girls. We need to feel connected to you—to know you went through the same thing before finding your Prince Charming and that there's some hope for us."

"Melissa, you might not believe it, but my husband was once my maintenance man."

"What?"

"Yes, girl. I had never been the type of woman to be tagging behind a man. I mean my momma had raised me right. A man chased you! You didn't chase the man. But something about Donnell. He used to have me banging on his door at all hours of the night. I couldn't get enough of him or that stick!"

"I know that's right, Pat. Tell it, boo. Preach!" yelled Brit.

Laughing, Pat said, "Girl! Lucky for me he was also a good man all around. He wasn't only gifted in the sack, but gifted in the heart, mind, and spirit."

"Aw, that is so sweet. Melissa ain't mad at you though." She smirked. "So I guess we can't get too stank with you then. A married couple's bedroom business is private. What about you, V?"

"Ryan!"

"Well damn, don't hold back."

"Sorry. But girl, wasn't nothing like him. Ryan was, well, you know, how can I say, um, you know," she began whispering, "well endowed."

"All right for well endowed! Melissa ain't mad at ya. Question is, did he know how to use it?"

"Girl, you didn't hear me though. That was the Rock of Gibraltar, and I was the climber getting as, hey, what did that commercial say? 'A piece of the rock.' He was just so big and then on top of that so gentle. You know sometimes men who have been blessed with a little extra down there tend to be a little rough. To show you just how much you *can't* handle them. Not Ryan's ass. He was the gentlest lover I had. And like Donnell, he had me banging on dorm doors at two and three in the morning. He maintained all the machinery. Kept the pipes in good working condition. I was devastated when he settled down. Girl, I was singing Vesta Williams's 'Congratulations' for months, but not too soon after that, I was singing the praises of Mikki Howard because I had a 'Love Under New Management'!"

"Girl, you're just as crazy as they come, but that's an interesting point. What do you do when your maintenance man settles down? Let's hear from a few callers. K103.5. Who's on the line?"

"Hey, Melissa. My name is Angie calling from Fort Worth. I've been single for five years now, but I have yet to run out of maintenance men."

"Single for five years, girl! Yeah, you know you need some working it out. I can see going without for a month, two, maybe even six, but sixty months? There's no way in hell, so y'all know somebody's laying the pipe over in Fort Worth. So Angie, have you ever had a maintenance man settle down on you?"

"Sure. One of my maintenance men just got married, matter of fact."

"So how did that work out? Was breaking it off tough?"

"Who said anything about breaking it off? I could tell, just by looking at homegirl that she wasn't throwing that stuff right, so he's back home. I'm getting with the brother tonight—okay!"

"And on that note, let's take another caller. Angie, you ain't no good, girl. No good! K103.5, who's this?"

"Divas! This is Francine, a.k.a. Frenchie, from Arlington. Girl, I had my best maintenance man—I mean my *best* maintenance man—settle down on me. And girl, it was a heartbreaker. But out of respect for the sister about to settle down with my plumber—that's what I call him, girl, 'cause he was plunging the hell out of this [*beep*]— I decided to end it, and we went our separate ways. We had handled each other's needs for the duration of their non-married relationship, but once he decided to tie the knot, we, excuse the pun, cut our knot."

"Okay, Frenchie. I can't say I agree with y'all continuing to work it out throughout his dating another woman, but at least you drew the line when they jumped the broom. Okay!"

"I know that's right, Melissa," said Pat. "What happened to both of you just waiting until you were committed and experiencing the joy of being together after not being with anyone during your courtship? Maybe I'm just old fashioned!"

"Caller, are you there? Did you hear what my girl Pat said about just holding off?"

"Yea Melissa, I heard. Granted, I can't deny I wasn't being the best kind of woman, but this is the twenty-first century, and come on, girl, you know if he ain't getting it in the relationship he's damn well getting it somewhere else, and hell, why should I deprive myself? He might as well be with me. I got needs too, and trust, it was only a sexual thing—he knew it and I knew it. I didn't want him for a husband, and he definitely didn't want me for a wife. And I'm here to tell you, that big [*beep*] was good as [*beep*]. And afterward, after the nasty that is, he got his [*beep*] and got out, 'cause I had [*beep*] to do."

"Okay! Dallas, I expected it to get nasty in here, but, *damn*, not that nasty! Magic," Melissa was cracking up laughing, "have you ever been a maintenance man?"

"Ha-ha, back at 'cha! Whatchu talking 'bout, Melissa. I'm just the DJ. What you pulling me in this for?"

"Well for obvious reasons. You are a man! Well, at least I hope so! You are a man, right Magic?"

"Aiight Melissa, don't start f-ing with me. It's nothing but all man right here!"

"Okay then, I knew that! But your girl just wanted Dallas to know that this chocolate morsel with those size thirteen feets was nothing but nicca!" Melissa laughed. "Now tell us if you've ever been the maintenance kind—the plumber, the electrician, the cable man, the pipe layer, or whatever the name may be?"

"First of all Melissa, I ain't ever heard this until tonight. You know y'all women be having names for stuff we ain't never even heard of before! But to answer your question, yes, I have been a maintenance man. I got a few clients around town as we speak. Mmm-huh, we need to hurry this show the hell up, so I can get the hell out of here, 'cause the tension and smells up in here is getting a brother worked up for real though."

We all cracked up at that. Though Magic wasn't the cutest thing walking, he did have some plump lips and big-ass feet. He could probably fuck a woman down real good, and I mean real good—sweaty, nasty-talking, and some good ole pussy-licking fucking down.

"And how would those women rate you, Magic?"

"Tens all around, Melissa. Ten for size, ten for technique, ten for stamina, and ten for 'da ability to put they asses to sleep."

"Whew, hot damn now! I done heard it all this evening, Dallas. We got the world's sexiest, if not lustful, damn poem read to us; hooked Jessie's crazy butt up with what sounds like one of Texas's most successful physicians; and now we done heard what goes down in Magic's bedroom. I don't know about y'all but I have had enough! This is Melissa Morgan signing off. Magic, the maintenance man, put us on a little something. Dallas, we will see you next week. Until then, maintenance men, keep doing what you do. Hold those glasses up, I'm pouring this just for you! Magic, play Xscape's 'My Little Secret,' and take us out of here as we end another quiet storm on none other than the Power Station—K103.5. And remember family, pray for me, 'cause I'm praying for you:

Now I lay you down to sleep,
I pray the Lord your soul to keep;
When in the morning light you wake,
May he teach you the path of love to take.
Good night my people and remember it's all about love."

As nice as Dr. Houston had made me feel, I walked out of that studio without his number in hand. Something about the excitement of talking about and listening to the stories about the Divas' e-dates and maintenance men made me, for a moment, forget him altogether. By the time I got back to the studio that little piece of paper would be crumpled up in the bottom of a trash can somewhere. "Humph, if it's meant to be, we'll find each other somewhere down the road."

Chapter Ten

Remembering Past Loves

September 2008. It was Saturday again. And I can't lie, I was grateful. I couldn't wait to lean back on Dr. Wilma's couch and spill my guts. Lol! I needed some help sorting things out. As much as I loved my girls, they weren't doing much in the way of fixing my mess of a life. Maybe *The Love Forum* was helpful to an extent, but I mean everybody on the panel was as messed up as me! Plus, they were my good girlfriends, so they couldn't give me the objective perspective I needed. Dr. Wilma had been where I'd been—or at least I had the feeling she had (how else did she know so much?)—and she was a successful, intelligent woman, which meant she was where I wanted to be. She was seated at that beautiful antique carved wood desk when I entered.

"Oh. Hello, Jessie. It's nice to see you again. Have a seat and take all of life's weight off. Relax yourself. Would you like something to drink? Coffee or water? I'd offer you a little wine, but that's only for spa visits."

"Ha! No thank you, Dr. Wilma. I don't need a thing to drink. I want my head on straight for this visit."

"Oh? Did you have a tough couple of weeks?"

"Not really tough . . . just a lot to think about. I mean you know I've been participating in that radio show—*The Love Forum*. It's just the whole time I'm sitting up there on that panel, discussing my love life with all of Dallas, I'm beginning to realize I really don't have any strong examples of good love in my life. Even Big Momma—the strongest human being I know didn't know good love. My own father rolled out on my mother so long ago I don't even know what he looks like."

"Well, what about your girlfriend Pat?"

"Yeah, I guess Pat's life is cool, but we're not as close as me and the other girls." I had forgotten all about Pat hinting that her marriage was on the rocks, on top of her issues with her health. "Don't get me wrong, I love Pat. I'd go to war for her, but since her marriage and the birth of her children, she hasn't been as, you know, available as my other girls. I haven't really had the opportunity to be around her like I probably should be. Birds of a feather flock together, right? I need to be around that kind of bird, huh?"

"Well maybe you two could arrange to spend a little more time together? Really, though, I want to spend this session discussing you, Jessie. Naturally, your girlfriends are a very big part of your life. I think this tends to be the case with single women more so than women involved in relationships, but I think your personality is strong enough that you aren't completely influenced by their presence. If you don't have any examples of good love around you, you need to be that example yourself. So, if you don't mind, I'd like you to open up to me about your past relationships. Are you sure you won't take me up on that offer for something to drink? You're gonna be doing most of the talking today."

"Um, I guess I'll take some water, Dr. Wilma. Thanks."

She poured me a tall glass, and of course I was checking out the shoe game! I liked Dr. Wilma so much because she was quality, all the way down to the floor, but she wasn't any designer's mascot. I *knew* those shoes were Jimmy Choo! Oh, despite the size of my bank account, I do keep up with the fashion world! But Dr. Wilma didn't flaunt it. I appreciated that. Especially living in a world where everything has to shine to be worth something. To say the very least, Dr. Wilma was classy.

I sipped my water.

"Jessie, tell me a bit about your relationship history. Sum it up for me. I'm not rushing you. Take your time. But pull out the most important elements of your past relationships and tell me about them. I'm trying to determine the theme, if you will, of your romantic commitments."

"Well, I've had three major ones in my adult life. It's funny you're asking me this right now, because I swear I've been thinking real hard about each of them lately. Trying to make some sense of my current state. Vince was one."

"Tell me about him."

"I was at Club NV and Vince approached me. Not much of a story there, except he had his shirt unbuttoned with a gold chain and his chest hairs sticking out."

"Was that a problem?"

"Dr. Wilma!"

"Okay! I don't like my men showing the chest hair either. I just wanted to be sure. Didn't want to insult you. Go on . . ."

"After we fixed that—I told him he better not come out the house like that again—we started what seemed to be a great relationship. We were both young and naïve, and I remember staying over his place while he was supposed to be working security at an apartment complex. That nut would call in pretending to be at the job while we were sitting in his living room watching movies, eating, and . . . well, you know . . ."

"Mmmm. I guess what the residents didn't know wouldn't hurt them was his philosophy?"

"That was before GPS and employee tracking was all the rage. It was a fairly safe neighborhood, so I guess Vince thought he could take that risk without it catching up to him. I can't pretend that I was pushing him to go! Like I said, we were young."

"So why did it *seem* to be a great relationship?"

"Well, it took a sour turn one night. I was over there and we hadn't eaten dinner yet. One of his friends stopped by to help him hookup his entertainment system, and I decided to go out and pick up something for everyone. I ended up going to KFC and getting one of their family meal packs. You know men are extra greedy, Dr. Wilma."

"I know sweetie. I call my son Baby T-Rex he eats so much."

"So I get back and let them know I had picked up dinner. Out of nowhere, the friend starts going off about how I didn't ask him what he wanted to eat before I left. He was like, 'If you're going to offer something you should have at least asked if I wanted anything before you went out.' Of course I was taken aback. I had just gone out for *my* dinner, but decided on the family pack, enough for everyone, in case they were hungry. But do you know this fool keeps at it? Berating me in front of Vince over some damn chicken that I didn't have to buy him in the first place? He would not let it go. But you know, his ignorance could not compare to the fact that Vince did not say one word. He didn't say one thing."

"So this friend is berating you in front of your man and he says nothing about it?"

"Nope! I guess getting that entertainment system wired was more important."

"So what did you do, Jessie?"

"I kindly picked up my purse, said 'You all have a nice night,' and left."

"Please don't tell me you left the chicken."

"I did, Dr. Wilma, because at that point, it wasn't about the dinner."

"I understand. But just the thought of those two watching TV on the newly wired entertainment system eating my bird, bought with my own money, rubs me the wrong way. Did he at least go after you?"

"Well, yes, he did do that. And of course it was a heated argument ending with me telling him not to touch me. I got in my car and left. After that, things fell apart pretty quickly. I didn't call, and after I ignored a handful of his calls, neither did he. I finally saw him many months later at a happy hour downtown and we talked and hashed out some things. He told me to stop by his place afterward. At that point, I didn't have anyone so I said what the hell, everyone deserves a second chance. But that turned out to be the biggest mistake. I made a complete and total fool of myself."

"What do you mean?"

"Well, he gave me the address to his new place, told me how to get there, and what time he would be back home. We basically made arrangements to meet up."

"And?"

"When I got there, I knocked on the door and his roommate answered and he had this puzzled look on his face. I mean, he knew who I was as they had been friends for some time—and no, I know what you're thinking, it wasn't Mr. I-Don't-Want-This-Chicken. Anyway, he asked if Vince knew I was coming by. Mind you now, I'm still at the front door. So he says, 'hold on,' and he goes in and knocks on Vince's bedroom door. This boy comes back, stuttering, saying Vince is, um, occupied. He was letting me know in his own little way that there was someone there. Vince's ass didn't send a message for me to come back; he didn't get up to talk to me himself . . . nothing. His roommate shook his head and just said sorry and closed the door."

"Hmmmm. I guess that could be considered a humiliating experience. Did you two connect after that?"

"No! To say the least, I was truly outdone—and done!"

"Okay. You said you've had three relationships. Tell me about another."

"Next was Gary."

"And how did you guys meet?"

"Believe it or not, we met at a gym."

"That's not too hard to believe. You seem to take very good care of your body."

"Thanks, Dr. Wilma, but I really can't claim any credit. I'm not the workout type. All this just comes naturally. These are all Big Momma's genes! I say believe it or not because I was just going through a little phase where I called myself going to the gym every day. Honestly, I had only been going a few days when I met him."

Man, Dr. Wilma was taking me back. I remembered how Gary approached me and everything. I was all sweaty with no makeup. My hair was pulled back in a raggedy looking ponytail—in a pink knocker, like I was a high school girl with no regular salon appointment! I had sweat stains all in my crotch and along my back. Embarrassing!

He said, "How you doing?" anyway though.

I have to admit, I wasn't in the mood. The guys at the gym were always staring, like the women there were meat loaf they wanted to sop up with a biscuit. I wasn't trying to be anybody's meat loaf. Still, he was easy on the eyes. I said, "I'm fine, how are you?" Kind of interested. Kind of not.

"Cool. Just trying to sweat a couple of pounds off before I run out of here and drink it back on."

He brought my smile out of hiding. I liked his bluntness, and damn, those eyes. His teeth were white and straight as a picket fence. "Maybe you should try some of the sports drinks, like Gatorade or some of the vitamin waters?" I said.

"Yeah, maybe. I know you were killing that StairMaster in there, though."

"Ha! I guess. Um, were you beside me or something?"

"Oh, no. I was just checking you out from the weight room."

"Uh, okay. Let me find out I got a stalker at the gym!" I laughed and he joined me.

"Oh no, ma. Don't get me wrong, I'm not a freak or anything. I just thought you was funny. You were stepping like you were trying to make the machine pick up and move. You kinda reminded me of Sophia in *The Color Purple*—on a mission, marching to kick Harpo's ass or something like that."

He had a sense of humor. Damn I needed a laugh. I had been cracking my own damn jokes for going on two years. And for real, I wasn't all that funny. I always liked a man who wasn't afraid to make fun of me too. I know that sounds crazy, but it's true. I guess it's a sister thing. You know sometimes you take yourself so seriously and it feels good to be laughed at a bit. Really. "Was I that bad?" I said.

"You definitely were going to town, but by the looks, you definitely know what works for you. Sophia never looked liked that."

"Well thanks for the compliment . . . I think."

"It's definitely a compliment. Trust." He let those chestnut colored eyes wander all over me. And I let him. Down to the sweaty crotch and all!

"Well, look, I've stayed my limit. I guess I'll see you around the gym sometime." I wanted to let him see what I was working with back there. I was about to walk my bottom, round as the goddamn moon, across the gym floor like Iman—with way more junk, of course.

"No doubt. Yo, be careful out there. Don't march over anyone trying to get back to the locker room, aiight?"

"I'll try not to." I walked away giggling. I can't lie. I was trying to walk a little softer, not like Ms. Sophia going to whoop Harpo's ass, and keep my sex appeal, too.

I saw Gary a few more times in the gym before he finally decided to push up. We were both in the gym's co-ed sauna when he finally asked me on a date. For some reason, I was so impressed by the way he had taken his time. I loved the anticipation of it all—waiting to see what flirty thing he would say to me in the gym, how he would look my whole body over. I felt like tongue kissing him every time I talked to his fine ass, so you can guess how that first date went down. I maintained, but damn it was hard. After dinner and dancing, we went back to my house for a nightcap. Before I knew it, my panties were dangling off one ankle and Gary's bald head was between my knees. He ate that thing like it was Sunday dinner. I climaxed three times. I have NEVER came off the strength of a little head. Quite honestly, I'm usually bored. Like cleaning my nails while the dude is down there *thinking* he's working it out. But Gary? He should quit his day job and eat pussy full time. Number one, he's soft. Just light licks. Small sucks on the clitoris. Number two, he doesn't treat you like a damn ice cream sundae he wants to hurry up and get to the bottom of. Needless to say, I was ready to go after that third orgasm. I leaned over and started rummaging through my nightstand for a condom. There were none! Grrrrr. I wanted to scream. I literally had to bite my lips and hold it in. Then I thought he might have one. I mean he should have. Running around sticking his head in random women's coochies, right?

I said, "Gary? You have protection?"

He said, "Naw, baby. But I'm safe."

"Oh no, nigga. I don't get down like that."

"I'm safe, Jessie. Trust me. Now let me in."

He put his hands on my knees and spread my legs open. I

was sitting there open as a butterfly while he unbuttoned his pants and let out the most wonderful looking dick. I mean it was just pretty. Smooth skin. A good-sized head. Length just right. And looking into his beautiful-ass eyes made it NO better. He had himself positioned just so . . . so the head was right at my hole. Peeking down into it. Knocking at the door. *Knock, knock! Who is it?* But I pushed him back.

"I can't do it, babe. Believe me, I want to. What you just did with those lips right there? That tongue? That was magical. Best I ever had. But I can't do it. It's a no go. I'm not trying to make any new feet for shoes I can't afford, and I don't want any unwelcome guests funking up the cooch. You dig?"

He pushed the issue, though. That was the ultimate turn off. Number one, I don't like a man too desperate. It's pussy. If you start treating it like it's crack and you can't live without it, then I begin wondering what you do with all your extra time. If you can't control yourself enough at that very moment, why should I believe you can control yourself at any other? Chances are you're fucking everything in a skirt. And then the fact that he was willing to fuck raw on our first go—hell, our first date—made me beyond suspicious. I jumped into my panties quicker than he could blink and was standing in the refrigerator looking for some juice while he moaned and groaned about some damn blue balls. He left with an attitude, but called me not thirty minutes later. We arranged for our next date, and you best believe he had a pocketful of rubbers. We made love the whole night through, and I must say the oral sex was a good indication of what was to come. The brother did not disappoint. Lying on Dr. Wilma's couch, I started getting a little hot remembering it all. I sat up a minute and gulped down half that water.

"Take your time," Dr. Wilma said. "We have plenty of it. So tell me, aside from the sex, what went right? Or wrong?"

"Well the sex was magical. He came around and no matter what had transpired between us—we could have just stabbed each other and called each other's mommas bald headed bitches—we couldn't keep our hands off each other."

"Did you stab each other? Did you talk about each other's mothers?"

"Well, not specifically. I was just generalizing. My point is, it was a volatile relationship. We were always fussing about something."

"What? Specifically?"

"Well, I didn't tell you this before, but Gary lived in New York. He had an apartment in Dallas—because he did so much business here—but it wasn't his primary residence. And if Gary was in New York, then he was nowhere to be found. I couldn't reach him if I was dying."

"And how did that sit with you?"

"I thought he was cheating. I thought there was another woman. And this was the topic of 99 percent of our discussions. Now, they usually ended up with my legs stretched from one corner of a room to the other and Gary all in and between them, but once that was said and done and I came down off of that sex high, I was blue again. After awhile, the time we spent apart became more and more frequent. My heart broke into a million little pieces. Still, if he was in town, I'd sweep those pieces up into a little dustpan, pour 'em down my shirt, and pretend I was working with a whole beating muscle. When we made love, Dr. Wilma, I would hold him so tight. Inside my head, I'd be saying things like, *God, please. Make him love me*. I'd try to fuck him so good. Make the sex the best he ever had . . . just so he'd stay. Just so he'd see in me what I saw in him. I mean, I put aside all sexual limitations for him Dr. Wilma. You know us black girls don't be playing with our reputations."

"Don't I know it. What do you mean though? Elaborate."

"I mean. Look, I'm sort of embarrassed to say this."

"If you're safe anywhere on this earth, Jessie, it's with me. You can speak your mind here . . . tell me all your secrets and they are perfectly safe."

"Well . . . there was oral sex."

"Jessie. You're a thirty-three-year-old woman. Why are you ashamed by that very adult act?"

"Well, not so much the oral sex, Dr. Wilma, as the extent of it. I mean, I'd swallow his semen. Let him ejaculate in my face and on my breasts and stomach . . . that sort of thing."

"Still very adult acts, unless of course you felt you were being pressured, or performing in some way you didn't wish to."

"I guess Big Momma raised me to believe you only do those sorts of things for your husband, and I just gave him all those pleasures without any real commitment from him."

"I see. Well I wouldn't beat myself up about it too bad. Were you hoping the relationship would develop into something more? Tell me more about that."

"It continued in that way for quite some time. I mean with him disappearing for weeks, and sometimes months, at a time and then popping back up as if nothing had happened. We'd argue for a while and then I'd be right back in his bed again. One night—actually the last night we ever slept with each other (after I had sucked his dick and had a mouthful, to say the least)—he jumped in the shower and left his phone sitting on top of the television set."

"Uh-oh."

"Uh-oh is right. I mean I'm generally not the sort to be going through my man's shit. I let him do him, until I feel like I'm being lied to, you know? To say the least, I felt like I was being lied to."

"So what did you do?"

"I looked through it. I picked it right up and started pushing all sorts of buttons. I looked in the call log and didn't find anything there, but when I started reading the text messages, my heart just dropped into my shoes."

"What did you see, Jessie?"

"Number one, the message was from someone Gary thought enough of to name 'Wifey.' Her real name wasn't even in there. No need for it, I guess. She was so far up the totem pole she just snatched that title and it was known exactly who she was. Well, he had a whole host of messages saved in there from 'Wifey.' Some freaky stuff. You know, her talking about what she was going to do with him when he 'got home.' Those two little words—'got home'—put a few more cracks in my beat-up heart. I was wondering, *Do they live together? Is he fucking married?* Of course there were 'I love you' messages. I mean, what could I expect from 'Wifey'? But you know, Dr. Wilma, it was the little messages that cut the deepest. Messages like, 'Babe, pick up some milk on your way.' I mean they were a couple. He bought her maxi pads and nail polish. I was crushed."

"And did you confront him?"

"No, I didn't. Really, I knew I didn't have the clout. I was his every few months fuck. I knew that. It's what I had been for over a year. He never talked about committing to me. I had never been to New York, or even invited for that matter. I mean, I didn't even know what his middle initial stood for. I just left. He was still in the hotel shower. I collected my things, threw a mint in my mouth, and walked out the door. I wouldn't see him again for a very long time."

"And tell me about when you did see him, Jessie. Close your eyes, take a deep breath, relax, and recall that meeting."

I shut my eyes, and the image of Gary in that strip club was clear as the palms of my own hands. I'd been on the phone with V, contemplating whether or not I was even going to hang out with her. Gary had been text messaging me throughout the day. I hadn't heard from him in so long, but as soon as that number came across the screen of my phone, I felt this tugging at my heart. It was like a bit of string was wrapped around it and someone was just lightly pulling, lightly tugging. I told V we had been text messaging back and forth. He wasn't being too concrete, but he was leading me in a way that let me know he wanted to see me. And as usual, it had been a long while since I'd had the pleasure of a big dick in me, so I can't deny I was pushing for a rendezvous myself. Wifey or no wifey, I had some unfulfilled needs.

V said, "Girl, I don't even know why you're messing with that trifling Negro. He's been in town ever since Friday. And he's just now talking about seeing you? At two thirty on Sunday? Think, Jessie. First of all, he didn't come down to see your crazy ass. Know that. Second, he calls you in the afternoon, not saying he wants to spend any time with you, but asking about your plans later on in the evening. You're his backup, Jessie! You don't see that? If his first boo doesn't come through, then he's gonna come calling on your crazy ass—knowing you'll be home, just waiting for him to call."

"I know. You're right, girl." V wasn't lying. She called it how she saw it and her vision was crystal clear. I had to figure out what to do with myself. No sense sitting in the house whining and crying about the dick I wasn't going to get. "So what you doing tonight, V?"

"I heard about this party. Cover charge only ten dollars, free drinks, free food, and best of all, a free dick show to boot. Holla!"

"Girl, you ain't right." I laughed at her wild tail. Vanessa very rarely turned down a "dick show" as she called them. "So what time is it?"

It was at eight, she said. It would go until they kicked our asses out. We decided to get there around ten. We knew we would be the first ones there, but we thought that was a good plan so we'd be able to eat without the other vultures eating up everything in site, and, for V's sake, we'd be able to get seats right up front. I asked her if DeDe was going.

"Now Jessie, you know good and damn well DeDe is the one that told me about the party. You know Ms. Kravitz knows everything to know about anything in this city. Now I'm gonna give you the address. And don't be all upset and frowned up when you get there either—I know you—it's just a building, girl. As for Ms. DeDe, she will be in the house promptly after her shift ends at her part-time job."

We were right. We were practically the first ones there. V and I pulled up at almost the exact same time. And I be damn—I was wondering what she meant by "it's just a building." All right for us pulling up to what used to be a church that they turned into a public venue. Suddenly, my stomach was in knots . . . this was a bad omen. Something in the wind just didn't feel right about this one, but nevertheless, we strolled in, and just like she said she would, V went straight to the buffet table.

"Go on, girl. I ain't mad at you."

Gradually, everyone started coming in, and around midnight, there was a full house of people. And although the Tabernacle looked like a church on the outside, it no way resembled one on the inside (except for the stained glass windows). DeDe never showed up. She probably had gotten a last minute phone call from Malcolm and ditched us. The place was kicking though. Upstairs, everyone was dancing to a mix of House, Hip Hop, and R&B. Downstairs, the scene was R&B, Funk, and Reggae. And there we sat, me and V, on the front row, breathing in air so thick from the fusion of cigarettes and blunts, we were getting our own little high.

Angie Stone's "Wish I Didn't Miss You" echoed throughout the room. "Girl, that's my jam!" I yelled, and you could just feel the mood—raw anticipation and emotions and a whole lot of heat and pinned-up lust. It kinda reminded me of those ole Spelman days partying with the sexy-like-a-mothafucka strippers, and to tell you the truth, with the drought I was in, it kinda made me want to relive those days.

By the time the strippers were on stage and hopping their naked asses all through the audience, I was drunk as a skunk. I had three or four shots of vodka with lime up in me, and I was fantasizing about bringing one of those big-dick niggas home. I got up to use the bathroom (either I was gonna pee or try to masturbate in the stall) when lo-and-behold who grabbed me by the wrist and pulled me so close I could name his cologne— Ralph Lauren Polo Double Black.

"The hell you doing down here looking at these tired-ass niggas for? You got a real man right here. You like to see them strip, don't you? Here, hold my drink." Like a fool, I took Gary's drink out his hand. Lawd, this was not a good time. I was not in the best shape for fighting off temptation. And damn that big dick was pushing into my thigh like a big-ass bag of quarters. I probably should've looked on the floor to make sure I wasn't leaking.

"You want me to strip for you, baby? Here. Let a real nigga show you how to strip. Where your money at? Come on. Get those dollars ready."

We were sort of in the corner. Not a whole lot of people were paying attention to us as everyone was doing their own thing. I was getting tempted. I can't lie. I wanted to drop down to my knees and whop him off right there, for old time's sake. And just like old times, I felt like a whore. Why did this nigga have this effect on me? Do you know he straight undid his pants and pulled out that hard-ass dick? He pointed that shit right at my pussy, through my dress. The only thing holding it back was some thin-ass silk.

"Now this is a real nigga's dick. Not those sissy boys' you giving all your hard earned money to. Come here." He took my free hand—the one not holding his drink—and wrapped it around his dick. It felt like home. My pussy was wet as a goddamn river. "I miss you, boo. How you been? You miss me?"

I couldn't understand it. What was it about this man? He knew exactly what strings to pull to get me. Well, I can't even say that, because he was honestly doing some inappropriate shit—some shit I wouldn't tolerate from nobody else—but something about him doing it just pushed all my damn morals out the window. Big Momma would not have been proud, and in a used-to-be church on top of that! Believe me, not proud at all! And I knew it. I knew this place was nothing but the devil and so was Gary, but I threw all of that out the window and thought, *If loving this man is wrong—right now, I don't want to be right.*

"Let me put this big boy back before these freaks start bum rushing me. You liked that shit didn't you? You wanna suck that shit, don't you?"

I started laughing. "Ah boy, it was all right."

"Girl, you know you all wet and shit. You need me to call a mop over here? No, fuck that. Keep that shit wet. Meet me upstairs."

"I'm hanging with my girls, Gary. And you ain't been nowhere to be found for three days. Now all a sudden you got time to get up?"

"Girl, quit playing. Would you rather hang with your girls or hang with your boy—who you haven't seen in months? Those bitches'll be there. Come on, Jess. Meet me upstairs. It's not like I'm tearing you away from them. Shit, look at V doing her thing. Come on and meet me upstairs, baby."

You would've thought I'd be talking myself out of following that fool up those stairs. First of all, what did I think I was about to do? Fuck him in the middle of the club? But I was happy as I could be following behind his big-dick ass.

We got up there and there was a couple sitting on one of three couches. We took the one furthest from them. I thought I should probably keep an eye on them in case one or the other ran out of breath the way they were kissing so hard and not coming up for a bit of air. I might have to call the damn medics.

Gary said, "I thought you was supposed to be at home in a couple of hours waiting for my call? That's what you said when I texted you earlier in the day."

"I know, but V's not ready to go yet. What time is it?"

"It's almost two thirty, baby. And you know I woulda been real disappointed if I had called and you weren't available. You not working tomorrow, are you?"

"No, I'm off. Why? You plan on spending the day with me or something?" Right then, Angie Stone's "Wish I Didn't Miss You" started playing, and I yelled, "Hey! That's my jam!" Throwing my hands in the air, I started grooving to Angie's sweet jam.

He started laughing and said, "Look at this shit."

The nigga took his hand out his pocket, lifted his hand up, and showed me a goddamn wedding band. He looked like he was disgusted. He said, "I'm married now."

He took the breath from me. I couldn't speak for a good thirty seconds. I know I must have looked like a fool sitting there with my mouth hanging open. The entire weekend flashed through my mind: his misleading text messages; his pulling his dick out and rubbing it all on me; me actually contemplating sucking it—in the middle of the goddamn strip club; his begging me to follow him upstairs, me being the silly bitch that

I am and doing it. All I could say was, "Well shit, ain't this 'bout a bitch!" And although I loved the beat to Angie's song, I guess I couldn't have even fathomed how much the lyrics would mean—until that moment—and all I could think of was how I wish I hadn't missed, better yet, met this fool.

He said, "Yeah. So I'm trying to settle down now. You know, do things the right way."

I had yet to pick up my jaw and by the time he had said that unbelievably dumb shit, a woman was walking in our direction. She was about a six, and I'm being generous. God knows I'm not the type to ever jump on the woman when the man is to blame, but I cannot pretend that finding out she's much less fine than me doesn't piss me off. Number one, she was wearing a pair of what had to be Payless pumps. Bright red—not a good red, like a hooker red—some loud mess that drew all attention to the size of her feet. A size twelve, easy. I'm not lying. She had a black dress that I would have let slide if when she finally made her way over to our couch I didn't see lint balls all over it. Matter of fact, it was like she had on a lint dress with a few bits of black in it. She looked like one of those alley cats walking around with their fur all snatched out. Her makeup was overdone. Of course she had on stupid red lipstick to match those big-ass boats she was calling shoes. And she had sleep the color of her eyeliner all in the corners of her eyes. Ewwww! According to that look on her face, she was not pleased. Little did she know, I was not pleased having to look at her ass.

I hadn't really noticed Gary jump off the couch I was so soaked up in that troll walking towards me. But when I finally came to my senses, I noticed his body language had gone from sex magnet to herb ass nigga. He was all hunched over and looking in her eyes like a dumb-ass puppy dog. I honestly can't even remember what happened from there. I have some memory of Gary saying something like, "She ain't nobody, baby. That's an old friend." And of him being pulled away like the puppy dog he was looking like. The next thing I knew I was back downstairs with V.

"Where is Gary?" V said.

I didn't even know V had seen him. "I don't know. He's upstairs somewhere."

"Well let his ass stay up there. I'm almost ready, Jess. Let me just look at these big-dick motherfuckers a couple more minutes. For real, I can't even afford that. These men done wiped my wallet clean."

I heard V's words, but I didn't *hear* them. My insides were torn apart. Did I just see what I thought I saw? The man whose balls I had once licked the whole circumference of . . . the man whom I had told all about Big Momma and her illness . . . the man whom I prayed to God would one day marry me . . . had not only just flashed me a tacky-ass wedding ring, but flashed a tacky bitch to match? And was calling her wife?

"I don't know about you, Jess, but these niggas done made a sista hot! Maybe you just ought to give Gary one more chance. At least take him home and let him take care of you once more. You know what I'm saying? Get some for the both of us, 'cause it looks like your girl is about to be romancing the damn vibrator herself. You know me. I ain't never been the misery loves company type. If you got a chance to get you some, go on. Ha! And you and I both know you been a little vacant in between those thighs for some time now. I think you worse off than me."

The sad thing is—the thing I'm most ashamed to admit— is that even after seeing him with that broke down woman, even after seeing him turn from a man to a little boy right before my eyes, is that I wanted him to come over. My heart was aching right through my chest because I wanted that man in my bed. Not hers. I started racking my brain thinking about all the positions I could fuck him in . . . to show him my pussy was better. That I was better. That it was me he wanted, not her busted ass. Then I started thinking about all the ways I would curse him out if given the chance, but for real, I knew that wouldn't happen. I knew he wouldn't come over. "Wifey" was no longer in New York waiting for him to bring her the milk, she was traveling with him now. She was in *our* city.

We left the club and my stomach was in one big knot again. I couldn't shit it out, couldn't sleep it out, couldn't cry it out. So I cleaned. I cleaned like the nigga was coming over. Like he was gonna drop that pumpkin off and come over to my place with the glass slipper in his hand, *Cinderella* style. Desperation is a terrible thing. Desperation will have you believing a married man you haven't seen in months, who just told you goodbye in the worst kinda way, would be over your house in a few. It was around four when I finished. Everything from the tub to the goddamn floors was scrubbed clean. I jumped in the shower so I'd be fresh to touch. While I was in there I scrubbed myself with the same determined arms I used to scrub the floors. I thought I was trying to wash off the dirt I'd gathered from that cleaning spree I had just gone on, but what I was really doing was trying to wash off the shame. Another nigga. I had fallen in love with another sorry nigga who didn't love shit on me. He ain't even love the dirty-ass sex tricks I performed. I started crying. No, crying isn't even the word. I started balling. Like a brand new baby. I cried and cried until that shower water went from lukewarm to freezing cold. I walked out the tub and landed on my bed buck naked and sopping wet. I fell asleep like that. My heart had been re-broken. And sad to say, with each heartbreak, my heart became a little more hardened.

I woke up later that morning but still early, as if I was going to work. My eyes were swelled up like two boiled eggs, and I was coughing and sneezing something horrible. I mustered up enough strength to let out the dog. Paid a few bills online. Cried a little more, well a lot more. Watered the plants. Played solitaire. Ignored a few phone calls. And finally fell asleep in my love seat. It was a call from V that woke me.

V said, "Wassup, girl? It is too nice out here. Almost sixty-five degrees in January!"

"Hey, V. What's going on? What time is it?"

"Almost twelve. I'm out here riding around with the windows down like a white girl . . . 'bout to catch a cold. Volume pumping. I know you ain't still in bed? Ooooh, my bad.

Oh my goodness! Where's my manners?" She started whispering. "Is Gary's black ass over there?"

"No, girl. Gary's black ass is full of shit."

"Oh, now he's full of shit? He wasn't full of shit last night when you was letting him grind all over your pretty ass. Don't even act like you don't want that man. If I ain't told you a thousand times, you got to show the man a little interest, Jess. Damn! He's not just going to assume that you want him! Um, how did Kelly Price put it—you should have told me—"

"V, Gary is not the one, okay?"

"Yeah right. You may not talk about him that much, but just by the way you look at him when you two are together is enough for me. You are hooked, side-swanked, as they say, bit, and whatever else you want to call it." V started singing off key to the tune of Jungle Fever, "*You got Gary fever . . . you got Gary fever.*"

I wasn't in the mood to be reminded of how far down my feelings for Gary went, and I certainly wasn't in the mood to hear that ridiculous singing, even though V could hold a tune. But I still wished the sandman, from that TV show, *Showtime at the Apollo*, would come get V's ass right then. I was hearing the sirens in my head.

"Girl, you're so crazy. You must have been up mighty early. I guess that vibrator didn't keep you up too late."

"I did what I had to do and then took my ass to sleep. Bing, bang, boom. I'm just coming from the mall. Returning all that shit I wore last night. You know how I do."

"V, you're crazy. Certified!"

"Yeah, well I was just hoping they didn't smell the arm pits on that thing."

I hung up with V feeling worse than I did before she called. Her pointing out how I fell apart in that man's presence just brought all those feelings back to the surface. I started thinking about what had gone down at the strip club. I mean did I really see a wedding ring? Did Gary even say he was married? I mean why would he have brought me upstairs knowing his wife was there? Maybe I had hallucinated. I mean I had had a whole lot to drink. I was still a little hung over. I needed to know what was what. I picked up the phone and dialed his number. Of course he didn't answer, and my heart sank and shattered all at once. I was trying to imagine how I was going to put it back together again when his deep and beautiful voice came on the answering machine.

"You've reached Gary Thomas. I'm unable to take your call at the moment, but if you leave a detailed message, including the time you called, and the best time to reach you, I will get back to you as soon as possible. God bless."

Looking back, crying into that answering machine was the stupidest thing I could have done, and lord knows if I could have helped myself, I would have. But something like what comes over you in church took over me. Yes, I am comparing those feelings to what happens to me when I'm in the face of God. It was that real. I broke down worse than I had broken down the night before when I was ripping through that house cleaning like a crazy savage.

"Please, baby. Please, baby, tell me you're not married. Gary baby, I can't take this. Please call me back and tell me that ugly bitch I saw in the club is not your wife when I'm supposed to be your wife."

And it just got more and more humiliating from there. I was so out of control there was snot dripping off the handset by the time I finished. And I did not finish on my own! The fucking answering machine cut me off.

At least I had enough sense not to call back a second time. Really, I don't even know if it was sense. The phone rang and it was Melissa, so she interrupted any plans to call again. I broke down further as soon as I heard Melissa's voice. I told her how everything went down. How I thought I had dreamed it and all that.

"Lord, are all my friends stupid? I mean all of them? Jessie! Come on now. Do you really think you hallucinated? Since when do you hallucinate, Jessie? I've known you a whole bunch of years now and I have never even heard of a bad dream you had. Now all a sudden you're imagining entire scenarios while you're wide awake?"

I was blocking out Melissa's words. I got up off that love seat and poured a tall glass of Merlot. I gulped it down, stared in the distance awhile, then hit play on my DVD player. *Love and Basketball* was in there. My day off was coming to a slow end. My eyes were still big as two boiled eggs and the beautiful story about to unfold before me in this movie was not gonna help. Still, I couldn't turn it off. All while the beginning credits rolled, Melissa went on and on. I heard a few snatches here and there. Things like, "you're stupid" and "wake up." I needed Big Momma just then. Big Momma would tell me everything Melissa was telling me, sure. She'd tell me I was trying to keep something that didn't want to be kept, and she might even call me out my name, but there would be some old love underneath. Melissa loved me, but her love was new, and new love never ever compares to old love. I wouldn't feel like a perfect fool before Big Momma. Here I had another girlfriend explaining to me how wrong my life was, but offering no options for fixing it.

"Girl, what you watching?"

"*Love and Basketball.*"

"I knew you were. I'd know Sanaa's voice anywhere. I love that damn movie. But, Jess, it is a movie. You know that, right? It is a *movie* called *Love and Basketball.* You ain't Sanaa, and Gary's dirty dog ass sure ain't . . . what's his name? That fine brother. Omar Epps. Gary certainly ain't Omar's fine self."

"Melissa, what am I going to do?"

"Girl, you're a hopeless romantic. You fall hard, too soon, for every Tom, Dick, and Harry. But regardless, you gonna do like every other woman on this earth has done since the beginning of time and will continue to do until the end—you gonna get over that shit!"

"You say that like I'm about to make some brownies. Like all I got to do is take three steps and my heart is gonna be whole."

"No I didn't either. I didn't say it was going to be easy. And I didn't say you'd accomplish it in three steps. You're not listening. I said you're going to get over it. And you will. You're not the first woman to experience this shit and please believe you won't be the last. You won't be anywhere near the last."

"Yeah. I guess you're right."

"I know I'm right! If you meant one thing to him, Jess—one thing—he would have made every attempt to get back to you. You sobbed like a goddamn crazy woman on his answering machine. For all he know, you might have slit your damn wrists! You might have three hundred Tylenol swimming in your stomach right now. But is that nigga beeping in on the other line? Did he send a text to your BlackBerry? A 'hey baby, is everything, okay?' No! I'ma act like Big Momma on your tail and say—people tell you exactly who they are! Listen the first time. Gary is telling you, flat out, no questions asked, he wants no parts of you. Ring, ring! Anybody home upstairs?"

"I hear you, girl. Loneliness will make you do some stupid shit, won't it?"

"You know I know. I been dumb as two rocks trying to cross the street over my *fair* share of men. So you know I'm not talking to you from some high post. I've been there, Jess. I'm not telling you this to hurt you. I'm telling you this because I love you. You deserve better. You got to move forward, no matter how hard it is. You are Big Momma's grandbaby . . . damn near her child. The last thing you are, is a weak-ass, whining little girl. You're a full-grown woman. Built tough enough to see this little shit through and a whole lot more after it. Trust. I have seen you at work. I got to get going, but I want you to cheer up. I'll call you in the morning to see how you're doing . . . make sure you got your ass up and got to work on time. And real talk, Gary really wasn't all that. I mean I know he had some nice eyes and big dick, but that shit comes a dime a dozen. I just rode past a nigga with some nice eyes and big dick. You want me to put him in the trunk for you?"

"No!"

"Oh, okay. That's what I thought."

Melissa was always on the money. Well, at least when it came to relationships! I didn't know why I deliberately chose to disregard everything she said. As much sense as it made, I just couldn't get it through, as Big Momma would say, "my thick head." I could even hear her in the background: *Girl, no matter how drunk you thought he was, I'm telling you, he was not just messing with you that night, and his drunk ass not knowing what he was doing, told you the truth. I know it hurts, baby girl. But you need to move on now. You're a beautiful woman, and you need to realize that he belongs to someone else. There's no need of fighting for something that's already taken. Okay, baby? . . . And, Jessie, a church?*

I had almost forgot I was still in the comfort of Dr. Wilma's office. Her voice shocked me back to the present.

"So, what finally came of Mr. Gary?"

"Well, I remained in my little personal hell for about two more weeks. I kept putting the events of that night through my imagination and questioning them until I wore myself out. I even wrote my ideas down at one point. Separated a piece of paper into two columns. Put 'reality' on one side and 'fantasy' on the other. I couldn't sort it out without him, though. I finally broke down and called again. This time he answered. Funny thing, it was two weeks to the day that everything went down—a Sunday."

"Go on."

"Well, when I called, he was on his way to BV's—a little meeting/gathering spot in downtown Dallas, you may have heard of it—and told me to give him a minute, that he would call me right back. I'm embarrassed to say I was excited and feeling special when he did call back, right. I didn't have time to think about the fact that he was still in Dallas and hadn't dialed me. There wasn't time to get upset about that—even though I would cry and cry over that later."

"What do you mean? Why?"

"Because, Dr. Wilma, either he had been in town all that time and hadn't bothered to reach out to me, or he was now officially living in Dallas . . . and hadn't bothered to reach out to me."

"Oh, okay. I see."

"So he calls back, and I just asked him flat out, 'Are you married?'"

"And what did he say?"

"He told me no. He laughed, asked me what the hell I was talking about. 'Why was I tripping?' he asked."

"Were you satisfied with that answer?"

"Honestly? At the time, yes. It was exactly what I wanted to hear. I wanted to believe he wasn't married. And really, whether or not he was became the secondary issue."

"What was the primary issue?"

"He stopped calling. I mean altogether. I tried calling him back a few days later and his number had been changed. It didn't matter if he was married or not because he was through with *me*. I wouldn't see him for a good couple of years."

I remembered seeing that pretty-eyed, big-dick man like it was yesterday.

"Excuse me," he said. "Um, I don't believe it. Jessie? Is that you?"

"Yes, it's me, Gary. How are you?" You know my eyes walked themselves right down to his chunky ring finger.

"I'm fine. Yeah, made that move to the DC metro . . . Dulles is home now . . . here picking up some relatives. You look really good, Jess. I mean you always did."

I wanted to know who this damn Harvard graduate was talking to me. Since when did Gary talk all proper? The Gary I knew threw a 'nigga' in every time he got a chance—sometimes for no reason at all. But his speech was no longer my concern.

"Oh, thanks," I said. And thanked God in heaven I had put on a full face of makeup. My lashes were like *ping, pang, pow!* And of course the body and clothes were doing what they did too—making all the boys come to the yard.

"Life must definitely be treating you well. You certainly have a glow about you."

Before he could finish listing my many positive attributes, a woman was running towards us yelling, "Gary, Gary! They're on a different flight, baby. They're coming into gate sixteen. Oh, excuse me." She had noticed me standing there. "Hello. How are you?"

"I'm fine. Thank you for asking. And yourself?"

"I'm doing well."

If this was the girl I'd seen in the strip club all those years ago, those shots of vodka were definitely playing tricks on me. She was not only pretty, she was verging on beautiful. Just what I would expect to be Gary's type.

"I see Gary still doesn't have any manners," I cleared my throat, "introducing special people." I extended my hand. "My name is Jessie."

"Hello, Jessie. I'm Monica. And you're right about that! Are you leaving or coming?"

"Oh, I'm passing through on business. Heading back to Dallas and just happened to run into Gary . . . my old running partner. I see DC is treating the both of you well."

"Girl, it's all right. Nothing spectacular. Nothing like New York, where we're from, but it is home though. You know they say home is where the heart is." She looked into Gary's eyes, and he did not meet that glance very easily. There was certainly some hesitation. With him sitting there looking so stupid, like a deer in headlights and not opening his mouth a peep, I thought I should get going.

"Oh look. My business partner is in line to board. Listen, it was nice meeting you, Monica."

I shook her hand once more and thought, *Why the hell are we doing all this handshaking?* It was like I was going above and beyond to prove I was nobody. And why the hell was I doing that? I guessed I was a nicer woman than I thought. I guess there was no reason to destroy that woman's perception of her dirty-dog husband. And then, maybe she wasn't the chick from the strip club and maybe he had changed his ways. Whatever the case, it wasn't up to me to figure all of it out. Still, I gave Gary a small hug . . . shake things up a bit. You know, let her get a glance at how round and brown I was back there. She obviously didn't have a Big Momma in her lineage to bless her with the curves! I mean you need a little ass to go with the beauty, right?

Gary said, "Have a safe flight, Jess."

And his wife said, "Yes, please do. And it was nice to meet you."

I thanked them for the well-wishes, turned around, and pretended to hurry to my gate. A little speed would make the hips swivel a little more. They'd take a few dips with a light jog. Ooh, I wanted to turn around, but didn't. I knew he was watching me, and that she had to be, too. At that moment, I took a deep breath, and as Terry McMillan put it, "exhaled." And just like that, everything fell into place. I had peace of mind and a strong end to that chapter of my life. I knew I had far to go, but at least that was said and done.

"You're doing fine, Jessie. I hope that by talking about your past loves you're gaining some insight into your patterns, but also your strengths. It's clear to me that while you have suffered some significant injuries at the hands of men, you're committed to being treated with care and respect. That is very important, and it's a quality that is not easily learned. That said, I know you've had at least one other significant relationship. Why don't you take a sip of your water and tell me about it."

I took a gulp, not a sip, because the man left to discuss was a heavy load to carry. Not that I had known him long—I hadn't, but I was hoping and praying, with my whole being, that he was the one. Michael Todd Crawley was like the water I was drinking. Tall, transparent (so far), and refreshing. He was healthy fluid in a world of nasty, fattening soda.

"Well Dr. Wilma, Michael is my latest project. He's handsome with a body to die for. He's the reason I'm finding myself back in the gym lately."

"And how did you meet him, Jessie?"

"Oh, well he's my friend Tracy's husband's brother. Tracy is my sorority sister and coworker at DataComm. Well, actually, she's a Daisy Chain executive, but we're working on that skin care line I told you about. She had a little get-together, a while back, and her husband arranged for me to meet Michael there. I guess it was sort of a blind date, but we had known of each other. Dr. Wilma, he lit up the room. He was the handsomest thing there. I know I'm a pretty woman. Folks have been telling me that all my life, but when I tell you I felt like the luckiest person in the world when I realized he was there for me. Ooh! So he's divorced. He has a six-year-old daughter, and she and his ex-wife live in Atlanta. From what I can gather he's an excellent father. He's always checking on her, pays her private school tuition in addition to regular child support, and his house is just crowded with her pictures."

"You've been to his house already?"

"Yes. You think it was too soon?"

"Too soon for what? Did you sleep with him, Jessie?"

I took another sip of water. Suddenly it seemed like I didn't have enough of the water I didn't even want in the first place. "Well, no."

"What's the 'well' for?"

"I wanted to, Dr. Wilma."

She wrote down something in her notebook.

"Oh God, Dr. Wilma. You think I'm a ho."

"I most certainly do not. I can't believe you accused me of that. I'm trying to find out what's going on inside of you, Ms. Lady. I fully understand that you are *not* your choices or your fleeting thoughts. Thinking about sleeping with him—even wanting to— is something totally different from sleeping with him, and even if you did, I wouldn't think any different of you. You're safe here, Jessie. I told you that. Now go on. Finish telling me about Michael."

"Okay, well, like I said, I met him at the get-together. We stayed in the main sitting area for about twenty minutes and then we went on the back patio. We wanted to be alone. We talked for three hours. It was . . . it was . . . just magical. I felt like an itty- bitty little girl in his presence. It felt like love at first sight, Dr. Wilma."

"Okay. Go on."

"I didn't hear from him for two weeks after that first encounter. I was so devastated."

"Why?"

"We had had such a connection. I stared in his eyes and held his hand. I even kissed him back on the patio. It was such a strong connection. I went to sleep giggling. I couldn't believe he didn't call the next day or the next. And then when I finally broke down and called he didn't return my call for, like I said, two weeks. And even then, I had to chase him down."

"What do you mean?"

"I asked Tracy to call me and tell me the next time he would be at their house. He was coming over for dinner one Tuesday night and I just happened to 'stop by'—looking like the brown skin Beyoncé, no less!"

"And so, did that 'accidental' visit get things going again?"

"Yes, we've talked . . . or texted every day since. I have a date with him tonight!"

"Oh really? I'm happy to hear that. I am a little concerned about his disappearing like that, though. Did he explain why he hadn't returned your calls or followed up on that first meeting?"

"He was very up-front. He said he had had an emergency with his ex-wife down in Atlanta—something about her threatening suicide—and he went to make sure that she was okay and his daughter was safe."

"I see. And was this suicide attempt because of him?"

"No, I don't think so. At least he didn't say anything like that. I mean his being so up-front I didn't really want to push for details, you know?"

"I understand that. And it might not even be your business. But if the relationship develops into something more, I want you to remember that. I want you to question him. His past relationships will be very helpful in determining the path your own relationship will take."

"Okay, Dr. Wilma. I'll remember that. I definitely want this to go somewhere. He is like the man of my dreams!"

"Don't rush it. Slow your roll, sweetheart. I'm certainly not telling you to suppress your feelings, but I want you to go about this the right way, understand?"

"Yes, ma'am, I do."

"Okay, well it looks like our time is up. I want you to have fun tonight. Don't think too much about the future. Don't tell that man you want to have his babies or anything!"

"Ha! I won't."

"All right. I'll see you next month."

"Thanks, Dr. Wilma."

Chapter Eleven

Trouble in Paradise

October 2008. After her session with Dr. Wilma, Jessie decided it was time to put her muscles to work—crossing her legs while she watched television eating pizza and wings didn't count. She was on her way to the gym to get that much-needed workout when Tracy called her phone. Her heart rate sped up a bit, like she was already on the elliptical. Again, she remembered that she had yet to have that oh-so-important conversation with DeDe. If she was honest with herself she'd admit that she had been avoiding it all. Still, maybe Tracy would give her the push she needed.

"Hello?" she said.

"Hey, Jess. How are you?"

"I'm fine, Tracy. It's nice to hear from you. Girl, I am so excited about the next phase of this Daisy Chain project."

"Yuck, Jess! Let's not talk business right now." Tracy began laughing. "I'm calling to check on you and Michael, and also to ask you a fairly awkward question."

Jessie thought, *Oh boy. Here we go.*

"What is it, girl?"

"The girl DeDe, that's on *The Love Forum* with you . . . she's the one dating the married man, right?"

Both Jessie and Tracy knew the answer to that, but it didn't make the moment any less uncomfortable. Jessie's palms were sweating she was so nervous. She put on her thinking cap—she couldn't let Tracy know she was hip to the situation.

"Yes, girl. And I know what they say—birds of a feather flock together—but I do NOT, in *any* way, shape, or form, condone that. And the funny thing about De is she never did before this guy either."

"Well, you wouldn't happen to know who he is?"

"She's been very secretive about him," Jessie said without hesitation. She didn't want to be responsible for Tracy's broken heart. That was on DeDe's, and especially Malcolm's, hands.

"She hasn't even told us a name, and girl, I can't pretend I even want to know. It's like as soon as she starts talking about that dude, I check out, you know? I just don't want no parts in it. But Tracy, why you asking me this? You think you know the man she's dealing with or something? Please don't tell me it's one of your girlfriend's husbands or something!"

"Actually, if I can be honest with you, and I am real sorry to involve you in this, Jessie, but I hope you can relate to my pain woman-to-woman, I think she's dating Malcolm. It's my husband I'm concerned about."

"What? Oh no! Tracy, I am so sorry to hear that."

"Girl, it is what it is. So you say she hasn't said anything about who it might be?"

"No, she hasn't. Look, I'm not going to lie to you, I'd be real uncomfortable getting in the middle of this if it is true, but I promise you I will speak with DeDe, without asking any questions, and remind her that her actions have hefty repercussions." She needed to get Tracy off the phone before she told another lie.

"That's all I can ask for. Jessie, I'm getting to the end of my rope. I've been carrying the financial and emotional responsibility of this marriage for a very long time now. I can't continue to wait on him to get control over what's in his drawers. Anyway, how are things coming along with you and Michael?"

"Girl, now you got me worried. Does Michael have any of those same tendencies?"

"I can't lie, he's been known to chase the ass. I mean, when Malcolm hooked you guys up, he was entertaining somebody he calls Sweets."

"What do you mean?"

"I mean, remember when Malcolm called him in front of us that day? Come to find out he was in some woman named Sweets's face. But you know what? I'm on the verge of becoming a bitter woman, which means I don't put it past any man and that you probably shouldn't be asking my opinion. I will say that Michael has never really brought any woman around me other than his wife. I hadn't even heard this girl Sweets's name before—and with a name like Sweets, we just thought she was some ho he was embarrassed to bring to the house. I don't know if that means he's monogamous or that he deals with a whole lota whores he's scared to show the family. Anyway, girl, like I said, I'm the last person you should be asking those sorts of questions. My marriage might be falling apart, after all. But let me get offa here. If it's not your girl DeDe, it's someone else. I got some more research to do. Oh, and Jessie? Word to the wise. Tell your girl she really don't want no parts of an affair with Malcolm Crawley."

"Oh okay, Tracy. Well, like I said, I will have that little pep talk with De."

"Thanks, girl."

Jessie didn't take two breaths before she had DeDe on the line.

"What's up, Jess? To what do I owe this honor?"

"You owe it to your trifling ways."

"Huh? What are you talking about?"

"That damn Malcolm, of course. DeDe, Malcolm is my soror's husband!"

"And what, Jessie? I mean we already knew he was somebody's husband. So what? Because that somebody has a name now it's more real to you? It has been very real to me for over a year now."

"So tell me how you knowingly are destroying a marriage, De?"

"First of all, it is not me that's doing the destroying. Malcolm owes your soror, not me. I have no obligation to her. She ain't my wife. And please don't think she's little Ms. Goody Two-Shoes over there either. I think that bitch has been following me."

"Huh? Why you say that, De?"

"What kind of car does she drive, Jess?"

"A BMW—like her husband."

"Don't call him that. Yeah, that's what I thought. I've been seeing a red beamer almost everywhere I go."

"Look, De, I don't know what you're talking about, but did you stop to think that maybe you deserve to be followed around? What would you do if your husband of a decade had a mistress? And what about your obligation to her as a fellow human being? Talking about you don't owe her. If you don't owe her, who the hell does?"

"What? Jessie what are you talking about? You—"

"You know what, I'm obviously not going to be able to get through to you. That's clear. I'm not going to try to change your thinking. Your own fucked-up life experiences have led you there and it looks like they will not be easy to undo! I'm gonna give you this as a cautionary warning. Tracy is on the verge of shutting down your whole world. I just got off the phone with her, and she is not pleased."

"You told her about me?"

"Now why would I do that? I, unlike you, know where my loyalty lies. I told her I didn't know if you were the woman Malcolm was having an affair with but that I would have a little talk with you. Now, after this call, I want nothing more to do with this, De. Get your shit together. Drop that zero, find a man of your own, and stop treating your fellow women like they're trash. Because little do you know, that behavior is a reflection of what you think about yourself. You obviously don't think you're special enough or important enough to have your own man."

"Oh lord. Here we go with this lecture. Just because I'm involved with a married man does not mean I don't have self-esteem. It means I'm getting some help with my bills, some good dick, and none of the other bullshit that comes with maintaining a relationship."

"You go on and tell yourself that, sweetie. Whatever you need to justify your behavior is all right with me. But don't say you haven't been warned. This shit is about to blow up in your face. And as Big Momma used to say, 'What goes around comes around—and it feels much worse coming than going.' Goodbye, love. I'm about to jump on this treadmill."

"Yeah, whatever."

Hanging up with Jessie, DeDe began to think the affair with Malcolm was more trouble than it was worth.

+++

Brit had been working for American Airlines for some time. Her momma hated it, of course. She was forever worried about Brit crashing into the Atlantic or a range of mountains, despite Brit telling her over and over, "Ma! Flying is safer than driving! You got more of a chance of crashing than me!" She didn't have to sit in a cubicle all day, she got to travel like a diplomat or something, and she met all sorts of wonderful people. Not to mention her profession *encouraged* flyness. She could never look too pretty. And since Brit wasn't the sharpest crayon in the box, pretty was about all she had. American Airlines was good for her lashes. They kept her looking good. Considering all the wonderful people she met, including the richest of the rich (she worked first class mostly—don't let anybody fool you into believing looks don't matter. Brit's pretty tail was in first class because she made the gentlemen smile, and a happy customer was a returning customer), she never found love in the sky. Oh, plenty of men offered. She had a wallet full of business cards with personal cell numbers scribbled along their backs. She'd been offered all sorts of gifts and trips and dinners. But Brit could not, for the life of her, shake her obsession with thugs. She was bougie as she wanted to be. High class as she could be on her flight attendant salary and well educated, even if she lacked all common sense. Still, nothing set Brit's heart in motion like an all out thug. This attraction played its part when she took her car to be serviced some nine months ago at Don Maxville Pontiac.

Brass was a piece of work, no doubt. His body alone made women open up like a book, but even that was put to shame when he smiled. Those teeth were white as rice, his lips plump as a plum split in two (and as juicy). And when you looked above it, at his eyes—well, let's just say Brass never knew ugly by name, only in passing. Those deep eyes were almost attacked by his eyelashes. They were long and wild from one end of his lids to the other. They were almost feminine. But his muscles and walk and talk hushed any ideas about femininity. He was only a driver. He literally took Brit's car from one building to the next (a job that couldn't have earned him more than ten dollars an hour), but he could have been the janitor for all Brit cared. She laid eyes on him and about offered to have his babies right there in the dealership's service center. As a matter of fact, she asked Brass if she could call him.

"Please tell me you don't have a woman. Please tell me I can take you out tonight." She couldn't believe the words coming out her mouth, but Brass could. It was an offer he got weekly. And the other brothers on the job hated him for it. He was always in an argument and always getting called out his name, put in his place. They liked to remind him he was a "dime a dozen driver," as the head mechanic was always pointing out. But Brass didn't have to say much. He pushed a brand new Honda Accord—purchased by his last lover, Rasheeda—always had on the freshest kicks, and was never seen with a bag lunch because some fly honey was forever scooping him up at twelve noon sharp taking him out to lunch.

Aside from his women paying much of his way, Brass had yet to give up his criminal past. He was out on parole for a drug trafficking charge and was excited every time he took a deep breath and felt the fresh air coursing his lungs, but nothing about those breaths was romantic enough to keep him from his hustling ways. Since the moment his feet landed on free concrete he had been raping folks with a booming check-chasing scheme. Using his slick talk and slicker ways, Brass had people all across North America (yes, Canada and Mexico, too) wiring money to their mothers, daughters, sisters, and grandbabies in need. By the time they'd figured out they had wired a complete stranger, and not their mother or daughter, he was long gone and nowhere to be heard of.

Brit got involved in it all accidentally. As much as Brit would have liked to believe she was a "down chick," she didn't fit the bill. Number one, Brit wasn't smart enough to understand the ropes, let alone know them. And then, a down chick played her role. She chilled in the background, sexed her man when he wanted it, cooked his meals when he needed, went out on the town on occasion, but she didn't ask any questions. Brit couldn't handle that last requirement. It was partly because she was worried about Brass cheating on her, partly because she was plain old nosey. But Brass saw her nosiness as an opportunity. By telling Brit about the check-cashing scheme, he could explain away all the late-night phone calls and put Brit's heart to rest about "all those bitches" calling his name when they were out in public. She had to hear "Brass" in a sexy drawl every place they went. And always when she turned around it was some young chicken-head or old-ass cougar curling up her lips at him. He explained that he needed "those bitches" to run for him. He said he only used women because police and everybody else were less likely to suspect them as doing some shady shit. (Really, he only used the women he was fucking, and because he was fucking so many, his supply of runners never ran out. He credited his "magic stick" with making them stupid enough to follow his every command.) So he told Brit a little about the scheme to get her off his back about the women, but what he didn't expect was that she would jump on board so easily. He broke it down to her like this, "We both gonna win, baby. You replace all those hungry-ass bitches and your heart is put at ease, and I keep my plan going ahead full speed. You're a flight attendant, baby! You're in ten, fifteen area codes a week! You can handle the business of eight bitches." Brit didn't really understand what he was talking about, but she got the part about the bitches getting out of his life. She took him up on his offer to run the Western Union scheme and he did everything he said he'd do, except he kept his other bitches for both other check-cashing opportunities and for sucking his dick when Brit was away. But November 8 was the beginning of the end for Brit.

Brit was sitting at the bar in Mo's Lounge waiting for Brass to join her. In her purse she had four thousand dollars. While she had convinced herself she was doing all this for her man, she couldn't deny she was always nervous. She always felt like she was going to get caught and sometimes couldn't think of the right thing to say when things got heavy. Walking up to the cashier, rocking whatever color wig the gig called for, pretending to be some smart businesswoman, or something, never became easy for her. Somehow, though, she always pulled it off. They say God looks out for fools and children, and Brit hadn't been a child since the eighties. She had probably scored 50,000 for Brass by that time. He walked into the bar looking good enough to eat. She shifted on her seat to prevent the new moisture in her panties from staining her pants.

"Hey, baby boy."

"Hey."

"You looking good. Why don't you pull me in the men's room real quick."

"Girl, stop playing. You got my money?"

"Well damn, Brass. I can't get a 'hello' before we you start asking me about this stupid money?"

"Brit, come on now."

"Brass, we aren't gonna eat? You don't want to spend any time with me?"

"Yeah, Brit, damn. You a greedy bitch to be so damn skinny. Shit."

"Why do you call me that, Brass? I asked you not to do that."

"Sit down."

The couple sat at the bar and ordered some drinks. Brit asked for a Cosmopolitan and Brass got a Grey Goose and cranberry. No doubt they would have made some beautiful babies, and Brit even considered "forgetting" her birth control a couple of times, but the last thing she wanted to do was trap a man. She would just put some good pussy on him and let him come home on his own.

"Where the money at?"

"In my purse."

"Give it here."

"What's wrong with you? You're acting like a crackhead, Brass. I'll give it to you after we eat. Can't you drink your drink and talk to me. Why are you treating me like those other women? This is me. Brit, remember? I'm your woman, right?"

Brass almost said, "Not no more," but bit his tongue. He wanted that money in his palm before he broke the news. So he chilled. He ordered two more vodka and cranberries and ate a double order of chicken wings. He complimented Brit on her hairstyle and shot the shit with her for a half hour or more. He let her bring up the money.

"Well here, baby. Since you're dancing all out of your seat over there."

She handed him an envelope, but held on to it until he kissed her.

"That little peck, Brass? No you didn't! You better give me some tongue."

They slobbed each other down right there at the bar, turning the bartender's stomach. As soon as Brit let go of the envelope, Brass smiled wide as Brit's hips.

"Ha, ha! That's what I'm talking about." He clapped his hands and stuffed the package in his jean pocket. He finished off his last drink.

"Look here, girl. It's been fun. No lie. You a ride or die bit—I mean woman. But, ah, it's time for me to take my life in another direction."

"Huh?" Brit stared at him without batting an eye. She wanted to be sure to catch every word that was about to come out his mouth.

"I met somebody."

"You met somebody? What are you talking about, Brass?"

"I got something new going for me right now. I'm not feeling this thing between you and me no more."

"Nigga, are you telling me that after I just risked my freedom and put four thousand fucking dollars in your hands that you leaving me?"

"Something like that. Look, me and Esther got a plane to catch to Mexico."

"And the bitch name is Esther? How old is she? A hundred-eight?"

"Ha ha ha. Watch your mouth, ma. That's my baby you talking about."

"Your baby, Brass?"

Brit looked around for something to hit him with, a drink to dump on him, something, but they had finished every last drop and all she had at her disposal was a fork and a butter knife. Brass followed her eyes.

"I wish you would. Now look here. I'm about get up from here and walk to my car. You better not say a fucking thing or I will beat your ass right here in Mo's, and you know I will."

Brass scooted his chair back and began walking towards the door.

"Brass, what about this fucking check?"

"Oh, handle that for me."

Brit watched him walk out that door with all the money and all her self-respect. She didn't understand what had just happened. She definitely hadn't seen it coming. She couldn't contain herself, and even though she was the type to always be crying for a man, she generally didn't like to do it in public. She busted out crying right there at the bar. She had disgusted the bartender with all that kissing, though, and he didn't even bother to ask if she was okay. He just said, "Will that be all?" right in the middle of her crying. "Can I get you your check?" She thought, *I hate all these bastards*, tossed a fifty on the table, and ran out of there.

+++

While Brit was having her heart balled up between Brass's hands, Pat was experiencing something similar. Only Pat wasn't supposed to be feeling what Brit was feeling. She was the married one. She was off the market and supposedly resting assured in the sanctity of a blessed union. But Donnell might as well have been named Brass the way he was acting. The kids would be home from school soon, but Pat had some things she needed to get off her chest. She went into the den to join Donnell in front of the TV.

"Donnell?"

Donnell didn't even look up. "What, Pat?" He sounded like she was pestering him.

"What's the matter with you?"

"Ain't nothing the matter with *me*."

"You saying something is wrong with me?"

"Pat, why did you wait until the kids were on their way home to come in here bothering me with your shit?"

"Bothering you? Donnell, I'm your wife. How am I bothering you? I admit, I could have come in a little sooner, but you have not been easy to talk to lately. Baby, what's wrong?"

"Pat, leave me alone."

"Leave you alone? Donnell, why are you talking to me like this?"

Donnell was quiet as the ugly paint on the walls (Pat was not the most handy when it came to interior decorating). He looked his wife in the eyes and felt nothing. "I'm going to get the kids off the bus."

He walked past Pat, leaving her with tears welling up in her eyes and her jaw trembling in pain. She watched her husband walk out the front door and had the overwhelming feeling her marriage was over.

Later that night, when the children were asleep and all the dishes were washed, Donnell said something about having to take a walk. He never came home. He stayed the night with his mistress, and when he finally did grace the hall of his and Pat's lovely house, he smelled like jasmine. A fist full of tears clogged Pat's throat, and Donnell went to work without so much as a word to his wife.

+++

Now Jessie's situation on the other hand was looking a little like love. She and Michael had gone to an early afternoon movie—a romantic comedy with Halle Berry—and were headed to dinner. She was having a hard time containing her excitement, which she knew wasn't the smartest thing. Big Momma had warned her about getting too hype over a man, and especially about showing it. She recalled the advice with ease.

"Jessie, girl, you got to hold on to something. Don't give it all up. Keep something for yourself or else they start taking advantage. Trust me, baby. Trust me on this one."

Jessie knew that advice meant she probably should enjoy herself at dinner, even go dancing with him, but she most certainly should not give up the goods. By the time she had finished her salad at dinner, though, she knew that thought was out the window. She wanted Michael worse than anything.

"Why you looking at me like that, girl?"

"Like what?"

"Like you ready to jump my bones."

"Maybe I am."

"Damn! Let me find out I got a woman that sees what she wants and goes for it."

"I'm not usually that kind of woman. But, boy, you just bring it all out of me."

"Well that's real nice to know. Damn! A woman in the streets and freak in the sheets, I likes that."

After a little dancing and a whole lot of drinking, Jessie found herself in Michael's condo fighting off the feelings of sex bubbling up in her like champagne. His condo was beautiful. The décor was high fashion to say the least and even the details were taken care of. Jessie felt like she couldn't have done a better job of decorating it.

"Michael, your house is beautiful, baby."

"Well, thank you, ma'am. Would you like something to drink?"

"Whatchu got?"

"Whatever you like. I have a full bar over here. Come join me."

They walked past a black baby grand piano, resting atop a white sheepskin rug, into a small alcove with a leather bar and several wood stools. She couldn't believe he had the skills to pull it all off. "Who did this for you, boy? I know you had to have an interior decorator."

"Naw, just have that knack I guess. I put the hardwoods in, did the painting and wallpapering, put the blinds in, all the way down to the furniture, you know, your boy got skills."

"Oh, okay. I'm impressed." *Damn*, Jessie thought, *the boy can even do the handy-work around the house.* "Well, you need to come to my place and put some things together."

"Aiight, baby girl, so what's going to be your drink of choice? Can you even handle another drink? Those eyelids are looking a little heavy. I don't want to get to a point where you can't make sound decisions."

"And what sort of decisions will I be making tonight?"

"You never know."

They drank a little more. He had made Jessie a watermelon martini. She couldn't even tell if it tasted good. She was coming up on stone drunk, let alone tipsy, and the liquor was just running down her throat without a thought or taste. What she was aware of was the longing between her thighs. She wanted this man. She wanted to put something on him, hook him. Change his life for him like she knew he was going to change hers.

"Let me play something for you."

Michael walked over to the piano, placed his drink on it, and began strumming the instrument like he was petting it. This was Jessie's cue. She pulled her dress up over her head like it was a t-shirt. Michael was playing something soft, something beautiful, and didn't notice his date was standing in her hot pink underwear set, running her feet over his sheepskin rug. She called his name. He looked up, and his fingers froze over the keys.

"Damn, baby. You're beautiful," he said.

She thought, *And this nigga knows just what to say out his mouth*. She unhooked her bra and tossed it beside her dress. Her breasts were like firm Jell-O, only far prettier and the color of caramel. He turned around on the piano's bench and watched her make her way towards him. The longing in his pants was visibly raging, and just like Pat, Jessie knew she had found her Rock of Gibraltar. Jessie sat on top of him with her legs straddled on each side of him. She could feel his hardness between her legs, throbbing, jumping within his pants.

Giving soft whimpers of pleasure, Jessie whispered, "Michael, I want you so
much, I'm yours . . . I want to make love with you."

"Mmmm, you want me, huh? I want you too, Jessie. You're so beautiful, so perfect. I knew you were made for me the first moment I saw you."

He kissed her and it felt like love. It felt like love and heaven mixed up. His big hands took up the whole small of her back. Her body-frame fit perfectly inside of his. His tongue massaged her neck and collarbone and then made its way to her nipples. If she was honest with herself, she was fighting back the urge to tell this man she loved him. And for a minute she had Big Momma in her head. She had to hurry up and push her out though, before she started messing with her high. Michael was beyond sexy, but even he couldn't sustain her fever through Big Momma's image and voice. She stood up so that Michael could undress (*god he had a perfect body*), and waited for him to remove her panties. He knelt before her, and she got butterflies in her stomach. He bit her panties and pulled them all the way down to her ankles with his pretty, pearly-white teeth. Jessie quietly looked at him: her panties in his mouth; the shape of his head; the lobes of his ears; his thick neck and broad shoulders; his chest (slightly hairy); and his manhood (which curved slightly to the left). His manhood was hard for her, announcing its excitement as it leaked its juice on to the white rug. He slowly kissed her feet, her legs, her thighs, her hips, and she trembled when his tongue slowly caressed her lips, parting them (she didn't even remember opening her legs). All she could feel was his lips, tongue, and hot breath loving her.

He slowly moved back to the piano bench and said, "No, just stand there, I want to look at you . . . sexy! You're pure sexy, girl. Come here."

Jessie's body was flawless, without a doubt. It was never something she hid or was uncertain of, but with Michael, she felt like art walking. The way he touched her, with such care, his large hands felt like silk on her bare skin, and his soft caresses confirmed her beauty to her. She felt perfect in his presence. Straddling him again, the tips of his fingers gently found their home and rhythmically made soft circles around her clit. She soon felt the head of his dick pushing its way in at her pussy's entrance, and although Jessie was engulfed in his many pleasures—his embrace, his fingers, his lips, his tongue, the aroma of his breath—her mind snapped in a cold second.

"Mike . . . Michael . . . you got a condom?"

"Yeah, baby, but I don't want to use it. I want to feel you. I want you and that warm juice, all over me."

Jessie didn't even hesitate, that would scare her later, but at that moment she wanted to feel Michael, too. She didn't want to deny him good pussy. Pussy with a condom was okay, but there was something about sex without it that was better, and she wanted to rock his world. To convince him, with one fuck, that she was the one. She let him enter her and felt him in her throat. Without realizing it, she shouted, "Damn!"

"You like that, baby? Is it big enough for you?"

In between moans of pleasure, she said, "Yes!"

"Then ride it, baby, ride this dick like you mean it."

Jessie rode him like tomorrow wasn't coming. They made love for what seemed like forever. On the piano bench and then on the floor, until, eventually, she became engulfed with emotions and was left shivering, moaning, panting—fulfilled. Michael lifted her up in one full swoop (with him still inside of her), and carried her into his bedroom where he softly laid her down, and with a clap of his hands, the lights dimmed and R. Kelly began singing from the speakers embedded in the walls.

"Not this pervert!" Jessie said, and they laughed together. She couldn't remember the last time she laughed while making love. She was having sex with this man! She was having fun, and she reveled in the moment, in this man, in their lovemaking. When it came time for him to climax, she grabbed his ass with both her hands and pushed him deep into her. She held his body tight as he began to moan and shake.

He lay on top of her (and inside of her) for what seemed like eternity. Jessie caressed his head, neck, and shoulders, kissing him ever so gently, until he soon fell to the side of her and the new lovers lay in silence contemplating what they had done.

Jessie was not proud of sleeping with him on their first 'official' date and hoped that decision would not come back to haunt her. She hoped she had nothing to worry about going condom free, either. She was on birth control, so an unexpected surprise in that area wasn't likely, but she knew better than to go unprotected with a stranger. But somehow, Michael didn't feel like a stranger. His beautiful house, his success, his beauty—all that likely disqualified him from any diseases . . . or so Jessie thought. Still, she prayed, *God, I hope he's clean.*

When Jessie woke the next morning there was breakfast on a silver tray before her. Her head was aching from a hangover, and she was thirsty as the desert. She grabbed a glass of water and gulped it down, and then proceeded to drink a glass of orange juice on top of that. As she ate her scrambled cheese eggs, pancakes, and sausage, she listened to Michael singing in the shower (not bad). She was half done with her plate when he emerged from the bathroom fully dressed. He was wearing the sharpest black suit with a bold, colorful stripped tie. She wanted to fuck him one more time off the strength of that getup alone.

"Morning!" Feeling a little embarrassed, she said, "I'm sorry. I'm so hungry. Have you eaten?"

"Good morning, yourself, beautiful. Yes, I ate while you were asleep, you were sleeping so peacefully, I just couldn't bring myself to disturb you." He smirked while heading towards the bed. "So you just wake up pretty as shit, huh? Makeup scribbled all over your face, hair all over, smelling like pure sex, and I still wanna kiss all over you."

"Thanks." Jessie smiled, suddenly aware of her morning breath. She quickly returned to her thoughts of Michael, though. He was saying all the right things, and if her memory served her correctly, the dick was good. "Ummm, breakfast is wonderful, baby. Don't tell me that on top of being the businessman, slash handyman, slash designer, slash good lover, you can cook, too?"

"Naw, cooking ain't one of my things, but I'm glad you're enjoying it. Martá made it."

"Martá?" Jessie cocked her head and looked at Michael like he was stupid.

"Yah, baby. Martá. My cook."

"Oh!" Jessie laughed.

Laughing with Jessie, but serious at the same moment, "You got to get that under control, baby girl."

"What? What are you talking about?"

"That attitude. You don't think I would disrespect you, or another woman, by having y'all in my house at the same time do you? And then on top of that having one make breakfast for the other?"

"I know. That is pretty silly. I'm sorry, Michael. It's just, you know, I've been really . . ." *Girl don't say it.* "Well I guess it's a female thing."

"Yah, right. I understand, baby girl." He made one hell of a smirk. "But I ain't your past. I'm a brand new man, and I'm going to expect that you treat me as such."

And I thought, *I know that's right. Tell it to me like it is, baby.*

"Well, look here. Take your time. Take a shower. Consuela took care of your dress, and it's hanging behind the door in the bathroom. I'm flying out to Houston for an early afternoon meeting. I gotta get this money if I'm gonna be taking your expensive tail out every night."

"Every night?"

"Yeah, every night. You trying to get rid of me or something?"

"Hell no! I'm holding on for dear life."

"Okay, okay. Sounds like we're on the same page."

"Michael?"

"Yeah, baby?"

"I didn't give it up too soon, did I?"

"Give what up? Oh! You mean the butt? Girl, we are grown-ass adults. And this ain't 1975. I'm all for the woman's movement. Matter of fact, I love it! Now y'all don't hold on to the drawers so tight for so long!"

"Whew! Okay, baby. Have a wonderful day at work. Give me a call when you get a chance, okay?"

"You got it, baby girl. I'll be back in town by six, be waiting for me."

He leaned across the beautiful silver breakfast tray and planted the softest, sweetest kiss on Jessie's head. She had to look at her hands to make sure her inside shaking hadn't made it to the outside.

She watched her future husband walk out the door with the biggest, most beautiful, morning-breath-smelling smile on her face.

She just couldn't go to work today (so called in), she took her time getting up, watched a little TV, and wandered around the house a bit. Neither the cook nor the maid spoke very good English, but they were polite, respectful women, and they didn't look at her like she was just another skank staying the night in Michael Crawley's condo. Either Michael had trained them well or he really wasn't a man whore. She explored both levels of the beautiful condo and all the surrounding grounds, including the pool and tennis court. She had struck it big. She knew she had struck it big when she thought about Michael being penniless . . . and it still didn't matter. If he was flat out broke, he made her feel wonderful, more so than any man before. And as Big Momma always told the girls, "sometimes you have to be behind a good man, more so when he's down than when he's up," and with that thought, Jessie knew—well-to-do or penniless—she would still be with him. If this thing right here worked out, it would make all the past heartache worth it! She could forgive every sorry black man to ever cross her path if Michael ended up being all he was cracked up to be.

Except that by nine o'clock that night Jessie was almost in tears. She had waited hours for him to call, and then called a few times herself. She texted him, "Hey, baby. What's going on? Give me a call, I'm a little worried," and he hadn't responded. By ten o'clock she was frazzled, wondering if he was okay, rethinking every moment they were together, second-guessing every decision. She hadn't believed, nor could she stand the fact that she had slept with him so soon (and raw on top of everything) . . . and now maybe he was through with her . . . never to call again.

Chapter Twelve

The Love Forum
Break up to Make Up

November 16, 2008. The week spent without Brass was one of the worst Brit had experienced in a long time. Seriously, she had suffered from a mild depression in those few days. Who would have known that walking into Mo's for a salad and a drink would end with her contemplating taking her life. It wasn't a thought that lasted more than a minute or so, but it had crossed her mind and she hated herself for it. Why was she caught up in trying to reform another low-down dirty-dog? Hadn't she learned her lesson? But that thought didn't even have time to marinate because Brass was knocking at her door that next Sunday morning, and it would be a Sunday Brit would not soon forget.

Brass, after noticing Brit had changed the door lock, picked the lock and walked into her apartment all buffed, tattooed, and clean shaven. He had a brand new glittery watch on his left wrist that made Brit's right eyebrow rise slightly higher than the left. She thought, *I know this mofo is not sporting a brand new Movado!* It was large and black-faced with a single diamond, shining bright like Easter Sunday. Brit became more enraged as she stared at him, then the watch, then back at him.

"Negro, I know you ain't just walk through my door. I know you just did *not* walk through my front door! If this ain't 'bout a bitch, what the hell do you want, Brass?" She held her hand to her ear, "What, what, what—I didn't hear you! What the fuck are you doing in my house? And I know you just did not break in here! Un-uh, no motherfucker. Don't even speak, I don't want to hear your lies." She shook her head and walked up to him, pointing her finger in his face, yelling, "You're a sorry-ass man, a sorry-ass excuse for a man! I can't believe you actually came back here, like the door was going to be open for you to just walk on in—like nothing happened!"

Brass sported a puzzled look and stepped back with each of Brit's forward steps. "Brit, girl, whatchu talking 'bout? Watchu doing?"

"Oh don't play!" Standing there with her hands on her hips, back arched, and head rolling. "Don't you remember, baby . . . packing your suitcase . . . taking seven pair of underwear . . . thirteen shirts . . . two pair of socks . . . the hundred-fifty dollar Christian Audigier jeans that I bought you, and sporting the new Guess watch I got you for your birthday—where is that at? Huh?"

Brit's voice, harsh and riveting, had a tone that Brass only occasionally had a chance to hear, and when he heard it, it meant he was in deep shit. Standing there with her hands on her hips and head tilted to the side, Brit tapped her foot looking at Brass half crazed, but right under all that tough talk and nasty attitude was a tender heart beating to the sound of Brass's voice. And at that very moment, through all her rage, Brit was begging and pleading with God that that man, the man she adored only behind God himself, was there to make up with her. She didn't give a shit if he had blown that bitch's back out all week, if the trick was having his baby—she just wanted her man back. Please God, let him be here to get me back, but only after I give him a piece of my mind first.

"Brit, come on, baby. Don't be mad, you know I love you, girl." Brass knew how to get to Brit, and as he smiled and showed those pearly whites as he started his roll, "Yah, I fucked up, and I know I've been fucking up lately, but I love you like there's no tomorrow, girl, and I'm lost without you, baby."

"Un-uh, don't call me *baby*. You lost that privilege when you walked out the door, going on some Mexican cruise, yah motherfucker, cruise your ass on out of here!"

"Brit, what you saying, baby? It's me, Brass! You know everything I do is for you, baby. How I'm going to front my business in Mexico if I can't get down there and make my connections and shit? How I'm gonna make that cheese? Come on, baby. You know I used that bitch. What I'm gone be doing with some fucking ugly trick down in Mexico? But hell, the trick was on me! Turns out she couldn't do shit for me—I mean us."

"Did you fuck her, Brass?"

"Almost, baby. I ain't gonna lie. I almost fucked her, you know I had to play that role, but I couldn't do it. I let her suck my dick, but I ain't fuck her."

"How many times, Brass?"

"A couple. What do that matter? I ain't fuck her. You ain't got nothing to worry about. This here dick still belong to you." He walked up to her and put her hand right down those hundred-fifty dollar Christian Audigier jeans. "That's all for you." He began to kiss her passionately, and her mind wandered a bit—she started to imagine him doing the same to the other woman, but rather than disgust her, the thought gave her a strange determination to keep her man. So when Brass asked to "enter her backdoor," Brit bit a pillow in pain and had anal sex for the first time. All the while she was hoping the demonstration of devotion would keep him in her bed and not wandering off into another woman's.

In not thirty minutes, Brass and Brit were an item again.

"Brit . . . Brit . . . you sleep?"

"No." She moved closer to Brass as they spooned, firmly nestling her backside into this crotch. "Just hold me."

"You love me, right?"

"Yes, boy, you know I love you."

"Good, 'cause I need you to show me how much you love me. I need you to help me out, need you to wire some money to a new business account in Mexico. Don't need much, just enough to get my share of the funds into the account to get the ship up and running."

"Brass, I thought you said that the trip to Mexico didn't work out?"

"Yah, it didn't, not totally. I had ole homegirl open an account, but she didn't have any money to put in the shit. Baby, this is my break. I can make it big with this one, all I need is you. Once this shit right here takes off, we gonna be living large."

"How much do you need, Brass?"

"'Bout five thousand."

"Five thousand dollars! Boy, have you lost your mind? I don't have that kind of money, where am I going to get that from?"

"C'mon, baby, think. What about your 401K? Your company stock option plan? American is doing good. You can borrow against that, baby. Trust me, this deal is a fat calf. The money is going to be flowin' in like the Mississippi—fast, steady, and endless. Brit, baby, I can't do this without you. You always talking 'bout being behind yo man, now's the chance."

"Brass, I don't know."

"Okay, baby, just think about it. You know your boy loves you, right?"

+++

The Divas were gathered around the now famous wood table in the DJ booth at K103.5. Each of them was looking flawless, as usual, but inside things were not as pretty. Jessie was aching to her bones over not hearing from Michael—and on top of that feeling, she missed him. She had been longing to hear his voice, feel his touch, be in his company. Pat felt her so-called perfect marriage slipping through her fingers. She was expecting the worst, and her intuition was in high gear and working double time. Either Donnell was having an affair, or right on the verge of having one.

"Break Up To Make Up" by the Stylistics was playing in the background. Really, the only one it applied to was Brit, and she was the last person that should have been making up.

"103.5, 103.5, 103.5, this is your girl V, sitting in the pilot's seat tonight while Melissa and Quentin celebrate, ugh, 'I met you on this day' anniversary. Well ladies and gentlemen, you know I got my girl's back and have to represent. The love forum's got issues tonight. Now my girl Brit just made up with her boo Brass, who just returned from a Mexican cruise with another woman. Yes, y'all, and he was living with Brit when he went on the cruise. Chile, I can't talk about it anymore . . . I'm all talked out. My girl has to tell you the rest. I'm just too outdone!"

"You know what, V, you can be outdone, because at the end of the day, this is my life and Brass is my man. What goes down over at 235 Charles is our business."

"Brit, girl, you ain't never lied. If *you* like it, I love it! Now just tell the listeners how it went down. I'll let them call in and set your silly behind straight."

"You and the listeners can kiss my ass. Oh, sorry, D-town. What I should say is that I know there are plenty of women out there who can relate to what I'm going through. And V, you're right, my man did leave and go on a weeklong cruise while we were living together. But he did *not* sleep with her!"

All the women laughed into their microphones. Jessie and Pat, even as upset as they were, were heaving and coughing so hard, tears swelled up in their eyes and burst down their faces as they held their stomachs and slapped their knees cracking up.

Brit said, "What? What are y'all laughing at? He didn't!"

"And how do you know this, Brit?"

"Ya'll are really starting to piss me off! I know because he looked into my pretty brown eyes and told me so, he said they didn't [*beep*], well do it, and all that slut did, and he called her an ugly [*beep*], is suck his [*beep*].

V said, "Girl, I don't even know what to say, other than B-I-T-C-H, are you for real? Are you hearing yourself? Do you actually believe that mess? Girl, it couldn't have been me, because just like him, his [*beep*] would've been on a cruise too . . . floating, piece by piece, in the Gulf of Mexico. Car, clothes, and every little piece of nothing he had."

"Girl, I know that's right," said Jessie.

"Well, why wouldn't I believe him, V? I'm not saying Brass is perfect. And I know it was fuc—ooh, excuse me—I know it was messed up how he went on that vacation with that slut, but he is just not the type to lie. I mean the Negro told me what he was doing before he did it! I knew he was on the cruise because *he* told me. *He was on a business trip!*"

At the same time, all the Divas shouted, *"A business trip!"*

"Girl, I'm too through with you," said DeDe, shaking her head.

"Brit, your man works at a car dealership, and I'm not even going to go there with you on that one. What kind of business was he doing, with another woman, on a cruise to Mexico," questioned Darlene.

"Girl, I know that's right. What's he doing . . . making a porno," V said, cracking her own self up.

"Yah . . . the star, producer, director, and everything else," said DeDe, "guess he's going to market and sale it, too. Huh, Brit?"

"Brit, I'm not even going to go there with you on the business trip, baby, but you do understand that when that man left for the cruise he thought he wasn't going to have to come crawling back to you? You do get that, right? Pat, Jessie, somebody, break it down for this girl."

"I know that's right, V," Pat said. She wiped the remaining tears from her eyes and pulled the microphone closer. She spoke with fierce determination. "Look here, Brit, you know I love you. That's why me telling you . . . well, your judgment was dumb as hell, and I hope and pray that it doesn't offend you, 'cause what I just said, and what I'm about to say, is coming from a place of love. Brass—and I hope his sorry ass is listening right now—went to Mexico on that woman's dime thinking he had finally hit it big. Somehow or other he messed up that situation and baby girl kicked his tail to the curb. When he realized he had nowhere to go, he came crawling back to you. You get it? He was so honest when he told you where he was going because he didn't think he would be coming back! All that honesty dried up the minute he realized he ain't have nowhere to sleep. Trust and believe me, baby. Trust and believe me."

"First of all, Pat, I am not dumb as hell. I just love deeply, that's all. And I know my man. I know when he's lying. The fool lies for a living. He wasn't giving me any of that lying energy when he came home. He admitted to letting her pleasure him orally, but promised they didn't do anything else."

"If this don't sound like some old Stylistics's 'Break Up To Make Up' bull [*beep*]. Whooo, girl, you got my blood pressure up. Magic, bring that track back. Play it one more time for us. This story is so sad, it makes you take that song in a whole other way."

"You got it, V, and you are truly holding down the fort tonight. For all the peeps out there who like to breakup to make up, here's the Stylistics one more time, laying it down like only they can."

"V, you ain't have to put me out there like that."

"Oh, Brit, please. I'm not even going to have this discussion with you. We all knew what we were signing up for when got on this show. We're supposed to be an open book."

"That's not what I'm talking about. I know that. I'm talking about how you're not supporting me."

DeDe interrupted them, "Brit, none of us will *ever* support such foolishness, you hear? We're being the best friends we can be by showing you what's wrong with your thinking."

"What's wrong with *my* thinking? Girl, you fucking a married man that ain't never gonna leave his wife! I just saw Malcolm at the goddamn grocery store with his wife and kids!"

"So what, Brit? What that mean? 'Cause the nigga takes his family to the market mean something?"

While DeDe and Brit argued back and forth about their liaisons with married and cheating men, the station's intern, Jackie, took a call from one Dr. Xavier Houston.

"This is 103.5. How can I help you this evening?"

"Uh, yes. Hello. This is Dr. Xavier Houston. I'm trying to contact one of *The Love Forum*'s participants. Her name is Jessie Harris."

"Dr. Houston, thank you for calling, but unfortunately I can't connect you with Ms. Harris right this moment. If you would like to speak with her on the air, I'm happy to arrange that. Is this phone call related to *The Love Forum*?"

"Uh, yes. I guess you could say that. In a way, it is. But, I'd like to speak to her privately. Can I please leave a telephone number for her to contact me?"

"Sure."

Jackie took down Dr. Houston's information and immediately set it aside in order to prep the next caller for her on-air time. By the time the Stylistics were finished singing about making up to breakup, she had Lesley Smith on the line. Ms. Smith was nearly screaming over the phone lines.

"Please tell me you all are in that studio slapping the [*beep*] out of Brit. Is that girl crazy?"

"Tell her, Ms. Lesley Smith. What should she do about this damn fool, Brass?"

"She ought to kick his ass to the curb, V. And by the way, you doing a good job on here. Melissa better watch out!"

"Ha! Well, thank you, Lesley, but I'm not here to take my girl's job. Thanks for your advice though. Hello, caller two, you're on the air."

"Yeah, my name is Meeka. I just want to tell Ms. Brit that her man Brass is well-known in the hood."

"Oh lord, Meeka! What do you mean?" V asked.

"I mean, everybody know about Brass. He in a different woman car every time I see him, and he rides through here regularly!"

"You ever dealt with him, Meeka?"

"No, but let me just say he has tried to holler. And on more than one occasion, okay?"

"So you telling my girl Brit to watch out?" V said.

Brit interrupted before Meeka could answer."You know what, V? You and Meeka's ghetto ass can kiss my high yellow ass— calling up here sounding like a young-ass hood rat. I wish I would take the word of some dumb-ass little girl over my man."

"Uh-uh! What she say? What did that [*beep*] say?"

"All right, caller. Thank you for your input. Let's hear from someone else. Caller, you're on the air."

"Yeah."

"Uh? Your momma ain't teach you no manners? Hello? Your name? Something."

"Oh, my bad. Yeah. It's Rico. I thought I'd call up here and give this girl a man's perspective."

DeDe said, "Rewind! Brit is on my nerves as much as everybody else's, but she is a woman! Not a girl, Rico!"

"Okay, whatever, but she sounding like a little-ass girl right now."

"Rico, go on. What advice do you have for Brit?"

"Take it from a dog—your boy is playing you. Him and shorty got into a fight and he's using you, ma. He's prolly still . . . you know. Check his phone. See ain't I right. And after you do, you should let me take you out."

"Oh lord! Rico done turned into Rico Suave. Boy, you can't even form a complete sentence. Goodbye!" V said. "But complete sentence or not, he's speaking the truth, Brit. From the look on your face I see you're not buying it though. Let me take another caller. Maybe one more voice of reason will penetrate that hard head. Caller, talk to V."

"Hello? This is Tangie. I just want to send a bit of support Brit's way. Brit, you nor I, nor none of those lovely ladies on this panel, have any idea what is in Brass's heart. He made a mistake. It happens to the best of us. If you choose to give that man another chance, it's just that—your choice."

"Bonk! Wrong answer, Tangie!" V said.

Brit hurried to interrupt, "Thank you, Tangie. Finally, someone who sees where I'm coming from."

"Magic, I don't know about you, but I can't take this anymore. All this stupidity floating all around in here is making me nauseous! Go on and put a little something on for us. We need to cool off in here."

"You got it, V. Here's a little James Brown. 'The Big Payback.' Since Brit will be needing this song in the near future! We'll be back just as soon as we pass some water around this table. Breathe ladies, breathe!"

V took the headphones off and walked around the table to Brit. She walked with such determination the other women in the room thought she was about to smack Brit. But instead of swinging, she just put her finger in Brit's face.

"Look, I know what's going on here. You're hurt. Just like I was hurt last month when I was all upset about my weight. I didn't want to hear what y'all had to say to me, but it was the truth. What we're telling you is nothing but the truth. The truth hurts, but it is exactly what you need to hear! And for real, I don't know why you all waited for Melissa to go on vacation to start acting up in here! I am a first-time DJ, and I'd think you would pay me a little more respect than that. Can you believe her, Jessie?"

"I sure can't, V, but love'll do that to you."

"So what you saying, Jess? You think her behavior is right?"

Before Jessie could answer, Brit said her piece, "Whatever Jessie thinks, I know you better get your big ass out my face and go over there and sit down. You ain't nobody's momma, V."

V rolled her eyes but made her way back over to her seat.

Jessie said, "Well, you know me, V. I'm not one to judge. I never have been. I want what's best for my girlfriend, but I also understand giving a man a second chance. You nor I know what's going on in Brass's head. He just might be serious. He may have made a terrible mistake, as we all have in our personal lives, and is now realizing he must make amends."

"Okay, Jessie. I can dig that. And despite Brit calling me all out my name, I love her, too! I only want the best for you, girl."

"Jackie, I'm ready for our next caller. I want to see what Dallas is talking about. Magic, are we ready to go?"

"Sure are, V. In five . . . four . . . three . . . two . . . one."

"Welcome back to K103.5. This is your girl V standing in for the sweet Melissa Morgan who is off on a date somewhere with her boo. Caller, you are on the line."

"Yeah. Hello. I'm calling to make a dedication."

"Okay. What's your name, caller?"

"My name is Mrs. Cole."

"Mrs. Cole, do you have a first name?"

"Oh, it's not my first name that really matters. Ask your girl DeDe what I mean."

"Ooh! Oh my goodness, DeDe, do you know what this caller is talking about?"

"No, I'm sorry. I don't."

"Oh, now the name doesn't ring a bell? Well, let me say this Ms. DeDe, I'm Malcolm's wife. You do know Malcolm Crawley, am I right? You did just sleep with him a few days ago, am I right? I'm the woman whose name is on the marriage certificate and on all the birth certificates of his kids. I'm the woman whose mouth you're stealing the food from by living up in that condo he's helping you pay for. And that cheap-ass Benz you're so proud of, I would like to point out how low down the list you are. Baby girl, that's a C class, okay? I'm pushing the 750. I got handbags that cost more than that bucket you're driving, but woman-to-woman, I'd like you to break it off. A man is a man. You can't expect but so much out of them, but as a woman, who I'm sure would like to be married one day herself, I hold you to a higher standard. One day, honey, you will find your soul mate and you will marry him and you will want him to be faithful to you and your family. And you will hope and pray another woman, such as yourself, won't come and break that family apart. That said, I would like to dedicate Shirley Brown's 'Woman to Woman' to you. I hope it inspires some compassion in you for me, and if not for me, than my children, and if not for my children, then yourself. Good night, ladies."

The wife was so swift with the phone, the station was left with a dial tone for some time before Jackie realized what had happened and muted it. The women all looked across the table at DeDe. "Damn!" Laughter erupted inside and outside the studio booth and the Divas expressions said it all—Girl, we feel so bad for you.

"Whew lawd, the mirror is cracked, and DeDe, girl, I think I need to reach down here and pick up your face, 'cause it's broke and on the floor. Well—I'm so embarrassed for you girl—do you have something you'd like to say to this caller, Ms. DeDe?"

"No, V, I don't. I have no idea what that caller is talking about, and if I did, I'd hope she'd have enough respect for herself not to call a radio station and broadcast her business all across Dallas. That is just tacky."

"Hmmm. Sounds like you may have an idea what Mrs. Malcolm Crawley is talking about. And don't I recall correctly you singing a song about a married man on our first show?"

"Play the damn song, V."

"All righty, then. Girl, you don't have to bark at me, I'm not the one that called," V said laughing hysterically. "Whew! Lawdy! All I got to say is that a hit dog will holler! Umph . . . Umph . . . Umph! You heard the lady, Magic. Put that Shirley Brown on and let's get out of here. Dallas, we will speak with you in exactly one week. Until then, we wish you luck in your pursuit of sweet love. And don't forget to leave the married men just where they are—in bed with their wives."

The ladies walked out of the studio that night with none of their issues resolved and each of them, without sharing it with the others, was considering the true purpose of the love forum. Was it truly there to help them, or was it just gossip made public? DeDe was particularly disturbed by Malcolm's wife calling in. She thought he was more careful than to let on about what was going on between them. And more important than that, she sure didn't sound like a woman who was getting left. She had a whole lot of ownership in her voice. Talking about Mrs. this and Mrs. that. De was beginning to think Malcolm's stories about leaving his wife were really a joke, just like Brit had said. And Brit was doubting her situation just as much as DeDe was doubting hers. Maybe Brass had lied about sleeping with that woman. And what if he left her again? She didn't think she could handle that. And then Pat and Jessie were no better off themselves. While their business hadn't been blasted all over the airways, their hearts didn't know the difference. They were still broken, and the women were still returning to lonely houses—Jessie's was missing a man altogether, but Pat's man was missing his heart. And then Ms. Melissa, who was supposedly the example for all the ladies to look to, was on her back in a hotel suite celebrating her anniversary and thinking, *I want to marry this man . . . but does he want to marry me?*

+++

V and her nine-year old son Jerome, Jr., lived in a small but cozy brick ranch house in East Dallas. As they sat in the living room, V watched Jerome play video games on the TV. As she watched him, she noticed her husband, his father, in him. She noticed the same tall lanky frame. The shape of his head. His small ears and how thick his eyebrows were. And although she loved her son to death, there was a part of her that hated him— that hated her husband.

"Jerome?"

"Yah, Ma."

"Have you talked to your father?"

"What do I need to talk to him for?"

"Well . . . I just thought maybe you've talked to him lately."

"Naw, but Granny called about cousin Willie."

"Sweets? What does he want?"

"Something about a business plan. Granny said don't be mad at her, but she thought about you when he was talking about it with her."

"Mmmmm, okay? Well . . . when was the last time you talked to your father?"

"Maaaa! I'm playing!"

"Boy, you heard me!" Staring at him, thinking, *just like his father*!

"Don't know . . . a couple of months I guess."

"Mmmm, that's not good! Maybe you should call him . . . hand me a game controller."

"Oh, you ready for another butt-whipping?" Laughing and reaching for a game controller.

"Watch your mouth boy!" Moving down to the floor and snuggling against Jerome. "And the last time we played, I let you win."

"Yah ma, right!"

As V played with her son, she thought about Jerome Sr., and how devastated she was when he left. More devastated over the fact that he left, than the situation which caused him to leave.

V and Jerome played in silence. Their brief conversation was actually the most she'd talked to her son in quite some time—and she knew it. She realized that although she was right there in the same house with her son, she was just as distant as his father. At that moment, V knew that her hate for her husband was killing her relationship with her son. And she thought *what type of man am I raising to send out into the world? Will he be distant to his wife, his children . . . to me?* With those thoughts floating around in her head, V let Jerome win. Got up, and silently cried as she walked down the hall to her bedroom. She opened the door and closed it behind her, turning the lock—securing herself inside. She paced the floor, replaying her life over and again. Going over every decision and choice she ever made. V knew she needed to change. She could hear her mother talking to her clear as day, *"Vanessa, you need to get over this and move on. All this hate you have festering inside of you is gonna eat you up alive. And the person it's gonna destroy, in the end, is you."* Contemplating what to do, without even realizing it, she had increased her pacing double speed. As minutes turned into hours, V threw her hands in the air, as if to give up. Exhausted, she had reached that point of total despair. She heard a voice in the back of her mind, say, *let it go, give it to him.* Overwhelmed, she dropped to her knees . . . rocked back and forth . . . and cried. As the tears rolled down her face, she began to pray:

Lord, I have a lot of work to do, but I'm willing to take the first step. Guide me father, guide me and help me make the right decisions. Help me to forgive father, help me Lord, Jesus.

She needed to forgive her husband and bring him back into the life of her son. And she needed to put all her resentment behind her and call Sweets. She needed to move forward, "I need to start a brand new chapter in my life . . . Lord, give me strength!" V sat on the bed. Took a deep breath. Covered her heart with one hand and picked up the house phone with the other.

+++

Brit walked into her apartment and knew something was wrong before she crossed the threshold. Brass's sneakers were not lined up along the wall by the door. She locked the door and put her bags down. She walked as fast as she could to the bedroom where she found Brass stuffing all his clothes into what looked like a brand new Louis Vuitton suitcase.

"What you doing, Brass?"

"Now why the fuck would you get on that stupid-ass radio show telling all my fucking business?"

"What? Your business? Brass, you knew I was going to be on that show. The only thing I did was tell exactly what happened. Now what are you doing? And who was that little-ass girl that called up to the station talking about you're well-known in her neighborhood?"

"Look, I know you know I live the sort of life where I can't have my business all out in the street. Even if I wasn't going back to Esther, I'd still be leaving your ass. That was real fucking stupid getting on that dumb-ass show and telling all my fucking business. You one dumb bitch."

"You going back? You going back to her? So what was all that you love me, you sorry, you can't believe you left me shit? What was that, Brass?"

"That was me not wanting to fuck up a good thing. I was gonna let you be the little something on the side, but your damn ass wanna go on the radio and tell my life story. You had my girl blowing up my cell phone wanting to know why you was saying I was your man."

"Oh, you're not my man, Brass?"

"Naw, ma. I ain't. I ain't your man. I got a new woman now. Her money is long, her hips is wide, and the brand new F-150 she bought me is outside waiting for me to put this beautiful Louie luggage she just got me in the trunk. Look sweetie, you cute. And your head game is something serious. Believe me. I wish you'd suck my dick real quick before I get in my new car, but it's over, ma. And don't bring your silly ass up to the job, and don't say my name one more fucking time on that dumb-ass radio show. You sound stupid by the way. You sound like a desperate ho. Oh, and the five Gs did the trick, the shit is about to pop big time. Mexico is the ticket, baby, you came through on that shit. I'll try—and I said try—to get you the money back. I'll even try to throw in an extra dollar or two for interest. It's been wild, girl . . . Peace . . . I'm out."

Brass collected all his beautiful luggage and walked right out of Brit's door. She was so shocked (let alone humiliated), she couldn't even bring herself to cry. She just felt numb. She looked at herself in her bedroom mirror, and with all her beauty, she suddenly felt very ugly. She stood in front of the mirror for hours. Eventually her eyes lost focus. Her worst fear had come to life and hit her like a ton of bricks—she was without a man. She felt invalidated—worthless—alone and betrayed. Betrayed by the one man she loved so deeply. And she asked herself over and over again, *How? How could he do this to me?*

+++

Jessie, on the other hand, had been so blessed to receive a text message from Michael. It read: *Hey, baby. I was out of town. Had to go see about my baby girl. You know how that goes. Can I see you tonight?* Her little eyes lit up and she started flipping through the clothes in her mind's closet. What would she wear? She started to text back: *Hell yeah, nigga. Bring your big-dick ass over on the double*, but heard Big Momma in the background. So she typed, *That would be nice*, instead.

She made a lasagna. She knew it would be tasty, because it was one of her specialties, and after she'd prepared it she could just throw it in the oven to bake while she got herself together for her future husband. She showered and shaved all the crevices. She brushed her teeth three times to be sure and gargled with burning Listerine. Her mouth smelled like pure mint when it was all said and done. She decided on a silk tank and a nice pair of slacks to wear. The pants highlighted her behind and hips, hugged her like they didn't want to let go, but didn't make her appear too slutty. She knew she had already given the butt up, but didn't want to give the impression that it belonged to him (though she wanted him to claim it). The tank top was conservative in its material and high cut, but seductive in the way it hung on her shoulders. She sprayed herself with a light musk and piled on the mascara and gloss. No foundation or anything like that, because he would be so up close and personal with her that she didn't want to appear too made up— it would make her look too desperate. Plus, she knew no man wanted to kiss a face smothered in foundation. When she was happy with her appearance, she went to check on the lasagna, which was piping hot and ready. She allowed it to cool, and made a fresh tossed salad and some garlic bread to accompany it. Just when her dinner was complete, she heard a knock at the door. She felt like a little girl all over again. She peeked at herself in the mirror in the hall and opened the door.

He was standing there looking like the most beautiful sculpture. His hair was cut low and the waves were just popping. She was getting seasick looking at them and almost laughed at that—"seasick" was how her friends at Spelman had always described a fly brother's waves. His suit was fresh and so clean looking, even with the cufflinks removed and the tie loosened. He was so sharp. And she wanted to love him so bad. She wanted him to love her even worse.

"Well hello, Mr. Crawley. How nice to see you."

"Hey, baby. You look beautiful. That is absolutely no surprise."

"Thank you. You don't look so bad yourself."

"Girl, let me in. And give me some sugar before you feed me."

He came in, and Jessie closed the door behind him. They embraced and kissed a long while. His mouth tasted fresh, which turned Jessie on. He took his tongue out of her mouth and smacked her behind before asking where the bathroom was. Jessie showed him and went about her business of setting the dining room table. Granted, Jessie's home did not compare to Michael's—she wasn't anywhere near his career success—but it was well kept, and she was proud of what she had accomplished with it . . . especially considering the constraints of her budget. Plus, she was looking to be upgraded. Michael could speed that process along. She had no complaints about that!

After he'd cleaned up in the bathroom, the two sat down to eat. Michael raved about Jessie's cooking, and she thought hard about how he made her feel in his presence. He was perfect, when she could get her hands on him. When he disappeared, though, she didn't know the next time she'd catch him. It felt like he was always slipping through her fingers. Nevertheless, she wound up making love to him again. And again, she didn't use protection—even though he had disappeared for a time, and she had no idea where he'd gone. She wanted to feel nearer to him and did not want some rubbery condom interfering with that. And just when she thought things couldn't get any better, he made love to her a hundred times better than the first time. She couldn't keep her moans under wrap and hoped, the whole hour through, her neighbors couldn't hear her. He ate her pussy like it was his favorite hobby, and she loved it. He rubbed his climax out on to the sheets, while his head was still buried between

Jessie's legs. She had climaxed several times, topping their first time. His sex was so good, it left her exhausted. Exhausted to the point where she couldn't hold her eyes open long enough to feel the dozen kisses he laced her with. When she finally woke up from her two-hour nap, he was holding her with both his arms and all his strength. She wondered what was so different about this time that he held her with such power? Maybe he was falling for her just as much as she was falling for him?

Chapter Thirteen

It Hurts Like Hell

Just an hour ago Pat had decided to tell Donnell about the cancer diagnosis. She realized, in one depressive moment, she needed the support of her husband. But now her lips were sealed. Nothing about cancer would come out of them, just sounds of deep pain. She and Donnell sat on opposite sides of their king-sized bed with their backs facing one another. Pat's shoulders shook with distress. She was crying, and the tears seemed to come from her gut, work their way through her aching insides, and finally show their heads in her red eyes. She kept saying, "Why? But why? Tell me why, Donnell?"

Donnell, her husband of ten years had just told her, with eyes dry as earth, "I want a divorce."

It wasn't so much the words themselves that knocked the wind out of Pat, but the way his lips failed to move, how emotionless his eyes were. She knew they had been having problems. She had been feeling Donnell slowly withdraw from her, and then completely ignore her over the past six months. And then that mess he pulled the other night—not coming home—was what almost put her over the top. She wouldn't have thought he could top that. That his coldness would end like this, with him asking for a divorce, she could not have imagined. Sitting on what felt like his bed (he kept referring to everything in their house as *his*), she recalled their wedding day and how he had stared into her eyes. She thought, *This man is looking into my soul . . . and he likes what he sees*. She recalled the discovery of both pregnancies. How they had jumped around like two fools who had just won the lottery. She thought about making love with him, the last time she could actually call it that. She imagined his hand on the small of her back and cried harder, because from what he was saying, she would no longer know what that felt like.

"Baby, what did I do?"

"I don't want this no more, Pat. I don't know what to tell you. I just don't want this shit. I want you to pack up and leave. You got to go."

"But baby, why? Why are you doing this to me?"

"You really want to know? You want to know why? The woman I love asked me the other day, 'Baby, why do I have to spend Thanksgiving alone?' And I thought to myself, 'Why does she?' I'm tired of living this lie. I am not in love with you. I am in love with someone else, and with her is where I want to be."

Pat felt blood rushing throughout her body and then felt a sudden drop in her stomach. *The woman he loves? Why should she have to be alone?* She blinked several times in disbelief. Had she heard what she thought she heard? Here her husband was looking at her like he didn't even know her. Like he hadn't proposed to her and married her and watched her deliver their children. She got up from the bed to look in the wall mirror. She needed to see her face before she said a word. Maybe she didn't look the same. He was looking into a stranger's eyes. She had to see this woman. At the mirror she saw Pat Carter. Eyes a little swollen, sure. She had been crying for hours. Waist a little bigger than last year and the year before that (she had birthed two big head babies), but Pat nonetheless. Why was this man talking to her like he didn't know her? Why was he talking about loving a woman and her name wasn't Pat? Then just like that, she was overcome with a feeling of disgust. Suddenly, she could not stand being in his presence. All that she had given him? All those years? All that love? She had to get away from him. She didn't even want an answer to any of those questions. Not one. She said, "I got to go. I can't be here. I can't be nowhere near you! I just can't." She ran from the house without so much as checking in on the kids. She drove straight to Melissa's. In the driveway, she finally allowed herself to feel, really feel, the pain of it all. And she couldn't walk. She couldn't even bring herself to unlatch the seatbelt.

+++

Melissa noticed Pat's car pulling into her driveway and knew it couldn't be good news. Number one, Pat's schedule was so precise and orderly she didn't make unexpected stops. Number two, it was taking her forever to come in. Within the space of five minutes, Melissa peeked out of the window twice, just to see Pat's shadow not moving a lick. She threw on a house robe and ran to the car.

Before she could open her mouth and fuss at Pat for sitting in her driveway like a stalker, it all registered. Her girlfriend was sitting in that car with a face tore up in pain. The tears were coming by the gallon. She picked up the pace and opened the car door. She kneeled at Pat's side.

"What happened, baby girl? What happened?"

Through the tears, Pat said, "He leaving me, Melissa. He said he don't love me no more, and how come she got to spend Thanksgiving alone."

"What? Who is she?"

"I don't know, but she the one who got his love. Me? I'm old news."

Pat started to laugh sarcastically. Melissa just stared at her. She knew that laugh. That, *I can't believe this shit* laugh. Soon it turned into a full-bodied, slap your knee thing, and Melissa had to fight back her own tears.

"Come on, girl. Get out of this seat. Come in this house with me."

She stood up and unstrapped her girlfriend. She pulled her out of the car. "Come on, honey. We gonna work this out."

"Naw, we ain't, Melissa. Ain't nothing you or me or anyone else on this Earth can do. Nothing is going to work out. Not a thing."

"Hush, girl."

Melissa pulled Pat along like she was a doll baby. Except for her legs, nothing else moved. Her face was absent of all emotion, and her tears had somehow dried up. She just stared into the distance as Melissa sat her down, and then began dialing the telephone. While Melissa listened to the ringing on the other end, Pat hummed a made-up tune. Whatever the song was, it had no hope in it.

"Hello? Pastor Levine?"

Pastor Levine was on the other end, and having just finished his dinner, was thrown off a bit.

"Yes? This is Pastor Levine."

"Pastor Levine, this is Melissa Morgan. You know, I head the youth council at Greater Antioch?"

"Yes, yes. I know you, Ms. Melissa. What can I do for you? Is everything okay?"

"Well no, Pastor Levine. I really hate to ask you this, but I have a friend in need—it's Ms. Pat. You know, Donnell's wife."

"What's wrong?"

"Well Donnell . . . he just left her and—"

"No need to explain. Where is she?"

"She's here with me, at my house. I live at 135 Bailey . . . unless you want us to come to you?"

"No, no. I'll be right there."

It didn't take the pastor long to get there, but in that time, Melissa witnessed Pat fall deeper into what looked like an instant depression. She was aching to her core over watching her friend go through this. She couldn't believe Donnell. If he could do this to Pat, what in the world would Quentin do to her . . . and they weren't even married yet.

Pastor Levine crossed the front door's threshold looking mighty strong. Just his presence put Melissa at ease. She looked over at Pat to see if she felt this godly man's aura. But Pat was unmoved. She was staring off into space somewhere thinking unthinkable things.

"Pat?"

She ignored him.

"Pat, you don't have to answer me. You don't even have to look at me. But I want you to hear me. God has not left you. God is with you at this very moment. He is the reason you haven't collapsed. That you're able to still hold yourself together."

Pat started laughing that hysterical laugh again, and Melissa was flushed with embarrassment. The laugh was quickly stifled though when Pat looked into Pastor Levine's eyes and saw that he wasn't fazed by it.

"What God done for me, Pastor? What I got, Pastor? You tell me that." She looked around as if searching for something.

She stared into the pastor's eyes with both power and pain. All hope had been drained from her. Melissa dotted her eyes with her pointer fingers as tears welled in them.

"I've known you since I came to be the pastor of Greater Antioch. I know you, Pat. We go back. I've watched your marriage from a distance, your children, you yourself. And I know you're no weakling. I know you're hurting and the pain is great. I know you're used to your strength seeing you through. But no matter how strong you are in your faith, things will go wrong for you. And whether or not this here situation is a test of your faith or not, greener pastures lie ahead. They lie ahead."

Melissa thought Pat might start laughing again, but she didn't. She just cried, and then she whispered, "I'm through with Greater Antioch. I'm through with Greater Antioch, and I'm through with God himself." She folded into herself like there was not a bit of wind left in her. Pastor Levine approached her softly and sat next to her. He motioned for Melissa to join them. Melissa took a seat, and together they flanked Pat, as if to shield her from what harmed her. They bowed their heads, and Pastor Levine, in a low but firm voice, prayed with them into the wee hours of the morning.

+++

While Pat was busy losing her life, DeDe was busy making a mess of hers. That damn wife calling into the station and embarrassing her like that had put her in another state of mind. She was beginning to wonder if Malcolm was worth all the trouble. His dick was big, but a black man with a big dick came a dime a dozen. The myth was true! She had decided to put the fire to Malcolm's ass. She was going to put her house up for sale, and see if that didn't encourage him to do as he said he'd do and get rid of that old bag.

She had started the whole process with Darlene. DeDe was happy to help her homegirl out. If DeDe could sell the thing and put a little extra dough in Darlene's pocket, that was all the better. But maybe Darlene was too damn busy or something because the calls were not coming in. DeDe had a point to make, and she needed to make it fast. And then maybe, in her heart, she was sincere about selling the house and getting the hell out of Texas. She needed to be somewhere where her career could flourish, and banking on some foolish man leaving his wife just didn't appear to be the wisest move.

Things took a turn when she discovered that a fine-ass colleague of hers—Shawn Wyatt—was dipping into real estate on the side. She decided to kill two birds with one stone and ask him to sell her house while slowly but surely pushing up on him. Maybe he could help loosen the hold Malcolm had on her. She sure as hell hoped he wasn't gay. She approached him in the teacher's lounge one day.

"Hello, Mr. Wyatt. It's nice to see you."

"Oh hello, Ms. Kravitz. Nice to see you, too. How are you?"

"I'm fine. Actually, I'm not. I'm trying to unload a condo. I heard you do real estate on the side?"

"I sure do. Where is the condo located?"

"Downtown Dallas."

"One of those condos in that area they've been revitalizing?"

"Yes, sir! You think you could help me get it off my hands? Keep this between me and you, but I'm looking into a career change."

"Oh really? Might I ask what you plan to do?"

"I'm a singer, actually. I'm looking to move to L.A. to pursue my career full time."

"Oh, okay. Well I can definitely be of some assistance. When can we get together?"

"How about tonight? I'm trying to get the ball rolling."

"That sounds good. Write down your address for me. I'll come by to see the property, and we can get things started."

While this conversation was taking place, Darlene was calling DeDe. When her phone went straight to voicemail she tried again and then finally settled for leaving a message. She told DeDe she needed to see her about a potential homebuyer coming by to see the condo that night. DeDe checked the message a little later but decided Darlene had missed her opportunity so deleted the message. She didn't bother calling Darlene and letting her go honestly. She just figured Darlene would figure it all out herself.

That night, DeDe made sure she was dressed to kill without looking like she had dolled up especially for Mr. Wyatt. She threw on a velour sweat suit that hugged her in all the right places and touched up her makeup. She was a neat freak, so cleaning the house wasn't anything she had to worry about. She did, however, have to worry about Malcolm stopping by. Him seeing Shawn Wyatt in her kitchen, even if he was a real estate agent, would not be good. Especially if you were looking through a psycho's eyes. She sent him a text message to assure he would stay his ass wherever he was. *I'm gone to the movies with Jessie*, she wrote. He said, *Okay*, and DeDe went about her business.

Mr. Wyatt came through her door looking sharp as Denzel. She thought, *I could definitely get with this. Time to get me a man I can have to myself. Somebody I don't have to worry about getting up to leave in the middle of the night. Somebody I can spend holidays with. Somebody who doesn't have a wife at home waiting to call up to radio stations and put all my business in the streets.* They sat at the kitchen table to go over the details of the selling process, but DeDe wasn't listening. She was busy batting her eyes and did not pick up on the fact that Shawn, as he insisted she call him, was paying her no mind. She had to stop all her flirting though to explain why she already had a For Sale sign on her lawn.

"Oh, I had another real estate agent, but she wasn't getting the job done. I think you can handle it much better."

"Oh, okay. Well I'm going to leave you with these documents. Look them over, call me if you have any questions, and I'm going to start scheduling some open houses as soon as possible."

Denzel-Look-A-Like left, put a new For Sale sign up in the yard, and DeDe had not the slightest idea that he was going straight home to a beautiful family he wasn't giving up for any amount of easy pussy in the world. Shawn was no Malcolm, and DeDe would have no opportunity to harm his wife or his children. He took his wedding vows seriously.

Well no sooner had DeDe closed the door behind him did Darlene drive by her house. Darlene saw the sign indicating that someone, not her, was selling DeDe's condo. She thought she saw her For Sale sign in the garbage. She said, "DeDe's trifling ass done went behind my back to sell that house. She just underhanded all the way around, I guess." She sped off, too through with her "friend." And on top of that, she was feeling a little uneasy about Miguel's work visa. It would be expiring soon, and Darlene was begging and pleading with God that he wasn't just sticking with her to earn his citizenship. It sure didn't feel that way, but if he popped up asking her to marry him too soon, she was going to be something kinda suspicious.

DeDe was in the house recalling how her evening had gone. She was staring at herself in the mirror making sure she looked as good as she thought when her cell phone rang. She hoped it was Shawn, but when she saw an L.A. number on the ID and realized it was Electra Sounds, she thought, *Well this kind of call is just as good!*

"Hello? DeDe Kravitz speaking."

"Uh yes, Ms. Kravitz? This is Rebecca Haines from Electra Sounds. I'm Alicia Myer's assistant."

"Oh. Hello, Rebecca. What can I do you for?"

"Well Ms. Kravitz, I'm sorry to call you with this news, but it looks like Electra Sounds will no longer be extending you the invitation to join our label."

"What the fu—I mean, excuse me, I mean what? What do you mean?"

"Ms. Myers seems to think your current situation—you know, the affair—is not a healthy image for our label. We're interested in promoting family-friendly music, and well, women who are involved with married men just don't fit into our formula. I'm sorry to call you with this news. I've heard that you're very talented."

"You're damn right I'm talented. Excuse me, Rebecca, but why do these . . . these allegations . . . because that's what they are . . . have any bearings on my contract with Electra Sounds?"

"Are you saying they aren't true? Actually, that really doesn't even matter. Unfortunately, once the rumor wheel gets to churning there's really nothing we can do about it. We here at Electra Sounds are just not interested in the bad-girl image. We promote family and music that reflects sisterhood."

"Rebecca . . . you don't understand. This is my only chance. I'm getting up there. Honey, you really don't get it. You sound about what, twenty-five?"

"Yes, ma'am. I just turned twenty-five this year."

"Well Rebecca, I know that you can't really relate, but please just try to imagine what it's like to see your life slipping away. Please, is there anything I can do?"

"Hold on, Ms. Kravitz Let me speak to Ms. Myers and see what she says."

DeDe stayed on hold with one hand pressing the phone against her ear, and the other hand holding her up against the wall. She was not ashamed to pray out loud. "Please, God, please. One more chance. Grant me one more chance. I'm putting Malcolm's ass to the curb. No more hurting his wife. No more harming his kids. Just please, God. Give me this one more chance. I won't disappoint you anymore."

"Hello, Ms. Kravitz?"

"Yes, Rebecca. I'm here."

"Ms. Myers said we might be able to work out a PR plan if you can figure out a way to clear up this rumor. She said she'll give you a call in the morning so you guys can discuss the possibility."

DeDe yelled out, "Hallelujah, Rebecca! Bless your little twenty-five-year-old heart. Tell Ms. Alicia Myers she has nothing to worry about! I'm cleaning this thing up starting right this minute."

The minute she hung up with Electra Sounds, DeDe dialed Malcolm's house number. And when his wife answered, she didn't hang up either.

"Tracy?"

"Yes."

"Tracy, this is DeDe."

+++

The Divas certainly had a lot going on. While DeDe's and Pat's lives were being flipped all around and upside down, Jessie was experiencing something similar. She was sitting on her couch, her hands resting in her lap, just staring off into space thinking.

It's funny how love works when you think you've found someone who could make you complete, someone who, at first appearance, you totally understand and they seem to totally understand you. It's funny how two people can meet and connect so well, and how Cupid's arrow pierces you so deep. But then you find out his arrow is only a flesh wound for the other person, and damn that arrow sho' does hurt.

I mean, how can this guy make me feel so beautiful and so terrible at the same time? That first night, I fell asleep with a "cheese" smile on my face. I fell asleep thanking Jesus. I said it out loud! You've answered my prayers, Lord, I said. And even after he talked me out of my panties that first date—well let's be honest, I talked myself out of them—and even after he disappeared, and even as I can't find him right this moment, I still want him. It's like the worse he treats me the more I like him. I guess after being played and rejected by so many men— most recently those two cornballs Marcus and Rodolfo—it just makes the situation that much worse.

Marcus and Rodolfo were two more disappointments on the list that was Jessie's heartbreak. Marcus she had met twice. The first time was almost a decade ago. He was what you'd call pretty. Down to his pinky toes. Just a good-looking sharp young brother who made the girls swoon. For whatever reason, they never hit it off. But some ten years later she saw him again at Club NV. At first, she thought he worked there as maybe a bartender or security personnel, but then she noticed him cleaning up. Clearing the tables of their drinks and even mopping up. That was a little disturbing because she didn't want a janitor for a man, but she was trying to keep an open mind and maybe a blue collar man not only worked hard on the job, but also in his relationship. One thing led to another that night and in a few weeks Marcus was spending the night for the first time. He arrived with two bags in his hands—one with food from Subway and the other with a change of clothes and toothbrush. They had history, having met so long ago, so there was really no need to act all crazy about him coming over just *knowing* he was welcomed overnight. She was up late that night, working on a project for DataComm, so he went on up to bed and went to sleep. During the week he was easy to find. He might have even been classified as a bug-a-boo he called so often, so when that next weekend approached, and Jessie couldn't reach him, she got a little suspicious. When she finally got a hold of him, he told her that he had been with a friend who was visiting from California. They had hit all the local spots—comedy clubs and restaurants and things like that—and Jessie didn't want to go the psycho-girlfriend route. She was trying to step outside of her comfort box. She had entertained a man with a service job, and therefore, was going to try something a little different herself; she wasn't going to jump to conclusions and assume he was doing dirt. Only he started behaving in ways that couldn't be denied. He'd damn near stalk her until Thursday night. Then the phone calls stopped, and she couldn't get a response from him if she texted, "I'm dying." And sure enough, as soon as Sunday night rolled around he materialized talking about, "Can I come over?" It didn't take Jessie long to figure out her house was being used as a crash pad. She dropped him, and her new take on dating men who didn't meet her expectations.

Then came Adolfo. She met him online unexpectedly. She had opened up a Facebook account to reconnect with old friends from college and he had sent her a friend request. He was a stranger, so she wasn't sure why he was reaching out to her. She wrote to him before welcoming him into her friends.

Jessie: Hello. Um, I'm sorry. Do I know you?

Adolfo: No, ma'am, you don't. But you're beautiful. Your profile picture is plain old intriguing. I wondered if we could try to get to know each other. We live in the same area.

She accepted the friend request, and they shared a few flirtatious e-mails before deciding to meet in person. He was an attractive man, well groomed, and fairly intelligent. His conversation was nice, and he did all the right things—opening doors, pulling out chairs, picking up the tab. But he was a DJ and his schedule was a nonstop list of demands. "I promise we're going to get together next weekend," was his signature line. Really, she only caught up with him online. He'd see that she was visiting her Facebook page and instant message her. *What's going on, baby?* or *How you been?* And then he'd go into some story about how he had several parties to play or was entertaining some houseguests. Sooner than later, Jessie kicked him to the curb. She was left twiddling her thumbs wondering if love was even looking for her, let alone going to find her.

Then came Michael, and it seemed he had already lost interest in her. She was hating herself for having slept with him so quickly, but knew, even in retrospect, that she couldn't have helped it. She should have probably left well enough alone, but Michael was a challenge, and Jessie never backed down from a challenge. Plus she had just this overwhelming connection with him. And the connection was not weakened by his piss poor habits—like hanging out with his boys nonstop. Just that previous week she couldn't get a half-hold on him. Every time she called or texted, the answer was one of a few: *I'm busy. With the boys, call you later. I'm too sleepy and don't feel like driving over.* And yet she was waiting patiently for him right that moment. When the doorbell rang, her heart jumped a bit faster. The butterflies came alive in her stomach. She opened the door to what seemed like God's best work.

"Hey, baby girl. Don't you look beautiful. Just what I needed to see. Pretty in pink."

Jessie wore a pink fitted housedress. Her eyes lit up with his words.

"Hey, handsome. I feel the same way. You are a sight for sore eyes."

"Sore eyes? What are those eyes sore about?"

"They haven't rested on you in damn near two weeks, that's what."

They made their way into the kitchen where Jessie had prepared dinner. His salad and bread were waiting for him.

"Hell yeah, baby. Something smells good. I am so hungry."

"Well good, 'cause there is plenty of chicken and rice and veggies."

"All this for me?"

"All this for you. You better recognize! You could have this every night of your life if you knew how to act."

"Well, that might be more of a possibility now."

"Whatchu mean?"

"I just went on medical leave."

"Medical leave? Is something wrong, baby? Medical leave for what?"

"You know, I'm just tired. I need a break. I been working so hard. I been giving that damn insurance company all my time. All my energy. I just really want to focus on me."

"But Michael, you can't just up and take a medical leave."

"You can when you are as valuable to the company as I am. Now pass me some Ranch dressing and let's get this dinner going."

Jessie and Michael ate and then made love till the early morning hours. She thought she might be in love. As a matter of fact, she was almost sure.

Michael was out of the door before Jessie could put a piece of bread in the toaster for him the next morning. His cell had been vibrating all night, and his shoulders looked a little tenser each time it vibrated. At one point, he even said, "Nigga stop fucking texting me!"

And Jessie asked, "Who, baby? Who's bothering you?" But Michael didn't answer. He only grabbed his things, forgot to kiss her or say goodbye, and flew out the door.

Chapter Fourteen

The Love Forum
I'll Do Anything for Love

November 23, 2008. Melissa and Quentin sat down at the bar. They were in Carrabba's waiting for a table. Melissa was starving and kept looking up from her stool to see if the waiter was coming towards them. Coming up on five months pregnant, her belly had been demanding she eat a little more—actually a lot more. She definitely wasn't excited about telling Quentin the news. Deep in her heart, she knew her little gumdrop, as she called the baby, wasn't going to solve their problems, wasn't going to give its father that push he needed to marry her, and really, she didn't even want to think about it. Still, her mind kept wandering back to that damn Doretha, and she couldn't help but feel something in her gut telling her to just totally disregard her. She hated the hold Ms. Doretha had on her and did not want to believe any bit of what Ms. Doretha had told her. She wished she'd never spoken to Ms. Doretha's crazy ass. The bartender was a cute young girl with hair down to her waist. Well, a weave down to her waist. It looked good though. Melissa almost asked for her beautician's number when the girl asked for their orders. She needed an excuse to explain why she wouldn't be drinking. She didn't want this to be the way she told Quentin. Suddenly, she wasn't thinking about her hunger or hair weaves or even stupid psychics.

Quentin said, "I'll take a rum and coke. Thanks."

"And you, Miss?"

"Um. I'll just take a Sprite. Thank you."

Melissa was thinking, *Damn where is that waiter at?*

"You ain't drinking, babe? What? My baby ain't getting it popping after a long day of work? That ain't like you, Lis."

"Yeah. How was work today?" She was trying, not so subtly, to change the subject.

It worked, though. "Tough. You know that damn Keith Jackson has been working my nerves with his ass-kissing ass."

"Ass-kissing ass? Ha! Well damn, babe. He must be putting in on heavy."

"I can't stand that nigga. And you *know* I ain't one to hate, Lis. But I just don't like a man who doesn't depend on his work ethic to speak for him. What the hell a grown-ass fucking man got to be complementing another man for?"

Just then the waiter came over and offered to lead them to their table. Quentin grabbed his rum and coke, and Melissa trailed behind him deciding to just to come out with it. She didn't waste anytime after the waiter left to get their appetizers.

"Q?"

"Yeah, babe? What's going on?"

"Q, I'm pregnant."

Quentin coughed and almost spit out his sip of drink.

"Oh lord, Q. Don't start coughing and shit. Don't tell me you don't want this baby." She thought, *Please don't tell me you don't want this baby!*

"What, girl? Calm down. You jumping to the wrong conclusion. It's just you told me this shit in the middle of me sipping my drink."

"Well, what are you thinking?"

"I think . . . um . . . I think we been having some problems, and you know that, but still, I think it's wonderful news, baby. Maybe this is the sign we need to get ourselves together and stop all that fussing we been doing. Come over here and sit with me."

Melissa slid out of her seat and joined Quentin on his side of the booth. Inside, she was a mess. She wanted to holler out in joy and say, "See there! You old dumb witch! You don't know what you're talking about." But she held back.

Quentin said, "That's why you not drinking, hunh? And why you been wearing all the baggy clothes . . . not letting me lift your shirt. You been to the doctor?"

"Yeah, of course. I'm five months."

"What the fu—five months, Melissa? Five months!" He pushed away from her and stared at her with confusion and hurt in his eyes.

"Yes. Five months, Quentin. I'm five months."

"Why the hell would you wait five months to tell me I'm having a baby? What kind of shit is that?"

"The fuck does it matter, Quentin? Does this new information change your life in any way?"

"Huh? What kind of dumb-ass questions are you asking? Does it change my life, Lis? Are you serious right now? I'm about to be a father. I am about to be somebody's father, and you give me, what, four months to prepare for that? What kinda shit you on, girl?"

Melissa positioned herself so that she was facing Quentin. Now the hurt in her eyes matched his. They were two tore-up looking things.

"Q, look. I love you. You know that. You knew six months ago I wanted to spend the rest of my life with you."

"What you saying?"

"I'm saying you haven't handled your business. And at this point, it's obvious you're not going to. If you had any intention of marrying me, you would have made it happen whether or not you knew about this pregnancy. Honestly, it really doesn't matter to me. I just want my mozzarella sticks." But she didn't just want her mozzarella sticks, she wanted him to marry her. Melissa almost sickened herself stooping to these games. She never thought she was that kind of woman. But desperation brings out a whole other side.

+++

Meanwhile, Quentin was looking at the mother of his child like, *mozzarella sticks?* He almost said it except the disinterest in Melissa's eyes was obvious.

"I love you, baby girl. And having a child with you is going to be the answer to one of my many prayers for us. You're going to be a wonderful mother, and I'm so happy that I'm the one who will share that experience with you. And I don't give a fuck about that little shit we been arguing about lately either, but—"

"But what, Quentin? You're 'not ready,' right?" Melissa gave the "not ready" the parentheses fingers. She rolled her eyes and touched her stomach.

"Well, yeah. I'm just not ready for all that, babe. I'm not ready for marriage . . . to be a husband . . . But what does that mean? That it has to be the end of us? Having a baby don't have to stop nothing. Us not being married don't have to stop nothing. I'm just not ready for that title yet."

"But you're ready to be a father? You not ready for a title, for a wife, but you ready to take care of a brand new human being?"

"Well, I really don't have a choice in the matter, now do I?"

"Uh-uh. Don't do that. Don't put this shit on me, Q. Don't put your irresponsibility on me."

"Well, I mean, did I have an opportunity to protest this? To say, no, I'm not ready for fatherhood? Look . . . I don't want to talk about that. What's done is done. What I do have a choice about is my marital status. And Lis, no baby is going to pressure me into that. I just don't want that right now."

"Right now? Well when then, Quentin? When is a better time to get married then when you have a son, or daughter, on the way?"

"Girl, it's the twenty-first century! Why you talking that backward stuff? We don't have to be married to start a family. I mean marriage will come. I want you to be my wife. We'll probably be married in the next few years. But I'm not ready to take that step just this moment."

"I might not have a few years."

"What? What's that supposed to mean?"

"Look, Quentin, I don't know how many times I've told you all I want is a family. To be married, and to bring three or four babies into this world—and to do that with you would be my dreams materialized. I don't have either of my parents. I have no immediate family here. You know that. You're all I have. You're all I love. And still you have no desire to dedicate your life to me. And finally . . . finally . . . I get that through my thick skull."

The waiter set their mozzarella sticks and salads on the table. They were quiet while he did so. In that space of time, Melissa felt her heart break. It split right down the middle. The evening was not going as planned. She had told herself over and over not to get her hopes up, but there was something inside her—that same something that dismissed everything that crazy psychic lady had said—telling her to believe. She had so wanted him to hear her news and then drop down on one knee . . . do the right thing. Make the fantasy she was living in her head a reality. She was having a hard time understanding him breaking her heart like that—even with the hours of pep talks she'd given herself. And now, where before she had been Starvin' Marvin, now she couldn't force a cheese stick down her throat. She excused herself and went to the bathroom.

In the stall she put the toilet seat down and sat on top of it. She put her face in her hands and just cried. She cried so long a lady knocked on the stall door.

"Hello? Are you okay in there, honey? Is there something I can get for you?"

"No, thank you. I'm fine. I just need a minute."

Melissa gathered herself and ran a cold paper towel across her face, gave her eyes a minute to rid themselves of the red. She smoothed her clothes with sad hands and went back to join her baby's father, not her future husband, at dinner. It was going to be a long night. And Melissa didn't know if she had the faith to get through it.

+++

DeDe had called Malcolm's wife and assured her that she no longer had anything to worry about. "At least not from me . . . look, I'm sincerely sorry for any pain I may have caused you, but effective today, I am calling off this relationship with your husband." Of course she had tried to get some details out of DeDe, and DeDe, despite the fact that she had been so comfortable being the other woman, actually understood Tracy's need for information. But she also felt like that was Malcolm's duty. *He* had married her. Those details should come from him. She was serious about her promise though. So much so she told the wife before she told Malcolm. She had called him right after and let him know he might want to stop at the jeweler on the way home, pick up a little something, because wifey was gonna hit the roof. He called her all kinds of stupid bitch, which made her real happy that he had put her condo and car in her name. The last thing she needed was someone coming to collect. Maybe she was stupid for dealing with a married man, but she wasn't stupid enough not to put everything in her name.

Now she was moving on. And the sexy real estate agent was a key part of her plan. While at work the Monday after he put her house on the market, DeDe conversed with a colleague she also considered a friend—Lola.

"Lola, girl. I need you to do me a favor."

"Oh lord. I know your ass, De. What's up?"

"Call this number for me."

"What number? Who you trying to hook up with?"

"Shawn Wyatt. You know he does real estate on the side? He ain't here today, and I want him to take me out some time . . . see if we can't get something going."

"Girl, you crazy. And what you want me to say? He gonna be like why this grown-ass woman don't call me herself?"

"He ain't gonna think that, Lola. He's gonna think it's cute. Now call him for me. See if he wants to meet out for drinks tonight."

Lola took out her cell phone and dialed the number. While she listened to the ringing she watched DeDe dancing around like a little girl whispering, "I got a boy-friend. I got a boy-friend." Lola was shaking her head like—girl, you are crazy—when a man answered the phone.

"Hello, Shawn Wyatt?"

DeDe came close and put her ear to the backside of the phone as Lola carried on with the conversation. She could hear everything clear as day.

"My name is Lola and I'm DeDe's friend."

"DeDe?"

"Yes, DeDe. You're selling her condo for her."

"Oh yes. Ms. Kravitz. Is she okay?"

"Oh, she's fine."

"Um, I'm sorry, Lola, was it? Can you hold on one second."

The women listened while they heard some mumbling in the background. Shawn came back to the phone and asked Lola how he could help her.

"Well, I'm calling because my girl DeDe really thinks that you're quite attractive, and she'd like to get to know you. Would you be available for drinks tonight?"

"For drinks? Uh, no. Excuse me again."

This time DeDe and Lola could hear clearly. There was a woman in the background yelling, "Who the hell is that? What the fuck did she just say?" Before they knew it, the woman was on the phone.

"Who is this calling my husband?"

"Uh . . ."

"Guess what, baby girl, you don't even have to tell me. Check this. Mr. Wyatt is good and locked down with a bucket load of kids. Can you fit all five of them in your car? I didn't think so. And 'side from being a good faithful husband, Shawn has a crazy-ass Puerto Rican wife who has no problem putting a bitch in check, if you catch my drift. You know what they say about us little Spanish bitches—we'll cut a tramp without a second thought. So do yourself a favor honey, go on and lose this number. If he *was* your real estate agent, he is no more. Bitch, it looks like you're back at the drawing board 'cause my husband won't be selling anything of yours."

She hung up. DeDe and Lola heard the sharp clip of the call disconnecting and just stood there frozen in the silence, staring at each other like they were having a contest to see who could go the longest without blinking.

Lola broke the quiet with a short giggle. And when she couldn't hold it anymore, she busted out laughing. She ran around the classroom, holding her stomach and mouth in good pain.

"Girl! You didn't know that man was married with five kids?"

"No, Lola! I didn't. I told you I was trying to clean up my image. Now why would I go from Malcolm's no good ass to the same setup? He don't have no pictures on his desk! How he got five kids and a wife and no pictures up?"

"He don't have enough desk space for all those damn kids, that's why. Lord, DeDe you just can't win! You are attracted to married men like they honey and you the bee!"

Groaning, DeDe said, "Shat-up bitch. Whew! You never lied, Lola. But who is gonna sell my house now?"

"You better get Darlene on the phone."

"I think I messed that connection up, Lola. I was ignoring Darlene's calls trying to get in Mr. Wyatt's drawers. And now look at me. Nobody to sell my house, and nobody to help pay that big-ass mortgage either. Maybe I shouldn't have let Malcolm go so soon!"

"Maybe . . ."

DeDe said that stuff about not letting Malcolm go so soon, but she didn't mean it. First and foremost she had made a promise to God, but then she also had a promise to herself to live up to. The simple fact was that that little cuss out by Mr. Wyatt's wife was her final wake-up call. She was putting men on the back burner. They wouldn't get one more ounce of her energy. She was only giving herself to her music and to loving acts that showed she had some respect for herself.

+++

Michael was finally showing Jessie some consistency. She had gotten some good lovemaking every day for a week straight. He had only been with his boys one night, and even then he had invited her over later. She was on her way to the house when he called her on her cell phone.

She said, "Hey, babe. I'm right around the corner. I'll be there in a minute."

"Okay."

"What you call me for? You need something? Need me to stop at the store or something?"

"No. I'll see you when you get here."

Jessie thought that was a little strange and Michael had seemed a little worried. Jessie pushed on the gas a little harder. Maybe something *was* wrong.

She pulled into Michael's driveway and noticed that his car wasn't there. She thought that was weird. Maybe he had been in an accident. When she got to the door, it was Michael who let her in, and that was strange too because where was the maid? But Jessie didn't have time to ask any of those questions because Michael started talking before she could even get settled.

"Jessie, have a seat."

They were by the fireplace in the living room. Michael was drinking something with a deep brown hue. His forehead was wrinkled up in worry. Instinctively, Jessie wrinkled up her own face. Her eyebrows looked like they were going to kiss they were so close. She sat down on one of the plush love seats and tried to meet Michael's eyes. But he wouldn't look at her.

"Michael, what's wrong? Is everything okay? Is your daughter all right?"

"Yeah, yeah. Mikala is fine. Thank you. Look, Jessie, there's really no easy way to say this. I just got to come out with it. Jessie, I have syphilis."

I have syphilis. Jessie could not have dreamed that those words would have ever come out of his mouth. And instantly the world slowed down around her. It was like her senses shut down. She couldn't feel the leather cushions beneath her. She couldn't smell Michael's potent liquor even though she had noted its sharpness the moment she walked through the door. She couldn't taste the chewing gum in her mouth. And she could not see Michael standing before her. There was a man there, certainly, but he was a stranger. Nothing about him was familiar. Not his frown, his beard, the way he stood.

"Who are you?" she said in an almost whisper.

And while he stood there looking stupid, pretending to really wrestle with the question, Jessie recounted in her mind the times they had made love—none involved using a condom. She knew syphilis, if treated early, was curable, and that it had virtually little lasting effect on the body.

"How long have you had it? How long have you known you had it?"

"I just found out today, baby."

"Baby? Baby! Don't call me no fucking baby, Michael. You dirty-ass- motherfucker."

"Jessie, watch your mouth now."

"I'm not watching shit, nigga. Does this mean you been fucking other bitches the whole time you were screwing me? That's why I couldn't ever get up with your ass—why you was always nowhere to be found. Your ass was fucking."

"No, Jessie. That's not true. The doctor told me I could have contracted this several months ago."

"Could have? You don't even *know* when you got it, Michael? You still sound like a fucking whore, just like your damn brother. I guess the apple truly don't fall far from the tree."

"I know you better watch your mouth in my house before you get put out."

"Oh, okay. So first you gonna burn my ass. Maybe make it so I can't have babies. Maybe give me fucking brain damage—oh yeah, I know about STDs Michael—and then you gonna put me out the house? You're a class act, Michael. A typical ass nigga. You got a little change and a little vocabulary, but you the same as all the rest of these sorry motherfuckers running around here. If I didn't have enough going for me, I'd cut your ass."

Jessie got up from the love seat and dashed for her bags like she was running in the Pen Relays. She grabbed her stuff and darted to the door holding back tears and the overwhelming desire to spit right between Michael's eyes. She got in her car, but didn't have the strength to start the engine. She began to shake uncontrollably. Before she knew it, tears were streaming down her face mixing with mucus, and in less than a minute, she was a hysterical mess. She didn't even realize Michael had opened her car door. He pulled her from behind the steering wheel, scooped her up like she was a bag of laundry, and carried her back into his house. He walked her to his bed and laid her there. She was still crying, and he left for a moment to get tissues and a warm rag. He wiped her eyes, nose, and cheeks. And then he wiped her whole face, even as the tears continued to fall, with the warm rag. The whole time he was saying, "I'm sorry, baby. I'm sorry. I wasn't fucking around, I swear. This infection came from a long, long time ago. I only made love with you."

Before Jessie could even really register what was going on, Michael was kissing her. And what was probably crazier than the fact that he had his tongue down her throat was that she was letting him stick it there. She was naked soon thereafter and whispering, "I can't do this with you. I can't do this." But Michael swept her fears aside like they were a few strands of hair in her face.

"I got antibiotics, babe. For both of us. You didn't give me a minute. My boy, I mean my doctor sent me home with medicine. It'll be gone in a matter of days. Let me make love to you. Let me make it up to you."

And crazy as it seemed, Jessie made love to Michael again, without a condom, as if her life hadn't just flashed before her eyes, as if she had not just had her heart broken into three pieces. Jessie did not orgasm, but Michael did, and once he released everything in him, he fell beside her leaving her to her thoughts. She just didn't know anymore. She didn't know if any of this was worth it.

+++

Inside the studio the Divas were a little tense, to say the least. Darlene was avoiding DeDe over that trifling shit she had pulled. DeDe should have been feeling sorry but instead was contemplating her own loneliness and her new determination to beat it, the fact that Electra Sounds had not called her back, *and* how to make next month's mortgage payment without her sugar daddy Malcolm. Both Melissa and Jessie were reserved, their thoughts not focused on the show but on their separate personal matters. Pat was barely holding it together as Donnell had not returned any of her calls and had only texted to say the children were doing fine. Brit hadn't been married to Brass, but you couldn't tell her heart that. It was as disfigured as Pat's, and she had noticed what looked like FBI agents or something following her everywhere she went (they were outside the studio at that very moment). And then V had her same old fat-girl worries. She had just eaten a large pizza by herself before coming to the studio, and she was disgusted over her lack of control. Looking into the faces of those skinny women was not helping the matter. DJ Magic had to get things going. If he had left it up the Divas, they would have been sitting there all night, their eyes fixed on their microphones, and nothing coming from their mouths but sighs and small breaths.

"Good evening, Dallas. This is your boy Kirk 'Magic' Wonder. I'm in the studio with a bunch of the quietest ladies you ever did see. Yes, y'all, these women are actually lost for words. Now, I ain't no expert on women. All my exes will tell you that, but I do know when something's wrong with them. And ladies and gentlemen, something ain't right up in the K103.5 studios. Let me put on a little Beyoncé to cheer the ladies up. I suspect they need to be reminded they're their own best friends."

Magic spinned Beyoncé's "Me, Myself, and I" and took off his headphones to give a pep talk.

"I don't know what's going on. I have no idea why y'all sitting around this table acting like somebody done killed your best friend, but get your shit together. We got a show to do."

"He's right, y'all. We got a show to do," Melissa said. "And this show is supposed to help us through what we're going through right now. Let's let it be our therapy."

Jackie, Melissa's intern, walked over to Melissa and whispered something in her ear. "Well all right, Jackie. That's just what we need. Keep that caller on the line for me."

Beyoncé finished up the ballad, and Melissa put her game face on. "Hello, Dallas. Magic wasn't lying when he said the ladies and I are not at our best this evening, but we realize the love forum was designed just for times like this. We're gonna let y'all get all in our business in just a moment, but right now, we have a surprise caller on the line with a dedication. Jackie, what's the dedication?"

"Well, Melissa, this gentleman called and specifically requested that we play Gerald Levert's 'Mr. Too Damn Good,' and this goes out to one of our ladies on *The Love Forum*. He said that this comes from his heart, and that he wants to be the smile on your face . . . your sunny day . . . your breakfast in bed . . . your 'Mr. Too Damn Good' for you. He says listen to the words, baby, 'cause I'm going to be so good to you, your 'Mr. Too Damn Good' to you."

At that very moment, all the Divas perked up in their chairs, and each one of them, in the back of her mind, was hoping that the dedication was for her. As Magic began playing the song, Melissa began singing to the music, "Ah shucks now. Sing, Gerald, sing. Whew! 'Mr. Too Damn Good.' Yes!"

As the music played—and Melissa stopped singing and listened intently herself—all the Divas were bobbing heads, snapping fingers, and completely wrapped up in the lyrics, music, and mood. Each one secretly yearning for the caller to be her 'Mr. Too Damn Good.' And as the music faded, Melissa finally ended everyone's anticipation by saying, "Hello? Caller, are you there? This is the ever-so-sweet Melissa Morgan."

"Hello? Yes. Melissa? This is Miguel."

Darlene said, "Miguel? Hey, baby! Whatchu doing calling up here?"

"Yeah, Miguel, whatchu calling up here for?" Melissa echoed.

Miguel, clearing his throat, softly said, "*Oye bebé, usted es el amor de mi vida.*" Everyone turned and looked at Darlene, who was sporting a big smile on her face.

Melissa, beside herself by now, cried, "Girl, are you going to tell us what he just said?"

"Oh my god, Lis. He said, '*Hey, baby, you're the love of my life.*'" And all the Divas, at the same time, sighed and looked at Darlene with a special look and listened attentively as Miguel began to speak.

"Darlene, I know you've been hurt, and I know you're grappling with our love, but I want to be the one who eases your pain and helps you catch that love. When you feel like you can't go on, I want to be the one who provides the words of encouragement. When you stumble and fall, I want to be the inspiration that picks you up and puts you on solid ground. When your heart is empty, I want to be the fuel that fills you back up. Baby, I know there's baggage—and we all have some—but I'm willing to carry that baggage. And if you let me,

I'll show you that it's not too heavy nor is the load too great. Darlene, let me be your 'Mr. Too Damn Good.' I love you so much, baby. And I want to marry you. I'm calling to ask you to spend the rest of your life with me. I want to make you my wife. And I hope that you will say yes and consider moving to Brazil with me."

"What! Oh my God! Miguel! Are you serious? Are you for real?" He had answered all her prayers in one swoop, and his asking her to move to Brazil confirmed that the love was genuine. He wasn't just trying to get a green card.

"Yes he is for real, girl!" Melissa said. "Look out the window! You gonna marry the man or what?"

"Hell yes I'm going to marry him!"

Miguel yelled out like a little girl, "Yes!" and then said, "I love you, miss. I'm waiting right outside. I'm on my way up with the ring."

"Okay, okay! Dallas, you hear that? It took a Brazilian man to get it right. And he calls her 'miss,' okay! Darlene had to let go of the brothers to get this thing right. Magic, get that Larry Graham ready. This is going out to our newly engaged couple Miguel and Darlene. Congratulations and have a ball living this brand new life together. Here is the Dream Lovers' classic 'When We Get Married.' And when this beautiful song is through, we'll let you know how big . . . and clear—don't forget the clarity, y'all—the ring is."

The women left their sadness in their seats, if only momentarily, and jumped up to congratulate Darlene. DeDe was the first over there, and Darlene was so distracted that she fell into DeDe's hug without a thought about DeDe pulling that mess with the condo. By the time all the hugs had been given out, Jackie was opening the studio door to let Miguel in. In his hand was a typical ring box—a navy green velvet—but inside was anything but a typical ring. On his knees he revealed a ring as big as a cherry. The ladies put their hands over their eyes in mock disbelief. They started saying, "It's blinding me! I can't see!"

Melissa was back on the air by that time. "Well ain't this just about a [beep]! Dallas, the official word is in. The ring is a *banger*. I don't even know if Darlene's little skinny fingers can hold that mofo up! What do the Divas think?"

Jessie said, "That is a beautiful ring, Darlene. And broke as I am, you know I know jewelry, girl. He pulled out all the stops. He did not take that purchase lightly."

"Ooh, thank you, Jessie." Darlene was gawking at the ring like it was mesmerizing her. "I don't think I can make it through the rest of *The Love Forum*, y'all. I'm sorry. I need to get out of here and be alone with my fiancé."

"No, no, baby. Do your duty. Stay on this show and tell Dallas what real love is. I'm going to sit right over here in this corner and stare at your beautiful face. I'll be here waiting for you when you get done."

Melissa said, "Okay, Miguel. Don't come up in here being God's gift to women. You just rubbing it in now. Magic, I need to dedicate a song to my damn self! This is for my boo—you know who you are. I think I need to let the other person know how I really feel. Magic break me off a little new school, another Beyoncé joint, but this one ain't about no friendship. Magic put on that 'Single Ladies (Put a ring on it),' and let's see if I can't drive my point home."

Magic laughed at Melissa. "No doubt, M&M. I got you covered. Damn, Miguel done started something up in here tonight! I don't wanna hear none of my women's mouths either."

The Love Forum addressed the concerns of listeners later that night. They called in, and the women and Magic pushed forward as if the studio wasn't a collection of broken, healing, and hopeful hearts. The ladies went home—some to pure misery, others to loneliness, and one to pure bliss.

Chapter Fifteen

Sweet V's

December 13, 2008. V and her cousin Sweets stood in the middle of Sweet V's in awe. Darlene, using her banging real estate skills, found this beautiful historic building with floor-to-ceiling windows, distressed brick walls, and restored wood floors in the ideal location—downtown Dallas in Deep Ellum, just around the corner from the new metro station, and a few blocks down from Baylor Medical (the ideal spot for foot traffic). The interior décor (thanks to Sweets) was high chic with a less is more theme. It was just beautiful—from the custom made taupe wall curtains to the black and chrome salon chairs to the stainless steel and black slate fountain (which took up one whole wall). All the stylists' stations were complete with brand new appliances, styling tools, and all the fixings a beautician could want. The wood floors were polished so well they sparkled. V had always strived for independence—as far back as elementary school when she ran a lemonade stand for three straight summers on her momma's front lawn. Each year she made enough to buy her own school clothes—without being told what to buy and when to buy it—and she decided then that she didn't want to take orders from anybody. That ambition had been diluted a bit by the destruction of her marriage, but now, after some serious soul searching, she was back on course. Now Sweet V's—her and Sweet's full-service beauty salon—was a reality. The cousins gave each other a long hug, said some encouraging words to one another, and headed to opposite ends of the building to do some tidying up before the people started arriving for the grand opening. V was putting things here and there, wiping off the tops of things, and humming to herself when she was swept with a wave of gratitude. She took a seat and said a small prayer.

"Lord, I want to thank you, from the bottom of my broken heart, for seeing me through this. I was taking my husband's choices so personal. It was like he was a mirror of me. Anything he did, I assumed responsibility for. But that day is no more. And I give the glory of that to You. I trusted in You, who I should have trusted in from the beginning, and now I can accept that man for who and what he is, I can now appreciate his choices as having nothing to do with me, and I can step into my destiny and be all you intended. Thank you, Lord. Thank you."

"Amen," Sweets hollered. "Now come on here, girl. We got to open this joint up."

The partners headed to the front to open the doors for their first official day of business.

"Sweets! Can you believe this?" V was just overcome with excitement. She couldn't contain herself.

Sweets was extravagantly gay because, as he said, that was the only way to do it. He looked at his cousin like she was crazy. "What do you mean can I believe it? Of course I can, V. I ain't no slouch, and you ain't too bad yourself."

"Yeah, I know, but it was so much work."

"As is anything worth having. Now come on and welcome your crazy girlfriends in here."

The Divas were walking up the street when V and Sweets reached the door. One by one they filed into the salon. Their mouths opened in astonishment.

"Well damn, V! You weren't playing!" Melissa said.

Jessie backed her, "Yeah, V. This is just . . . I have no words . . . it's phenomenal. You are definitely putting the fire to my ass. I have got to get it together."

"Well ladies, you know what they say," Sweets interrupted. "If you can conceive it, then you can achieve it."

Just then, a rush of people entered the salon. V and Sweets had meticulously planned the opening—down to the six varieties of dip for the vegetables. There was food and wine, a manicurist, and a masseuse for any of the women needing to relieve some stress. Naturally, the sweet Melissa Morgan would be broadcasting live, right from the salon. As she, Magic, and Jackie set up, the wash girls took their respective clients and began to prepare their hair for the styling process. Before long, K103.5 was on the air and Melissa was up to her usual antics.

"Dallas, it's your girl Melissa, and me and the Divas are broadcasting live from Sweet V's—the brand new full-service beauty salon co-owned by the one and only V. Yes, the fabulous Vanessa and her too-fly cousin Sweets are open for business. Come on down, Dallas. We're on Gaston, right at the corner of Texas street. Get your hair done, have a glass of wine, get those cracked-up feet done, and let the masseuse work his magic on you . . . speaking of Magic . . . Magic, honey, please set this thing off right and play a little something for us."

As Magic went into a thirty-minute commercial-free stint, the other Divas took their seats in the salon chairs. As they were being rolled, conditioned, or blow-dried, they sparked up the sort of conversations a beauty salon always invites.

"You know, I just want to say I'm very proud of you ladies for going on the air, without fear, and sharing with the world your love woes. I know that has to be tough," one patron, getting her toes done, said.

"Yeah, having the world all in your business is not easy," DeDe said with a laugh. She was thinking about getting a few streaks to spice things up a bit.

"But it's helpful, though. I know just listening to *The Love Forum* I've wizened up a little," the woman said.

"But have the Divas wizened up is what I want to know. What about you, Ms. Jessie?" Sweets tapped Jessie on the shoulder just after he fastened her last roller into place.

"I don't even know, Sweets. I don't know if I'm wiser or not. I do know this man spends absolutely no time with me, and I spend my time nursing my heart. And I know my little heart feels more cracked than before. Does a broken heart equal wisdom?"

Sweets said, "I think so. First of all, you got to be grateful you can still feel pain. When something terrible goes down, and you can't feel the hurt, then you know there's a problem with your heart. Tin Man, honey, okay!"

"True," Jessie said.

Darlene said, "I don't see what in the hell a broken heart has to do with wisdom."

"Well you must not have had yours broken, love," Sweets said. "Now me? My heart is aching right this very minute."

"Aww, Sweets. I'm sorry to hear that," DeDe said. She gave her stylist the signal to go ahead with the highlights. "What happened?"

"This man is just all over the place. I can't pin him down. One minute he's ready, the next he isn't. He's still playing both sides of the fence, trying to pretend he's not gay as a jaybird. I'm discovering as many women's numbers as I am men's."

"Well how long y'all been together, Sweets?"

Just then V came through, making sure each of the clients was comfortable.

"Too long," V said. "Who wants wine?"

The clients raised their hands, and Sweets rolled his eyes. "Don't start with me, Ms. V. You just keep doing what you're doing . . . Todd and I have been together a few years, and I've lived through a slew of his bitches and stable of man whores, too. I know he's fucking around on me, and if this trick keeps texting him talking 'bout some damn 'Michael' I'm gonna go crazy."

Jessie felt her heart jump. *Did he just say Michael?*

V said, "I'm surprised Todd didn't hook up with my ex-husband. They would have been perfect for each other."

"Not that I'd put it past him, but I never heard anything about your hubby and mine, V."

While the other women chimed in on the conversation, Jessie whispered to Sweets.

"Sweets, what did you say about Michael?"

"Michael, honey. That's what his latest trick is calling him, I guess."

"Why wouldn't he just use his real name?"

"Well because 'Todd' is known for what Todd does. You see what I'm saying?"

Jessie went quiet for a while, just thinking. After a few minutes she came to the conclusion that "Michael" was about as common a name as they get. Nothing in Michael said "down low." He'd been married. He had a baby girl. His only problem was disappearing for days at a time, and she had seen that behavior time and again—and it absolutely always had to do with the brother chasing women, not men. Not to mention, he was just too manly to go that way. In a space of five minutes, Jessie had gone from having heart palpitations back to just plain old sad. Gay or not, Michael was still hurting her.

Sweets must have read Jessie's aura, because out of nowhere, he made a request. "Magic, play a little something for me." He placed his hand under Jessie's arm, motioned her out of her seat, and walked her to the dryer.

"What you want to hear, Sweets?" Magic said.

"It's not for me, Magic. Put on that Spinners remake for me. 'Love Don't Love Nobody' . . . I think Jean Carne sang it. Dedicate it to Ms. Jessie for me." Then he whispered into Jessie's ear, "Don't worry about it, baby doll. All God's doing is prepping you for the real love of your life."

Jessie was moved by his gesture, and at the same time, a little embarrassed that she was wearing her pain so obviously. She sat under the dryer with all those rollers taking up all the space above her and called Big Momma's name in her head. *I need you, Big Momma, and bad.*

Chapter Sixteen

The Final Forum

It was Wednesday when Jessie went to visit Michael at his condo. She was almost done with her antibiotics, and they had been speaking regularly, though they hadn't seen each other since he revealed he had syphilis. Jessie had also tested positive at her gynecologist, and the doctor said there was nothing to do but to continue to take the prescribed medicine and to return in a couple of weeks for a follow-up visit. She had decided that while there was a true possibility that Michael was sleeping with other women, she was going to give him the benefit of the doubt (even though he was Malcolm's brother). She appreciated his honesty and his desire to take care of her health, and well, she wanted to believe that he was falling for her as desperately as she was falling for him. But, still he was distant. He wasn't available. She could hold him with her hands, but not with her heart, because while he was sitting before her, his mind was elsewhere.

Jessie had noticed, for the second time, that his car was missing from the driveway and that there was no help around the house. She kept asking him, "What's wrong, baby? What is it?" But these questions held no weight because Michael not only didn't feel any drive to answer them, but he felt no drive to even acknowledge Jessie's presence.

They sat watching the end of *Boomerang* on BET (Jessie couldn't have guessed that Michael was nervous about the cable service being cut right in the middle of Eddie Murphy begging and pleading because he hadn't been able to pay the bill). Jessie just sat there on the verge of crying. She knew he was slipping through her hands. The whole time they were watching the movie Michael hadn't once stroked his finger across her thigh—which was in plain sight (she was wearing a little black mini-skirt)—like he normally would've. He did, however, begin a discussion on music after the movie ended though. Stacey

Lattisaw was playing on the screen during the credits. They talked about Stacey and Johnny Gill, and Jessie asked Michael to look up "Giving My All to You"—her favorite Johnny Gill song—on YouTube and play it for her. After he played, it he seemed like he was loosening up a bit. She was thrilled when he played Whitney Houston's "I Will Always Love You" and pointed it out as his favorite song. She thought he was warming up to her and maybe he wasn't slipping through her fingers. As a matter of fact, she thought, *Is this Negro trying to tell me something*? The dead butterflies in her stomach almost came to life, and the two of them spent the rest of the time listening to music and acting like, well, friends. At the end of the night they embraced like it was their last embrace—his arms seemed to say, *Goodbye, love. Goodbye*. Little did she know it would be the last time he'd hold her.

The next day Jessie was at work, doing more work than they paid her for, when she got a text message from Michael. It read: *My job denied my medical leave and then I was fired. I have no car if you hadn't noticed—they took it back. I had to let go of Martá and Consuela. I think I might lose my house*. The message stopped her mid-step. She took a deep breath and then ran to her cubicle. She sat down and collected her thoughts. What Michael was telling her might have turned off the average woman. The fact was that this was a turning point in the relationship—she was on the verge of love, but not dipped all the way in it. She could leave now while the going was good. What use was he with no job and no house and no car? He had failed Melissa's most basic test. But she felt an overwhelming need to comfort him.

She texted back: *It's gonna be okay, baby. We're going to get through this together*. Jessie still had no idea why he had been seeking medical leave, but she had an uneasy feeling. She thought about how he had given her syphilis and begged God to protect her from anything worse. *God, I swear to you. I won't ever let another man touch me without a condom if you protect me this one time. God, please*. The fact that she didn't feel comfortable asking Michael about his health should have been evidence enough that she probably shouldn't have been sleeping with him, but she could not untangle herself. She was happily, if nervously, stuck in his web. She wanted this thing to work worse than anything she'd ever wanted.

That night, she tried to contact Michael. She wanted to comfort him in his time of need. She wanted to cook for him, maybe even loan him a little money (lord knows she didn't have much to spare), but he did not respond to any calls or texts. She decided to drive by his house, just in case he was sulking and falling into a depression, but he was nowhere to be found. She even walked around the perimeter of the complex to look in his windows. He wasn't there, and she felt a mixture of emotions. She went to bed worried about him and sent a final text before closing her eyes in sleep: *I'm praying for you. I hope I can see you in the morning. I have tickets to the museum.* Naturally he didn't respond, and Jessie fell asleep held by her own embrace.

Waking up the next morning she did what she had done every morning for over a month—she lunged for her BlackBerry to see if it was flashing, if Michael had texted or called. If she was honest with herself she didn't expect to see his number across the screen, but still, her heart sank a little more every time she woke, stared at the phone, and saw that no one in the whole world had bothered to think of her. She texted Michael once more to see if he would join her at the museum. She was shocked to receive a response, but was even more surprised to read the message: *Who the fuck is this texting Todd at this time in the morning?*

She read the text several times, checking the phone number over and over again. It was Michael's number, she was sure, and she knew just who "Todd" was. Jessie knew without any hesitation that she was about to text back Sweets. *Oh Big Momma, why? Why me?*

She typed: *Who is this?* Despite knowing exactly who it was and that he would confirm her suspicions, she just had to know. She had to.

Sweets responded: *This is his man, bitch.*

His man? Jessie typed.

Yes, boo. His man. Now again, who the hell is this texting Todd at this time in the morning? He's asleep!

Jessie couldn't bring herself to type another word. She had had her worst fears confirmed and there was no denying it. She set her phone down and got into the shower to let the running water drown out her crying. When she got out, Sweets had left one last message. Her stomach was one big knot as she read it: *Look here, bitch. You're one of many, okay? His name ain't no Michael, he don't love you, and your future together is NONEXISTENT. Do yourself a big old favor and lose his number.* If she were high yellow, Jessie would have turned beet red. If she were the queasy type, she would've purged last night's dinner all over the floor. Jessie grabbed her chest, feeling a true physical pain—the hurt was manifesting itself in her bones—and slumped to the ground. She curled herself into a ball and began crying again.

In the hour spent on the floor hugging herself, Jessie recounted her whole experience with Michael, trying to determine if she had missed any signs. How in the world did she fall for a gay man? But as she racked and racked her brain she came up with nothing. Sure he was giving her the unfaithful signals—nowhere to be found, distance, a lady's man when in her presence—but nothing . . . not one thing that would make her believe he had an alternative lifestyle. She was still sniffling when she felt Big Momma's presence in the room. Big Momma told her to get up off that floor. She asked Big Momma, *I can't get a minute?*

And Big Momma, sweetly, but firmly, said, *No, baby. You can't. You got to see your way through this and the first step is walking out that door. Now, baby girl, now!*

Jessie went to the museum. Even with the devastating news still on her mind. Her eyes were vacant as she perused the beautiful building all alone, but the point was that she hadn't stopped living for anything for more than an hour. Her imagination was giving her terrible things to think about—HIV and the utter falseness of their relationship. She felt foolish. When Michael actually called, it threw her off. She had subconsciously ended the relationship, so to hear his voice on the other end of the phone was startling. It was around three. She was on her way to get some Mexican food for a late lunch. Despite her stomach's nervousness, she knew she had to eat. But with the appearance of those digits, Mexico, its food, and any thoughts of eating went out the window. And while Jessie knew she had all the proof she needed, she needed to hear it from Michael himself.

"Hello?"

"Hey, baby. It's me. What's going on? I'm sorry I couldn't get to the museum this morning, but you know me . . . I really don't do the mornings."

She had forgotten all about the museum being a joint visit.

"Oh no, it's fine."

"So what's going on?"

"Michael, I got some strange messages from your phone number this morning."

"Huh? What messages?"

"Well, there was someone texting me saying that your name wasn't Michael. Whoever it was said your name was Todd."

"Todd? What the hell? You must have me mixed up with someone else, baby girl. Did you check the number?"

"Yeah. Several times. It was yours. The person said you bat for the other team, Michael. He said you were gay."

And as Jessie expected, Michael was silent. The silence was brief, but noticeable, and in that time she was able to bite her lips closed and pinch her eyes shut to hold back the tears.

"Look . . ."

She thought he was about to confess and ran to a nearby bench. *God, Big Momma, I need both of y'all for this one.*

"I don't know who the hell was texting you, but it was no one from my camp, and they certainly not saying what you say they said. And I'ma tell you what—if I was near you right now, I'd slap the shit out of you for saying that dumb shit to me."

While Jessie hollered and screamed and said, "I don't know who the hell you think you're talking to," and threatened Michael, his heart was busy trying to beat itself outside of his chest. He looked down to see if his shirt was waving under the power of the blood being pumped through him. His slick words and bravado certainly didn't reflect what was going on in his head. That dumb-ass nigga Sweets had picked up his phone while he was sleeping—again. He was a sneaky-ass nigga and so caught up in the idea of them being together full time. He had been telling Sweets for over a year now that he was not coming out. He liked things the way they were, and if Sweets couldn't get with it, he was going to have to get lost. Not only that, but if Michael was to come out, he wouldn't be that hounding man's dude. Sweets was too damn desperate and possessive—worse than a damn woman. And Michael was beyond tired of talking his way out of these types of situations. Jessie was the third woman in a year Sweets had pulled this shit on. Jessie was still going off on the other end of the phone when Michael regained his composure.

"Look, Jessie. I'm sorry. I didn't mean to be so disrespectful, but what you're accusing me of is some serious shit. You can't just go around calling men gay. That's nothing to play with. I love pussy. And I thought you understood that. I have no idea what could have happened. I don't know where these mysterious messages came from, but, baby, you got to believe me, they have nothing to do with me."

Jessie had been here plenty of times before—you present your boo with some incriminating evidence; you have a pair of purple drawers pinched between your nails so as not to get some other woman's coochie juice on your hands; you KNOW the things aren't yours because you're a size extra small and these things are an extra large; you're yelling and screaming, talking about, "I hope the pussy was good nigga, 'cause you're on your way out the door"; and somehow, some way he convinces you that they're his mother's panties and that she stopped by the apartment to shower the other day. Then all a sudden the two of you are cuddled up before a movie and you don't even remember the words purple or panties. She knew Michael was feeding her a heap of bullshit, but his words, the tone of his voice, how genuinely angry he seemed at her accusation made her want to believe absolutely everything he said.

"Baby?"

"Yeah, Michael?"

"Have I ever lied to you? Have I ever been dishonest? Didn't I come to you the moment I found out I had that disease? Didn't I take care of you? Don't you know all my deepest, most shameful secrets? I told you about my ex-wife trying to commit suicide—I ain't never told nobody that! My very best friends don't know that shit. My momma don't even know I been laid off, but you . . . you, Jessie. You know these things, and it's because I trust you, baby. And I'm going to need you to trust me in return. I don't know what went down with my phone. A couple of my homeboys stayed over my house last night. Maybe those fools got in my shit and are playing a game, I don't . . . I'll ask them, but girl, don't do this to me. Don't doubt me this way."

Jessie bought it all—hook, line, and sinker.

"Michael, I'm sorry. I'm sorry I doubted you. You just don't understand what it was like getting those messages this morning. Boy, I had written you off."

"I can imagine. That shit ain't funny! But, babe, I'm telling you, I'm not that nigga. I'm a man. And I love women. I'm trying to love you . . . if you'd let me."

If Michael didn't have a pot to piss in or a window to throw it out of, he had game. Throwing in the "wanting to love her" line sent Jessie's mind in a whole different direction. She wasn't thinking about that damn Sweets.

"You just don't know how happy it would make me to see you today, Michael. I would love to spend the night with you."

"Okay, well let me see if I can't work that out. I'm going to give you a call later, okay? And I'm going to get to the bottom of this text message bullshit, too."

"Okay, baby."

But that promise to call was never realized. Jessie waited by the phone, patient as a spider, but Michael never bothered to call. She went to bed for the third night in a row with no one to hold her and a dozen unanswered questions. Saturday night was no different as Michael chose to hang with the fellas once again.

The only thing that distinguished Sunday from that whole disappointing weekend was that Michael had sent a text message.

Jessie picked up her BlackBerry half annoyed, half yearning for his attention, really wanting to hear that he'd cleared up that whole gay incident. His text message read: *Jessie, I really don't think there is any point in trying to pursue anything here. There's just too much confusion. I don't see anything positive coming out of this. God bless you and all that you do. THIS IS TOO MUCH WORK WAY TOO SOON!*

"Well I ain't need to see that shit in all capital letters!"

She put her own fingers to work: *I agree, Michael. That's why I told you to take care of yourself at your house Wednesday. We're obviously at different points in our lives. You know, I'm employed. You're not. I have a car. You don't. You're diseased. I'm not. Then again, we do agree on one thing, don't we? We both love MEN!*

She held down the delete button (she saw Big Momma's face and heard her voice say be the lady that you are). She didn't want to get nasty, even though she was hurt . . . and confused. She tried it again: *It's time I followed my instincts and not my heart. This was really over some time ago. You knew that better than I did.*

Despite the fact that Jessie had kept it respectful, almost kind, Michael came back with his teeth drawn: *Yeah. I kinda knew we were wasting our time.*

Jessie was flushed with the thought, *Unfucking believable, bitch-ass nigga!* She let it go though. She put the phone down, took a bath, and when she got out, she dialed V and Melissa and put them on the three-way speaker.

V said, "Mmm. Ain't that a bitch. So that fool wants you to believe those text messages just materialized out of thin air? What the hell? Is his BlackBerry a goddamn Ouija board or something? He got ghosts sending his text messages? Then he going to play you for the weekend, spending time with his homies, and if you would have planned something for Sunday, you either would have been stood up or treating his ass to something he couldn't afford, just for him to break it off with you afterward. Well you a smart bitch for handling the breakup in such a classy way. I knew I taught you how to handle your business. Now if we can just teach Brit a thing or two."

Melissa had a slightly different take on the situation. "Uh-uh, girl. Your man—in less than forty-eight hours—has broken two of our four coveted rules. Does he have a job? No. Does he have a car? No. His ass almost don't have a house! It leaves you to wonder if he's actually divorced. Didn't you say he was Malcolm's brother! Humph, two damn peas in a pod—if he ain't chasing the dick, oh please believe he's chasing skirts! And, Jess, you know your sister is saving the last of the three Ds for last. Baby girl, besides those so-called mysterious text messages . . . I mean even if they were from one of his homeboys playing around, what man spends that much time with his homeboys instead of trying to find something lasting? Or, at the very least, trying to get some butt? Either he's really immature, your successful future has scared him off and he doesn't think he can compete now that he's been fired and thus treat you like you're accustomed to being treated, or, and I hate to say this, that other life you're suspecting? It's alive and well. Whatever the hell is going on, one thing is for sure, that breakup sounds pretty fishy, almost like it was premeditated. He suddenly wanted to breakup when it was time to explain those suspicious-ass messages? He knew exactly what ticked you off, and he was just waiting for the perfect opportunity."

Jessie didn't want to bring this up to the girls, but she was considering just letting it all go. She didn't have much more to say to Michael or Todd or whoever he was. She didn't plan on confronting him or getting to the bottom of anything.

"Oh hell no!" Melissa and V shouted at the same time.

Melissa said, "Jessie! What the hell are you talking about? You don't just let no shit like this go, girl! This nigga has crossed you. He crossed you, and now you got to cross his confused ass back. Playing those kinds of games, I wouldn't be surprised if his ass gave you a disease or something."

Now Jessie was wishing she hadn't said a thing. She must have taken too long to answer.

Again V said, "Oh hell no! That nigga burnt you, didn't he? I bet that nigga *is* a flaming fucking fag. Who's he seeing, my ex-husband?"

"V, shut up. You don't know what to say out of your mouth," Melissa said.

"Oh, bitch, please, like I don't have experience in that department! Hello, ex-husband? What should I have said?"

"Look, that's not the issue. The issue is making sure Jessie is safe. Look, Jess, you know my homegirl is a gynecologist over at the county hospital. Let me get you an appointment over there. We'll make sure you check out, and then whatever you decide to do—confront this nigga or not—I will support you . . . fully."

"Thank you, Lis."

"Yeah, I guess I support you, too."

"Thank you, V. I really appreciate it."

"We just don't want to see you hurt. You know that. And if that means busting out the brass knuckles, then so be it. But Ms. Jessie is ever the lady, and I can ride that train, too."

"'Preciate it, Lis. I'll talk to you divas later."

Jessie got off the phone not feeling any better. Maybe she was being completely gullible buying his story about not knowing anything about the text message. She could get to the bottom of it all and dial-up Sweets, but she just didn't want that man all up in her business—which was precisely why she left out that very important detail when on the phone. And when it was all said and done, Jessie found herself sitting at her kitchen table with a mug of hot chocolate contemplating how she might have saved the relationship. For days after, she thought and prayed and questioned herself about how she could have handled the situation differently, but she continued to come up blank. Maybe she gave up too much of herself, was too available, too nice. No doubt putting sex into the mix didn't help things (Big Momma always said, "Sex too early won't hurt a good relationship, but it will hurt a bad one"). But even considering all that, at the end, Michael just seemed like an asshole. She decided to be honest with herself and own up to the fact that he had probably done everything that he had done intentionally. He knew exactly what set her off. That inconsiderate bullshit of choosing the boys over her and failing to call and at least say, "Hey, I'm not going to make it." It was like he figured three straight days of rejection with a final push at the end would put her over the edge. Whether he was gay or not he sure as hell was mean. And, she couldn't help but ask herself, *Am I better off?*

+++

December 14, 2008. Wow, the last show was finally here. We sat around the table, and Melissa cued to us that we were on the air in five . . . four . . . three . . . two . . . one. The Supremes' "Someday We'll Be Together" began to play, and we all looked around smiling—some smiling more than others, but smiling nonetheless—and Melissa began singing and DeDe followed: "*Just to kiss your sweet, sweet lips baby, hold you ever, ever so tight and I want to say someday we'll be together . . .*"

Soon we were all singing: "*Ah, yes we will, yes we will, someday, we'll be together.*"

"103.5, 103.5, 103.5!" Melissa let out a big sigh. "This is your girl, the ever-so-sweet Melissa Morgan, and as Boyz II Men put it, we've come to the end of the road baby. Yes D-town, we've reached the last broadcasting of *The Love Forum*. Here with me tonight are all the Divas, looking ever so pretty I might add—thanks to Sweet V's beauty shop! Dallas, say hello for the last time to Brit, DeDe, Darlene, V, Pat, and Jessie, along with our emotional guru, Dr. Laura, who has definitely kept it real and on point for us. Oh, and we can't forget our boy, the bad boy of radio himself, Mr. Kirk 'Magic' Wonder, doing what he does best—" Melissa began laughing, then said, "Keeping the Divas in check! So K103.5 listeners, it's been an interesting six months. Whew, to say the least! We've met some interesting characters, had some relationship meltdowns, an engagement, numerous revelations, and drama, and more drama, and more drama topped off with extra drama, but thank God, Ms. Celie, we're all here!" We all cracked up at Melissa's crazy tail—that girl and *The Color Purple*.

"And what have those six months told me? Humph! Now I know why there are so many angry sistas in the world, that's what. But rather than put my girls through the pain of retelling their lot of sad stories again, I'm just going to quickly sum it up for you. Pat's husband Donnell, who we thought at the beginning of the forum was the best damn thing since sliced bread, has not only filed for divorce, but put my girl out of the house. Well, let me be accurate. He didn't put her out, but he didn't offer to leave, knowing full well her babies are in that house. Jessie's pretty ass got a breakup text—not even a call, let alone a damn dinner date and some diamond earrings for the road—and is struggling to come to terms with that. We remember Brit's drama with that dirty-ass dog Brass—well he left her ass again. DeDe finally let go of a certain someone and tried to get it cracking with someone else, but that other someone's wife stepped in and karate chopped that plan in half. V is going through her own woes, self-induced maybe, but woes nonetheless. And as for myself, life and love has thrown some curveballs my way. My beloved, on discovering that I'm expecting—yes, Dallas, your girl Melissa is going to be a momma—was not inspired to jump the broom. On the other hand, our girl Darlene shared a wonderful experience with the K103.5 family. Her boo, Miguel, proposed right here on *The Love Forum*, but it may be bittersweet for the Divas, as she may be leaving the states to make Brazil her home. So Darlene, you are the only one holding down the fort. You're the only one with some good news. And what do ya know? Your man is two shades *behind* black. K103.5, what's really going on between the brothers and sisters when it comes to relationships?"

I was a million miles away despite being right there in the studio booth with the ladies. They all had their own problems, and my heart was aching for them, but my focus was on my own terrible situation. I felt the tears well in my eyes, and I knew, in that instant, that it was all too much for me. My eyes started stinging from fighting to hold back my tears, and I felt chills take hold of me. Just when I thought I would lose control—I felt my cell phone vibrate. It was enough to distract me for a moment, and when I looked down at the text, I felt God was behind it. It was Dr. Wilma. She wrote: *Melissa told me you're wearing your grief. Do you need to talk? I'm here at the office, come see me.*

Without much explanation, I left the final forum. I wish I could have been there to say goodbye properly, but I couldn't stand the pain. I was obviously wearing it like a garment because the Divas didn't stop me. They just sent me off with encouraging words and sympathetic smiles.

+++

The Divas watched as Jessie walked out the door, and each said a little prayer for her. Each woman knew that whatever Jessie was going through must be heavy, as it wasn't like Jessie to skirt her responsibilities. They tried to continue with the show, and they did the best they could without her but the overall feeling wasn't the same. Still, the show had to continue. Darlene explained why her relationship had flourished while everyone else's had failed.

"You know what they say, Melissa. Black is wack! Ha! No, I'm just playing, but y'all cannot deny the trend here. I'm thinking it's time that my ladies look outside the race. The grass *is* greener on the other side. I'm just saying . . ."

"I don't know, Darlene. I'm not quite ready to go that route," Melissa said. "I'm going to give the brothers a few more rounds, but you do bring me to a good point. You know we're coming up on the holiday season. If you ask me, it's no surprise that Christmas is right around the corner and the majority of us are, what? Say it with me, Dallas—single!"

"Oh hell yes," DeDe chimed in. "I know all about this trick, Melissa. And I think I should be the one to run it down to the listeners since I wasn't dumped, per say, but was the one who did the dumping."

"Puhlease, DeDe," Darlene said. "What the hell does that matter? Your ass just wants some more airtime on the radio since beginning your campaign to clean up your image."

"Dallas, I'm going to let Darlene pass on that one because, as she said, I'm trying to clean up my image. That said, ladies, if your man inexplicably starts picking little pointless fights right about now, talking about y'all need a break, asking you why you wearing that short-ass skirt for other men to see when he the one who bought it, or huffing and puffing about how much money he don't have—please don't be surprised when you get the 'I need some space' text. He is trying to save money! He does not want to put in on a gift for you. Do *not* be fooled. Do *not* take that fool back without a ring in hand. Holla!"

"So you're saying don't take him back, DeDe? Okay. What do you think, Darlene?"

"You know me, Lis. I don't like that phony mess. If you can't afford a gift, just say that. I mean if we're supposed to be in a relationship, communication of that kind should not be an issue."

"Yeah, but what if by admitting to not being able to get a gift, it makes a man feel less than a man?" V said.

"If you can't feel less than a man with your woman then maybe you don't have the right woman. I'm who you're supposed to be able to be vulnerable with."

"I know that's right, De."

"I hope Dallas is listening!" Melissa thumped the microphone with her finger. "Hello? Is this thing on? Do not throw your relationship away over a Christmas gift!"

V said, "I don't know about that. I mean, what man can't afford a Christmas gift? Does he have a car full of kids? Well if he does, I don't want him anyway. I mean, does he have a problem saving? Does he make minimum wage? All those factors make me not want his ass in the first damn place. I'm here to speak for the women who don't play that. Don't walk through that door Christmas morning without a gift in your hands. If you're empty-handed, just don't even come."

"Well damn, V. You just contradicted my whole argument," Melissa said.

"No, Lis, I gave another perspective. Men know what kind of women they have. He knows if his girl is gonna cut his ass over a gift, and he knows if he's got a 'ride or die' chick."

"Hold up, V," Brit demanded. "So if you have all these stipulations on what a man can and can't have then you should be able to understand why some men don't want an overweight woman."

"Oooh!" Melissa said. "And on that note, we're going to switch the subject."

V just stared at Brit, and Brit was taking that look like a real woman. Away from the mic she said, "Look, V. It is what it is."

V said, "You damn skippy. But I got something for your ass. I got something for all you skinny bitches. Ms. V is about to let go of all this excess baggage weighing her down. The Chinese food spot ain't gonna hear my voice for a long-ass time."

Melissa spoke above the whispers, "Well let's say your man does break up with you right before the holidays. Do you take him back afterward?"

Pat did not find this conversation the least bit comical. Her voice was man-deep when she said, "Hell to the *no*, you don't take that man back. He can't just walk in and out of your life whenever he got the feeling. This ain't Macy's! Ain't no revolving door. It's one way in and one way out, and you can only use each door one time."

"All righty then. Looks like we got our final answer to that one. Let's go to the phone lines to answer this next question. What if you are fortunate enough to have a man who doesn't play those games. You can count on him to be around for Christmas, right. So what do you ask him for? Ladies, call up and let us know what the best Christmas gifts are. While we're waiting for you, let's listen to Ms. Janet 'If You're Nasty' Jackson. Magic, put on that 'What Have You Done For Me Lately.' You know, just in case we got a couple of brothers out there suffering from relationship amnesia."

The callers had all sorts of suggestions for the best Christmas gifts from brand new Lexuses to spa visits to quality time. That segment of the show put a few smiles on a few of the ladies' faces, but most of them were still struggling through their pain. Even Melissa was just sort of coasting through the segments.

"Okay, Dallas. It's time to get a little serious again. I hate to do this to you. I wish we could just talk about brand new cars and diamond bracelets, but if we did that we would not be serving the love forum's purpose."

"Oh lord, Melissa! What you about to hit us with?" DeDe asked.

"Well, I'm thinking about Jessie's situation. What the listeners don't know is that Jessie is no longer in the studio with us. She couldn't stick it out. Our girl's heart is broken—though she probably won't admit it. But her situation has made me put on my thinking cap. I'm wondering about what you do when you're still in love with someone who has, in essence, moved on. What do you do in that situation? Do you get even, or do you simply keep moving forward? Unfortunately, Jessie was the victim of a trifling breakup. Now y'all know if I tell you it was trifling then it was trifling. This so-called breakup was premeditated. I mean that trifling-ass saboteur—I won't name names—did our girl dirty. Callers, give me a ring and let me know your thoughts. What should our girl Jessie do?" Melissa would never reveal the true details surrounding Jessie and Michael, but she thought hearing some suggestions about how to get over a breakup might help her help her friend. The callers' answers to the breakup question varied, but kept the other ladies of the forum in high spirits despite their individual circumstances.

"I'ma tell you what. Jessie better carry her pretty ass over to his crib and bash in all those damn windows."

"Now why would she get even? She is better than that. Let that cornball float on. Float on, Negro! Float on! Don't nobody over here want your black ass anyway!"

"Forget what all those other callers say, Melissa. You tell Jessie put on the freakum-girl dress, get a pint of light liquor—whatever she likes—and make that call. Yes, *that* call. Nothing makes you feel better than sex with an ex! And then she can take her tail to work the next day and make that money!"

"Well, Dallas, you certainly have no shortage of opinions!" Melissa was finishing up that segment with a slight growl in her stomach. She had eaten two bowls of cereal before sitting down in the booth, but the baby was demanding a refill already. She wanted the remainder of the show to hurry along. Her little pooch was turning into quite the gut, and her eating habits were partly to blame. "Now, DeDe, you know you've got some explaining to do."

"What you mean, Melissa?"

"What do I mean? Stop playing, girl. You need to explain why you got wives calling up to my station!"

"Oh."

"Yeah, 'oh.' Well?"

"I'm gonna keep it funky, Lis. Yes, Dallas, I was dating a married man, but it did not start out that way. Malcolm did not reveal his marital status to me until *well* into the relationship."

"How 'well'?"

"Well! I mean we had been dating for six months before I had my suspicions confirmed."

"Oh, so you knew?"

"In retrospect, I can say I did know, but at the time I kept pushing the idea out of my head. I did not want him to be married. I needed him not to be married. I mean, I was in—"

"Oh lord, De! You were in love with him?"

"Damn Melissa, I feel real messed up saying this on the air knowing good and well he has a family out there, but yes. I mean, I was with him for a whole year. Washing his socks and making his dinner like I was the wife! You know he helped me buy my condo and Benz."

"Yes, girl, I know. So what were the signs you ignored? Ladies! Listen up!"

"The holiday thing, of course. I *never* got a holiday. Certainly not a Christmas or Thanksgiving or Valentine's Day, but not even a damn Labor Day!"

"Oh no, De. And what did he say to explain that behavior?"

"Well, he's a busy and successful man. Work was always the reason behind his absence, and then, what can I say, the day after was *always* on point. A nice little gift and then lots of wild lovemaking."

"So when did he come out with it, De? Oh, hold on, De. Jackie is telling me the Mrs. is on the line! Do you want to take this call? You know what, I'm not even going to make you answer that on the spot. Magic, put that Shirley Murdock on, you know the one! We're gonna take a small break and see if we really want to go this route."

Magic threw on that Shirley Murdock, and the ladies just stared at one another across the table.

Pat was trembling when she spoke, "Well shit, bitch. This is what the fuck happens when you break up happy homes."

"No you don't, Pat," V said. "You don't take your troubles and put them on DeDe. I ain't saying she right. I ain't saying she right at all. But number one, she is God's child just like you and me are. Number two, she is righting her wrong. And number three, which might even be more important than one or two, she is your friend."

Pat put her head down and started to sob. Brit ran over to comfort her.

"What you wanna do, De? You want to take this call on air? You got a lot to think about! You got a career to build, babe! I mean the call could go beautifully. She might not be calling up here to act like a fucking lunatic. She might put the blame where it belongs—on her husband. But what if she doesn't? What if y'all get to fussing and carrying on, on the air? Electra Sounds might never call you back, girl. And I can't lie, my ratings would be through the roof. But I'm not willing to risk your career over this. You been hungry for this a looooong time."

"Number one, I don't know *what* the fuck this bitch is calling up here for. I called her ass before I called Malcolm. I had this talk with her already. She can't have nothing but bad in mind."

Pat said, "Can you blame her?" But nobody paid her any mind.

"Oh, so this bitch is calling up here trying to start some shit. Oh okay. I got something for her ass! Magic, keep that music going for a while. We gonna pretend like we on the air and see just what this tramp is trying to do. I'm the last one to be breaking up a marriage, but you ain't gonna call up to my station trying to set some shit off with *my* girls! I mean what more do she want? You broke the shit off! Jackie, put that woman through."

The women assumed their seats around the table and everyone but Brit and Pat looked ready to pounce.

"Hey, Dallas, this is your girl the sweet, sweet Melissa Morgan. We're back with a doozy. You know our girl DeDe was involved with one Malcolm 'Cole,' a married man. Well DeDe broke it off but his wife is on our phone lines. Hello?"

"Yes, I'm here."

"Good evening, Tracy. How can we help you?"

"Yeah. Look. I'm just calling up this bitch to tell all of Dallas that that bitch is burning! Yes the fuck she is. That bitch's dirty ass gave my man two diseases! Yes two, and one of those, bitches, ain't got a cure if you know what I'm saying."

"You broke-down bucktooth bitch! Ain't nobody burn your husband. I never even fucked the nigga raw. So what are you talking about?"

"Yes you did, bitch. He told me about the pregnancies. Bitch, you been pregnant three times and ain't got one kid. So what that tell you? And bitch, you better keep an eye on that cheap-ass Benz 'cause I'm coming for it. And your little-ass condo is about to be my rental property 'cause I know you can't make those payments by yourself. Any of you, bitches in there need a place to stay? What about the Pat chick that don't have a house anymore? Or V's single, fat tail. Or better yet, DeDe, you can stay there. Bitch, make the rent check out to Mrs. Cole, and on the memo line put—For the woman I wish I was."

"And on that note, get this crazy-ass bird off my phones, Jackie."

Jackie disconnected the call. The women were silent for a short while before V busted out laughing. No one else really thought it was funny though.

"Well I'm definitely going to the gym. Random bitches calling up here talking about how fat I am. And you better be glad Melissa got that good head on her shoulders, DeDe. 'Cause, honey, all your business was about to be in the streets! And why you ain't tell us about all those babies and diseases, girl? I just drank after you."

"Shut up, V. You know that crazy-ass bitch was lying."

Melissa said, "Damn, DeDe! Your career was nearly down the drain!"

"Yeah, Lis. Thanks, girl."

Just then, Dr. Laura walked into the studio, and Jackie took a call. Because they had not been on the air, Dr. Laura had no idea about what had just transpired. The women said their hellos, and Jackie got Dr. Laura's tea while holding the phone to her ear. No one felt compelled to bring Dr. Laura into the drama.

Magic was about to cue Melissa to get ready to return to the air when Jackie yelled, "Don't go back on yet!"

Magic was swift with the ones and twos, and at that point, used to all the twists and turns the evening had taken, so he just threw on Monica's "Sideline Ho." DeDe gave him a look, and he winked at her.

Melissa said, "What happened, Jackie? Don't be stopping the show for that crazy-ass wife of Malcolm's!"

"It's not that, Ms. Melissa. Ms. Pat, your son—"

"My son what?" Pat jumped out of her seat and all the ladies, including Dr. Laura, were on guard. "My son what, little girl?"

"Ms. Pat, he's in the hospital. They say he drowned."

"What!?" Pat hollered like she had watched Matthew drown. She shot out of the studio like lightning. And all the women, Melissa included, flew out behind her.

"Me and Dr. Laura and Jackie gonna hold it down, girls! Go take care of that boy," Magic yelled to their backs. While the Divas were making wind with their legs and Pat's heart was feeling like it was resting in her throat, Magic got on the air.

"Dallas! I know y'all are out there jumping in your seats! Got the radios turned up and everything, but I am sorry to disappoint you gossip hungry fools! The conversation took place off the air and let's just say the ladies have settled their differences! DeDe is a single woman who has learned from her past mistakes and who has vowed to never break up another home again—willingly that is—and of course, she will keep her ears and eyes open for all the signs she ignored before. I am your boy Kirk a.k.a Magic, and I will be holding down the remainder of the show. I know what y'all are thinking! The ladies trashed the studio and are on their way to the police station in cuffs. Nope! I will just say that one of our beloved Divas is having a family emergency and needs your prayers. While we are hoping and praying, the lovely Dr. Laura is going to weigh in on all this drama. Dr. Laura, please help us make sense of this mess."

"Good evening, Magic. I'm happy to hold down the fort with you. I guess I'll go on and start with Melissa's drama. Of course I want to congratulate her on her pregnancy. And before I weigh in on the other ladies, I would like to offer the host of the forum a few words. Ladies in the Dallas listening area, please take heed if you're in a similar situation."

"Dr. Laura, I don't know Melissa very well . . . I mean, we're brand new friends, but I do know that she is a very open-minded woman who is always looking for an easier, better way to do things. So on her behalf, I will welcome this advice."

"Well Magic, Melissa, and listeners in her predicament, you may not find this easy to hear, but Melissa's man *telling* her he didn't want to be married instead of going with the flow, marrying her, and then breaking her heart later deserves all of Dallas's applause! That honesty is not easy to come by. Now, on another note, I'd give him a time limit. Make a decision. Ladies, ask yourselves—how long are you willing to wait for marriage? And I would not suggest anything more than eighteen months. If he does not have himself together in that time, you need to move on with your life. Just remember, you aren't the first single mother and God knows you will not be the last! A broken family does not have to have any less love than an unbroken one. Now for Melissa's sake, I hope he pulls it together, but her focus, and the focus of all of Dallas's pregnant single women should be their health and the health of those unborn babies. Amen! Listen to me amening myself! Now for Jessie's situation. I hope Ms. Jessie has the strength to be listening to this right now, wherever she is."

"She's probably helping with that family emergency, Dr. Laura."

"Oh yes, forgive me, Magic. I am not being insensitive. I've just been working hard all week."

"I'm sure the ladies understand, Doc."

"Good. Jessie . . . sweetie. I'm going to come at her from a spiritual perspective because I'm quite sure she's aware of all the mistakes she's made. If I was talking to Jessie right now, if she was sitting across from me, I would say to her, 'Jessie, honey, I want you to promise me that you will not internalize this experience other than to appreciate the lessons you've learned from it. In other words, I want you to know that his rejection of you does not, by any means, determine your self-worth. The queen, Ms. Aretha Franklin, was not lying when she said, "A Rose is Still a Rose." Just because *this* man did not want you does not mean no other man will.' And, on another note, I just want to say how foolish he is! Girl, you're drop dead gorgeous. That goes for Ms. Pat, too." Dr. Laura shook her pointer finger like Pat was still sitting across the table. And then felt a sudden rush of sadness for her.

"And what about DeDe, Dr. Laura. Can you get in her ass please?"

"Ha! Magic, I think you and I are enjoying our new jobs a little too much. Listen, Dallas, I'll say this about DeDe—she is one of many. Women have been sleeping with married men since the beginning of time. That act is old as prostitution. Now we agree that the husband is the one who owes the wife his fidelity, and I think that's how mistresses justify what they're doing. Now, I'm not gonna fuss at the brothers this evening because our focus is De, but black men y'all know better! But back to the mistress's role. Listen to me, women. You deserve to be the wife. Do you hear me? I'm going to say those words one more time. You deserve to be the wife. Figure out what it is in you that says you deserve second best. Figure it out—and fix it!"

"Amen, Dr. Laura! You are preaching tonight. Jackie is telling me we have a caller on the line, someone who wants to send a message to Ms. Jessie. Caller, are you there? Introduce yourself, please."

"Uh, yes. Hello. Good evening, Dr. Laura. I have been thoroughly entertained by this program though I admit tonight was a little disheartening. I'm sorry to hear that so many of the women are suffering from broken hearts, and that those broken hearts are the responsibility of my fellow brothers. My prayers are also with the women and their current emergency. I'd like them to know that there are still good brothers out there. There are those of us who don't cheat, lie, or betray—and we have jobs! My name is Dr. Xavier Houston, and I want Ms. Jessie to know that I find her captivating and that I am waiting for the opportunity to connect with her. I'm confident that I can heal that broken heart of hers."

"Well hot damn, Dr. Xavier Houston! Do you have a brother?" Jackie had put on a pair of headphones and was talking into the mic.

Magic said, "This doctor has our interns getting in on this! Jackie, your tail is too young for any of the doctor's brothers. And I'm going to tell your mama! Ha!"

"And on that note—such a lovely note to end the show with," Dr. Laura said, jumping in like a regular disc jockey, "I want to thank Dr. Houston bunches and bunches for giving the women of Dallas a sprinkle of hope—I am going to ask Magic to give you some Ted and Sheri. Magic, put on that 'Come Ye Disconsolate' and dedicate that to all the lovely women of *The Love Forum*—DeDe, Jessie, Pat, Brit, Darlene, V, and Melissa. Stay strong my sisters. Dry your last tear because it's going to be all right in the morning: *You met somebody. Said he'd love you for life, but what he did not tell you is that he already had a wife. Somebody's been cast aside, kicked to the curb . . . well you need to find you some scripture 'cause the healing is the way, God can heal, God can heal it . . .*" Dr. Laura sang the forum off the air and sipped her tea like a regular old pro.

Chapter Seventeen

No More Tears

When I arrived at Dr. Wilma's office it was late in the evening, and security ensured that everyone checked-in before navigating through the complex. I slowly made my way to Dr. Wilma's suite and discovered she had left the door open for me. As I walked through the door, a chime announced my arrival, and she greeted me with a big hug and wonderful smile. I needed that.

"Hello, Jessie. Despite everything, you look wonderful as always. Please, the Sanctuary awaits you!"

I didn't know how to contain my hurt. Tears just started rolling down my face as we walked into her office. The fireplace was glowing and she had positioned two chairs in front of it. We sat down, and without saying a word, she poured me a glass of wine. I took the glass and tilted it against my lips, trying my best not to down it. Dr. Wilma must have noticed my attempt at some restraint and smiled. As I sipped, she said so eloquently, "You know, Jessie, there are some women who will never love or know unconditional love before they leave this earth. Yes, we may meet someone; we may have a wonderful time; we may even go that extra step and get married and start a family. The marriage may last for two months, two years, or even twenty years, and though we care about that person, and love him or her in our own way, that deep spiritual connection may never exist and we may never get to feel it at all. But there are some people—I call them the lucky ones—who will experience a love that seems not only blessed, but touched by God."

I let that notion play in my mind as we sat there. The fire was warm and the wine was easing some of my pain. For a while she just held my hand, and the only noise was that of the crackling fire. After I calmed down, she asked if I wanted to talk about how I was feeling and the words just started pouring from my mouth like water flowing from an open faucet.

"Dr. Wilma, I thought he was the one. From the first time we met to the times we spent just talking about, humph, seemingly nothing now, but we were in sync. I could read him. I knew exactly what he was thinking and he could read me as well—we were one in the same. Now, as I look back, I don't think he ever really cared about me. It's as if I was just, as my Big Momma would say, 'naïve to love.'"

"Well Jess, remember when you first came to see me and we associated songs with your life? If you recall, when I asked you what song summed up your love life you said Luther Vandross's 'A House is not a Home,' but Natalie Cole was running a close second with 'I'm Catching Hell.' If one song could best describe the way you feel right at this moment, what would it be?"

I didn't have to think long. It was Me'Shell Ndegéocello's "Fool of Me." I must have been a million miles away, thinking out loud, 'cause the next thing I knew, I heard Me'Shell singing. Out of nowhere, Dr. Wilma had produced the song and it floated from the speakers. And as quickly as the song materialized, so did Dr. Wilma's hand. She was right at my side, holding it firmly, as the tears flowed down my face. I looked at Dr. Wilma and noticed that my sister, she was crying too, but smiling. Bewildered, I asked, "Dr. Wilma, why are you crying?"

And she answered, "Sometimes the best way to show love and understanding for someone is not to cry with them, but to cry for them. I'm crying for you, Jessie. I feel your hurt. I know your heart is so heavy with pain, but one thing is for sure—you'll get through this, as we all have, and I'll be there to hold your hand each step of the way. You don't have to suffer through this alone."

Before I could reply, I received a text: *Come to Dallas Children's Hospital when you can. All the Divas are here with Pat . . . Matthew has been hurt!!!*

+++

Every one of the women, minus Jessie (who was on her way), bombarded Dallas's Children's Hospital's emergency room in one forceful movement.

"Matthew! Matthew! Where is my son? Where is my son?" Pat screamed. She started banging on the security officer's desk, but she couldn't ask the question again because she fainted—hitting her head on the desk on the way down. The ladies ran to her side, but the hospital staff reached her before the women. They had Pat on a gurney within five minutes of her busting through the hospital's doors. The women were a mess. None of them could gather their nerves and all eyes were on them. The emergency room was filled with a lot of shady looking characters, but their injuries couldn't compare to what the Divas had brought through the door—a sense of drama and a whole lot of lashes, gloss, and heels. Melissa noticed a woman staring at them harder than everyone else in the waiting area. Then she looked to the woman's side and saw that Pat's daughter, Chanté, was sleeping snuggled up in the crook of the woman's arm. Melissa thought, *That's Donnell's mistress. That bitch got a lot of fucking nerve being up in this damn waiting room with Pat's daughter—who Pat herself hasn't seen in months—on her arm.* Jessie walked through the sliding glass doors as Melissa walked over to the woman. Jessie said, "I got the text message. What happened? Is Matthew okay?"

While DeDe filled Jessie in, Melissa began a conversation with the woman holding Chanté. "I'm going to keep this as ladylike as possible. Number one, bitch, you ain't worth the bail money. Number two, little Chanté there loves her auntie Melissa and I don't want her to wake up and see me whooping your ass. That might scar her for life, especially since she lives in a gated community and don't know a thing about the hood. But can you please tell me what the fuck is going on here? And why the fuck are you in this waiting room with the married-man-you're-fucking's daughter? Can you tell me that?" Melissa was trying to keep her voice down and not wake Chanté.

"Look, I don't want any trouble. And I can understand how it might seem inappropriate that I'm here, but what things seem like and what they are, are two separate things. I am Donnell's woman now."

The woman was decent looking. She looked like she probably knew what to do in the kitchen with those hips taking up all the seat beneath her, but more important than any of that, she looked like the type of chick who spent her whole days and nights gassing up her man's head. Like, "Ooh, baby, you look so handsome today" and "You the smartest man I know." She probably made Donnell feel like the most important man on the planet—even if it meant diminishing her own character.

"How you gonna be somebody's woman when he got papers on him saying he belongs to a whole other living, breathing human being?" Melissa asked. The woman was holding on to Chanté like she was her daughter or something.

"Come on now," she said. "You know things ain't always what they seem on the surface."

By the time she got that out of her mouth Jessie and the other women had made their way over. They stood over the woman with Chanté almost in her lap, and all of them were thinking some version of *Why the fuck does this bitch have our baby Chanté up under her like that?* They might have pulled her out behind the hospital and taught her a few lessons if Té didn't look so cute and comfortable with her.

"Man, Melissa, fuck this girl's explanation for breaking up Pat's marriage." DeDe had the nerve to say that, but it was clear she was sincere. DeDe had finally seen, first hand, the effects of an affair. "Chick, just tell us what the hell happened to Matthew."

"Well, he did drown."

The women all shook in anguish. Each one put her hands over her face and began crying. In her mind's eye, each woman replayed the drowning, and it was the saddest, most horrible picture. With all their commotion, they woke Chanté, who was now looking around bewildered.

"But he was revived. He was revived. They're stabilizing him now."

"Oh God! You playing games, woman. Who just says, 'He drowned,' and then don't clear that up with 'but he was revived'? I see your trifling-ass ways shining through and the topic of discussion is children! I feel really sorry for Pat having to go against you," V said. She was opening and closing her fists in a way that said, just give me five minutes with this wench.

"That didn't come out right. Y'all are going to have to forgive me." She was rubbing Chanté quiet and the little girl seemed perfectly comfortable in her embrace. "It's just that I've been sitting here beating myself up about this for hours. All I been focusing on was the drowning . . . and how I could let that happen to little Mat. I mean, you're right, the reviving is the most important part, but like I said, I just can't believe I was so irresponsible."

The women, even if they didn't want to admit it, were absolutely convinced of the woman's sincerity. They didn't even know her name and God knows they didn't want to sympathize with her, but they started to consider how they themselves would feel if they had made such a grave mistake. As they were standing there contemplating whether or not Donnell's mistress deserved the benefit of the doubt, Donnell walked his trifling tail up into the huddle of women.

"Matthew is fine," he said. "He's fine. He's stable. He has suffered no permanent injuries. He's just shook-up a bit."

The woman holding Chanté burst into tears and Chanté, with her little self, rubbed the woman's arm as if she loved her.

"It's okay, Valerie. It's okay." Donnell wanted more than anything to hold his girlfriend. To caress her in the same fashion that Chanté was doing, but he didn't want to hear from the mouths of all Pat's friends. He was just about to ask where Pat was when Jessie interrupted his intentions.

"Well thank God in heaven. God is good all the time. Now on to Pat. What are they saying about her?"

Donnell looked confused. "Pat? What do you mean?"

"Donnell, they just rushed Pat back there." Brit pointed beyond the metal doors that led to the area with the hospital rooms and doctors. "She fainted the moment she ran in here."

"What the hell? I don't know. Let me go check." Donnell ran to check on his wife, and Valerie held her hand to her heart still silently sobbing about Matthew. The women found a fairly secluded area where they could sit together and discuss things.

"That nigga done broke her heart, y'all. She came in here and took two breaths thinking about her child and her husband, and then she collapsed, hitting her damn head on the desk as she went down." Shaking her head as she closed her eyes in disbelief. "This is some fucked-up shit!" Melissa said.

"Well I'm just grateful—beyond words—that Matthew is okay. God, y'all just don't understand the crazy thoughts that were running through my head on the trip over here. Imagining a child's funeral is just not the sort of daydreaming I want to do."

"You ain't lying, Jessie. I want no parts of those sorts of dreams. And what about this Valerie bitch? Over there crying and shit like she ain't responsible for this mess." V said as she stared at Valerie with one of those *if looks could kill* stares.

Jessie said, "What happened, Melissa? What did she do? What happened with Matthew?"

"I don't know exactly, but she obviously feels some guilt over the matter. She must have been keeping the kids while Donnell was at work. The point is, Matthew drowned—even if he was revived—on her watch."

DeDe said, "Yeah, and I know y'all think I'm the last one who ought to have something to say, but I think she is sincerely sorry. I mean look at her over there holding on to Chanté like she really loves her! I mean damn! How long was Donnell having this affair that his mistress all in love with the kids and shit already?"

"Had to be a long while, De," Darlene said. The circumstances at hand had helped her forgive any indiscretion of DeDe's and DeDe was glad for it, though she didn't want their friendship to be mended over Matthew's near death.

The women remained in the waiting area for some time, eating snacks and drinking sodas from the vending machines, watching the news, but most importantly watching Valerie. They needed to sum her up really well so that when Pat asked about her they'd have a true estimation of her. The fact was, however inappropriate their relationship was, it seemed that Valerie and Donnell had a sincere, working love. This made DeDe particularly sad because it was so clear that Donnell was going to leave Pat. There was no turning back. He did not love her friend anymore.

Jessie was able to return to her thoughts of Michael's down low activities now that Matthew was okay and it was likely Pat had just suffered a momentary meltdown. Melissa saw the worry on her girlfriend's face and pulled her aside.

"Come on, take a walk with me."

The best girlfriends told the crew they'd be back soon and were out the sliding glass doors before the other women could ask where they were going. Jessie and Melissa waited until they were almost to the end of the hospital's parking lot to begin the conversation.

"We never talked about Doretha, you know," Melissa said.

"Yeah. She's no joke, huh?"

"No, not at all."

"Why you say it like that, Lis? Everything okay?"

"What I'm about to say to you is gonna be tough to swallow, Jessie. And it's gonna seem like I'm the bearer of bad news. In a way I am. In another way, I bear blessings."

"You're scaring me, Melissa." Jessie grabbed her girlfriend's arms, and Melissa looked away into the city distance to gather herself. She wanted to focus on the positive and looking into Jessie's eyes was drawing her closer to the sadder elements. Jessie let go of her arms and placed her hands on Melissa's belly.

"It's nothing to do with the baby is it?"

Melissa bit her lip and the tears just about fell from her eyes, but she pulled it together.

"It does. Jessie, Doretha revealed to me that Quentin wouldn't marry me. Before that, before even I knew, she told me I was pregnant with Meli." Smiling and looking down at her bulging belly. "Meli is short for Melissa . . . Jessie . . . she told me I was pregnant with a baby girl."

"Oh, Lis. Girl, you don't believe that do you? That woman doesn't know what she's talking about. She's just filled with hocus-pocus, and a whole lot of drama."

"I didn't want to, but Jess, the truth is, Doretha has never been wrong—and I am pregnant. She hasn't been wrong about your life, has she? I don't even know the extent of your reading, but I know it was on point."

Jessie took a minute to consider her reading.

"Jessie, Quentin isn't going to marry me, and in a very short while, he won't even have the opportunity."

"What?"

"Jess, I'm not ever going to hold Meli. I'm not going to make it to see her birth. I won't be on this earth much longer. Being in this hospital is making that reality so real for me."

"WHAT? What in the world are you talking about, Melissa? You are talking crazy. Don't say that!"

"Jessie, calm down. I know this is a lot to swallow. Believe me, I've been dealing with this for five months now, and I'm still struggling to come to terms with it. I will always be with you and the rest of the Divas. Always."

At that moment the women noticed that Brit was walking towards them.

"Look, I don't want to share this with anyone else. Jess, I just want you to know that true love is going to come your way . . . and it will arrive in the strangest package, but don't question it. I want you to promise me that you'll be open to it. More importantly, I want you to trust that I am okay with it."

"Huh?"

"I'm okay with it, sista girl! You have my blessings."

Jessie couldn't ask Melissa to clear up what she'd said because Brit joined them.

"They're sending Matthew home with Donnell and his ho. The police came with child welfare to investigate and make sure he wasn't being abused or neglected and concluded that he wasn't. You know I wanted to be like, 'What about his father leaving his mother after ten years of marriage for some pussy. Then kicking her out of the house and all that—that ain't abuse?' But I kept it clean, girls."

"You silly, Brit. And what about Pat?"

"That's why I came out here to get y'all. They said we can dip back there and visit with her for a while until they get her a permanent room."

"Oh, they checking her in?" Jessie asked.

"I guess so."

Before going into Pat's room the women stopped by Matthew's room and gave him soft hugs and kisses, told the little guy they loved him, did the same to Chanté, and gave Valerie and Donnell five looks of pure evil. Donnell didn't lift his head to meet any of their eyes, and Valerie looked like she didn't want to stir up anything either. She might end up with her head busted upside the emergency room curb. The couple left with the kids and the women found Pat looking not so great. She was pale—sort of ashy looking—and Melissa wondered if she had missed something over the past couple of weeks. Had Pat been looking this run down and she had ignored it? She had been on the run so much (ducking Ms. Doretha's predictions mostly), and Pat just stayed locked up in the guest room crying all day and all night. The only time she came out was to halfway curse out the pastor and for the forum, and then she was usually made up with a face full of makeup.

"Hey, baby girl," V said.

"Hey, y'all."

"What's going on, Pat? Why you look so tired, girl? What did they say?" Brit asked.

"They saying they got a whole battery of tests to run. The doctor isn't comfortable letting me walk out of here having fainted, being dehydrated, and looking like I do." Pat knew precisely what was wrong, but she couldn't bring herself to break the news to the Divas.

"Yeah, you do look bad."

"Well damn, DeDe," Melissa said. "Don't worry about Pat's feelings none."

The ladies laughed, and then spent the next hour worrying about Pat. Within that time Pat broke down crying about seeing her son in that hospital bed.

"Can y'all believe he got his woman keeping my kids, and we ain't even divorced? Shit, we ain't even legally separated! And why he ain't offered to give up that house so I can keep my own children? Especially now that this woman is responsible for my baby almost drowning!"

V said, "You know, Pat, I know that shit stings, but honestly, it's not for you to contemplate. Who knows why he's doing the shit he's doing? Who knows? But that's not for you to figure out. What you need to do—what you *have* to do is get yourself together. No judge is going to award you custody without a steady job, a place to stay, and your health."

"Yeah," Jessie said, "and your health definitely takes precedence at the moment. We got to focus on getting you well."

Pat almost lost her breath when Jessie said that. She was deathly afraid of her children suffering her lose.

"How could he do this to you, Pat? I thought y'all would be together forever . . ." DeDe was imagining Tracy sitting in Pat's place, and despite that evening's confrontation, she couldn't forgive herself for playing the same role the woman Valerie was playing in Pat's life.

The women had no answer for that, and no one even questioned DeDe's posing of the question. Eventually, the emergency room staff indicated it would be best if they let Pat get her rest, and they all went home, their hearts heavy as lead. The funny thing is, they didn't think things could get any worse until Donnell called Melissa two mornings later asking, "Did you know Pat has cancer?"

"What? Hell no I didn't know that! What are you talking about, Donnell?" Melissa said.

"A doctor called the house to confirm an upcoming chemotherapy appointment. He gave it some fancy name . . . I can't recall what he called it, but it's in her breasts. She's gonna require a mastectomy in addition to the chemo."

Things got even worse when Melissa asked, "Well can she count on you to be there, Donnell?"

Donnell said, "She's still on my health insurance, and from what I understand fighting cancer is quite expensive, so she should be grateful, but other than that, I can't commit to anything. I'm sorry. My life is moving in a different direction."

Melissa thought, *My poor girl. Poor Pat. When it rains, it pours.* When Pat came home from the hospital, Melissa—after helping Pat out of the Taxi—stopped her at the door with the news.

"Why didn't you tell anyone, Pat? You need support. This is too heavy a load to carry. I could have been going to those doctors' visits with you—"

"Girl, look at yourself. You're big and pregnant. You need support yourself. I have decided to bear this cross alone and that's what I'm going to do."

"Alone?"

"Yes, dear. Alone. No husband, no friends . . . certainly no God."

Pat walked past Melissa holding her belly and closed the guest bedroom door behind her.

Chapter Eighteen

Decisions

December 15, 2008. I hadn't planned on quitting that Monday morning. I walked through DataComm's revolving doors like any other Monday. Clean cut, makeup flawless, mind on trudging through the piles of paperwork and phone calls. It wasn't till I reached my cubicle and asked myself, *Why the hell am I still in a goddamn cubicle?* that I knew it was time to go. I didn't discuss the decision with anyone. Just put my coffee down, slipped out of my blazer, and walked to Harriet's office with more determination than my feet could handle. Harriet was on the phone and I waited to be invited in.

"Come on in, Jessie. How can I help you?"

"Thank you, Harriet."

"Have a seat. I've been meaning to call you in here to chat with me."

I couldn't help but think, *Oh lord! For what? To criticize every damn thing I've done in the last week, and then take credit for all my work?*

"Harriet, I'm going to be delivering my letter of resignation by the end of the business day. I just wanted to let you know before I did so."

"What?"

Oh . . . my . . . god. My mind must be playing tricks on me because Harriet actually looked a little concerned. If she was concerned, I figured it was only because she would have to do some of her own work for a change.

"Yes. I'm going to be venturing off on my own. DataComm has provided an undeniable foundation for what I hope will be a prosperous career, but I feel stifled here. I'm not moving up in the company as I expected I would be. I've been here for quite some time and I'm just not seeing the fruits of my labor."

"Jessie, recall that I just said I wanted to see you. Well, the fact is I wanted to talk about this very thing. I will be retiring from DataComm as soon as next month and it has been my fervent recommendation to the board that you replace me as vice president of marketing. I know it seems like I give you a hard time, and I can't pretend that I don't, but I see something in you like the fire that was in me twenty years ago. Your ideas are innovative, you're a hard worker, and quite honestly, you're beautiful. In this industry, beauty goes a long way."

"Wow. Thank you, Harriet. I appreciate that."

"Look, I understand that yearning to get out on your own. I once had it . . . until DataComm offered me a six-figure salary I couldn't refuse. I can only imagine what your starting salary will be."

"Really?"

"Yes, love. With the title 'vice president' comes many advantages! I can't pretend like there aren't some disadvantages, though. I have no husband, for instance. And my womb will never be filled with a bundle of joy—just gas and bloating. I'm too old now. I gave all that up in pursuit of a career, power, and all the glorious fruits of my labor that went along with the job. And now I'll be the first to tell you I love the feel of a Marc Jacobs bag dangling at my elbow—have you seen his new collection?—but I'd replace it in a hot damn minute with a beautiful baby. A baby boy, if God takes requests! Maybe venturing out on your own will allow you to have both—a successful career and a family. I don't know. But I don't want you to hand in that letter of resignation without seriously considering your new options."

I left Harriet's office and nearly ran out of the building. I couldn't breathe in that thick office air. The wind outside greeted me—it felt so good—and I leaned against the building to let it soothe me. I fought them, Lord knows I tried, but the tears overwhelmed me and were soon falling down my face. I stood there thinking, *That's going to be me someday. I'm going to be an old-ass Harriet with a ton of money and no children to spend it on. A big-ass beautiful house with a bedroom empty as a used can.* Still, I decided against handing in the letter of resignation just yet. I needed to talk it over with the girls and get Dr. Wilma's input before making any brash decisions. I collected myself and headed back to my cubicle, knowing one way or another I wouldn't be sitting in it for much longer.

Chapter Nineteen

Searching

December 20, 2008. If I was honest with myself I was happy as all get out to see Dr. Wilma. It was like walking into Big Momma's kitchen and finding some banana pudding in the refrigerator, and Big Momma herself sitting at the table with her smile and her look of love. Dr. Wilma gave me a hug and told me to go on and fix myself a beverage and make myself comfortable. "We have to step it up, Ms. Jessie. We're at the end of our sessions now, and I want to make sure that we make as much progress as humanly possible. I don't want to lose you without at least two drastic changes coming to fruition in your life."

"I'm ready to work, Dr. Wilma."

"You know I keep tabs on you as best as I can. And from what I understand . . . well . . . I'm completely aware that underneath that pretty pink blouse is still a broken heart. Am I right?"

I was thinking, *Well damn, Dr. Wilma, just jump right in there.* I was fighting back the tears.

"I don't know if it's broken, but it's damn sure at the breaking point."

"I want you to tell me about why you think you held on, and are still holding on to Michael."

"Dr. Wilma, before we go any further, I have to share something with you."

"What is it, sweetheart?" Dr. Wilma sipped her drink like I was about to tell her I bought a new skirt. She could not have known what was coming.

"Michael is on the DL."

I just knew Dr. Wilma was going to spit that drink out of her mouth. But she was cool as a cucumber. She swallowed and adjusted her glasses. "How do you know that, baby girl? Do you mean he's bisexual?"

"Well, yes. For real, he's on the down low."

"Oh, okay. He doesn't care to share his sexual liaisons on the 'other side,' but he has them nonetheless. How did you find out?"

"Well, there had been signs. Little things happening that made me a little wary. But I just pushed them aside because I didn't want to believe they were true."

"Jessie, honey, people operate out of their own pain. I can tell you, without even speaking with Michael, that he feels he is living in a world that will not accept him for the man he is. The African American culture is particularly judgmental of gay people. He must therefore lie to navigate his way through this life. I've seen it time and time again. I know it's difficult to understand right now, but by stepping in Michael's shoes you can come to a place of forgiveness."

"We just had such a strong connection, Dr. Wilma. How could I be attracted to a gay man? I mean he seemed to be everything I wanted in a man. Successful—I mean I know he just lost his job, but you don't get a house as beautiful as his without working hard and being good at what you do, so I know he'll be back on top soon. And was funny, handsome, sexy! Just easy to be with . . . and he has sex with men."

"Number one, please do not internalize *his* gayness. It is not a reflection on you."

"But how could I not see it, Dr. Wilma?"

"Well did he run around in panties snapping his fingers and asking to wear your lip gloss? Jessie, not all gay men are flamboyant. And then, it's important that we acknowledge the fact that Michael Todd is bisexual. That means he is attracted to both men and women."

"And I didn't deserve to know that?"

"Oh, you most certainly did. Now, on the other hand, I need you to realize that, minus his bisexuality and his dishonesty, anyone could come to you with the very same qualities—the success, the looks, the connection—and fill that man's shoes. Now, was it him you were in love with, or on the verge of being in love with, or his things? His qualities . . . the good ones, I mean."

"It certainly wasn't his things. He's losing them as we speak and that fact does not deter my heart. As for qualities . . . aren't qualities what make the person? Isn't he his qualities?"

"He is to a certain extent, yes. But what I mean is that the qualities that most attracted you to him ought not to be the generic ones you can pick up in a grocery tabloid story: rich, funny, sexy. They ought to be specific like the way he places his hand on the small of your back, or kisses your forehead to encourage you, or calls your name—things of that sort. Did he have any of those?"

"Well yes."

"What were they?"

"Um, when we slept together, he'd hold me through the whole night. Never let me go. If I got up in the middle of the night to use the bathroom he always asked where I was going as if he was scared he was going to lose me. And when I got back in the bed, he pulled me even closer and held me tighter than before."

"Ah! That's what I'm talking about. And what did that gesture do for you?"

"It made me feel safe, Dr. Wilma."

"Of course it did—"

"Until he got up the next morning and didn't call for three days."

"So do you see the problem then? That sense of security was fleeting; therefore it did not exist. You can't be safe with a man for eight hours of sleep and then have that safety wear off as easy as nothing. You can't be safe with a man who keeps secrets from you. Jessie, are you ready to let this thing go? Is this relationship over?"

"Yes, Dr. Wilma. I have no choice. I just can't continue to go through the pain of constantly being rejected any longer. I can't believe he did this to me."

"Well, baby girl, I want you to allow your reaction to be proof that he was not the man for you. He does not possess the compassion you need and require."

"You're right, but damn . . . it hurts so bad Dr. Wilma."

"Pain tells you something is wrong. You have to honor pain, Jessie. God knows it doesn't feel good, but it is your personal alert system. When you feel it, you know it's time for a change. Now please continue with me. Use this experience to feed your answer, too. How are your past relationships a reflection of your inner life?"

"Honestly, Dr. Wilma, I never thought of them in this way. I've always blamed the men in my life. They've done some pretty messed-up stuff to me. This is probably the worst."

"No doubt they have, and no doubt this is an extremely painful situation. I don't want you to think that by me asking you to tell me what their actions say about you means that I'm dismissing what they've done to you. Yes, their actions were terrible. In the same breath though, you've *allowed* them. Do you see where I'm going with this? What did your *allowing* Michael to disappear for days without any word say about you? What did your *allowing* his secrets say about your supposed 'surprise' discovery that he was on the down low?"

"It said I was willing to put up with that mess just so that I wouldn't feel like another man had left me. I was willing to ignore signs that he was not being honest in order to be held on the occasional night."

"Amen. And who was the first man to leave you?"

"My father."

"Okay. Describe for me what that was like . . . the pain of having your father leave you."

"Quite honestly, Dr. Wilma, it was the worst feeling in the world. I've never had anything top it—even with discovering I had been sleeping with the enemy. My father left me empty. I was ten when he remarried. By the time I was eleven he stopped calling altogether—he even changed his phone number. When I heard the operator come on the line to tell me the number was no longer in service, I wanted to kill myself. I took about four or five Tylenol. Looking back, I know those pills couldn't have done anything but maybe put me on the toilet, but when I lay down to sleep that night I begged God not to wake me up in the morning."

"Okay, good. Keep going. Can you make a connection between that incident—your father's abandonment—and your past relationships, including this most recent one?"

I was quiet for two whole minutes . . . combing my brain, putting together the pieces of the puzzle. Finally, with eyes full of tears, I spoke. "I've been fighting all this time— trying my hardest, my best, doing whatever I had to do—to make sure I never felt that feeling again. I . . . I never wanted to feel that hurt again . . . of being left like my father left me, Dr. Wilma." And at that moment it felt like the hurt and pain, of all those years, filled my chest, heart and soul and I broke down and began sobbing uncontrollably. Dr. Wilma gave me the strong silence I needed. Silence so that I could have a clear, quiet space to let it all out, and strength so that I knew I had something to fall back on. After many, many minutes of crying, I finally gathered myself and apologized to Dr. Wilma.

"What exactly are you apologizing for, sweetie? This has been your most significant session. You now see what it is you've been doing. Now we can work on fixing it."

Chapter Twenty

The Love Forum in Retrospect

December 28, 2008. Melissa felt like *The Love Forum* was still unfinished with the wrapping of the last show. Not one of the Divas, including herself, had actually been present for its closing, and she felt the listeners deserved more closure—not to mention they were blowing up her e-mail inbox with questions of who? what? where? when? Because of some scheduling conflicts, and some outright refusals (DeDe, Brit, and Pat had too many personal issues to attend another taping and Darlene and V just flat out refused). *The Love Forum in Retrospect* (as she had aptly named the show), featured only Jessie, Dr. Wilma (with Jessie's permission), Dr. Laura, and Ms. Doretha. The panel was well versed in the lives of the Divas, so it really didn't matter that most of them weren't there in the flesh anyway.

"D-town. This is Melissa Morgan, and rather than call myself sweet this lovely evening, I'm going to keep it real and tell y'all I'm fat!"

"You are not fat, Melissa. You're still every bit as sweet," Magic interjected.

"Well, thank you, Magic. I do appreciate that, but I guess you haven't noticed that I almost can't fit behind this damn mic!"

"Girl, hush," Jessie said. "You're beautiful. You're absolutely glowing."

"Y'all do make a girl feel good! Dallas, do you hear this? Even big and pregnant, eating everything in sight, the sweet, sweet Melissa Morgan is still beautiful."

Magic played Stevie Wonder's "Isn't She Lovely" in the background. And Melissa let out a big smile.

"Magic! I love you, boy!"

"And I love you back."

"Well, Dallas, as you know, the final forum didn't end in the way we'd planned. The Divas had a major emergency and

Pat's son, Matthew, took precedence. Shout out to little Matthew—sweetie, your auntie Lis is so happy you pulled through! So anyway, I thought we'd do one more show. Just to give our listeners a proper farewell and to let you guys know how each of the Divas is doing. In the studio with me today I have Ms. Jessie—flawless! I have Dr. Laura who saved the last show for us. I have Dr. Wilma who is Jessie's emotional therapist and has guided my girl towards healing her broken heart. And I have Doretha—my personal psychic who gave each of the Divas a reading so many months ago. Boy, Doretha, you ain't no joke. I tell you, sometimes I wish I didn't know your seeing-in-the-future tail! But Dallas, I must say, Doretha is always on the money. Anyway, I'm going to ask Magic to take us to commercial, and when we return my-ever-so-insightful friends and I are going to analyze each of the Divas' lives. Dallas, you won't want to miss this—trust me."

The women rode out the commercial break with very little conversation. Melissa, Jessie, and Ms. Doretha were living with the pure sadness of Melissa's future, and the doctors could feel that tension without much effort. Still, each of the women was committed to sharing the Divas' stories as they knew the stories might help other women in need.

"So Dallas, let's start with Ms. DeDe. She's unable to be with us this evening because she's busy soul-searching. Doretha, why don't you bring the listening audience up to speed on DeDe's progress."

"I'm happy to, Dear. Well, let's see. My vision tells me that after the hoopla at the radio station during the last forum, DeDe's heart was anything but at ease. She had a hard time dealing with Malcolm's wife calling up to the station. After all, she had tried to make peace with her. DeDe struggled with the idea that Mrs. Cole was still determined to hurt her. But, DeDe was determined to be honest with herself from that point forward and eventually realized why Mrs. Cole reacted the way she did. DeDe knows how much pain she must have caused Mrs. Cole and asked me to extend a public apology to her. Mrs. Tracy Cole, if you're listening, DeDe is sincerely sorry for all the pain she has caused you and your family and has committed herself to never causing that type of pain again."

"I'm not condoning anything that DeDe has done. I oppose affairs to the fullest. But should De be the sole bearer of guilt? I mean at what point are Malcolm, and yes, even Tracy, responsible for some of this?" Melissa asked.

"Sure DeDe fell in love with Malcolm before he admitted to being married, but the truth was she *knew* something wasn't right, just like Ms. Jessie here knew something wasn't right with Michael Todd. DeDe ignored her God-given intuition, and as a result, she participated in, if not the breaking up of a home, at least the committing of some serious damage to it. Still, you're right, Malcolm and Tracy must account for the roles they played. Malcolm is married to his wife, not DeDe, and I'm sure Tracy has been aware that something wasn't right in her marriage for a while. All of this is true. But we're here on DeDe's behalf. *DeDe* was living in a condo that another woman's husband was paying the utilities for. *DeDe* was driving a Benz that he was paying the insurance on, and during all of this, Tracy was home raising Malcolm's children and maintaining his home. DeDe is ashamed of herself. And as I said, she is committed to a new life. She is refusing Malcolm's calls."

"You mean that hobo is still calling her, Doretha? After all of this?"

"Oh yes. I did another reading for DeDe. He'll call for quite some time. Your listeners will be happy to know that DeDe will not entertain that foolishness."

"Thank God!" Melissa said. "So what's going to happen with DeDe career wise, Doretha?"

"She's in the studio. But she's not there to sing, but to write."

At this point, Dr. Laura interjected. "I think DeDe is determined to turn this whole situation around. She's giving all her troubles to God. She's giving them to Him, and she's going to use the gift He has given her to do His work. Gospel music is her calling, not anything else. She has seen the light."

"Amen, Dr. Laura. Amen." said Melissa.

"Now, Ms. Jessie . . . what about you? How has your love-life shaped up? 'Cause, Melissa and the K103.5 audience definitely wants to know the answer to this question, diva."

"Well, I've made a decision. I can't deny the lure of the vice presidency position at DataComm, and I'm quite sure my life would become a lot easier, at least financially, with it. But Melissa, I'm yearning for something more. I'm yearning for independence."

Melissa said, "Well, you are Big Momma's child."

"That's true, and it's not going do any good to have all my talent wasted at somebody else's company. Just as I developed that dynamite Daisy Chain campaign on my own, I'm going to develop many more.

"How are you going to make your money, Jess?"

"I'm going to work as an independent contractor until I've saved up enough money, or built a strong enough credit base to take out the necessary small business loans, to start my own company."

Dr. Wilma added, "But more important than the move to work for herself is Jessie's move to forgive. Before leaving therapy, I spelled out a twelve-step forgiveness process for Jessie. I explained to her, 'Baby girl, this is *not* going to be easy, but once you have accomplished it, you will be fit for love.' And I think that just the idea of healing herself in such a drastic way was enough to push her to quit her job and forgive Michael's indiscretions. Jessie is being prepared for her king and that is an exhilarating idea. Jessie, do you want to talk about your forgiveness list?"

"The first person on my 'to forgive list,' even before Michael, is Calvin Harris—my deadbeat father. Letting go of that pain scared me, I'm telling you, but I knew it had to be done. I let the courage required for that step push me right into my boss's office where I lay a beautifully written letter of resignation on her desk. I thanked Harriet for her wonderful guidance but let her know I had to branch out on my own. I have to see what this whole life thing is about."

"Amen, Jessie. I am so proud of you, girl. I know that great things are on the horizon." Melissa felt something lodge in her throat. She fought back the stinging feeling in her eyes as she thought about missing her best friend's . . . well, life—which made her contemplate the end of her own. She covered her emotions by saying, "Okay, so what about Ms. V? Dr. Laura, you wanna take this one?"

"Sure, Melissa. Well, V finally received a hit back from her E-Dating survey. I won't disclose the man's name, but I'll just say he was obese. V thought, 'Hell no! I do not want to be with his fat ass!' When his chunky picture flashed across the screen she was appalled. The first thing he asked her was, 'So what you like to eat?' Then he listed all his favorite foods, and the list took up two Internet pages."

Jessie couldn't help herself and said, "No he didn't, Dr. Laura."

"Yes, Jessie. He did. And it was that virtual interaction that made V realize she had to get herself together. How could she demand something of a man she couldn't herself provide? Not to mention she had been questioning how was she going to run a successful beauty salon and not feel beautiful herself? And it's not that she wants to be skinny—she doesn't. Anyway, V ain't built to be skinny."

"She sure ain't," Melissa said. "She's 'big-boneded' as they say. V is always going to be curvy. She's going to have a whole lot of hips and ass, and that just ain't to be avoided."

"So she laid out a plan for herself," Dr. Laura continued. "Nothing too drastic at first. She cut back to 2,000 calories and committed to exercising for thirty minutes, four times a week. She stepped up once she saw those first ten pounds drop off her easy as sweat, though. Dallas, you will be happy to know that V has lost twenty pounds, and in all the right places, too. She looks like America's Next Top Model, y'all. And the men are crawling out of the woodwork like roaches. She can't get a day to herself some weeks between the dates and the salon—which she would like to thank your listeners for the success of, Melissa."

"Oh, V knows she's more than welcome. That was the whole purpose of the forum—to take our lives to another level. But back to all these fellas sweating her . . ."

"Well, at first V was a little resentful . . . you know, about the sudden attractions. Then she remembered her reaction to her E-Dating survey, and she also took into consideration how good she felt about herself, being able to shop at the mall instead of the plus-size outlets, and she has committed to never losing control of her health again."

"That's just wonderful," Dr. Wilma interjected, giving Jessie a look that said, *All you guys are getting it together!*

"That brings us to Ms. Brit. Doretha, take the reigns please. You know we want to know what's up with this child."

Ms. Doretha said, "While DeDe's and V's and Jessie's lives are looking up, Brit's life has yet to be blessed with much optimism, Melissa. American Airlines downsized and Brit was one of the first to go."

"Oh no!" Dr. Wilma and Dr. Laura said in unison.

Ms. Doretha explained that Brit's supervisor pulled her into his office in an effort to let her down easy. The two of them had always gotten along. He thought Brit's work ethic was phenomenal and knew that her beauty and charm pleased the patrons—especially the big spending ones. He hated to see Brit go.

"Brit, we are so sorry to lose you," he'd said. "If I had any control over the situation, you know that you'd be right on that flight to Los Angeles. I really, sincerely wish you well."

"I cannot believe this, George. I have given this company so much of my life. I can't believe it would end like this. George, I honestly don't understand it. I mean both Leila and Heather have less seniority than me, and yet they're still here. Not that I wish unemployment on anyone—I don't—but I can't see how that's fair."

"I'm sorry. I thought you knew, Brit?"

"Knew what?"

"You're the subject of a police investigation. Something about fraudulent activity. That influenced the airline's decision to let you go rather than Leila or Heather."

Brit defended herself, and George looked like he wanted to believe her even if he didn't, but inside she was humiliated. She gathered her things and left the airport she had served for nearly eight years. She held back her tears, though. She wouldn't embarrass herself anymore than she had. She waited until she was safe and sound in her car to let out the wail of a child. What had she done? Why had she let a man grab a hold of her in such a way that he had jeopardized her whole future? She was crying so hard she didn't realize two uniformed men were standing at her car door. When she did see them she felt a sense of impending doom. However scared she was, she wasn't a dummy, and she knew to keep her mouth shut tight. She lowered her window.

"Yes?"

"Brittany Waites?"

"Yes, I'm Brittany Waites."

"I'm federal agent Williams and this federal agent Smith." They flashed their badges. "We'd like to ask you a few questions about your involvement with a Mr. Brasselton Drake. Are you familiar with him?"

"I am agents, but I'm not interested in speaking to you in the absence of my attorney."

The agents said a few words about innocent people not being afraid to talk, and Brit really wanted to defend herself, but all she heard was Brass's voice in her ear: *Don't say shit! That's just a tactic to get you to open up. The legal system is a game, girl.* She had to play it cool. They left Brit in the parking lot, she collected her thoughts, and then drove, below the speed limit, home. She wasn't going to give them any cause to get her inside any police station before she was prepared to be there. Afraid and non-trusting, she knew she needed to get home quick and get on her job search in a hurry. She needed to do that even before contacting her lawyer. She needed to land a job before her blemish-free record was compromised. She needed to secure a job before any background checks actually brought up something. At home she spent her entire evening searching through postings and submitting her résumé to several places.

"So, within a week she landed a position with Delta flying the Atlanta/DFW leg," Ms. Doretha told the listening audience. "She's going to have to move to Atlanta and start her life all over again, but she has no choice."

"Dallas, I think you're with me when I say we'll be praying for you, Ms. Brit. Just because you make poor choices in men doesn't mean you don't deserve happiness. Now, I think I'll take the liberty of updating our listening family on Pat's situation. We all know that Pat's marriage is over. We know that Donnell has moved on. What you may not know is that our lovely sister-friend has been diagnosed with cancer. Yes, Lord, what they say is true: when it rains, it pours. So without getting into it, because I really just want to give Pat her peace, let me just ask everyone to keep her in their prayers. Please, please keep this particular Diva at the top of your prayer list."

"I'm praying by the minute," Jessie said.

"So before we bless these people with forty minutes of continuous music, Doretha, please summarize the Divas' love lives and futures for us. We are hoping for the best. Fingers crossed, toes crossed, eyes crossed, all that! Oh, and K103.5 listeners, Jackie is holding up a big sign with Darlene's and Miguel's names on it and yes, the two are on their way to wedded bliss. They're getting married next year and my girl is in seventh heaven. Doretha, give us the news!"

"Dear, everything is on course and the Divas will not only survive but flourish. Melissa, love is coming for each of you. It may not arrive in the biggest or brightest package, or even in the package you've hoped for, but it is coming."

"Well hallelujah! A little bit of good news. I thought I might have to fire you, Doretha! Girl, I'm just playing. Magic, take us away with something good. We need it!"

Chapter Twenty-One

K103.5 New Year's Eve Party

December 31, 2008. Before the Divas knew it, New Year's Eve had arrived. As a group, they had had a hectic past few months. Melissa was well into her pregnancy and on the verge of dropping Quentin. They went out on the occasional date, and if she was feeling horny, she'd give him some, but she hadn't felt the urgency to invest in him. She had promised to give it a try and wait on him, but something in her spirit was telling her no. It wasn't that she blamed him for not wanting to marry her—how could she fault someone for their feelings?—but that she knew she deserved better than to wait around for someone to love her. Quentin didn't seem to notice the change in her feelings. And he seemed to be welcoming the baby with a whole lot of excitement. He didn't recognize that his phone calls weren't being picked up as often or that Melissa was less available, but at the K103.5 New Year's Eve party he did pick up on the fact that he was no longer Melissa's priority. She spent the whole night mingling among strangers and dancing with her girls. Even when he announced that he was leaving for the night, she just lifted her arm and tilted her head, like he was her homey. He went home with a heavy heart and began to wonder if he wasn't losing her. He went online and started looking at wedding bands.

V worked the party like a call girl. The men were falling at her new, slim feet. She collected a pocketful of phone numbers and gave each man a rating on his business card to remind herself of whether or not she wanted to call him. She had pocketed two ten-rated men and thought the prospect of two perfect looking men was a wonderful one. *Oh, they gonna hold me to these superficial-ass standards? I'ma hold their asses to it, too. Only fine brothers need apply!*

The other women, except Pat who had stayed at Melissa's house to nurse her broken heart, had a wonderful time. The

Dallas listeners had reserved a special place in their hearts for the Divas and the women were not only welcomed at the party but spoiled. Free drinks all night, free food, and wonderful conversation consisting of lots and lots of compliments. Each of them heard, "Bitch, you bad" on more than one occasion.

Perhaps the most significant highlight of the evening was when Dr. Xavier Houston walked through the door. In the first place, he had been dropped off in a Bentley. All eyes were on him from the moment his expertly stitched leather shoes hit the pavement. But rather than go straight to the bar or even dance a little bit, he walked right into the eyesight of Ms. Jessie Harris.

"I had no doubt you would be the most beautiful woman in here. Hello. My name is Xavier."

"The doctor? The doctor from *The Love Forum?*" *Oh my god—this is that fine brother from the old-school party. The one at the bar. The one who held his drink up when I was on stage,* Jessie thought. Jessie had taken her time with her appearance that night. Her makeup was model-like, her dress fit like her skin itself, and her hair was just one flowing movement hanging down her back. *Love weave! Sew it in!*

"Yes, the doctor from the forum. 'That strong cup of dark roast, café mocha style, waiting to be sipped.' And yes, I've been watching you since I saw you at the K103.5 old-school party. I've been waiting a long time for this opportunity."

"Oh? And what would this opportunity be, Dr. Houston?"

"The opportunity to prove to you your worth. I've been listening as you've given the most unworthy men your attention. You're worth so much more. I want to meet, better yet, exceed your expectations. Ready for that sip?"

Dr. Houston and Jessie danced the night away. The fact that she wasn't carrying all the excess baggage from her previous relationships made the evening even more fun. Michael, or Todd, could walk up in there and she wouldn't miss a beat. She danced harder than she'd ever danced. She felt the small hole in her heart slowly begin to seal up. And she did not even consider going home with Dr. Houston. What was more important was that he did not even consider asking her to. He shook her hand before getting whisked away in his Bentley. And Jessie thought, *Oh yeah. I'll look real good in that. That joint is going to look good against my skin.*

Back inside the party Jessie spoke with DK. DK told her, "Baby girl, that man told me right out his mouth that you are going to be his wife." As crazy as it sounded, Jessie wanted it to be true. Off the strength of one dance and few shared words, she wanted to marry that man as much as he wanted to marry her.

Chapter Twenty-Two

Confrontation

February 2009. Melissa was not spending much time at home, and though she constantly apologized for this, Pat was actually glad for it. She needed to be alone. She needed time to think: to think about her life; to think about what she gave up to be with the man she loved; to think about how she would move on; to think about what she would do to survive. Up until now, Donnell and the kids were her life. She gave up herself—for them—and now she felt like a gutted fish . . . lifeless . . . no inner being . . . dead. And as she went through each year of her life with Donnell, the anger and hurt became more unbearable, she was hurting beyond words, her heart was so heavy, and all she could think of was the jail she was in, rotting away, with no way out.

If Melissa was in her face, she couldn't hit the walls, slam the doors, punch the pillows, or scream like a madwoman. And anyway, she understood that Melissa needed to work as much as she could, while she could, to prepare for the birth of her child. It seemed like Quentin was going to be a good father, but then it had seemed like he was going to marry Melissa too. It was obvious men acted one way, and then, without notice, acted in another. Melissa was strong and proud, definitely nobody's dummy, and Pat wished she was a little more like her.

Pat hadn't seen her children in over two months, and although she loved them with all her heart and missed them dearly, they were becoming a fading memory. Even after Matthew's near-drowning, Donnell wouldn't let her near them, talking about how she was "unstable." Pat's anger was slowly wiping her children away . . . they were becoming a blur. All she could see was Donnell. All she could see was red. All she could see was his blood. His body—the body of a liar and adulterer—rotting in his own blood.

Melissa was at K103.5, as usual, and Pat had spent most of the day studying the gun her girlfriend kept in her nightstand.

She had never seen a gun before, and she noted how heavy it was. She thought it was quite shiny and wondered what it would feel like to shoot it. To shoot him. To shoot him—dead. As her anger boiled over like hot milk boiling over a pot's top, Pat didn't think about her children, or how much they would suffer with a dead father and a mother in prison. She just couldn't break away from her rage long enough to accomplish that. She had only one thought in her head—to kill him dead. And no amount of reality, no relationship—even that with her beloved children—was going to stop her. She wrote the words, *Gonna kill that cheating bastard* on a napkin, put the gun in her pocketbook, and left Melissa's. She drove to her husband's house, not even aware enough to be grateful that she was doing so during school hours. The fact that her children would not be home to witness the death of their father was one Pat was not even sane enough to consider. She had had a break with reality. She arrived to the house on autopilot. She could not recall making a single turn in the vehicle, could not recall parking, or opening the door to the house with the key beneath the patio doormat, could not recall the way Donnell jumped, like she was a stranger, when he saw her. Before she realized she was in the house, the gun was drawn, and Donnell was sitting at the kitchen table trembling in a bath towel, his skin still glistening with water. She didn't waste any time getting things started. She discharged a bullet in the kitchen wall. Donnell hollered out.

The moment Pat raised the gun to Donnell's head Melissa discovered the napkin note. She had come home to eat lunch since she had gotten into the habit of eating well-balanced meals for her pregnancy. She had moved to look in the kitchen cabinet for her prenatal vitamins and had seen the napkin on the counter. She read the scribble Pat had written, and then she ran into her bedroom. She opened her nightstand drawer to find it missing its most important and deadly content.

Melissa was on her cell phone with Jessie and out the door before anything really registered.

"Pick up, girl. Pick up. Please pick up, Jessie. Jessie? Oh my God, I'm so glad to hear your voice. Girl, where are you?"

"Melissa? What's wrong? Slow down. I can barely understand you."

"Jessie . . . girl . . . I can't believe it," Melissa said breathing hard and panting. "That crazy bitch . . . she's at Donnell's house . . . right now . . . fixing to kill his black cheating ass . . . if she hasn't done it already!"

"What? What the hell are you talking about! Who?"

"Pat's on her way to kill Donnell! I knew the bitch was going through—but I never thought she would snap cold like this. All I know is that my .45 ain't here and I just read a note saying she's *'gonna kill that cheating bastard.'*"

"Oh my God, are you for real! Naw, this can't be, we're talking about Pat. Pat would never go off the deep end like this. Girl, she's playing with you."

"Jessie, I don't think so. I got a funny feeling about this. Trust me. We got to get over there. I can't let my girl go down like this. We can't let her throw her life away over Donnell. And as much as it hurts me to say, we can't let Matthew and Chanté lose their father, even if he is a low-down dirty-dog."

"Okay, girl. I don't believe it but I'm on my way. Be there as soon as I can."

As Jessie made her way to Donnell's house, she dialed the girls up to see if anyone was close to Donnell's house. In a matter of minutes she, DeDe, Darlene, V, and Brit were on their way. They were all dialing Pat's cell phone, but she wasn't picking up. They ran all sorts of stop signs and red lights trying to get to her.

Jessie was the first to arrive. She found the front door open, and she slowly crept in to find Pat holding a gun raised at Donnell. Her hand was violently shaking, like an addict strung out on crack. Sweat poured out of every pore of her body as she paced the floor, wobbling like a drunk. Her voice, heavy, cracking at times, sent chills throughout the room. Jessie could see Pat's face, filled with unbelievable anguish. She looked like a different woman—a madwoman. As Jessie looked at Pat in all her hurt (Pat's face was drenched with both tears and sweat), her heart dropped, and her own eyes swelled with tears. Jessie stood there motionless. She watched in horror as Pat moved towards Donnell, grabbed his neck, shoved the gun down his throat, and began yelling at the top of her lungs.

"Nigga, you tell me why you did this to me. You better get to talking. Explaining. Something! You better tell me how you let me give you practically all my adult life—ten damn years— and then you just walk away from me? Walk away from me like I ain't nothing. Like I ain't had your babies and taken care of you all this time. You better get to answering."

Reacting to Pat's voice filled with pain Jessie found the courage to speak. "Pat, sweetie, it's me." And then Jessie found the strength to move, so she moved to stand firmly behind Donnell. Pat did not even acknowledge her presence. She didn't lift her head or smack her teeth or even blink. She continued her ranting.

"Nigga, I'm waiting. I'm waiting for some dumb-ass fucking excuse to come out your mouth. I'm waiting." She pulled the gun out of his mouth and fired at the floor.

Donnell jumped and said, "There is no excuse, baby. I was wrong. I can't believe I would throw our life away like that. I've been asking God to forgive me every day for that very thing."

"You lie! Fucking liar! You think I'm crazy, nigga." Pat looked up at the ceiling and shook her head. Her tone was sarcastic when she said, "You've been asking God to forgive you every day, huh?" Pat looked away. With a sad and somber voice, she said, "There is no God. If there was a God he would have heard my prayers, but they fell on deaf ears. 'Cause while I was praying, asking God to save my marriage, you were fucking that fat bitch's brains out! That's how I know there is no God, and how I know you're lying."

"Pat. Patricia honey, you know that's not true! You're just hurt and angry, baby," Jessie said while moving in front of Donnell to shield him from Pat. "Pat, can you hear me, sweetie? It's Jessie." She reached out to touch Pat who flinched. "Pat, you can't do this. It's not right. Yes, he hurt you. But what about Matthew and Chanté? Think about them. What are you going to tell them if you do this, Pat?"

"Jessie! Jessie," Pat said, sobbing uncontrollably. "He hurt me so bad, he hurt me so bad, he needs to hurt like he hurt me, Jessie. How? How can he just throw me away like this. Like I'm the leftovers from his plate; to be thrown away in the trash—like nothing—easily discarded. Like I wasn't the one who filled his belly for so many years."

"I know, Pat. We've all gone through some type of hurt, but you know what, baby," Jessie said beginning to cry as thoughts of Michael revisited her. "We'll get through. Today we're not what our men want. Maybe it's because we're not their fantasy anymore. Maybe because we don't peak their interest anymore. Maybe because we can't hold that intriguing conversation anymore. Maybe because the sex just isn't good anymore. There are so many maybes Pat, but one thing's for sure—we will get over the hurt and pain, whether we have the answers to those maybes or not. It may take a month, a year, or even several years, but with each day, the pain will lessen, the thoughts will fade, and we'll be able to move on with our lives."

"I don't have a life! What do I have, Jessie? I don't have a husband, no family—I haven't seen my children in over two months!—and I don't even know if I'll be around to see them next month, or even next year," Pat said through her sobbing. "What do I have to lose—what, Jessie? What? As far as I'm concerned, I'm already dead."

Without much commotion all the other women, minus Melissa, walked into the house and joined Jessie in careful stances. They didn't want to set Pat off and watch her life, the lives of her children, and even Donnell's, be destroyed right before their eyes.

DeDe said, "Pat. Pat, it's DeDe. I know I'm the last person you want to be hearing from right now, but I gotta tell you, Pat, it ain't worth it. Take it from the other woman. He is *not* worth it. Girl, I feel so low down after the pain I caused that family. Malcolm's wife helped me get it through my thick head the damage that I did, so I know what you're feeling. Not because I been through it, but because I caused it. Donnell is not worth you spending your life in prison. He is not worth your children growing up orphans. Pat, baby, I know you. You are an excellent mother. I know you do not want that for those babies. You ain't had them in your arms in over two months and look how crazy you going. What you gonna do without them for life? For life, Pat? Because they gonna put you away for life."

"Fuck that, Pat. Blow that bastard's brains out. You laid down with a dog and got up itching all over with fleas. Kill that bastard," Brit screamed at the top of her lungs. "Shut the fuck up, Brit," DeDe said. "Don't say another motherfucking thing. What kind of stupid shit is that to say?"

Pat's hand started shaking even more. Donnell whimpered.

"DeDe is right, Pat. Don't listen to nothing Brit just said. Brit is speaking out of her own pain right now. You got to forgive her. And you got to forgive Donnell—no matter how hard it is," Jessie said. "DeDe's right and you know it. You know your babies deserve better. And you know you are God's child. So what if Donnell don't value you no more? So what if he don't see your worth? He's a fool. Your husband—your true husband—who will stand by you and your children until the end of time is out there waiting for you as we speak. Do not deny him the pleasure of loving you, Pat. Do not deny him that. Do not deny your children you."

"*We* love you, Pat," Darlene said and started crying. Darlene's tears sparked the tears of each of the other women. They all cried together watching their girlfriend standing there, paralyzed by her rage.

"Pat, you know I love you," V said and started walking towards her. "You know I love you. I love you, Pat. I love you, girl." V repeated her litany of "I love you" until her hands were wrapped around Pat. She slowly worked her grasp up to the gun and whispered into Pat's ear, "Let it go, baby girl. Let it go. Lay it down. Give it to God. You bigger than this. You better than this." Pat let go of the gun. She sighed a big sigh and collapsed into V's arms that were no longer as plump as they once were, but still as soft to touch. V held her girlfriend up as easy as if she were holding a child. Jessie stepped in and took the gun from V.

Jessie said, "Donnell, I'm asking you, please, don't do anything that will make this worse than it is." She stared deep into his eyes to make sure he understood. "I think it's best we keep this amongst us. You know good and well you have torn this woman to pieces. You know you've broken her heart. The least you can do is forget this. Act like this situation never happened. Give her that at least. There has been far too much hurt already."

Donnell didn't get a chance to speak because Jessie's cell phone rang.

"Jessie Harris speaking."

The women and Donnell watched as Jessie's face turned from one of interest to that of stone. She lowered the phone and just stood there. She didn't move nor did she say a word, it was like she was paralyzed, frozen in time.

"Jessie, is everything all right? Jessie!?" cried V.

The only thing Jessie heard was Melissa's voice back at the hospital when Matthew was being revived. Melissa's voice was so clear, now Jessie understood.

V took the phone out of Jessie's hand and checked to see if someone was still on the line.

"Hello? Hello . . . this is the phone of Jessie Harris, may I help you?"

Everyone stood motionless, like statues, staring at V as if they knew something awful was on the other end of that line, and everyone listened, fixated to every word of V's conversation.

"Yes . . . yes . . . yes we know Ms. Morgan. Yes, Ms. Harris is here . . . I'm sorry, she's a little indisposed. Yes . . . oh no . . . no . . . no," V said. Tears began to swell in her already bloodshot eyes as she cried out, "Oh my God!" She hung up the phone and yelled, "It's Melissa! Oh God, she's been in a terrible car accident. They're airlifting her to Dallas Memorial hospital. Sweet Jesus, we got to get there now!"

Chapter Twenty-Three

The Storm

The women seemed to gasp collectively. And they each felt a sharp pain in their hearts. As low down as Pat's heartbreak went she was pulled out of it with the thought of losing her friend. And while Donnell had just had his life threatened (and it certainly did flash before his eyes), he was as concerned as the other women. At the same time, he wanted to extend a gesture of peace. He offered to take Pat to the hospital. She agreed and everyone rushed out of the house to their separate cars and raced to Dallas Memorial. They were rescued from one set of death's jaws and tossed into another.

In the car, Pat and Donnell shared very few words, but still, Donnell felt compelled to set the record straight.

"Pat, honey. I'm so sorry for how this all went down. I am truly ashamed of myself. We stopped communicating a long time ago, but that's not the point. I should have been more adult about the situation. I should have honored our past, and more importantly, our vows. I cannot express how sorry I am."

"Why did you keep me from my kids, Donnell? How could you do that? Knowing how I feel about Matthew and Chanté. And how could you put Matthew in that danger. How could you let him drown?"

"I kept you from the kids because I was so tired of the pain. I was so tired of coming in every day and dealing with the pain and the silence and the arguing. Valerie is wonderful with the kids. I know that's hard to hear and hard to believe since Matthew drowned, but that was a complete accident. Look, after this, I want you to move back into the house. I'm going to move out."

"To go live with her?"

Donnell was quiet for a while and studied the street before him. "Yes, Pat. Look, I love you. I always will. But I am no longer *in* love with you."

As Jessie made her way to the hospital to reach Melissa's side, she prayed. "God, please. God, please let us have her a little longer. Please let her live through this. Let her be the wonderful mother You and I know she will be and that she desperately wants to be. Please." Melissa was Jessie's best girlfriend, and just the thought of losing her, of facing life without her forced Jessie to tears. She drove in a blur as her tears prevented her from seeing clearly. It was a wonder she made it to Dallas Memorial at all. As she was parking she realized Quentin had probably not been called. K103.5 had only Jessie listed as an emergency contact. Melissa had refused to list Quentin "without a ring" as she had said. When she found a parking space and killed the ignition, she dialed him.

"Quentin, I have terrible news. I have terrible news . . ." Jessie couldn't even complete her thought. She was all choked up. She felt her throat closing as if it refused to let the words free.

"What is it, Jessie? What is it? What's happened? Don't tell me something has happened to my baby—to either of my babies. Don't tell me that, Jessie."

"Meet me at Dallas Memorial, Quentin." Jessie hung up the phone, unable to give life to the words. She didn't want to say them. She wanted to keep them off her lips so they could not be realized. She rushed into the hospital.

She found everyone in the emergency room waiting area. They were waiting to hear from the surgeons working on Melissa. All they had been told was "we're fighting for her life." Not twenty minutes after Jessie, Quentin walked in the door, and right behind him was a Dallas sheriff asking the group to accompany him into a separate room.

Jessie, Quentin, DeDe, Darlene, V, Brit, Pat, and Donnell stared at the man with hope clouding their eyes. He had no idea how important he was to each of them.

"As you know, Ms. Morgan was involved in a terrible, terrible accident. Ms. Morgan, while attempting to change lanes, to pass several cars, encountered some *black ice* on the highway. Unfortunately, she lost control of the vehicle and was unable to recover." Shaking his head and looking down, speaking somberly, "I'm sorry to inform you that Ms. Morgan crashed into the median wall at an exceedingly high rate of speed. No skid marks on the pavement. The odometer frozen at 112 miles per hour. Folks, when medical personnel arrived at the scene . . . there was debris everywhere . . . not too much left of the vehicle."

"Lord have mercy . . . sweet, Jesus!" cried V.

"The doctors don't know if they'll be able to save her or the baby. In any case, she has done irreparable damage to her body and unfortunately . . . to her brain."

Quentin cried out, "What? What the fuck? What the fuck is going on here? Where the hell was she going?" He started searching the faces of the people around him and it was in Pat's that he saw the most pain. He wouldn't take his eyes off her.

Pat said, "This is all my fault. This is all my fault," and grabbed her face in a tormented gesture, "I put Melissa here."

V went to comfort Pat and whispered in her ear, "You know that's not true, Pat. You know that. You God now? You have nothing to do with what God has in store for Lis."

"What the hell is she talking about?" Quentin demanded. "Where was my wife going?"

"Oh. I'm sorry," the sheriff interjected. "Are you Mr. Morgan? I wasn't aware Ms., I mean Mrs., Morgan was married."

Everyone got quiet then because Quentin wore his pain so plainly. It was contorting his face and causing his fingers to tense. She was not his wife after all, and he might miss the opportunity to make it a reality.

Jessie interjected, "Quentin and Melissa were considering marriage. He's the father of her child."

"Please tell me the baby is going to make it," Quentin said. He was crying at this point. "Please tell me I'm not going to lose them both."

"I'm going to have the physician come speak with you as soon as he's available."

The sheriff left the room and Quentin flew into a rage. "What the hell was she doing driving that fast? Where was she going? Where the hell was she going? Somebody in this room had better tell me something."

"She was coming to rescue me," Donnell spoke up.

"Save you from what? You a grown-ass man. What the hell was she coming to save you from?"

Pat said, "From me," and lowered her head. "I was going to kill Donnell. I left Melissa a note telling her my plans. She was rushing over to stop me. I am the reason this is happening to her."

"You're damn right. You're damn right you're the reason this is happening to her. I hate your goddamn guts, Pat. You crazy-ass bitch!"

"Hold on now. Just hold on. You don't have to talk to *my wife* that way. If you're honest with yourself, I think you'll find that you're really upset about not making that woman *your wife*."

Quentin couldn't stomach the reality of those words. He didn't even have the energy to respond to them. He just took a seat and buried his head in his hands. He would not lift it for a long while. He remained in that devastated position even as Dr. Xavier Houston, the resident trauma surgeon, stepped into the room and pulled Jessie into a conference. There he revealed to her that Melissa had slipped into a coma and that she was being closely monitored.

"Still," he said, "she has massive head injuries, and I do not use the adjective lightly. Jessie, her prognosis is grim. I think you should prepare yourself for the worst."

"What about the baby, Xavier?" Jessie barely got the words out of her mouth. She could not believe she was asking them and was puzzled about why it looked like God wasn't answering her prayers.

"Despite Melissa's condition, the baby is in fair condition. However Melissa progresses, we would like to keep Melissa on life support to bring the baby to full term. We will of course need the permission of her parents, or the consent of a living will. Otherwise, the courts will have to decide how we can proceed with this matter."

"This matter? This matter! You mean my goddaughter's life? My best friend's life?"

"Please, Jessie . . ." He placed his hand lovingly on her shoulder. "Please do not mistake my medical jargon for insensitivity. I am desperately concerned about Melissa and her baby's future. Believe me when I say I was just in there wrestling with all my might to save her—for hours. I believe it is from my efforts that have made it possible that she is surviving on life support this moment."

"I'm sorry. It's just—"

"No need to apologize."

"I don't understand why this has to be a legal matter. Shouldn't it be the hospital's policy to save the baby? Why would anyone have to think about that?"

"Well, let's cross that bridge when we get to it. She may very well have a living will."

"She doesn't, Xavier. She doesn't have one. I just had a conversation with her a few months ago about this. She just said, 'I have to get one,' but she hadn't had a chance. I guess we're at that bridge."

Just then, Quentin knocked on the door. They could see his distraught face through the door's window. Dr. Houston let him in.

"What's going on? Why wasn't I brought into this conference?"

"I'm sorry, and you are?"

"Why the hell does everyone around here keep asking me who I am? I'm Melissa's fiancé. I'm the father of the baby she's carrying."

Jessie let that ride since she was sure that as Melissa's "fiancé" he still had no legal rights. It was obviously making Quentin feel better to toss the word around.

"Oh, okay. I'm sorry. I wasn't aware that you were here. My name is Dr. Xavier Houston, and I'm the resident physician who was working on Melissa."

"What's going to happen to her?"

Dr. Houston re-explained the situation to Quentin who held his hands in clenched fists and bit his mouth shut to fight back the tears.

"What's going to happen to them?"

"Well, we feel that it's in the baby's best interest to keep Melissa on life support. This way he or she has a better chance of being born healthy. If we were to take her off of life support, both she and the baby would likely succumb. At least this way, we can hope to welcome your child into the world. Now, looking down the line I will tell you that you will need to legally intervene following the birth of the baby. Otherwise, the baby will become a ward of the state."

"A ward of the state? Is this because we're not married?"

"Well, yes. If she was married all these decisions would be made by her husband. I'm sure that you're near hysterical over the fact that you and Melissa's wedding day is determining what say you have over her life and the life of your child. I'm sorry for this legal issue. I know at the moment it's stupid and insensitive."

Quentin's face no longer resembled a face. Instead it was sadness come to life. The fact was that a wedding date hadn't determined his say in the matter because there was no wedding date. The guilt seemed to climb up his back and rest there like a bag of stones.

Jessie had long since stopped focusing on Quentin and his stupid regrets. She was beginning to understand the gravity of the situation and was contemplating a life without Melissa. More importantly, she was racking her heart and brain about the fate of her godchild. Dr. Houston not only noticed the hurt in her eyes but he matched her hurt with his own concern. While Quentin stared off into space and retraced his steps back to the waiting room, Dr. Houston gave Jessie his card. He hadn't given it to her at the K103.5 New Year's Eve party because he was scared she wouldn't use it, but this offer was not of the romantic sort.

"Please, please call me if you have any questions, or concerns, about Melissa. I promise that she and the baby will receive the best care. I'm going to go get back to her now, and I'll send some refreshments down for you guys while you wait."

"Thank you so much, Xavier . . . Dr. Houston. I can't even begin to express my gratitude."

Back in the lobby conference room, V pulled Jessie aside. "This ain't the best time for this, and lord forgive me, but if you let that man slip through your fingers one more time, you a stir-crazy fool. You dumb as a rock if you let him go. Now I'm going back to finish praying for Lis."

Chapter Twenty-Four

The Storm is Passing Over

After spending the entire night in the hospital, Jessie and the others were finally granted permission to see Melissa. The sight of her in that bed sent Quentin to the floor. He rocked and cradled himself like a newborn baby asking God, "Why? Why?" The women and Donnell stood around in a daze, obviously not able to comprehend what was happening. Melissa's bulging stomach was not comforting. They did not look at it and see the good—that at least the baby was likely to survive. Rather, they imagined the baby's life without Melissa and the lifetime of pain that would come from not having a mother. They were only allowed a short time with her, and Jessie and Quentin were the only ones allowed any private time with her. Jessie held her best girlfriend's hand and told her, "Little Meli will always have a home. I will raise her . . . I'll raise her up in a way that you would be proud of, Lis." She kissed Melissa's forehead and left Quentin alone with her so he could say his piece without feeling like Jessie's judging eyes were on him. He cried a good five minutes before he was able to contain himself.

"I . . . I . . . I can't believe you're on this bed right now. I cannot believe this. I can't believe I was just eating dinner with you not a few days ago, and now I'm begging God for your life. And I can't believe . . ." The room was completely quiet except for the hustling of all the machines keeping Melissa alive. They reminded Quentin of the ocean, and more specifically that time he and Melissa had gone to Jamaica and he had held her every night, even in the depth of that heat, like she was a limb of his, so tight. "I can't believe I let you get away from me. I regret I couldn't give you the one thing that would have made you happy . . . my hand in marriage. Baby, I regret I didn't swoop you off your feet, sit you on my bended knee—with your gorgeous, sweet, compassionate, successful self—and propose

283

to you. Who do I think I am? I know you're in there cursing me out, Lis. I know you. You saying, 'Nigga, I told you.' And Lis, baby, you're right. You are so right. I was so wrong. I was so wrong."

+++

The women could think of nothing better to do than go to church. They went to their separate homes and showered. Put on a little makeup because they all had the hunch it would run away with the tears. They were barely holding themselves together in the silence of their homes. In the face of the Lord they would be six beautiful brown messes. Except they arrived minus one—Pat had yet to show.

The pastor asked DeDe to sing something for the congregation. She was ashamed of herself because she saw it as an opportunity to turn her career around, and she knew that it was not the time to be making career moves, but the time to be mourning her friend. To make up for her selfishness she asked the pastor if V, Jessie, and Brit could join her. He said, "Of course" and welcomed them to the pulpit. As the girls made their way to the pulpit, they could hear Darlene's sobs and moans—muffled in Miguel's arms—as he held and comforted her. V was sick on the piano and the other girls could hold a tune, but really, she just wanted them behind her. She simply asked to be helped along as the women did not know the song she planned to sing. She sang "The Holy Light," the song she had been inspired to write on her last trip to the studio. It was an a cappella rendition, and as DeDe blew the roof off the church (and cried a whole lot in between), the other women established a melodic humming behind her and repeated her words—Kirk Franklin style—when DeDe raised her hand. V hit the keys with love and hope all over her fingers. The congregation erupted into applause at the song's completion and DeDe asked them to pray and pray for Melissa and the baby.

They remained in the pulpit as Pastor Levine called the congregation's attention. He said, "Sometimes our troubles are too large to bear and there comes a time when we need a shoulder to help us carry the load. Need I remind you of Jesus and that old rugged cross? Heavy was the load. And Simon the Cyrene stepped in and helped him carry that cross. Let me be that shoulder, that helping hand to help you carry whatever burden that may be too great for you to carry alone. Are there any troubled souls in the building this evening? Are there any troubled souls in need of that helping hand? If so, please step forward."

The organist began playing James Cleveland's song "God Is." Pastor Levine lifted his arms in welcome. He searched the faces of the congregation for someone who might be ailing. For someone who needed to lay down his load. Without notice, a voice belted out the most beautiful sound. The sound was both troubled and free, crippled and passionate. The women, the pastor, and the entire body of churchgoers turned to find its source. Standing in the last row of the church with her arms extended in the same welcome gesture as Pastor Levine was Pat. She was singing and letting an ever-flowing string of tears race down her face to the place on her shirt directly over her heart. Pastor Levine fell in love with the sight of her just then, in all that pain, in all that anguish. He knew that God had sent him this woman and that she would be his wife. She walked right into his embrace. Into her ear he said, "God never fails, and although your world seems to be falling apart, there is another bigger, better plan for you. One that involves the church, your faith, and a good man behind it all."

Chapter Twenty-Five

I Stood on the Banks of Jordan

Thursday, March 12, was a cold and dreary day in Dallas. It had been raining on and off for days, with the worst to come on Friday. It was fitting though, as we cried and were broken to pieces on the inside, it was as if God was crying with us on the outside. Thursday, March 12, 2009 . . . I'll never forget that day. It was bittersweet. The sweet was that Melissa, through a C-section, delivered a beautiful baby girl—Melissa "Meli" Morgan; the bitter was that Melissa didn't appear to be coming back to us, and as the psychic Doretha had predicted, Melissa would never hold her child. With this playing in my head, I asked myself, *Jessie, would you even want to know your future if this was the outcome?* And I wondered if Ms. Doretha's predictions, concerning the rest of us, would come to fruition.

+++

True to word, Friday morning was the worst. As the wind howled and lightning lit up the dark Dallas sky, the deafening, booming sounds of thunder shook the ground and rattled the windows of Melissa's room. The hospital staff, quickly, but graciously, gathered around and began the process of disconnecting her from life support. In the room were Quentin, her newborn daughter, Jessie, Pat, V, Brit, DeDe, and Darlene. When the nurse turned off all the equipment everyone remained silent, including the baby. They all watched as the steady rise and fall of Melissa's chest slowed and then stopped altogether. They had been holding hands and squeezed one another tightly as they let go of their beautiful girlfriend, who should have been a wife and mother.

As Jessie sat on the bed and ran her fingers through Melissa's hair, tears that she couldn't hold back if her life depended on it, streamed down her face. She sat there and reflected on their time together, their time as Divas, and their time as friends. As she kissed Melissa's forehead it dawned on her that it was Friday, March 13, and she thought, *What an unlucky day for my sista to leave us.* But she did gain some comfort knowing that Melissa was free to finally journey home, and then she realized that the Divas, Quentin, little Meli, the K103.5 family, and Dallas were truly the unlucky ones. As the text messages poured out announcing the end of Melissa's journey, the radio was set to come on as usual for Melissa to enjoy her favorite place in the world, K103.5. Not soon after the radio blared to life, DK's voice, smooth as it was, filled the room—it was like a little bit of sunshine peaking through a world of gray.

He sang, "*I saw her ship go sailing by, I stood there on the banks of Jordon, lord have mercy* . . . This is for my colleague, my friend, my homegirl, Melissa Morgan, who lost her battle this morning and went on to be with the Lord. Melissa loved James Cleveland and 'I Stood on the Banks of Jordan' was one of her favorite songs. This is for you, Lis. Rest in peace my sister, my confidant, my friend." Again, he sang along with James Cleveland, ". . . *she closed her eyes and she went on to glory with a smile, and while she did all I could do was stand there on the banks of Jordan, and her heart was heavy, as I watched the ship go sailing by* . . . K103.5 family, Melissa Morgan will be truly missed."

Chapter Twenty-Six

A New Beginning

June 27, 2009. I walked through the corridors of Spa Eloná with a head held high that last time. I admit, that first visit, my head was lifted, but that was in the name of observation. I was too busy looking at everything, trying to figure out and be closer to Dr. Wilma's success. But inside I was dying. That last visit meant a heart, and head, held high. It meant healing. We discussed the progress of my forgiveness campaign.

Dr. Wilma said, "So . . . who has been forgiven. Who now has your blessing to move on, out of your life, into the horizon."

"You make it sound so beautiful, Dr. Wilma."

"Well it is, baby girl. You're getting yourself back."

"I have forgiven my father. I've forgiven every man who has broken my heart. I have forgiven Michael Todd Crawley."

"Amen, baby girl. Amen."

On my way home, I picked up my cell to call Xavier, but ended up calling Quentin instead. As single dads come, he was making out just fine. I made my way over to his apartment every single day. I gave him a minute to collect his thoughts, or sleep (as he was getting up throughout the night for Meli's feedings), or tell me all the stories proud parents tell—like her holding that big head up and biting him with her gums. I also washed dishes and clothes and made dinner (good practice for my family life—and I was absolutely fine with that being far off in the future). Meli was Melissa personified down to her fingers, how they were always bent, like they wanted to fight. And while I sometimes got sad, I couldn't remain in that tiny depression because the little girl was so beautiful . . . and so loud! Ha!

While Meli and Quentin slept and I finished up my famous lasagna dish (thanks Big Momma) for that night, I dialed my girls back to back just to check on them. Losing Melissa had made me far more aware about what role I wanted my friendships to play. I needed my girls to know how I felt about them regularly. DeDe was first on the list.

"Hey, girl. What's new?"

"Jessie! Girl! I met someone."

"And you better have asked him if he gets down with the get down!"

"Aww shit! Now you see where I'm coming from. Now all a sudden it's okay to ask the down low question!"

"De, girl, I will never ever question you on that again."

"I asked him, Jess. You know I did. Even though I didn't have that vibe about him."

"What did he say?"

"Girl, I thought he was gonna slap me. But I like that reaction. I want him to get mad about the possibility. I wanna know that that shit pisses him off as much as it pisses me off!"

"I know that's right, De! But more important than any damn man, what did Alicia Myers say?"

"Oh, Ms. Myers is sweating me, Jess. She's on my nuts. The condo is, what? Sold!!! And your girl is on the next thing smoking to L.A. But I ain't going to L.A. to be on no Electra Sounds records! Guess who was listening to us in church that day? Remember right after we heard about Lis? God rest her soul. Girl, Dorothy Devine was in town visiting. She said I had been on her mind for weeks, and on behalf of Gospel Town records, she would like to offer me a deal, Jess! I got a record deal! No more teaching the little hoodlums!"

"Yay!" I had to catch myself before I woke up Meli. "That's what's up, De! Now don't forget where you came from, now. Remember the style of diamond I like. And you know a sista loves a Gucci bag!"

Next, I called Pat, who probably should have been who I called first. She had found out her cancer was potentially fatal. Breast cancer was generally treatable, but that was if you caught it early. Pat hadn't been so lucky. Still, she sounded like pure love when she picked up her phone.

"Hey, Jessie baby! Girl, God is good! He is good all the time. I'm going into my first chemo treatment in less than a week. I been seeing the pastor regularly, and he's been holding my hand every step of the way."

From Pat's story alone I was able to gather so much faith. She had seen the depths of pain. Had seen them, survived them, and lived to praise them—all while facing death. Pat's situation made Brit's look easy as Sunday morning.

"So, what's going on, Brit? What are they saying?"

"Sweetie pie, I love you. Jessie, you know I love you. But I am unable to discuss such foolishness over the phone. Whoever 'they' are, they're talking to my lawyer who is probably saying something like, 'We're gonna file harassment charges if you don't stop this nonsense.' Because your girl is now settled in her Atlanta apartment about to eat a homemade dinner of salmon and pasta. Girl, everything is gravy. Now let's talk about when you're coming down here to visit. Girl, girl, girl! The men down here are built like Brass, with that same swagger, but they work downtown and got corner offices! Holla!"

V had some wonderful news herself. I hadn't heard her so happy in so long. She said she was still dating all over the place and letting the men wine and dine her like they should have been doing when she was a little more plump. She said, "You know, Jess, if I was honest with myself and I had taken a look around me I would have seen that all my too skinny, beautiful friends were looking for love, too! I mean, not that y'all heartache should bring me joy, but it should have helped me realize I was looking for salvation outside of myself when I should have been looking within . . . seeking God."

Darlene's phone call was the most inspiring because it let me know love was not only possible, it was likely.

"November 15, sweetie. Pack your bags! It's in Brazil. Miguel said I have to meet his family before we become one, but he can't wait another year. So we're gonna kill two birds with one stone—and by the way, he ate the pussy!"

"I'm there, Darlene. Decked out in bells and whistles. Girl, I'm so happy for you. You so deserve it. The marriage and the head!"

"And so do you, Jess. So do you."

She sure as hell wasn't lying. I heard Meli crying and rushed to her crib. I was gonna sing her a lullaby, feed her hardworking daddy in her momma's name, and go on home to put the final touches on my first big account, Daisy Chain Cosmetics. When I made it to her crib, scooped her up in my arms, and held her close to my chest, I heard Quentin walk through the door. "Hey, how's the girls doing?" he asked.

"We're doing fine." Checking Meli's bottom as I cradled and rocked her back and forth.

Quentin, yawning as he came to plant his usual kiss on Meli's forehead, leaned over Meli and kissed me on the forehead. He thanked me for being there for him and Meli and wrapped his arms around the both of us—his forehead softly resting on mine. There we stood. Me, Meli and Quentin, wrapped in an embrace that seem to last for eternity—much longer than it probably should have. I didn't resist. Although, in my heart, I felt like I should.

On the ride home—as butterflies raced through my stomach—I kept replaying what happened between me and Quentin. Trying to get it out of my head—a little music should help—I flipped on the radio and heard no other than DK's voice.

"Evening, Dallas. This is your boy DK. I hope y'all are ready. The fellas are in the business. After listening to those women yap on and on about all they troubles in *The Love Forum*—rest in peace my beautiful baby-love Melissa Morgan—it's time for us to vent. Let me introduce you to our guests . . ."

I said, "Oh lord . . ." and shook my head.

Epilogue

May 12, 2009. It had been almost two months since Melissa passed away and my soul was restless. I needed answers, but didn't know where to turn . . . my mind kept going to Ms. Doretha. Lord, I can't believe that I'm actually walking down her driveway. But here I am, fifteen minutes late for my two o'clock appointment. As I approached the door, I stopped and just stood there—as if to collect my thoughts. I threw back my head, shut my eyes, and quietly reassured myself that I had made the right decision to come. Taking a deep breath, I reached for the doorbell—the chiming music was both beautiful and soothing. Soon afterwards, I heard Ms. Doretha's voice come over the intercom, "Dear, come in, the door is open. I've been expecting your early arrival."

As I entered, Ms. Doretha greeted me with a big hug. I hugged her back tight and we stood there hugging and consoling one another. We walked into the kitchen and sat down at the kitchen table. As I sat down, *I noticed a stack of blue envelopes—the top one had my name scribbled on it.* Before I could ask Ms. Doretha what the envelopes were, and most importantly, who were they from, she asked, "Dear, can I get you some green tea?"

I answered, "No, Ms. Doretha, I'm fine." And although green tea is my favorite, I was more interested in those blue envelopes than any tea. As I continued to stare at the envelopes with puzzled eyes, I thought, *Jessie, do you really want to know?*—

"Well, go ahead, Dear . . . they're for you."

"Ms. Doretha, what are they?"

"*My* Melissa—that sweet, sweet child—wrote them before she passed. She wanted me to give them to you when you were ready. I think you're ready, Dear."

"I'm sorry," turning around to face Ms. Doretha straight on, "I . . . I'm not understanding what's going on here. Ms. Doretha, what are these envelopes and what do they have to do with me?"

"Well, Dear . . . humph," shaking her head, "I went to see Melissa the day before she passed—well depending on how you look at it—the day before the accident. Sweet child, I just had to see my beautiful, sweet darling before she left this Earth. Plus, I knew she had some unfinished matters to address."

Ms. Doretha picked-up the stack of letters and placed them in my hand. She squeezed my hand tight and closed her eyes as if she was performing some sort of reading on me. Not saying a word, not even looking at me, she turned around and headed towards the stove. Out of nowhere—in a cracked and hurt voice—she told me that Melissa was with us. Startled, I asked, "Ms. Doretha . . . HERE . . . NOW!?"

"No Dear," as she walked back to the table, placing a cup of green tea in front of me anyway. "She's within our hearts. I know you need to know that she's alright and in a better place—and she is—but you also need to know that her earthly work is not finished. Dear, you're the vessel. Yes, Jessie, you're the vessel she will need to make her work complete."

"Ms. Doretha, I don't understand . . . what are you saying?"

"Dear, read the letter addressed to you, all the answers—for now—are within the letter."

I looked at Ms. Doretha while I slowly opened the letter. For some reason, I needed to see her eyes. I needed to figure out what she was thinking. Where she was coming from. *Hell . . . did she write these letters?* As I looked down, I felt chills all through my body. It definitely was Melissa's handwriting—I can recognize that chicken-scratch anywhere. I stared at the letter for awhile—too long I guess—and I heard Ms. Doretha say, "Well, what does it say, Dear?" I looked up at Ms. Doretha and was met with a slight smile and short nod. Visibly shaking—this was all beginning to be a little too much—I looked back down and started to read:

Dear Jessie,

If you're reading this letter, it means that you've seen Doretha. Girl, I told you she's the truth! You probably have a thousand-and-one questions on your mind so I'll start by saying that Jessie . . . you have been a true sista, soror, diva and friend. I have truly cherished our friendship, and girl, I love you so much. Jess, I truly believe that God puts us on this Earth for a reason and our steps, or journey in life, are already ordered. I guess my journey was to one, come into the Divas lives and show ya'll—and Dallas—the paths to Love. (Girl, I'm smiling ear to ear as I put the pen on this paper to write the next few words.) As well as, two, bring that beautiful girl, Meli, into the world. Jessie, I hope that she's a bundle of joy!

Well, you're probably wondering what in the world is going on. Girl, Doretha came by the house today— what a surprise that was?!—and I knew. I knew the time was near. I don't have time to write everything I want to say to you because I've written eight other letters—yours was the last. In the stack, there should be a letter for Quentin, DK, Magic, V, Pat, DeDe, Brit and Darlene. Yes girl, I was a writing fool today. Doretha sat with me and guided me through what life has to offer each of the Divas. I also have insight for DK, Quentin, Magic and my precious little Meli. Jessie, there is so much I want to accomplish and now I don't know if I have a couple of minutes, hours, days or what—that's the one thing I didn't want Doretha to tell me. But I'm at peace. Jess, I need you now more than ever. Please help your sista out by delivering the letters to everyone. If asked what the letters are for, just say that enclosed, are my parting words and wishes for each of them.

Jessie, DK should receive his letter first. He should (and will) continue The Love Forum with Magic—it should have a twist though. We've heard about all the Divas' relationship woes but what about the brothas. What were they thinking and feeling? What was going on in their heads? What are their views about relationships? Maybe it's time we started listening to what our brothas have to say—if we do, maybe the state of our black relationships can improve. Deliver the letter to DK. He has all the information he will need. I must tell you though; you'll experience great pain because of the new Love Forum—prepare yourself diva! Three men, your past (Michael Crawley), your present (Dr. Houston) and your future (by now your heart is telling you yes, but your mind is saying no) will play out a drama that will rock K103.5, Dallas and each of your lives—but all of you (according to Doretha) will find happiness in the end.

Well girl, I gotta go. Just know that through life, there are going to be joys, sorrows, laughter, and heartache. And yes, I know your heart is aching and the Divas' lives have changed tremendously, but keep the faith girl, you're going to have to press on day by day to reach your final destination. I'm not saying that it's going to be easy. But Jessie, on my short life on earth, I realized that finding love, whether true or not, takes you down many roads. Some roads may take you for the ultimate thrill ride—remember Marvin, girl. Others may just lazily wind you through the country-scape called life. A few may slowly lead you back to where you began—that would be Marcus (I know you're smiling). While others, without notice, abruptly end.

The Divas were blessed to travel down the same road for many years. Amazingly, we ended up in different directions in life. Relationships formed and relationships ended; marriages began and marriages died; love ones faded into memory and children sprung out of the midst. But most importantly, Jessie, in our own ways, we began to quench our desire for sweet, sweet love. Good-bye diva. I love you beyond words.

Melissa